Nora Roberts is the number one *New York Times* bestseller of more than 200 novels. With over 450 million copies of her books in print, she is indisputably one of the most celebrated and popular writers in the world. She has achieved numerous top five bestsellers in the UK, including number one for *Savour the Moment* and *The Witness*, and is a *Sunday Times* hardback bestseller writing as both Nora Roberts and J. D. Robb.

Become a fan on Facebook at
www.facebook.com/norarobertsjdrobb
and be the first to hear all the latest from Piatkus
about Nora Roberts and J. D. Robb.

www.noraroberts.com
www.nora-roberts.co.uk
www.jd-robb.co.uk

WITHDRAWN

By Nora Roberts

Homeport	Northern Lights	Black Hills
The Reef	Blue Smoke	The Search
River's End	Montana Sky	Chasing Fire
Carolina Moon	Angels Fall	The Witness
The Villa	High Noon	Whiskey Beach
Midnight Bayou	Divine Evil	The Collector
Three Fates	Tribute	The Liar
Birthright	Sanctuary	

The Born In Trilogy:
Born in Fire
Born in Ice
Born in Shame

The Bride Quartet:
Vision in White
Bed of Roses
Savour the Moment
Happy Ever After

The Key Trilogy:
Key of Light
Key of Knowledge
Key of Valour

The Irish Trilogy:
Jewels of the Sun
Tears of the Moon
Heart of the Sea

Three Sisters Island Trilogy:
Dance upon the Air
Heaven and Earth
Face the Fire

The Sign of Seven Trilogy:
Blood Brothers
The Hollow
The Pagan Stone

Chesapeake Bay Quartet:
Sea Swept
Rising Tides
Inner Harbour
Chesapeake Blue

In the Garden Trilogy:
Blue Dahlia
Black Rose
Red Lily

The Circle Trilogy:
Morrigan's Cross
Dance of the Gods
Valley of Silence

The Dream Trilogy:
Daring to Dream
Holding the Dream
Finding the Dream

The Inn Boonsboro Trilogy:
The Next Always
The Last Boyfriend
The Perfect Hope

The Cousins O'Dwyer Trilogy:
Dark Witch
Shadow Spell
Blood Magick

Many of Nora Roberts' other titles are now available in eBook and she is also the author of the In Death series using the pseudonym J.D. Robb. For more information please visit
www.nora-roberts.com or www.nora-roberts.co.uk

NORA ROBERTS

PRIVATE SCANDALS

piatkus

PIATKUS

First published in Great Britain in 2015 by Piatkus

1 3 5 7 9 10 8 6 4 2

First published in the United States by G. P. Putnam and Sons in 1993
Mass-market edition published in the United States by Jove in 1994

A CIP catalogue record for this book
is available from the British Library.

ISBN 978-0-349-40791-3

Typeset by M Rules
Printed and bound by CPI Group (UK) Ltd, Croydon, CR0 4YY

Papers used by Piatkus are from well-managed forests
and other responsible sources.

MIX
Paper from
responsible sources
FSC® C104740

Piatkus
An imprint of
Little, Brown Book Group
100 Victoria Embankment
London EC4Y 0DY

An Hachette UK Company
www.hachette.co.uk

www.piatkus.co.uk

To Pop

PART ONE

"'The time has come,' the Walrus said, 'to talk of many things.'"

LEWIS CARROLL

Chicago, 1994

It was a moonless midnight in Chicago, but to Deanna, the moment had all the makings of *High Noon*. It was easy to see herself in the quietly dignified, stalwart Gary Cooper role, preparing to face down the canny, vengeance-seeking gunslinger.

But damn it, Deanna thought, Chicago was *her* town. Angela was the outsider.

It suited Angela's sense of the dramatic, Deanna supposed, to demand a showdown in the very studio where they both had climbed ambition's slippery ladder. But it was Deanna's studio now, and it was *her* show that garnered the lion's share of the ratings points. There was nothing Angela could do to change that, short of conjuring up Elvis from the grave and asking him to sing "Heartbreak Hotel" to the studio audience.

A ghost of a smile flitted around Deanna's lips at the image, but there wasn't much humor in it. Angela was nothing if not a worthy opponent. Over the years she had used gruesome tactics to keep her daily talk show on top.

But whatever Angela had up her sleeve this time wasn't going to work. She had underestimated Deanna Reynolds. Angela could whisper secrets and threaten scandal all she wanted, but nothing she could say would change Deanna's plans.

She would, however, hear Angela out. Deanna thought she would even attempt, one last time, to compromise. To offer, if not friendship, at least a cautious truce. There was little hope the breach could be spanned after all this time and all the hostility, but hope, to Deanna's mind, sprang eternal.

At least until it dried up.

Focusing on the matter at hand, Deanna pulled into the CBC Building's parking lot. During the day, the lot would be crammed with cars—technicians, editors, producers, talent, secretaries, interns. Deanna would be dropped off and picked up by her driver, avoiding the hassle. Inside the great white building, people would be rushing to put out the news—at seven A.M., noon and five and ten P.M.—and *Let's Cook!* with Bobby Marks, the weekly *In Depth* with Finn Riley, and the top-rated talk show in the country, *Deanna's Hour.*

But now, just after midnight, the lot was nearly empty. There were half a dozen cars belonging to the skeleton crew who were loitering in the newsroom, waiting for something to happen somewhere in the world. Probably hoping any new wars would wait to erupt until the lonely night shift ended.

Wishing she were somewhere else, anywhere else, Deanna pulled into an empty space and shut off the engine. For a moment she simply sat, listening to the night, the swish of cars on the street to the left, the rumble of the huge air-conditioning system that kept the building and the expensive equipment cool. She had to get a handle on her mixed emotions and her nerves before she faced Angela.

Nerves were second nature in the profession she'd chosen. She would work with them, or through them. Her temper was something she could and would control, particularly if losing it would accomplish nothing. But those emotions, the ones that ran so strong and so contradictory, were another matter. Even after all this time, it was difficult to forget that the woman she was about to face was one she had once admired and respected. And trusted.

From bitter experience Deanna knew that Angela was an expert in emotional manipulation. Deanna's problem—and many said her talent—was an inability to hide her feelings. They were there, up front, shouting to anyone who cared to listen. Whatever she felt was mirrored in her gray eyes, broadcast in the tilt of her head or the expression of her mouth. Some said that's what made her irresistible, and dangerous. With a flick of her wrist, she turned the rearview mirror toward her. Yes, she mused, she could see the sparks of temper in her own eyes, and the simmering resentment, the dragging regret. After all, she and Angela had been friends once. Or almost friends.

But she could also see the pleasure of anticipation. That was a matter of pride. This bout had been a long time coming.

Smiling a little, Deanna took out a tube of lipstick and carefully painted her mouth. You didn't go one-on-one with your arch rival without the most basic of shields. Pleased that her hand was rock steady, she dropped the lipstick back in her purse, climbed out of the car. She stood a moment, breathing in the balmy night while she asked herself one question.

Calm, Deanna?

Nope, she thought. What she was, was revved. If the energy was fueled by nerves, it didn't matter. Slamming the car door behind her, she strode across the lot. She slipped her plastic ID out of her pocket and punched it into the security slot beside the rear door. Seconds later, a little green light blipped, allowing her to depress the handle and pull the heavy door open.

She flicked the switch to light the stairway, and let the door ease shut behind her.

She found it interesting that Angela hadn't arrived before her.

She'd have taken a car service, Deanna thought. Now that Angela was settled in New York, she no longer had a regular driver in Chicago. It surprised Deanna that she hadn't seen a limo waiting in the lot.

Angela was always, always on time.

It was one of the many things Deanna respected about her.

The click of Deanna's heels on the stairs echoed hollowly as she descended a level. As she slipped her card in the next security slot, she wondered briefly who Angela had bribed, threatened or seduced to gain entry to the studio.

Not so many years before, Deanna had rushed down that same route, wide-eyed and enthusiastic, running errands at the snap of Angela's demanding fingers. She'd been ready to preen like an eager puppy for any sign of approval. But, like any smart pup, she'd learned.

And when betrayal had come, with its keen-edged disillusionment, she might have whimpered, but she'd licked her wounds and had used everything she'd learned—until the student became the master.

It shouldn't have surprised her to discover how quickly old resentments, long cooled, could come rolling to a boil. And this time, Deanna thought, this time when she faced Angela, it would be on her own turf, under her own rules. The naive kid from Kansas was more than ready to flex the muscles of realized ambition.

And perhaps once she did, they would finally clear the air. Meet on equal terms. If it wasn't possible to forget what had happened between them in the past, it was always possible to accept and move on.

Deanna slipped her card into the slot beside the studio doors. The light blinked green. She pushed inside, into darkness.

The studio was empty.

That pleased her. Arriving first gave her one more advantage, as a hostess escorting an unwelcome guest into her home. And if home was where you grew from girl to woman, where you learned and squabbled, the studio was home.

Smiling a little, Deanna reached out in the dark for the switch that controlled a bank of overhead lights. She thought she heard something, some whisper that barely disturbed the air. And a feeling stabbed through that fine sense of anticipation. A feeling that she was not alone.

Angela, she thought, and flicked the switch.

But as the overhead lights flashed on, brighter ones, blinding ones, exploded inside her head. As the pain ripped through them, she plunged back into the dark.

SHE CRAWLED BACK INTO consciousness, moaning. Her head, heavy with pain, lolled back against a chair. Groggy, disoriented, she lifted a hand to the worst of the ache. Her fingers came away lightly smeared with blood.

She struggled to focus, baffled to find herself sitting in her own chair, on her own set. Had she missed a cue? she wondered, dizzy, staring back at the camera where the red light gleamed.

But there was no studio audience beyond the camera, no technicians working busily out of range. Though the lights flooded down with the familiar heat, there was no show in progress.

She'd come to meet Angela, Deanna remembered.

Her vision wavered again, like water disturbed by a pebble, and she blinked to clear it. It was then her gaze latched on to the two images on the monitor. She saw herself, pale and glazed-eyed. Then she saw, with horror, the guest sitting in the chair beside hers.

Angela, her pink silk suit decorated with pearl buttons. Matching strands of pearls around her throat, clustered at her ears. Angela, her golden hair softly coiffed, her legs crossed, her hands folded together over the right arm of the chair.

It was Angela. Oh yes, there was no mistaking it. Even though her face had been destroyed.

7

Blood was splattered over the pink silk and joined by more that ran almost leisurely down from where that lovely, canny face should be.

It was then Deanna began to scream.

Chapter One

Chicago, 1990

IN FIVE, FOUR, THREE . . .

Deanna smiled at the camera from her corner of the set of *Midday News.* "Our guest this afternoon is Jonathan Monroe, a local author who has just published a book titled *I Want Mine.*" She lifted the slim volume from the small round table between the chairs, angling it toward Camera Two. "Jonathan, you've subtitled this book *Healthy Selfishness.* What inspired you to write about a trait most people consider a character flaw?"

"Well, Deanna." He chuckled, a small man with a sunny smile who was sweating profusely under the lights. "I wanted mine."

Good answer, she thought, but it was obvious he wasn't going to elaborate without a little prompting. "And who doesn't, if we're honest?" she said, trying to loosen him up with a sense of comradeship. "Jonathan, you state in your book that this healthy selfishness is quashed by parents and caregivers, right from the nursery."

"Exactly." His frozen, brilliant smile remained fixed while his eyes darted in panic.

Deanna shifted subtly, laying her hand over his rigid fingers just under camera range. Her eyes radiated interest, her touch communicated support. "You believe the demand of adults that children share toys sets an unnatural precedent." She gave his hand an encouraging squeeze. "Don't you feel that sharing is a basic form of courtesy?"

"Not at all." And he began to tell her why. Though his explanations were delivered in fits and starts, she was able to smooth over the awkwardness, guiding him through the three-minute-fifteen-second spot.

"That's *I Want Mine*, by Jonathan Monroe," she said to the camera, winding up. "Available in your bookstores now. Thank you so much for joining us today, Jonathan."

"It was a pleasure. As a side note, I'm currently working on my second book, *Get Out of My Way, I Was Here First*. It's about healthy aggression."

"Best of luck with it. We'll be back in a moment with the rest of the *Midday News*." Once they were into commercial, she smiled at Jonathan. "You were great. I appreciate your coming in."

"I hope I did okay." The minute his mike was removed, Jonathan whipped out a handkerchief to mop his brow. "First time on TV."

"You did fine. I think this will generate a lot of local interest in your book."

"Really?"

"Absolutely. Would you mind signing this for me?"

Beaming again, he took the book and pen she offered. "You sure made it easy, Deanna. I did a radio interview this morning. The DJ hadn't even read the back blurb."

She took the autographed book, rising. Part of her mind, most of her energy, was already at the news desk across the studio. "That makes it hard on everyone. Thanks again," she said, offering her hand. "I hope you'll come back with your next book."

"I'd love to." But she'd already walked away, maneuvering

nimbly over snaking piles of cable to take her place behind the counter on the news set. After slipping the book under the counter, she hooked her mike to the lapel of her red suit.

"Another screwball." The comment from her co-anchor, Roger Crowell, was typical.

"He was very nice."

"You think everyone's very nice." Grinning, Roger checked his hand mirror, gave his tie a minute adjustment. He had a good face for the camera—mature, trustworthy, with distinguished flecks of gray at the temples of his rust-colored hair. "Especially the screwballs."

"That's why I love you, Rog."

This caused snickering among the camera crew. Whatever response Roger might have made was cut off by the floor director signaling time. While the TelePrompTer rolled, Roger smiled into the camera, setting the tone for a soft segment on the birth of twin tigers at the zoo.

"That's all for *Midday*. Stay tuned for *Let's Cook!* This is Roger Crowell."

"And Deanna Reynolds. See you tomorrow."

As the closing music tinkled in her earpiece, Deanna turned to smile at Roger. "You're a softy, pal. You wrote that piece on the baby tigers yourself. It had your fingerprints all over it."

He flushed a little, but winked. "Just giving them what they want, babe."

"And we're clear." The floor director stretched his shoulders. "Nice show, people."

"Thanks, Jack." Deanna was already unhooking her mike.

"Hey, want to get some lunch?" Roger was always ready to eat, and countered his love affair with food with his personal trainer. There was no disguising pounds from the merciless eye of the camera.

"Can't. I've got an assignment."

Roger rose. Beneath his impeccable blue serge jacket, he wore a pair of eye-popping Bermuda shorts. "Don't tell me it's for the terror of Studio B."

The faintest flicker of annoyance clouded her eyes. "Okay, I won't."

"Hey, Dee." Roger caught up with her on the edge of the set. "Don't get mad."

"I didn't say I was mad."

"You don't have to." They walked down the single wide step from the glossy set to the scarred wood floor, skirting around camera and cable. They pushed through the studio doors together. "You are mad. It shows. You get that line between your eyebrows. Look." He pulled her by the arm into the makeup room. After flicking on the lights, he stood behind her, his hands on her shoulders as they faced the mirror. "See, it's still there."

Deliberately, she eased it away with a smile. "I don't see anything."

"Then let me tell you what I see. Every man's dream of the girl next door. Subtle, wholesome sex." When she scowled, he only grinned. "That's the visual, kid. Those big, trust-me eyes and peaches and cream. Not bad qualities for a television reporter."

"How about intelligence?" she countered. "Writing ability, guts."

"We're talking visuals." His smile flashed, deepening the character lines around his eyes. No one in television would dare refer to them as wrinkles. "Look, my last co-anchor was a Twinkie. All blow-dried hair and bonded teeth. She was more worried about her eyelashes than she was punching the lead."

"And now she's reading the news at the number-two station in LA." She knew how the business worked. Oh yes, she did. But she didn't have to like it. "Rumors are, she's being groomed for network."

"That's the game. Personally, I appreciate having someone at the desk with a brain, but let's not forget what we are."

"I thought we were journalists."

"*Television* journalists. You've got a face that was made for the camera, and it tells everything you're thinking, everything you're feeling. Only problem is, it's the same off camera, and that makes you vulnerable. A woman like Angela eats little farm girls like you for breakfast."

"I didn't grow up on a farm." Her voice was dry as a Midwest dust bowl.

"Might as well have." He gave her shoulders a friendly squeeze. "Who's your pal, Dee?"

She sighed, rolled her eyes. "You are, Roger."

"Watch your back with Angela."

"Look, I know she has a reputation for being temperamental—"

"She has a reputation for being a stone bitch."

Stepping away from Roger, Deanna uncapped a pot of cold cream to remove her heavy makeup. She didn't like having her coworkers pitted against one another, competing for her time, and she didn't like feeling pressured into choosing between them. It had been difficult enough juggling her responsibilities in the newsroom and on set with the favors she did for Angela. And they were only favors, after all. Done primarily on her own time.

"All I know is that she's been nothing but kind to me. She liked my work on *Midday* and the 'Deanna's Corner' segment and offered to help me refine my style."

"She's using you."

"She's teaching me," Deanna corrected, tossing used makeup pads aside. Her movements were quick and practiced. She hit the center of the wastebasket as consistently as a veteran free-throw shooter. "There's a reason Angela has the top-rated talk show in the market. It would have taken me years to learn the ins and outs of the business I've picked up from her in a matter of months."

"And do you really think she's going to share a piece of that pie?"

She pouted a moment because, of course, she wanted a piece. A nice big one. *Healthy selfishness*, she thought, and chuckled to herself. "It's not as though I'm competing with her."

"Not yet." But she would be, he knew. It surprised him that Angela didn't detect the ambition glinting just behind Deanna's eyes. But then, he mused, ego was often blinding. He had reason to know. "Just some friendly advice. Don't give her any ammunition." He took one last study as Deanna briskly redid her makeup for the street. She might have been naive, he mused, but she was also stubborn. He could see it in the way her mouth was set, the angle of her chin. "I've got a couple of bumpers to tape." He tugged on her hair. "See you tomorrow."

"Yeah." Once she was alone, Deanna tapped her eye pencil against the makeup table. She didn't discount everything Roger said. Because she was a perfectionist, because she demanded, and received, the best for her show, Angela Perkins had a reputation for being hard. And it certainly paid off. After six years in syndication, *Angela's* had been in the number-one spot for more than three.

Since both *Angela's* and *Midday News* were taped at the CBC studios, Angela had been able to exert a little pressure to free up some of Deanna's time.

It was also true that Angela had been nothing but kind to Deanna. She had shown Deanna a friendship and a willingness to share that were rare in the highly competitive world of television.

Was it naive to trust kindness? Deanna didn't think so. Nor was she foolish enough to believe that kindness was always rewarded.

Thoughtfully, she picked up the brush marked with her name and pulled it through her shoulder-length black hair. Without the cover of heavy theatrical makeup necessary for the lights and camera, her skin was as elegantly pale as porcelain, a dramatic contrast to the inky mane of hair and the smoky, slightly slanted eyes. To add another touch of drama, she'd painted her lips a deep rose.

Satisfied, she pulled her hair back in a ponytail with two quick flicks of her wrist.

She never planned to compete with Angela. Although she hoped to use what she learned to boost her own career, what she wanted was a network spot, someday. Maybe a job on *20/20*. And it wasn't beyond the realm of possibility that she could expand the weekly "Deanna's Corner" segment on the noon news into a full-fledged syndicated talk show of her own. Even that would hardly be competing with Angela, the queen of the market.

The nineties were wide open for all manner of styles and shows. If she succeeded, it would be because she'd learned from the master. She would always be grateful to Angela for that.

"IF THE SON OF A BITCH THINKS I'm going to roll over, he's in for an unpleasant surprise." Angela Perkins glared at the reflection of her producer in her dressing room mirror. "He agreed to come on the show to hype his new album. Tit for tat, Lew. We're giving him national exposure, so he's damn well going to answer some questions about his tax evasion charges."

"He didn't say he wouldn't answer them, Angela." The headache behind Lew McNeil's eyes was still dull enough to keep him hoping it would pass. "He just said he won't be able to be specific as long as the case is pending. He'd like it if you would concentrate on his career."

"I wouldn't be where I am if I let a guest dictate my show, would I?" She swore again, ripely, then wheeled in the chair to snarl at the hairdresser. "Pull my hair again, sweetie, and you'll be picking up curlers with your teeth."

"I'm sorry, Miss Perkins, but your hair is really too short . . ."

"Just get it done." Angela faced her own reflection again, and deliberately relaxed her features. She knew how important it was to relax the facial muscles before a show, no matter how high the adrenaline. The camera picked up every line and wrinkle, like an old friend a woman meets for lunch. So she breathed deeply, closing her eyes a moment in a signal to her producer to hold his tongue. When she opened them again, they were clear, a diamond bright blue surrounded by silky lashes.

And she smiled as the hairdresser swept her hair back and up into a wavy blond halo. It was a good look for her, Angela decided. Sophisticated but not threatening. Chic but not studied. She checked the style from every angle before giving the go-ahead nod.

"It looks great, Marcie." She flashed the high-powered smile that made the hairdresser forget the earlier threat. "I feel ten years younger."

"You look wonderful, Miss Perkins."

"Thanks to you." Relaxed and satisfied, she toyed with the trademark pearls around her throat. "And how's that new man in your life, Marcie? Is he treating you well?"

"He's terrific." Marcie grinned as she gave Angela's hair a large dose of spray to hold the style. "I think he might be the one."

"Good for you. If he gives you any trouble, you let me know." She winked. "I'll straighten him out."

With a laugh, Marcie backed away. "Thanks, Miss Perkins. Good luck this morning."

"Mmm-hmmm. Now, Lew." She smiled and lifted a hand for his. The squeeze was encouraging, feminine, friendly. "Don't worry about a thing. You just keep our guest happy until airtime. I'll take care of the rest."

"He wants your word, Angela."

"Honey, you give him whatever he wants." She laughed; Lew's headache sprang into full-blown agony. "Don't be such a worrier." She leaned forward to pluck a cigarette from the pack of Virginia Slims on the dressing table. She flicked on a gold monogrammed lighter, a gift from her second husband. She blew out one thin stream of smoke.

Lew was getting soft, she mused, personally as well as professionally. Though he wore a suit and tie, as dictated by her dress code, his shoulders were slumped as if pulled down by the weight of his expanding belly. His hair was thinning out, too, she realized, and was heavily streaked with gray. Her show was known for its energy and speed. She didn't enjoy having her producer look like a pudgy old man.

16

"After all these years, Lew, you should trust me."

"Angela, if you attack Deke Barrow, you're going to make it tough for us to book other celebrities."

"Bull. They're six deep waiting for a chance to do my show." She jabbed her cigarette in the air like a lance. "They want me to hype their movies and their TV specials and their books and their records, and they damn well want me to hype their love lives. They need me, Lew, because they know that every day millions of people tune in." She smiled into the mirror, and the face that smiled back was lovely, composed, polished. "And they tune in for me."

Lew had worked with Angela for more than five years and knew exactly how to handle a dispute. He wheedled. "Nobody's denying that, Angela. You *are* the show. I just think you should tread lightly with Deke. He's been around the country-music scene a long time, and this comeback of his has a lot of sentiment behind him."

"Just leave Deke to me." She smiled behind a mist of smoke. "I'll be very sentimental."

She picked up the note cards that Deanna had finished organizing at seven that morning. It was a gesture of dismissal that had Lew shaking his head. Angela's smile widened as she skimmed through the notes. The girl was good, she mused. Very good, very thorough.

Very useful.

Angela took one last contemplative drag on her cigarette before crushing it out in the heavy crystal ashtray on her dressing table. As always, every pot, every brush, every tube was aligned in meticulous order. There was a vase of two dozen red roses, which were brought in fresh every morning, and a small dish of multi-colored coated mints that Angela loved.

She thrived on routine, at being able to control her environment, including the people around her. Everyone had their place. She was enjoying making one for Deanna Reynolds.

Some might have thought it odd that a woman approaching forty, a vain woman, would have taken on a younger, lovely woman as a favored apprentice. But Angela had been a pretty woman who with time, experience and illusion had become a beautiful one. And she had no fear of age. Not in a world where it could be so easily combated.

She wanted Deanna behind her because of her looks, because of her talent, because of her youth. Most of all, because power scented power.

And for the very simple reason that she liked the girl.

Oh, she would offer Deanna tidbits of advice, friendly criticism, dollops of praise—and perhaps, in time, a position of some merit. But she had no intention of allowing someone she already sensed as a potential competitor to break free. No one broke free from Angela Perkins.

She had two ex-husbands who had learned that. They hadn't broken free. They had been dispatched.

"Angela?"

"Deanna." Angela flung out a hand in welcome. "I was just thinking about you. Your notes are wonderful. They'll add so much to the show."

"Glad I could help." Deanna lifted a hand to toy with her left earring, a sign of hesitation she'd yet to master. "Angela, I feel awkward asking you this, but my mother is a huge fan of Deke Barrow's."

"And you'd like an autograph."

After a quick, embarrassed smile, Deanna brought out the CD she was holding behind her back. "She'd love it if he could sign this for her."

"You just leave it to me." Angela tapped one perfect, French-manicured nail along the edge of the CD. "And what is your mother's name again, Dee?"

"It's Marilyn. I really appreciate it, Angela."

"Anything I can do for you, sweetie." She waited a beat. Her timing had always been excellent. "Oh, and there is a little favor you could do for me."

"Of course."

"Would you make reservations for dinner for me tonight, at La Fontaine, seven-thirty, for two? I simply don't have time to deal with it myself, and I forgot to tell my secretary to handle it."

"No problem." Deanna pulled a pad out of her pocket to make a note.

"You're a treasure, Deanna." Angela stood then to take a final check of her pale blue suit in a cheval glass. "What do you think of this color? It's not too washed-out, is it?"

Because she knew that Angela fretted over every detail of the show, from research to the proper footwear, Deanna took time for a serious study. The soft drape of the fabric suited Angela's compact, curvy figure beautifully. "Coolly feminine."

The tension in Angela's shoulders unknotted. "Perfect, then. Are you staying for the taping?"

"I can't. I still have copy to write for *Midday*."

"Oh." The annoyance surfaced, but only briefly. "I hope helping me out hasn't put you behind."

"There are twenty-four hours in the day," Deanna said. "I like to use all of them. Now, I'd better get out of your way."

"'Bye, honey."

Deanna shut the door behind her. Everyone in the building knew that Angela insisted on having the last ten minutes before she took the stage to herself. Everyone assumed she used that time to go over her notes. That was nonsense, of course. She was completely prepared. But she preferred that they think of her brushing up on her information. Or even that they imagine her taking a quick nip from the bottle of brandy she kept in her dressing table.

Not that she would touch the brandy. The need to keep it there, just within reach, terrified as much as it comforted.

She preferred they believe anything, as long as they didn't know the truth.

Angela Perkins spent those last solitary moments before each taping in a trembling cycle of panic. She, a woman who exuded an image of supreme self-confidence; she, a woman who had interviewed presidents, royalty, murderers and millionaires, succumbed, as she always did, to a vicious, violent attack of stage fright.

Hundreds of hours of therapy had done nothing to alleviate the shuddering, the sweating, the nausea. Helpless against it, she collapsed in her chair, drawing herself in. The mirror reflected her in triplicate, the polished woman, perfectly groomed, immaculately presented. Eyes glazed with the terror of self-discovery.

Angela pressed her hands to her temples and rode out the screaming roller coaster of fear. Today she would slip, and they would hear the backwoods of Arkansas in her voice. They would see the girl who had been unloved and unwanted by a mother who had preferred the flickering images on the pitted screen of the tiny Philco to her own flesh and blood. The girl who had wanted attention so badly, so desperately, she had imagined herself inside that television so that her mother would focus those vague, drunken eyes just once, and look at her.

They would see the girl in the secondhand clothes and ill-fitting shoes who had studied so hard to make average grades.

They would see that she was nothing, no one, a fraud who had bluffed her way into television the same way her father had bluffed his way into an inside straight.

And they would laugh at her.

Or worse, turn her off.

The knock on the door made her flinch.

"We're set, Angela."

She took a deep breath, then another. "On my way." Her voice was perfectly normal. She was a master at pretense. For a few seconds longer, she stared at her reflection, watching the panic fade from her own eyes.

She wouldn't fail. She would never be laughed at. She would never be ignored again. And no one would see anything she didn't allow them to see. She rose, walked out of her dressing room, down the corridor.

She had yet to see her guest and continued past the green room without a blink. She never spoke to a guest before the tape was rolling.

Her producer was warming up the studio audience. There was a hum of excitement from those fortunate enough to have secured tickets to the taping. Marcie, tottering in four-inch heels, rushed up for a last-minute check on hair and makeup. A researcher passed Angela a few more cards. Angela spoke to neither of them.

When she walked onstage, the hum burst open into a full-throttle cheer.

"Good morning." Angela took her chair and let the applause wash over her while she was miked. "I hope everyone's ready for a great show." She scanned the audience as she spoke and was pleased with the demographics. It was a good mix of age, sex and race—an important visual for the camera pans. "Anyone here a Deke Barrow fan?"

She laughed heartily at the next round of applause. "Me too," she said, though she detested country music in any form. "I'd say we're all in for a treat."

She nodded, settled back, legs crossed, hands folded over the arm of her chair. The red light on the camera blinked on. The intro music swung jazzily through the air.

"'Lost Tomorrows,' 'That Green-Eyed Girl,' 'One Wild Heart'. Those are just a few of the hits that made today's guest a legend. He's been a part of country-music history for more than twenty-five years, and his current album, *Lost in Nashville*, is zooming up the charts. Please join me in welcoming, to Chicago, Deke Barrow."

The applause thundered out again as Deke strode out onstage. Barrel-chested, with graying temples peeking out from beneath his black felt Stetson, Deke grinned at the audience before accepting Angela's warm handshake. She stood back, letting him milk the moment by tipping his hat.

With every appearance of delight, she joined in the audience's

21

standing ovation. By the end of the hour, she thought, Deke would stagger offstage. And he wouldn't even know what had hit him.

ANGELA WAITED UNTIL THE SECOND half of the show to strike. Like a good host, she had flattered her guest, listened attentively to his anecdotes, chuckled at his jokes. Now Deke was basking in the admiration as Angela held the mike for excited fans as they stood to ask questions. She waited, canny as a cobra.

"Deke, I wondered if you're going by Danville, Kentucky, on your tour. That's my hometown," a blushing redhead asked.

"Well now, I can't say as we are. But we'll be in Louisville on the seventeenth of June. You be sure to tell your friends to come on by and see me."

"Your *Lost in Nashville* tour's going to keep you on the road for several months," Angela began. "That's rough on you, isn't it?"

"Rougher than it used to be," he answered with a wink. "I ain't twenty anymore." His broad, guitar-plucking hands lifted and spread. "But I gotta say I love it. Singing in a recording studio can't come close to what it's like to sing for people."

"And the tour's certainly been a success so far. There's no truth, then, to the rumor that you may have to cut it short because of your difficulties with the IRS?"

Deke's congenial grin slipped several notches. "No, ma'am. We'll finish it out."

"I feel safe in speaking for everyone here when I say you have our support in this. Tax evasion." She rolled her eyes in disbelief. "They make you sound like Al Capone."

"I really can't talk about it." Deke shuffled his booted feet, tugged at his bola tie. "But nobody's calling it tax evasion."

"Oh." She widened her eyes. "I'm sorry. What are they calling it?"

He shifted uncomfortably on his chair. "It's a disagreement on back taxes."

22

"'Disagreement' is a mild word for it. I realize you can't really discuss this while the matter's under investigation, but I think it's an outrage. A man like you, who's brought pleasure to millions, for two generations, to be faced with potential financial ruin because his books weren't in perfect order."

"It's not as bad as all that—"

"But you've had to put your home in Nashville on the market." Her voice dripped sympathy. Her eyes gleamed with it. "I think the country you've celebrated in your music should show more compassion, more gratitude. Don't you?"

She hit the right button.

"Seems like the tax man doesn't have much to do with the country I've been singing about for twenty-five years." Deke's mouth thinned, his eyes hardened like agates. "They look at dollar signs. They don't think about how hard a man's worked. How much he sweats to make something of himself. They just keep slicing at you till most of what's yours is theirs. They turn honest folk into liars and cheaters."

"You're not saying you cheated on your taxes, are you, Deke?" She smiled guilelessly when he froze. "We'll be back in a moment," she said to the camera, and waited until the red light blinked off. "I'm sure most of us here have been squeezed by the IRS, Deke." Turning her back on him, she held up her hands. "We're behind him, aren't we, audience?"

There was an explosion of applause and cheers that did nothing to erase the look of sickly shock from Deke's face.

"I can't talk about it," he managed. "Can I get some water?"

"We'll put the matter to rest, don't you worry. We'll have time for a few more questions." Angela turned to her audience again as an assistant rushed out with a glass of water for Deke. "I'm sure Deke would appreciate it if we avoided any more discussion on this sensitive subject. Let's be sure to give him plenty of applause when we get back from commercial, and give Deke some time to compose himself."

With this outpouring of support and empathy, she swung back toward the camera. "You're back with *Angela's*. We have time for just a couple more questions, but at Deke's request, we'll close the door on any discussion of his tax situation, as he isn't free to defend himself while the case is still pending."

And of course, when she closed the show moments later, that was exactly the subject on every viewer's mind.

Angela didn't linger among her audience, but joined Deke onstage. "Wonderful show." She took his limp hand in her firm grasp. "Thank you so much for coming. And the best of luck."

"Thank you." Shell-shocked, he began signing autographs until the assistant producer led him offstage.

"Get me a tape," Angela ordered as she strode back to her dressing room. "I want to see the last segment." She walked straight to her mirror and smiled at her own reflection.

Chapter Two

DEANNA HATED COVERING TRAGEDIES. INTELLECTUALLY SHE knew it was her job as a journalist to report the news, and to interview those who had been wounded by it. She believed, unwaveringly, in the public's right to know. But emotionally, whenever she pointed a microphone toward grief she felt like the worst kind of voyeur.

"The quiet suburb of Wood Dale was the scene of sudden and violent tragedy this morning. Police suspect that a domestic dispute resulted in the shooting death of Lois Dossier, thirty-two, an elementary school teacher and Chicago native. Her husband, Dr. Charles Dossier, has been taken into custody. The couple's two children, ages five and seven, are in the care of their maternal grandparents. At shortly after eight A.M. this morning, this quiet, affluent home erupted with gunfire."

Deanna steadied herself as the camera panned the trim two-story dwelling behind her. She continued her report, staring straight at the lens, ignoring the crowd that gathered, the other news teams doing their stand-ups, the sweet spring breeze that carried the poignant scent of hyacinth.

Her voice was steady, suitably detached. But her eyes were filled with swirling emotion.

"At eight-fifteen A.M., police responded to reports of gunfire, and Lois Dossier was pronounced dead on the scene. According to neighbors, Mrs. Dossier was a devoted mother who took an active interest in community projects. She was well liked and well respected. Among her closest friends was her next-door neighbor, Bess Pierson, who reported the disturbance to the police." Deanna turned to the woman at her side, who was dressed in purple sweats. "Mrs. Pierson, to your knowledge, was there any violence in the Dossier household before this morning?"

"Yes—no. I never thought he would hurt her. I still can't believe it." The camera zoomed in on the swollen, tear-streaked face of a woman pale with shock. "She was my closest friend. We've lived next door to each other for six years. Our children play together."

Tears began to spill over. Despising herself, Deanna clutched the woman's hand with her free one, and continued. "Knowing both Lois and Charles Dossier, do you agree with the police that this tragedy was a result of a domestic dispute that spiraled out of control?"

"I don't know what to think. I know they were having marital problems. There were fights, shouting matches." The woman stared into the void, shell-shocked. "Lois told me she wanted to get Chuck to go into counseling with her, but he wouldn't." She began to sob now, one hand covering her eyes. "He wouldn't, and now she's gone. Oh God, she was like my sister."

"Cut," Deanna snapped, then wrapped her arm around Mrs. Pierson's shoulders. "I'm sorry. I'm so sorry. You shouldn't be out here now."

"I keep thinking this is a dream. That it can't be real."

"Is there somewhere you can go? A friend or a relative?" Deanna scanned the trim yard, crowded with curious neighbors and determined reporters. A few feet to the left another crew was rolling tape. The reporter kept blowing the takes, laughing at his own twisting tongue. "Things aren't going to quiet down here for a while."

"Yes." After a last, sobbing breath, Mrs. Pierson wiped at her eyes. "We were going to the movies tonight," she said, then turned and dashed away.

"God." Deanna watched as other reporters stabbed their microphones toward the fleeing woman.

"Your heart bleeds too much," her cameraman commented.

"Shut up, Joe." She pulled herself in, drew a breath. Her heart might have been bleeding, but she couldn't let it affect her judgment. Her job was to give a clear, concise report, to inform and to give the viewer a visual that would make an impact.

"Let's finish it. We want it for *Midday*. Zoom up to the bedroom window, then come back to me. Make sure you get the hyacinths and daffodils in frame, and the kid's red wagon. Got it?"

Joe studied the scene, the White Sox fielder's cap perched on his wiry brown hair tipped down to shade his eyes. He could already see the pictures, cut, framed, edited. He squinted, nodded. Muscles bunched under his sweatshirt as he hefted the camera. "Ready when you are."

"Then in three, two, one." She waited a beat while the camera zoomed in, panned down. "Lois-Dossier's violent death has left this quiet community rocked. While her friends and family ask why, Dr. Charles Dossier is being held pending bond. This is Deanna Reynolds in Wood Dale, reporting for CBC."

"Nice job, Deanna." Joe shut down the camera.

"Yeah, dandy." On her way to the van, she put two Rolaids in her mouth.

CBC USED THE TAPE AGAIN ON the local portion of the evening news, with an update from the precinct where Dossier was being held on charges of second-degree murder. Curled in a chair in her apartment, Deanna watched objectively as the anchor segued from the top story into a piece on a fire in a South Side apartment building.

"Good piece, Dee." Sprawled on the couch was Fran Myers.

Her curly red hair was lopsidedly anchored on top of her head. She had a sharp, foxy face accented by eyes the color of chestnuts. Her voice was pure New Jersey brass. Unlike Deanna, she hadn't grown up in a quiet suburban home in a tree-lined neighborhood, but in a noisy apartment in Atlantic City, New Jersey, with a twice-divorced mother and a changing array of step-siblings.

She sipped ginger ale, then gestured with her glass toward the screen. The movement was as lazy as a yawn. "You always look so great on camera. Video makes me look like a pudgy gnome."

"I had to try to interview the victim's mother." Jamming her hands in the pockets of her jeans, Deanna sprang up to pace the room, wiry energy in every step. "She wouldn't answer the phone, and like a good reporter, I tracked down the address. They wouldn't answer the door, either. Kept the curtains drawn. I stayed outside with a bunch of other members of the press for nearly an hour. I felt like a ghoul."

"You ought to know by now that the terms 'ghoul' and 'reporter' are interchangeable." But Deanna didn't smile. Fran recognized the guilt beneath the restless movements. After setting down her glass, Fran pointed to the chair. "Okay. Sit down and listen to advice from Auntie Fran."

"I can't take advice standing up?"

"Nope." Fran snagged Deanna's hand and yanked her down onto the sofa. Despite the contrasts in backgrounds and styles, they'd been friends since freshman orientation in college. Fran had seen Deanna wage this war between intellect and emotion dozens of times. "Okay. Question number one: Why did you go to Yale?"

"Because I got a scholarship."

"Don't rub your brains in my face, Einstein. What did you and I go to college for?"

"You went to meet men."

Fran narrowed her eyes. "That was just a side benefit. Stop stalling and answer the question."

Defeated, Deanna let out a sigh. "We went to study, to become journalists, to get high-paying, high-profile jobs on television."

"Absolutely correct. And have we succeeded?"

"Sort of. We have our degrees. I'm a reporter for CBC and you're associate producer of *Woman Talk* on cable."

"Excellent launching points. Now, have you forgotten the famous Deanna Reynolds's Five-Year Plan? If so, I'm sure there's a typed copy of it in that desk."

Deanna glanced over at her pride and joy, the single fine piece of furniture she'd acquired since moving to Chicago. She'd picked up the beautifully patinated Queen Anne desk at an auction. And Fran was right. There was a typed copy of Deanna's career plan in the top drawer. In duplicate.

Since college, she had modified her plans somewhat. Fran had married and settled in Chicago and had urged her former roommate to come out and try her luck.

"Year One," Deanna remembered. "An on-camera job in Kansas City."

"Done."

"Year Two, a position at CBC, Chicago."

"Accomplished."

"Year Three, a small, tasteful segment of my own."

"The current 'Deanna's Corner'," Fran said, and toasted the segment with her ginger ale.

"Year Four, anchoring the evening news. Local."

"Which you've already done, several times, as substitute."

"Year Five, audition tapes and résumés to the holy ground: New York."

"Which will never be able to resist your combination of style, on-camera appeal and sincerity—unless, of course, you continue to second-guess yourself."

"You're right, but—"

"No buts." On this Fran was firm. She expended some of the energy she preferred to hoard by propping her feet on the coffee table. "You do good work, Dee. People talk to you because you have compassion. That's an advantage in a journalist, not a flaw."

"It doesn't help me sleep at night." Restless and suddenly tired, Deanna scooped a hand through her hair. After curling her legs up, she studied the room, brooding.

There was the rickety dinette she'd yet to find a suitable replacement for, the frayed rug, the single solid armchair she'd had re-covered in a soft gray. Only the desk stood out, gleaming, a testimony to partial success. Yet everything was in its place; the few trinkets she'd collected were arranged precisely.

This tidy apartment wasn't the home of her dreams, but as Fran had pointed out, it was an excellent launching point. And she fully intended to launch herself, both personally and professionally.

"Do you remember, back at college, how exciting we thought it would be to sprint after ambulances, interview mass murderers, to write incisive copy that would rivet the viewers' attention? Well, it is." Letting out a sigh, Deanna rose to pace again. "But you really pay for the kick." She paused a moment, picked up a little china box, set it down again. "Angela's hinted that I could have the job as head researcher on her show for the asking—on-air credit with a significant raise in salary."

Because she didn't want to influence her friend, Fran pursed her lips and kept her voice neutral. "And you're considering it?"

"Every time I do, I remember I'd be giving up the camera." With a half laugh, Deanna shook her head. "I'd miss that little red light. See, here's the thing." She plopped down on the arm of the couch. Her eyes were glowing again, darkened to smoke with suppressed excitement. "I don't want to be Angela's head researcher. I'm not even sure I want New York anymore. I think I want my own show. To be syndicated in a hundred and twenty markets. I want a twenty-percent share. I want to be on the cover of *TV Guide*."

Fran grinned. "So, what's stopping you?"

"Nothing." More confident now that she'd said it aloud, Deanna shifted, resting her bare feet on the cushion of the sofa. "Maybe that's Year Seven or Eight, I haven't figured it out yet. But

I want it, and I can do it. But—" She blew out a breath. "It means covering tears and torment until I've earned my stripes."

"The Deanna Reynolds's Extended Career Plan."

"Exactly." She was glad Fran understood.

"You don't think I'm crazy?"

"Sweet pea, I think that anyone with your meticulous mind, your camera presence and your polite yet strong ambition will get exactly what she wants." Fran reached into the bowl of sugared almonds on the coffee table, popped three in her mouth. "Just don't forget the little people when you do."

"What was your name again?"

Fran threw a pillow at her. "Okay, now that we have your life settled, I'd like to announce an addition to the Fran Myers's My Life Is Never What I Thought It Would Be Saga."

"You got a promotion?"

"Nope."

"Richard got one?"

"No, though a junior partnership at Dowell, Dowell and Fritz may be in the offing." She drew a deep breath. Her redhead's complexion flushed like a blooming rose. "I'm pregnant."

"What?" Deanna blinked. "Pregnant? Really?" Laughing, she slid down on the couch to grasp Fran's hands. "A baby? This is wonderful. This is incredible." Deanna threw her arms around Fran to squeeze, then pulled back sharply to study her friend's face. "Isn't it?"

"You bet it is. We weren't planning on it for another year or two, but hell, it takes nine months, right?"

"Last I heard. You're happy. I can see it. I just can't believe—" She stopped, jerked back again. "Jesus, Fran. You've been here nearly an hour, and you're just getting around to telling me. Talk about burying the lead."

Feeling smug, Fran patted her flat belly. "I wanted everything else out of the way so you could concentrate on me. Us."

"No problem there. Are you sick in the mornings or anything?"

"Me?" Fran quirked a brow. "With my cast-iron stomach?"

"Right. What did Richard say?"

"Before or after he stopped dancing on the ceiling?"

Deanna laughed again, then sprang up to do a quick spin of her own. A baby, she thought. She had to plan a shower, shop for stuffed animals, buy savings bonds. "We have to celebrate."

"What did we do in college when we had something to celebrate?"

"Chinese and cheap white wine," Deanna said with a grin. "Perfect, with the adjustment of Grade A milk."

Fran winced, then shrugged. "I guess I'll have to get used to it. I do have a favor to ask."

"Name it."

"Work on that career plan, Dee. I think I'd like my kid to have a star for a godmommy."

WHEN THE PHONE RANG AT SIX A.M., Deanna pulled herself out of sleep and into a hangover. Clutching her head with one hand, she fumbled for the receiver with the other.

"Reynolds."

"Deanna, darling, I'm so sorry to wake you."

"Angela?"

"Who else would be rude enough to call you at this hour?" Angela's light laugh came through the phone as Deanna blearily looked at the clock. "I have an enormous favor to ask. We're taping today, and Lew's down with a virus."

"I'm sorry." Valiantly, Deanna cleared her throat and managed to sit up.

"These things happen. It's just that we're dealing with a sensitive issue today, and when I considered it, I realized you would really be the perfect one to handle the guests offstage. That's Lew's area, you know, so I'm really in a bind."

"What about Simon, or Maureen?" Her brain might have been cloudy, but Deanna remembered the chain of command.

"Neither one of them are suited for this. Simon does excellent pre-interviews over the phone, and God knows Maureen's a jewel at handling transportation and lodging arrangements. But these guests require a very special touch. Your touch."

"I'd be glad to help, Angela, but I'm due in to the station at nine."

"I'll clear it with your producer, dear. He owes me. Simon can handle the second taping, but if you could just see your way clear to helping me out this morning, I'd be so grateful."

"Sure." Deanna shoved her tousled hair back and resigned herself to a quick cup of coffee and a bottle of aspirin. "As long as there's no conflict."

"Don't worry about that. I still have clout with the news department. I'll need you here by eight, sharp. Thanks, honey."

"All right, but—"

Still dazed, Deanna stared at the phone as the dial tone hummed. A couple of details had been overlooked, she mused. What the hell was this morning's topic, and who were the guests that needed such special care?

DEANNA STEPPED INTO THE GREEN room with an uneasy smile on her face and a fresh pot of coffee in her hand. She knew the topic now, and scanned the seven scheduled guests cautiously, like a veteran soldier surveying a mine field.

Marital triangles. Deanna took a bracing breath. Two couples and the other women who had almost destroyed their marriages. A mine field might have been safer.

"Good morning." The room remained ominously silent except for the murmur of the morning news from the television. "I'm Deanna Reynolds. Welcome to *Angela's*. Can I freshen anyone's coffee?"

"Thank you." The man seated in a chair in the corner shifted the open briefcase on his lap, then held out his cup. He gave Deanna a quick smile that was heightened by the amusement glittering out of soft brown eyes. "I'm Dr. Pike. Marshall Pike." He lowered his voice as Deanna topped off his cup. "Don't worry, they're unarmed."

Deanna's eyes lifted to his, held. "They still have teeth and nails," she murmured.

She knew who he was, the segment expert, a psychologist who would attempt to cap this particular can of worms before the roll of ending credits. Mid-thirties, she gauged, with the quick expertise of a cop or a reporter. Confident, relaxed, attractive. Conservative, judging by his carefully trimmed blond hair and well-tailored chalk-striped suit. His wing tips were polished to a high gleam, his nails were manicured and his smile was easy.

"I'll watch your flank," he offered, "if you watch mine."

She smiled back. "Deal. Mr. and Mrs. Forrester?" Deanna paused as the couple glanced toward her. The woman's face was set in a resentful scowl, the man's in miserable embarrassment. "You'll be on first . . . with Miss Draper."

Lori Draper, the last segment of the triangle, beamed with excitement. She looked more like a bouncy cheerleader ready to execute a flashy C jump than a sultry vamp. "Is my outfit okay for TV?"

Over Mrs. Forrester's snort, Deanna assured her it was. "I know the basic procedure was explained to all of you in the pre-interview. The Forresters and Miss Draper will go out first—"

"I don't want to sit next to her." Mrs. Forrester's hiss squeezed through her tightly primmed mouth.

"That won't be a problem—"

"I don't want Jim sitting next to her, either."

Lori Draper rolled her eyes. "Jeez, Shelly, we broke it off months ago. Do you think I'm going to jump him on national TV, or what?"

"I wouldn't put anything past you." Shelly snatched her hand away as her husband tried to pat it. "We're not sitting next to her," she said to Deanna. "And Jim's not going to talk to her, either. Ever."

This statement set the match to the smoldering embers in triangle number two. Before Deanna could open her mouth, everyone was talking at once. Accusations and bitterness flew through the room. Deanna glanced toward Marshall Pike and was greeted with that same easy smile and a lift of one elegant shoulder.

"All right." Deanna pitched her voice over the din as she stepped into the fray. "I'm sure you all have valid points, and quite a bit to say. Why don't we save it for the show? All of you agreed to come on this morning to tell your sides of the story, and to look for some possible resolutions. I'm sure we can arrange the seating to suit everyone."

She ran briskly through the rest of the instructions, controlling the guests in the same way a kindergarten teacher controls recalcitrant five-year-olds. With determined cheerfulness and a firm hand.

"Now, Mrs. Forrester—Shelly—Jim, Lori, if you'll all come with me, we'll get you settled and miked."

Ten minutes later, Deanna stepped back into the green room, grateful that no blood had been spilled. While the remaining triangle sat stonily, staring at the television screen, Marshall was up, perusing a tray of pastries.

"Nicely done, Ms. Reynolds."

"Thank you, Dr. Pike."

"Marshall." He chose a cinnamon danish. "It's a tricky situation. Though the triangle was technically broken when the affair ended, emotionally, morally, even intellectually, it remains."

Damn right, she thought. If anyone she loved cheated on her, it would be he who would be broken—in every way. "I suppose you deal with similar situations in your practice."

"Often. I decided to focus on the area after my own divorce." His smile was sweet and sheepish. "For obvious reasons." He glanced down at her hands, noting that she wore a single ring, a garnet in an antique gold setting on her right hand. "You're not in the market for my particular skill?"

"Not at the moment." Marshall Pike was enormously attractive, she mused—the charming smile, the long, slender build that had even Deanna, who hit five-ten in her heels, tilt her head up to meet the flattering interest in the deep brown eyes. But at this moment she needed to focus the lion's share of her attention on the sullen group behind him.

"The program will start right after this commercial." Deanna gestured toward the set. "Marshall, you won't be going on until the final twenty minutes, but it would help if you'd watch the show to formulate specific advice."

"Naturally." He enjoyed watching her, the way she revved in neutral. He could almost hear the engine gun of her energy. "Don't worry. I've done *Angela's* three times."

"Ah, a vet. Is there anything I can get you?"

His eyes slid toward the trio behind him, then came back to Deanna's. "A flak jacket?"

She chuckled, gave his arm a squeeze. He'd be just fine, she decided. "I'll see what I can do."

The show proved to be emotional, and though bitter accusations flew, no one was seriously wounded. Off camera, Deanna admired the way Angela kept a light hand on the reins, allowing her guests to go their own way, then easing them back when tempers threatened to boil over.

She pulled the audience in as well. With an unerring instinct, she offered the mike to just the right person at just the right time, then segued smoothly back to a question or comment of her own.

As for Dr. Pike, Deanna mused, they couldn't have chosen a more skilled mediator. He exuded the perfect combination of intellect and compassion, mixed with the concise, teaspoon-size advice so necessary for the medium.

When the show was over, the Forresters were clutching hands.

The other couple had stopped speaking to each other, and the two *other women* were chatting like old friends.

Angela had hit the mark again.

"DECIDE TO JOIN US, DEANNA?" Roger pinched her arm as he swung up beside her.

"I know you guys can't get through the day without me." Deanna wove her way through the noisy newsroom toward her desk. Phones were ringing, keyboards clattering. On one wall, current shows from CBC and the other three networks were flashing on monitors. From the smell of things, someone had recently spilled coffee.

"What's our lead?" she asked Roger.

"Last night's fire on the South Side."

With a nod, Deanna sat at her desk. Unlike most of the other reporters, she kept hers meticulously neat. Sharpened pencils stood points down in a flowered ceramic cup, a notepad aligned beside them. Her Filofax was opened to today's date.

"Arson?"

"That's the general consensus. I've got the copy. We've got a taped interview with the fire marshal, and a live remote at the scene." Roger offered her his bag of licorice. "And being a nice guy, I picked up your mail."

"So I see. Thanks."

"Caught a few minutes of *Angela's* this morning." He chewed thoughtfully on his candy. "Doesn't discussing adultery so early in the day make people nervous?"

"It gives them something to talk about over lunch." She picked up an ebony letter opener and slit the first envelope.

"Venting on national television?"

She lifted a brow. "Venting on national television seemed to have helped the Forresters' relationship."

"Looked to me like the other couple was heading for divorce court."

"Sometimes divorce is the answer."

"Is that what you think?" He kept the question light. "If your spouse was cheating, would you forgive and forget, or would you file papers?"

"Well, I'd listen, I'd discuss it, try to find out the reason it happened. Then I'd shoot the adulterous swine full of holes." She grinned at him. "But, that's just me. And see, hasn't it given us something to talk about?" She glanced down at the single sheet in her hand. "Hey, look at this."

She angled the sheet so they could both see it. In the center of the paper, typed in dark red ink, was a single sentence.

Deanna, I love you.

"The old secret admirer, hmm?" Roger spoke carelessly, but there was a frown in his eyes.

"Looks that way." Curious, she turned the envelope over. "No return address. No stamp, either."

"I just pulled the mail out of your box." Roger shook his head. "Somebody must have slipped it in."

"It's kind of sweet, I guess." She rubbed a quick chill from her arms and laughed. "And creepy."

"You might want to ask around, see if anybody noticed somebody sneaking around your mail slot."

"It's not important." She tossed both letter and envelope in the trash and picked up the next.

"Excuse me."

"Oh, Dr. Pike." Deanna set down her mail and smiled at the man standing behind Roger. "Did you get lost on your way out?"

"No, actually, I was told I'd find you here."

"Dr. Marshall Pike, Roger Crowell."

"Yes, I recognized you." Marshall offered a hand. "I watch you both often."

"I just caught part of your act myself." Roger slipped his bag of candy into his pocket. His thoughts were still focused on the letter, and he promised himself he'd slip it back out of her trash at the first possible moment. "We need copy on the dog show, Dee."

"No problem."

"Nice to have met you, Dr. Pike."

"Same here." Marshall turned back to Deanna when Roger walked away. "I wanted to thank you for keeping things sane this morning."

"It's one of the things I do best."

"I'd have to agree. I've always thought you report the news with clearheaded compassion. It's a remarkable combination."

"And a remarkable compliment. Thanks."

He took a survey of the newsroom. Two reporters were arguing bitterly over baseball, phones were shrilling, an intern wheeled a cart heaped with files through the narrow spaces between desks. "Interesting place."

"It is that. I'd be glad to give you a tour, but I do have copy to write for *Midday*."

"Then I'll take a rain check." He looked back at her, that sweet, easy smile at the corners of his mouth. "Deanna, I was hoping, since we've been through the trenches together, so to speak, you'd be willing to have dinner with me."

"Dinner." She studied him more carefully now, as a woman does when a man stops being simply a man and becomes a possible relationship. It would have been foolish to pretend he didn't appeal to her. "Yes, I suppose I'd be willing to do that."

"Tonight? Say, seven-thirty?"

She hesitated. She was rarely impulsive. He was a professional, she mused, well mannered, easy on the eyes. And more important, he had exhibited both intelligence and heart under pressure. "Sure." She took a square of notepaper from a smoked-glass holder and wrote down her address.

Chapter Three

"COMING UP ON *MIDDAY*, THE STORY OF A WOMAN WHO opens her home and heart to Chicago's underprivileged children. Also the latest sports report with Les Ryder, and the forecast for the weekend with Dan Block. Join us at noon."

The minute the red light blinked out, Deanna unhooked her mike and scrambled up from the news desk. She had copy to finish and a phone interview scheduled, and she needed to review her notes for the upcoming "Deanna's Corner." In the two weeks since she had pinch-hit for Lew, she'd put in more than a hundred hours on the job without breaking stride.

She whipped through the studio doors and was halfway down the hall toward the newsroom when Angela stopped her.

"Honey, you only have two speeds. Stop and go."

Deanna paused only because Angela blocked the way.

"Right now it's go. I'm swamped."

"I've never known you not to get everything done, and at exactly the proper time." To keep her in place, Angela laid a hand on her arm. "And this will only take a minute."

Deanna struggled with impatience. "You can have two, if we talk on the move."

"Fine." Angela turned and matched her stride to Deanna's. "I've got a business lunch in an hour, so I'm a little strapped myself. I need a tiny favor."

"All right." With her mind already on her work, Deanna swung into the newsroom and headed for her desk. Her papers were stacked according to priority: the precise notes to be transcribed and expanded into copy, the list of questions for the phoner and her cards for "Deanna's Corner." She turned on her machine and typed her password while she waited for Angela to explain.

Angela took her time. She hadn't been in the newsroom for months, she mused, possibly longer, since her offices and studio were in what CBC employees called "the Tower," a slim white spear that shot up from the building. It was a not-so-subtle way to separate the national and non-news programs from the local ones.

"I'm giving a little party tomorrow night. Finn Riley's due back from London this evening, and I thought I'd give a little welcome-home thing for him."

"Mmm-hmm." Deanna was already working on her lead.

"He's been gone so long this time, and after that nasty business in Panama before he went back to his London post, I thought he deserved some R and R."

Deanna wasn't sure a small, bloody war should be called "that nasty business," but she nodded.

"Since it's all so impulsive, I really need some help putting everything together. The caterers, the flowers, the music—and of course, the party itself. Making sure everything runs smoothly. My secretary just can't handle it all, and I really want it to be perfect. If you could give me a couple of hours later today—and tomorrow, of course."

Deanna battled back the sense of resentment, and obligation. "Angela, I'd love to help you out, but I'm booked."

Angela's persuasive smile never altered, but her eyes chilled. "You're not scheduled for Saturday."

"No, not here—though I am on call. But I have plans." Deanna began to tap a finger on her notes. "A date."

"I see." Angela's hand went to her pearls, where her fingers rubbed one smooth, glowing sphere. "Rumor has it that you've been seeing a lot of Dr. Marshall Pike."

The evening news might run on facts and verified information, but Deanna understood that newsrooms and television studios ran on gossip. "We've been out a few times in the last couple of weeks."

"Well, I wouldn't want to interfere—and I hope you won't take this the wrong way, Dee." To add intimacy to the statement, Angela rested a hip on Deanna's desk. "Do you really think he's your type?"

Torn between manners and her own schedule, Deanna chose manners. "I don't really have one. A type, I mean."

"Of course you do." With a light laugh, Angela tilted her head. "Young, well built, the outdoorsy type. Athletic," she continued. "You need someone who can keep up with the vicious pace you set for yourself. And a good intellect, naturally, but not overly cerebral. You need someone who can make his point in quick, fifteen-second bites."

She really didn't have time for any of this. Deanna picked up one of her sharpened pencils and ran it through her fingers. "That makes me sound sort of shallow."

"Not at all." Angela's eyes widened in protest even as she chuckled. "Darling, I only want the very best for you. I'd hate to see a passing interest interfere with the momentum of your career, and as for Marshall . . . He's a bit slick, isn't he?"

Temper glinted in Deanna's eyes, and was quickly suppressed. "I don't know what you mean. I enjoy his company."

"Of course you do." Angela patted Deanna's shoulder. "What young woman wouldn't? An older man, experienced, smooth. But to let him interfere with your work—"

"He's not interfering with anything. We've gone out a few times in the last couple of weeks, that's all. I'm sorry, Angela, but I really have to get back on schedule here."

"Sorry," she said coolly. "I thought we were friends. I didn't think a little constructive advice would offend you."

"It hasn't." Deanna fought back a sigh. "But I'm on deadline. Listen, if I can squeeze out some time later today, I'll do what I can to help you with the party."

As if a switch had been thrown, the icy stare melted into the warmest of smiles. "You're a jewel. Tell you what, just to prove there's no hard feelings, you bring Marshall tomorrow night."

"Angela—"

"Now, I won't take no for an answer." She slid off the desk. "And if you could get there just an hour or two early, I'd be so grateful. No one organizes like you, Dee. We'll talk about all of this later."

Deanna leaned back in her chair when Angela strolled away. She felt as though she'd been steamrolled with velvet.

With a shake of her head, she looked down at her notes, her fingers poised over her keyboard. Frowning, she relaxed them again. Angela was wrong, she thought. Marshall wasn't interfering with her work. Being interested in someone didn't have to clash with ambition.

She enjoyed going out with him. She liked his mind—the way he could open it to see both sides of a situation. And the way he laughed when she dug in on an opinion and refused to budge.

She appreciated the fact that he was letting the physical end of their relationship develop slowly, at her pace. Though she had to admit it was becoming tempting to speed things up. It had been a long time since she'd felt safe enough, and strong enough, with a man to invite intimacy.

Once she did, Deanna thought, she would have to tell him everything.

She shook the memory away quickly, before it could dig its claws into her heart. She knew from experience it was best to cross one bridge at a time, then to prepare to span the next.

The first bridge was to analyze her relationship with Marshall, if there was a relationship, and to decide where she wanted it to go.

A glance at the clock made her moan.

43

She would have to cross that personal bridge on her own time. Setting her fingers on the keyboard, she got to work.

ANGELA'S STAFF PRIVATELY CALLED her suite of offices "the citadel." She reigned like a feudal lord from her French provincial desk, handing out commands and meting out reward and punishment in equal measures. Anyone who remained on staff after a six-month probationary period was loyal and diligent and kept his or her complaints private.

She was, admittedly, exacting, impatient with excuses and demanding of certain personal luxuries. She had, after all, earned such requirements.

Angela stepped into the outer office, where her executive secretary was busily handling details for Monday's taping. There were other offices—producers, researchers, assistants—down the quiet hallway. Angela had long since left the boisterous bustle of newsrooms behind. She had used reporting not merely as a stepping-stone, but as a catapult for her ambitions. There was only one thing she wanted, and she had wanted it for as long as she could remember: to be the center of attention.

In news, the story was king. The bearer of the tale would be noticed, certainly, if she was good enough. Angela had been very good. Six years in the pressure cooker of on-air reporting had cost her one husband, netted her a second and paved the way for *Angela's*.

She much preferred, and insisted on, the church-like silence of thick carpets and insulated walls.

"You have some messages, Miss Perkins."

"Later." Angela yanked open one of the double doors leading to her private office. "I need you inside, Cassie."

She began to pace immediately. Even when she heard the quiet click of the door closing behind her secretary, she continued to move restlessly, over the Aubusson, past the elegant desk, away

44

from the wide ribbon of windows, toward the antique curio cabinet that held her collection of awards.

Mine, she thought. She had earned them, she possessed them. Now that she did, no one would ever ignore her again.

She paused by the framed photos and prints that adorned a wall. Pictures of Angela with celebrities at charity events and award ceremonies. Her covers of *TV Guide* and *Time* and *People*. She stared at them, drawing deep breaths.

"Does she realize who I am?" she murmured. "Does she realize who she's dealing with?"

With a shake of her head, she turned away again. It was a small mistake, she reminded herself. One that could be easily corrected. After all, she was fond of the girl.

As she grew calmer, she circled her desk, settled into the custom-made pink leather chair the CEO of her syndicate—her former husband—had given her when her show hit number one in the ratings.

Cassie remained standing. She knew better than to approach one of the mahogany chairs with their fussy needlepoint cushions until invited.

"You contacted the caterer?"

"Yes, Miss Perkins. The menu's on your desk."

Angela glanced at it, nodded absently. "The florist?"

"They confirmed everything but the calla lilies," Cassie told her. "They're trying to find the supply you want, but suggested several substitutes."

"If I'd wanted a substitute, I'd have asked for one." She waved her hand. "It's not your fault, Cassie. Sit down." Angela closed her eyes. She was getting one of her headaches, one of those pile-driving thumpers that came on in a rush of pain. Gently, she massaged the center of her forehead with two fingers. Her mother had gotten headaches, she remembered. And had doused them with liquor. "Get me some water, will you? I've got a migraine brewing."

Cassie got up from the chair she'd just taken and walked across the room to the gleaming bar. She was a quiet woman, in looks, in speech. And was ambitious enough to ignore Angela's faults in her desire for advancement. Saying nothing, she chose the crystal decanter that was filled with fresh spring water daily and poured a tumblerful.

"Thanks." Angela downed a Percodan with water, and prayed for it to kick in. She couldn't afford to be distracted during her luncheon meeting. "Do you have a list of acceptances for the party?"

"On your desk."

"Fine." Angela kept her eyes closed. "Give a copy of it, and everything else, to Deanna. She'll be taking care of the details from here."

"Yes, ma'am." Aware of her duties, Cassie walked behind Angela's chair and gently massaged her temples. Minutes clicked by, counted off by the quiet tick of the long case clock across the room. Musically, it announced the quarter-hour.

"You checked on the weather forecast?" Angela murmured.

"It's projected to be clear and cool, a low in the mid-forties."

"Then we'll need to use the heaters on the terrace. I want dancing."

Dutifully, Cassie stepped away to note the instructions down. There was no word of thanks for her attentiveness; none required. "Your hairdresser is scheduled to arrive at your home at two. Your dress will be delivered by three at the latest."

"All right, then, let's put all that aside for the moment. I want you to contact Beeker. I want to know everything there is to know about Dr. Marshall Pike. He's a psychologist with a private practice here in Chicago. I want the information as Beeker collects it, rather than waiting for a full report."

She opened her eyes again. The headache wasn't in full retreat, but the pill was beating it back. "Tell Beeker it isn't an emergency, but it is a priority. Understood?"

"Yes, Miss Perkins."

By six that evening, Deanna was still going full steam ahead. While she juggled three calls, she beefed up copy that would be read on the late news. "Yes, I understand your position. But an interview, particularly a televised interview, would help show your side." Deanna pursed her lips, sighed. "If you feel that way, of course. I believe your neighbor is more than willing to tell me her story on the air." She smiled when the receiver squawked in indignation. "Yes, we'd prefer to have both sides represented. Thank you, Mrs. Wilson. I'll be there at ten tomorrow."

She spotted Marshall coming toward her and lifted a hand in a wave as she punched down the next blinking light on her phone. "Sorry, Mrs. Carter. Yes, as I was saying, I understand your position. It is a shame about your tulips. A televised interview would help show your side of the dispute." Deanna smiled as Marshall stroked a hand down her hair in greeting. "If you're sure. Mrs. Wilson has agreed to tell me her story on the air." Tipping the receiver a safe inch from her ear, Deanna rolled her eyes at Marshall. "Yes, that would be fine. I'll be there at ten. 'Bye."

"Hot breaking story?"

"Hot tempers in suburbia," Deanna corrected as she disconnected. "I have to put in an hour or two tomorrow after all. A couple of neighbors are engaged in a pitched battle over a bed of tulips, an old, incorrect survey and a cocker spaniel."

"Sounds fascinating."

"I'll give you the scoop over dinner." She didn't object when he lowered his head, and met his lips willingly. The kiss was friendly, without the pressure of intimacy. "You're all wet," she murmured, tasting rain and cool skin.

"It's pouring out there. All I need is a nice warm restaurant and a dry wine."

"I've got one more call waiting."

"Take your time. Want anything?"

"I could use a cold drink. My vocal cords are raw."

Deanna cleared her mental decks and punched in the next button. "Mr. Van Damme, I'm terribly sorry for the interruption. There seems to be a mix-up with Miss Perkins's wine order for tomorrow night.

She'll need three cases of Taittinger's, not two. Yes, that's right. And the white wine?" Deanna checked off her list as the caterer recited from his. "Yes, that's right. And can I ease her mind about the ice sculpture?" She sent Marshall another smile when he returned with a cold can of 7-Up. "That's wonderful, Mr. Van Damme. And you do have the change from tarts to petits fours? Terrific. I think we've got it under control. I'll see you tomorrow, then. 'Bye."

With a long exhale, Deanna dropped the phone on its hook. "Done," she told Marshall. "I hope."

"Long day for you?"

"Long, and productive." Automatically she began to tidy her desk. "I appreciate your meeting me here, Marshall."

"My schedule was lighter than yours."

"Mmm." She took a deep drink, then set the can aside before shutting down her workstation. "And I owe you one for changing plans for tomorrow to accommodate Angela."

"A good psychologist should be flexible." He watched her as she straightened papers and organized notes. "Besides, it sounds like a hell of a party."

"It's turning out that way. She's not a woman to do anything halfway."

"And you admire that."

"Absolutely. Give me five minutes to freshen up, then I promise to focus all my energy on relaxing with you over dinner."

When she stood, he shifted so that his body just brushed hers. It was a subtle move, a subtle suggestion. "You look very fresh to me."

She felt the trickle of excitement run down her spine, the warmth of awareness bloom in her stomach. Tilting her head to meet his eyes, she saw the desire, the need and the patience, a combination that sent her pulse skipping.

She had only to say yes, she knew, and they would forget all about dinner, and all about relaxing. And for one moment, one very long, very quiet moment, she wished it could be that simple.

"I won't be long," she murmured.

"I'll wait."

He would, she thought when he moved aside to let her by. And she would have to make up her mind, soon, whether she wanted to continue along the comfortable, companionable road of this relationship, or shift gears.

"Having your head shrunk, Dee?"

She spotted the cameraman by the door, biting into a Milky Way. "That's so lame, Joe."

"I know." He grinned around the chocolate. There was a button that said AVAILABLE pinned to his tattered denim vest. He had holes in the knees of his jeans. Techs didn't have to worry about appearance. That was just the way Joe liked it. "But somebody's got to say it. Did you set up those two interviews for the morning? The tulip wars?"

"Yeah. Sure you don't mind giving up your Saturday morning?"

"Not for overtime pay."

"Good. Delaney's still at the desk, isn't he?"

"I'm waiting for him." Joe bit off more candy. "We've got a poker game tonight. I'm going to hose him for the double shift he stuck me with last week."

"Do me a favor, then, and tell him we're set, both women, ten o'clock."

"Will do."

"Thanks." Deanna hurried away to do quick repairs on her hair and makeup. She was applying fresh lipstick when Joe burst into the ladies' room. The door slammed back against the wall, echoing as he lunged at her.

"Jesus, Joe, are you nuts?"

"Get your butt in gear, Dee. We've got an assignment, and we've got to move fast." He grabbed her purse from the sink with one hand and her arm with the other.

"What, for God's sake?" She tripped over the threshold as he hauled her out the door. "Did somebody start a war?"

"Almost as hot. We've got to get out to O'Hare."

"O'Hare? Damn it, Marshall's waiting."

49

Fighting impatience, Joe let Deanna tug her arm free. If he had any complaints about her, it was that her vision wasn't quite narrow enough. She always saw the peripheral when the camera needed a tight shot.

"Go tell the boyfriend you've got to go be a reporter. Delaney just got word there's a plane coming in, and it's in trouble. Big time."

"Oh, God." She made the dash back into the newsroom with Joe on her heels. Bursting through the pandemonium, she snatched a fresh notebook from her desk. "Marshall, I'm sorry. I have to go."

"I've already gathered that. Do you want me to wait?"

"No." She dragged a hand through her hair, grabbed her jacket. "I don't know how long I'll be. I'll call you. Delaney!" she called out.

The stout assignment editor waved the stub of his unlit cigar in her direction. "Take off, Reynolds. Keep in touch on the two-way. We'll be patching you in live. Get me a goddamn scoop."

"Sorry," she called to Marshall. "Where's the plane coming in from?" she shouted to Joe as they raced up the stairs. His motorcycle boots clattered on the metal like gunfire.

"London. They'll be feeding us the rest of the information as we go." He shoved open the outside door and then plunged out into a torrent of rain. His Chicago Bulls sweatshirt was immediately plastered to his chest. He shouted over the storm while he unlocked the van. "It's a 747. More than two hundred passengers. Left engine failure, some problem with the radar. Might have taken a hit of lightning." To punctuate his words, a spear of lightning cracked the black sky, shattering the dark.

Already drenched, Deanna climbed into the van. "What's the ETA?" Out of habit, she switched on the police scanner under the dash.

"Don't know. Let's just hope we get there before they do." He'd hate to miss getting a shot of the crash. He gunned the engine, glanced at her. The gleam in his eyes promised a wild ride. "Here's the kicker, Dee. Finn Riley's on board. The crazy son of a bitch called in the story himself."

Chapter Four

SITTING IN THE FORWARD CABIN OF THE BELEAGUERED 747 was like riding in the belly of a dyspeptic bronco. The plane bucked, kicked, shuddered and shook as if it were struggling mightily to disgorge its complement of passengers. Some of the people on board were praying, some were weeping, still others had their faces buried in air-sickness bags, too weak to do anything but moan.

Finn Riley didn't give much thought to prayer. In his own way he was religious. He could, if the need arose in him, recite the Act of Contrition just as he had through all those shadowy sessions in the confessional as a child. At the moment, atonement wasn't on the top of his list.

Time was running out—on his battery pack on his laptop computer. He'd have to switch to his tape recorder soon. Finn much preferred writing copy as the words flowed from his mind to his fingers.

He glanced out the window. The black sky exploded again and again with spears of lightning. Like lances of the gods—nope, he decided, deleting the phrase. Too corny. A battleground, nature against man's technology. The sounds were definitely warlike, he mused. The prayers, the weeping, the groans, the occasionally hysterical laugh. He'd heard them in trenches before. And the echoing boom of thunder that shook the plane like a toy.

He used the last moments of his dying battery playing that angle.

Once he'd shut down, he secured the disk and the computer in his heavy metal case. He'd have to hope for the best there, Finn mused, as he slipped his mini-recorder from his briefcase. He'd seen the aftermath of plane crashes often enough to know what survived was pure luck.

"It's May fifth, seven-oh-two Central time," Finn recited into the recorder. "We're aboard flight 1129 approaching O'Hare, though it's impossible to see any lights through the storm. Lightning struck the port engine about twenty minutes ago. And from what I could squeeze out of the first-class flight attendant, there's some problem with the radar, possibly storm-related. There are two hundred and fifty-two passengers on board, and twelve crew."

"You're crazy." The man sitting next to Finn finally lifted his head from between his knees. His face, under its sheen of sweat, was pale green. His upper-class British voice was slurred more than a little with a combination of scotch and terror. "We could be dead in a few minutes and you're talking into some bloody machine."

"We could be alive in a few minutes, too. Either way, it's news." Sympathetic, Finn dragged a handkerchief out of the back pocket of his jeans. "Here."

"Thanks." Mumbling, the man dabbed at his face. As the plane shuddered again, he laid his head weakly against the seat and closed his eyes. "You must have ice water for blood."

Finn only smiled. His blood wasn't icy, it was hot, pumping hot, but there was no use in trying to explain that to a layman. It wasn't that he wasn't afraid, or that he was particularly fatalistic. But he did have the reporter's unique sense of tunnel vision. He had his recorder, his notebook, his laptop. These were shields that gave the illusion of indestructibility.

Why else did a cameraman continue to roll tape when bullets were flying? Why did a reporter jab a mike into the face of a psychopath, or run in instead of out of a building during a bomb threat? Because he was blinded by the shields of the Fourth Estate.

Or maybe, Finn mused with a grin, they were just crazy.

"Hey." He shifted in his seat and aimed the recorder. "Want to be my last interview?"

His companion opened red-rimmed eyes. What he saw was a man only a few years younger than himself, with clear, pale skin shadowed by a hint of a beard shades darker than the tousled mane of wavy bronze hair that swept the collar of a leather bomber's jacket. Sharp, angular features were softened by a mouth spread in an engaging grin that featured a crooked eyetooth. The grin brought out dimples that should have softened the face, yet only made it tougher. Like dents in rock.

But it was the eyes that held the onlooker's attention. Just now they were a deep, misty blue, like a lake dappled in fog, and they were filled with amusement, self-deprecation and recklessness.

The man heard a sound bubble in his own throat and was stunned to realize it was a laugh. "Fuck you," he said, grinning back.

"Even if we buy it on this run, I don't think they'll air that. Network standards. Is this your first trip to the States?"

"Jesus, you are crazy." But some of his fear was ebbing. "No, I make the trip about twice a year."

"What's the first thing you want to do if we land in one piece?"

"Call my wife. We had a row before I left. Silly business." He mopped his clammy face again. "I want to talk to my wife and kids."

The plane lost altitude. The PA crackled under the sounds of screams and sobs.

"Ladies and gentlemen, please remain in your seats, with your seat belts fastened. We will be landing momentarily. For your own safety, please put your head between your knees, grasp your ankles firmly. Once we land, we'll begin emergency evacuation procedures."

Or they'll scrape us up with shovels, Finn mused. The vision of the wreck of Pan Am flight 103 spread over Scotland played uneasily in his mind. He remembered too well what he'd seen, what he'd smelled, what he'd felt when he'd broadcast that report.

He wondered, fatalistically, who would stand in front of twisted, smoking metal and tell the world about the fate of flight 1129.

"What's your wife's name?" Finn asked as he leaned forward.

"Anna."

"Kids?"

"Brad and Susan. Oh God, oh God, I don't want to die."

"Think about Anna and Brad and Susan," Finn told him. "Pull them right into your head. It'll help." Cool-eyed, he studied the Celtic cross that had worked its way out from under his sweater to dangle on its chain. He had people to think about, as well. He closed his hand over the cross, held it warm in his hand.

"It's seven-oh-nine, Central time. The pilot's taking us in."

"CAN YOU SEE IT YET? Joe, can you see it?"

"Can't see a goddamn thing through this goddamn rain." He squinted, hefting his camera. Rain ran off the bill of his fielder's cap and waterfalled in front of his face. "Can't believe there's no other crews here yet. It's just like Finn to call the son-of-a-bitching story in so we'd get an exclusive."

"They'll have heard about it by now." Straining to see through the gloom, Deanna shoved sopping hair from her eyes. In the lights of the runway, the rain looked like a hail of silver bullets. "We won't be alone out here for long. I hope we're right about them using this runway."

"We're right. Wait. Did you hear that? I don't think that was thunder."

"No, it sounded like—there!" She stabbed a finger toward the sky. "Look. That's got to be it."

The lights were barely visible through the slashing rain. Faintly, she heard the mutter of an engine, then the answering wail of emergency vehicles. Her stomach flipped over.

"Benny? Are you copying this?" She lifted her voice over the storm, satisfied when she heard her producer's voice come through her earpiece. "It's coming down now. Yes?" She nodded to Joe. "We're set. We're going live," she told Joe, and stood with her back to the runway. "Go from me, then follow the plane in. Keep on the plane. They've got us," she murmured, listening to the madhouse of the control room through her earpiece. "In five, Joe."

She listened to the lead-in from the anchor, and her cue. "We've just spotted the lights from flight 1129. As you can see, the storm has become very violent, rain is washing over the runways in sheets. Airport officials have refused to comment on the exact nature of the problem with flight 1129, but emergency vehicles are standing ready."

"What can you see, Deanna?" This from the anchor desk back in the studio.

"The lights, and we can hear the engine as the plane descends." She turned as Joe angled the camera skyward. "There!" In the lightning flash, the plane was visible, a bright silver missile hurtling groundward. "There are two-hundred and sixty-four passengers and crew aboard flight 1129." She shouted over the scream of storm, engines and sirens. "Including Finn Riley, CBC's foreign correspondent returning to Chicago from his post in London. Please, God," she murmured, then fell silent, letting the pictures tell the story as the plane came into clear view.

It was laboring. She imagined herself inside as the pilot fought to keep the nose up and level. The sound must have been deafening.

"Almost," she whispered, forgetting the camera, the mike, the viewers as she kept her gaze riveted on the plane. She saw the landing gear, then the bright red, white and blue logo of the airline slashed on the side of the plane. There was only static in her earpiece.

"I can't hear you, Martin. Stand by."

She held her breath as the wheels hit, skidded, bounced off the tarmac. Held it still as the plane slid and swayed, chased down the runway by the flashing lights of emergency vehicles.

"It's skidding," she called out. "There's smoke. I can see what looks like smoke under the left wing. I can hear the brakes screaming, and it's slowing. It's definitely slowing, but there's a problem with control."

The wing dipped, skimming the tarmac and shooting up a shower of sparks. Deanna watched them sizzle and die in the wet as the plane swerved. Then, with a shuddering bump, it stopped, diagonally across the runway.

"It's down. Flight 1129 is on the ground."

"Deanna, is it possible for you to assess the damage?"

"Not from here. Just the smoke I spotted at the left wing, which corroborates our unofficial reports of left-engine failure. Emergency crews are soaking down the area with foam. Ambulances are standing by. The door's opening, Martin. The chute's coming out. I can see—yes, the first passengers being evacuated."

"Get closer," the producer ordered. "We're cutting back to Martin to give you time to get closer."

"We'll move closer to the scene, and bring you more on flight 1129, which has just landed at O'Hare. This is Deanna Reynolds for CBC."

"You're clear," her producer shouted. "Go."

"Goddamn!" Excitement pitched Joe's voice up an octave. "What pictures. What pictures. It's fucking Emmy time."

She shot him a look, but was too used to the cameraman's style to comment. "Come on, Joe. Let's see if we can get some interviews."

They dashed toward the runway as more passengers slid down the emergency chute into the arms of waiting rescue workers. By the time they reached the huddle of vehicles, and reset for broadcast, there were half a dozen people safely out. One woman sat on the ground, weeping into her folded arms. With the singlemind-edness of a newsman, Joe rolled tape.

"Benny, we're at the scene. Are you getting this?"

"Absolutely. It's good film. We'll be putting you back live. Get me one of the passengers. Get me—"

"Riley," Joe shouted. "Hey, Finn Riley."

Deanna glanced back toward the chute in time to see Finn make his slide to earth. On hearing his name called, he turned his head. Eyes narrowed against the driving rain, he focused on the camera. And grinned.

He landed easily, despite the metal case he clutched. Rain dripped from his hair, skimmed down his leather jacket and soaked his boots.

In an easy lope he covered the ground from chute to camera.

"You lucky son of a bitch." Joe beamed and punched Finn on the shoulder.

"Good to see you, Joe. Excuse me a minute." Without warning, he grabbed Deanna and planted a hard kiss on her mouth. She had time to feel the heat radiating from his body, to register the shock of electricity from his mouth to hers, a quick burst of power, before he released her.

"Hope you don't mind." He gave her a charming smile. "I thought about kissing the ground, but you look a hell of a lot better. Can I borrow these a minute?"

He was already tugging her earpiece free. "Hey."

"Who's producing?"

"Benny. And I—"

"Benny?" He snagged her mike. "Yeah, it's me. So, you got my call." He chuckled. "My pleasure. Anything I can do for the news department." He listened a moment, nodded. "No problem. We're going live in ten," he told Joe. "Keep an eye on that for me," he asked Deanna, and set his case down at her feet. He dragged the hair out of his face and looked into the camera.

"This is Finn Riley, reporting live from O'Hare. At six thirty-two this evening, flight 1129 from London was struck by lightning."

Deanna wondered why the rain running off her clothes didn't sizzle as she watched Finn make his report. *Her* report, she corrected. Two minutes after hitting the ground and the sneaky bastard had usurped her, stolen her piece and delegated her to gofer.

So he was good, Deanna fumed as she watched him leading the viewers on the odyssey of flight 1129 from London. That was no surprise. She'd seen his reports before—from London, yes, and from Haiti, Central America, the Middle East.

She'd even intro'd a few of them.

But that wasn't the point.

The point was that he'd snatched her piece away from her. Well, Deanna decided, he might have upstaged her, but he was going to discover that stealing her newspiece wasn't a snap.

Interviews were her strong point, she reminded herself. That was her job, she told herself, struggling to cool off. And that's what she would do. Brilliantly.

Turning her back on Finn, she hunched her shoulders against the downpour and went to look for passengers.

Moments later, there was a tap on her back. She turned, lifted a brow. "Did you need something?"

"Brandy and a roaring fire." Finn wiped rain from his face. He was in gear, fueled by the chaos and the immediacy of the report. And the simple fact that he wasn't a dead man. "Meantime, I figured we'd round out the piece with some interviews. Some passengers, a few of the emergency crew—some of the flight crew, if we're lucky. We should be able to get it in for a special report before the late news."

"I've already lined up a couple of passengers who are willing to talk to me on air."

"Good. Take Joe and do it, while I see if I can finagle an interview with the pilot."

She snagged his arm before he could pivot away. "I need my mike."

"Oh. Sure." He handed it over, then offered the earpiece. She looked like a wet dog, he mused. Not a mongrel, no indeed. One of those classy Afghan hounds that manage to maintain dignity and style under the worst of circumstances. His pleasure at being alive went up another notch. It was a pure delight to watch her glaring at him. "I know you, don't I? Aren't you on the *Sunrise News?*"

"Not for the past several months. I'm on *Midday*."

"Congratulations." He focused on her more intently, the misty blue of his eyes turning sharp and clear. "Diana—no, Deanna. Right?"

"You have a good memory. I don't believe we've spoken before."

"No, but I've caught your work. Pretty good." But he was already looking beyond her. "There were some kids on the flight. If you can't get them on mike, at least get them on camera. The competition's here now." He gestured to where other newsmen were milling among the passengers. "Let's work fast."

"I know my job," she said, but he was already moving away.

"He doesn't seem to have a problem with self-esteem."

Beside her, Joe snorted. "He's got an ego the size of the Sears Tower. And it isn't fragile. The thing is, when you do a piece with him, you know he's going to do it right. And he doesn't treat his crew like mentally deficient slaves."

"Too bad he doesn't treat other reporters with the same courtesy." She spun on her heel. "Let's get pictures."

IT WAS AFTER NINE WHEN they returned to CBC, where Finn was greeted with a hero's welcome. Someone handed him a bottle of Jameson, seal intact. Shivering, Deanna headed straight for her desk, turned on her machine and started writing copy.

This, she knew, would go national. It was a chance she didn't intend to miss.

She tuned out the shouting and laughing and back-slapping and wrote furiously, referring now and then to the sketchy notes she'd scribbled in the back of the van.

"Here." She looked down and saw a hand, wide-palmed, long-fingered, scarred at the base of the thumb, set down a glass on her desk. The glass held about an inch of deep amber liquid.

"I don't drink on the job." She hoped she sounded cool, not prim.

"I don't think a swallow of whiskey's going to impair your judgment. And," he said, drifting easily into a rich Pat O'Brien brogue, "it'll put some heat in your belly. You don't plan on operating heavy machinery, do you?" Finn skirted her chair and sat on the edge of her desk. "You're cold." He handed her a towel. "Knock it back. Dry your hair. We've got work to do."

"That's what I'm doing." But she took the towel. And after a moment's hesitation, the whiskey. It might have been only a swallow, but he was right, it put a nice cozy fire in her stomach.

"We've got thirty minutes for copy. Benny's already editing the tape." Finn craned his head around to scan her screen. "That's good stuff," he commented.

"It'll be better if you'd get out of my way."

He was used to hostility, but he liked to know its source. "You're ticked because I kissed you? No offense, Deanna, but it wasn't personal. It was more like primal instinct."

"I'm not ticked because you kissed me." She spoke between her teeth and began to type again. "I'm ticked because you stole my story."

Hooking his hands around his knee, Finn thought about it and decided she had a small, if not particularly salient point. "Let me ask you a question. Which makes better film? You doing a stand-up, or me giving a play-by-play of the flight minutes after evacuation?"

She spared him one heated glance, and said nothing.

"Okay, while you're thinking it over, we'll print out my copy and see how it reads with yours."

She stopped. "What do you mean, your copy?"

"I wrote it on the plane. Got a quick interview with my seat-mate, too." The reckless amusement was back in his eyes. "Should be good for human interest."

Despite her annoyance, she nearly laughed. "You wrote copy while your plane was going down?"

"Those portable computers will work anywhere. You've got about five minutes before Benny comes along and starts tearing his hair out."

Deanna stared after him when Finn walked off to commandeer a desk.

The man was obviously a lunatic.

AND A DAMNED TALENTED one, she decided thirty minutes later.

The edited tape was completed, the graphics set less than three minutes before airtime. The copy, reworked, rewritten and timed, was plugged into the TelePrompTer. And Finn Riley, still in his sweater and jeans, was seated behind the anchor desk, going national with his report.

"Good evening. This is a special report on flight 1129. I'm Finn Riley."

Deanna knew he was reading the news, since she had written the first thirty seconds herself. Yet it felt as though he were telling a story. He knew exactly which word to punch, when to pause. He knew exactly how to go through the camera and into the home.

It wasn't an intimacy, she mused, worrying her earring. He wasn't settling in for a cozy chat. He was . . . bringing tidings, she decided. Carrying the message. And somehow staying aloof from it.

Neat trick, she thought, since he had been on the very plane he was describing.

Even when he read his own words, words he had written while

plunging through the sky in a crippled plane with its port engine smoking, he was removed. The storyteller, not the story.

Admiration snuck past her defenses.

She turned to the monitor when they switched to film, and saw herself. Hair dripping, eyes huge, face pale as the water that rained over her. Her voice was steady. Yes, she had that, Deanna thought. But she wasn't detached. The fear and terror were there, transmitted as clearly as her words.

And when the camera shifted to capture the plane skidding on the runway, she heard her own whispered prayer.

Too involved, she realized, and sighed.

It was worse when she saw Finn on the monitor, taking over the story minutes after escaping the damaged plane. He had the look of a warrior fresh from battle—a veteran warrior who could discuss each blow and thrust concisely, emotionlessly.

And he had been right. It made better film.

At commercial, Deanna went up into the control booth to watch. Benny was grinning like a fool even as sweat popped onto his wide, furrowed brow. He was fat and permanently red-faced and made a habit of tugging on tufts of his lank brown hair. But he was, Deanna knew, a hell of a producer.

"We beat every other station in town," he was telling Finn through the earpiece. "None of them have any tape of the landing, or the initial stages of evacuation." He blew Deanna a kiss. "This is great stuff. You're back in ten, Finn. We'll be going to the tape of passenger interviews. And cue."

Through the last three and a half minutes, Benny continued to murmur to himself, pulling at his hair.

"Maybe we should have put him in a jacket," he said at one point. "Maybe we should have found him a jacket."

"No." There was no use being resentful. Deanna put a hand on Benny's shoulder. "He looks great."

"And in those last moments in the air, some, like Harry Lyle, thought of family. Others, like Marcia DeWitt and Kenneth

Morgenstern, thought of dreams unfulfilled. For them, and all the others aboard flight 1129, the long night ended at seven-sixteen, when the plane landed safely on runway three.

"This is Finn Riley for CBC. Good night."

"Up graphics. Music. And we're clear!"

A cheer erupted in the control booth. Benny leaned back in his swivel chair and lifted his arms in triumph. Phones started to shrill.

"Benny, it's Barlow James on two."

A hush fell over control, and Benny stared at the receiver as though it were a snake. Barlow James, the president of the news division, rarely phoned.

Every eye was on Benny as he swallowed and took the phone. "Mr. James?" Benny listened a moment, his ruddy face going ghostly, then flushing hot candy pink. "Thank you, sir." Opening his mouth wide, Benny flashed a thumb's up and set the cheering off again. "Yes, sir, Finn's one in a million. We're glad to have him back. Deanna Reynolds?" He swiveled in his chair and rolled his eyes at Deanna. "Yes, sir, Mr. James, we're proud to have her on our team. Thank you very much. I'll let them know."

Benny replaced the receiver, stood and did a fast boogie that sent his belly swaying over his belt. "He loved it," Benny sang. "He loved it all. They want the whole eight minutes for the affiliates. He loved you." Benny grabbed Deanna's hands and spun her around. "He liked your fresh, intimate style—that's a quote. And the fact that you looked good soaking wet."

With a choked laugh, Deanna stepped back and rammed straight into Finn.

"Two pretty good qualities in a reporter," Finn decided. He caught a whiff of her hair as he steadied her, rain and apple blossoms. "Nice job, guys." He released Deanna to shake hands with the control crew. "Really terrific."

"Mr. James said welcome back, Finn," Benny said. As he relaxed again, the pudge of his belly sagged comfortably at his belt. "And he's looking forward to beating your butt at tennis next week."

"In his dreams." Out of the corner of his eye, he saw Deanna descending the stairs. "Thanks again."

He caught up with her in the newsroom just as she was shrugging into her coat.

"It was a good piece," he said.

"Yes, it was."

"Reading copy isn't one of my priorities, but reading yours was a pleasure."

"It's certainly a night for compliments." She swung her purse over her arm. "Thanks, and welcome back to Chicago."

"Need a lift?"

"No, I've got my car."

"I don't." He flashed her a smile. Dimples winked out, charmingly. "Probably hell getting a cab in this weather."

She studied him. In her heels, she was about the same height he was, and she got a good, close look at those innocent blue eyes. Too innocent, she thought, especially in combination with that quick, dashing grin and the wink of dimples. He *wanted* to look innocent, she decided. Therefore he did. Neat trick.

"I suppose, as a professional courtesy, I could give you a ride home."

Her hair was still wet, he noted, and she hadn't bothered to repair her makeup. "Are you still ticked at me?"

"No, actually, I'm down to mildly miffed."

"I could buy you a burger." He reached out to toy with one of the buttons on her jacket. "Maybe I could talk you down to slightly steamed."

"These things generally run their course. In any case, I think your homecoming's been exciting enough. I've got a call to make."

She was involved with someone, Finn realized. It was too bad. Really too bad. "Just the lift, then. I appreciate it."

Chapter Five

FOR SOME, ORGANIZING A PARTY WAS A CASUAL AFFAIR. Food, drink, music and good company were tossed together and left to mix in their own way.

For Deanna, it was a campaign. From the moment Cassie had passed the torch to her barely twenty-four hours earlier, no detail was left unattended to, no list unfulfilled. Like a general rousing troops, she inspected the caterer, the florist, the bartender, the housekeeping staff. She arranged, rearranged and approved. She counted stemware, discussed the playlist with the band and personally tasted Van Damme's chicken kabobs in peanut butter sauce.

"Incredible," she murmured, her eyes closed, her lips just parted as she savored the flavor. "Really, really incredible."

When she opened her eyes, she and the slim young caterer beamed at each other.

"Thank God." Van Damme offered her a glass of wine as they stood in the center of Angela's enormous kitchen. "Miss Perkins wanted cuisine from around the world as her theme. It took a great deal of thought and preparation, in a short amount of time, to come up with flavors that would complement one another. The ratatouille, the deep-fried mushrooms à la Berlin, the tiny spanako-pita . . ." The list went on.

Deanna didn't know ratatouille from tuna fish, but made appropriate noises. "You've done a wonderful job, Mr. Van Damme." Deanna toasted him and drank. "Miss Perkins and all of her guests will be delighted. Now I know I can leave all of this in your hands."

She hoped. There were half a dozen people in the kitchen, rattling pans, arranging trays, bickering. "We have thirty minutes." She took one last glance around. Every inch of Angela's rose-colored counters was filled with trays and pots. The air was thick with delicious smells. Van Damme's assistants rushed about. Marveling that anyone could function amid the confusion, Deanna escaped.

She hurried toward the front of the house. Angela's lofty living room was all pastels and flowers. Delicate calla lilies streamed out of crystal vases. Fairy roses swam in fragile bowls. The floral theme was continued with the tiny violets dotting the silk wallpaper and the pale pattern of the Oriental carpets spread over the floor.

The room, like all of Angela's trim two-story home, was a celebration of feminine decorating, with soft colors and deep cushions. Deanna's practiced eye scanned over the sherbet-colored pillows on the curved-back sofa, the arrangement of slender tapers, the presentation of pale pink and green mints in crystal candy dishes. She could hear the faint sounds of the band tuning up through the closed terrace doors.

For a moment, she imagined the house as hers. More color, she thought. Fewer frills. But she would definitely enjoy the lofty ceilings and curved windows, the cozy fireplace set with apple wood.

She'd want some art on the walls. Bold prints, sinuous sculptures. And a few well-chosen antiques to mix with edgy modern pieces.

One day, she mused, and shifted a vase an inch on a tabletop.

Satisfied, she took a final tour of the main level. She had just started across the foyer to the staircase when the door chimes pealed. Too early for guests, she thought as she turned to answer.

She sincerely hoped it wasn't a last-minute delivery she'd have to deal with.

Finn stood on the porch with dusk gathering behind him. A breeze wafted up, played with his hair and brought Deanna the scent of man and nightfall. He grinned at her, letting his gaze roam up from the toes of her sneakers to her tousled hair.

"Well, hi. Are you covering tonight's event?"

"So to speak." He'd shaved, she noted. And though he hadn't bothered with a tie, the slate-gray jacket and trousers made the casual look elegant. "You're early."

"By request." He stepped inside and shut the door at his back. "I like your party dress."

"I was just going up to change." And he was blowing a hole in her schedule. She caught herself playing with her earring and dropped her hand hastily. "Why don't you come in and sit down. I'll tell Angela you're here."

"What's your hurry?" he asked as he followed her into the living room.

"No hurry. Do you want a drink? The bartender's in the kitchen, but I can handle something simple."

"Don't bother."

He sat on the arm of the sofa as he glanced around speculatively. Deanna was no more suited to the ornate femininity of the room than he was, Finn decided. She made him think of Titania. And, though he couldn't say why, Titania made him think of wild sex on a damp forest floor.

"Nothing's changed around here in the last six months. I always feel as though I'm walking into the royal gardens."

Deanna's lips twitched. She quashed the disloyal urge to laugh and agree. "Angela's fond of flowers. I'll go get her."

"Let her primp." Finn snagged Deanna's hand before she could walk out. "She's fond of that, too. Do you ever sit down?"

"Of course I sit down."

"I mean when you're not driving a car or writing copy."

She didn't bother to tug her hand free. "Occasionally I sit down to eat."

"That's interesting, so do I. Maybe we could do it together sometime."

Deanna lifted a brow, tilted her head. "Mr. Riley, are you coming on to me?"

He sighed, but the laughter stayed in his eyes. "Miss Reynolds, I thought I was being so subtle."

"No."

"No, I'm not being subtle?"

"No, you're not. And no." Now she did slide her hand from his. "It's a nice offer, but I'm involved with someone." *Maybe*, she added to herself. "And if I weren't, I don't think it's wise to mix personal and professional relationships."

"That sounds very definite. Are you always very definite?"

"Yes." But she smiled. "Definitely."

Angela paused in the doorway, set her teeth against temper. The picture of her protégée and her lover smiling intimately at each other in her living room had her gorge rising. Though the taste of fury was familiar, even pleasant, she took a deep breath, fixed a smile on her lips.

"Finn, darling!" She flew across the room, a curvy golden blossom stemmed in pale blue silk. Even as Finn rose from the sofa, she threw herself into his arms and fastened her mouth possessively on his. "Oh, I've missed you," she murmured, sliding her fingers up into the thick tangle of his hair. "So much."

She had an impact, Finn thought. She always did. The offer of unapologetic sex was there in the press of her body, the heat of her mouth. His body responded even as his mind took a wary step in retreat.

"It's good to see you, too." He untangled himself, holding her at arm's length to study her. "You look wonderful."

"Oh, so do you. Shame on you, Deanna." But she didn't take her eyes off Finn. "For not telling me the guest of honor was here."

"I'm sorry." Deanna resisted the urge to clear the huskiness from her throat. She wished now she had left the room the moment Angela had entered, but the greedy, knowing look on the woman's face as she raced to Finn had rooted Deanna to the spot. "I was just about to."

"She was going to mix me a drink first." Finn looked over Angela's shoulder to Deanna. There was still amusement there, Deanna noticed. And if she wasn't mistaken, a faint touch of embarrassment.

"I don't know what I'd do without her." Turning, Angela slid one arm around Finn's waist, cuddling her body back into the curve of his in a way only small, soft women could manage easily. "I can depend on Deanna for absolutely everything. And do. Oh, I forgot." Laughing, she held out a hand for Deanna, as if to invite her into the charmed circle. "With all this confusion, I completely forgot about the excitement last night. I was nearly sick with worry when I heard about the plane." She shuddered, and squeezed Deanna's hand. "And I meant to tell you what a terrific job you did on the remote. Isn't it just like Finn to hop right out of the center of a near disaster and do a report?"

Deanna's eyes flicked up to Finn's, then back to Angela's. There was so much sexual heat in the room she could barely breathe. "I wouldn't know. I'm sure the two of you would like some time alone before the guests arrive, and I really need to change."

"Oh, of course, we're keeping you. Deanna's a tiger for timetables," Angela added, tilting her head up to Finn's. "Run along, dear." Her voice was a purr as she released Deanna's hand. "I'll handle things from here."

"Why don't I fix that drink?" Finn shifted away from Angela when Deanna's quick footsteps rapped up the stairs.

"I'm sure there's champagne back there," Angela told him as he walked behind the rosewood bar. "I want to toast your homecoming with the best."

Obliging, Finn took a bottle from the small refrigerator built into the back of the bar. He considered several different ways to handle the situation with Angela as he removed the foil and twisted the wire.

"I tried to phone you several times last night," she began.

"When I got in, I let the machine pick up. I was pretty wiped out." The first lie—but not the last, he decided with a grimace as he popped the cork. Bubbling wine fizzed up to the lip, then retreated.

"I understand." She crossed to the bar, laid a hand on his. "And you're here now. It's been a long six months."

Saying nothing, he poured her wine and opened a bottle of club soda for himself.

"Aren't you joining me?"

"I'll stick with this for now." He had a feeling he'd need a clear head tonight. "Angela, you went to an awful lot of trouble. It wasn't necessary."

"Nothing is too much trouble for you." She sipped the wine, watching him over the rim.

Perhaps it was the coward's way to keep the bar between them. But his eyes were direct, steady and cool. "We had some good times, Angela, but we can't go back."

"We'll be moving forward," she agreed. She brought his hand to her lips, drew the tip of his finger into her mouth. "We were so good together, Finn. You remember, don't you?"

"I remember." And his blood pounded in response. He cursed himself for being as mindless as one of Pavlov's dogs. "It's just not going to work."

Her teeth nipped sharply into his flesh, surprising, and arousing, him. "You're wrong," she murmured. "I'll show you." The doorbell chimed again, and she smiled. "Later."

HE FELT LIKE A MAN LOCKED behind bars of velvet. The house was crowded with people, friends, coworkers, network brass, associates, all happily celebrating his return. The food was fabulous and exotic, the music low and bluesy. He wanted to escape.

He didn't mind being rude, but understood if he attempted to leave, Angela would create a scene that would reverberate from coast to coast. There were too many people in the business here for an altercation to go unreported. And he much preferred reporting news, rather than being reported on. With that in mind, he opted to tough it out, even with the inevitable messy showdown with her at the end of the interminable party.

At least the air was clear and fresh on the terrace. He was a man who could appreciate the scent of spring blossoms and newly cut grass, of mingling women's perfumes and spicy food. Perhaps he would have enjoyed being alone to absorb the night, but he'd learned to be flexible when there was no choice.

And he had the talent for listening and exchanging conversation while his mind wandered. For now he let it trail to his cabin, where he would sit by the fire with a book and a brandy, or hunch over his bait box making new lures. Alone. The fantasy of being alone kept him sane through discussions of ratings and programming.

"I tell you, Riley, if they don't beef up Tuesday nights, we're going to face another cutback in the news division. Makes me sick to think about it."

"I know what you mean. Nobody's forgotten the body count from two years ago." He spotted Deanna. "Excuse me a minute, there's something I have to do." He squeezed through the crowd on the terrace and slipped his arms around her. When she stiffened, he shook his head. "This isn't a come-on, it's a diversion."

"Oh?" Automatically, she matched her steps to his as he danced. "From what?"

"From a diatribe on network politics. Tuesday night's schedule."

"Ah." She ran her tongue around her teeth. "We're a little weak there, as I'm sure you know. Our lead-in for the late news is—"

"Shut up." He smiled at her when she laughed, and enjoyed the fact that they were eye to eye. "You're a long one, aren't you?"

"So I've been told. You know, of course, that as the guest of honor, you're required to mingle."

"I hate rules."

"I live for them."

"Then consider this dance mingling. We'll even make small talk. I like your dress." It was true. The Adolfo gown's simple lines and bold red color were a welcome change from Angela's overly fussy pastels and lace.

"Thank you." Curiously she studied his face. She could almost see the pain rapping at his temples. "Headache?"

"No, thanks, I have one already."

"Let me get you some aspirin."

"It's all right. It'll pass." He drew her closer, laid his cheek against hers. "Better already. Where are you from?"

"Topeka." She'd nearly sighed, nearly closed her eyes before she snapped back to attention. He was entirely too smooth, she decided, though the adjective seemed odd when she was pressed tight to a body that was tough as iron.

"Why Chicago?"

"My roommate from college settled here after she got married. She talked me into relocating. The position with CBC made the move easy."

She smelled fabulous, he mused. The scent of her hair and skin made him think of spiced wine and quiet smoke. He thought of his lake, dappled in starlight, and the musical call of crickets in high grass. "Do you like to fish?"

"Excuse me?"

"Fish. Do you like to fish?"

She drew back to look at his face. "I have no idea. What sort of fishing?"

He smiled. It wasn't just the puzzlement in her eyes that caused his lips to curve. It was the fact that she was so obviously considering his question as seriously as one on world politics.

"You made the right move, Kansas. Curiosity like that should take you right to the top in this business. God knows you've got the face for it."

"I prefer to think I've got the brains for it."

"If you do, then you know that looks matter in television news. The public likes their death, destruction and dirty politics delivered by an attractive medium. And why the hell not?"

"How long did it take you to get that cynical?"

"About five minutes after I landed my first on-the-air job at the number-three station in Tulsa." Finn's thoughts veered forward; it would take only an inch to taste her ripe, sexy and serious mouth. "I beat out two other candidates because I looked better on tape."

"And your work had nothing to do with it?"

"It does now." He toyed with the ends of the hair that rained over her shoulders.

His fingers felt entirely too good against her skin, Deanna realized, and shifted gears. "Where did you get the scar?"

"Which one?"

"This one." She moved his hand between them, tilted the scar up.

"Oh. Bar fight. In . . ." His eyes narrowed as he tried to place the incident. "Belfast. A charming little pub that caters to the IRA."

"Mmm." As a precaution she kept his hand in hers. However intimate the gesture looked, it prevented him from touching her. "Don't you think it's undignified for a well-known television correspondent to brawl in bars?"

"I'm entitled to some entertainment, but it was a long time ago." The scarred thumb brushed gently up the side of hers, down again, toward the wrist, where her pulse began to stutter. "I'm much more dignified now." And he smiled, drawing her closer.

Every muscle in her body turned to water. "I don't think so."

"Try me." It was a low, murmured challenge she had no answer for. "Someone's looking for you."

Shaking off the mood, she glanced over her shoulder and spotted Marshall. When their eyes met, he smiled and held up two glasses of champagne.

"I guess that's my cue to let you go." Finn did, then captured her hand for one last moment. "Just how seriously involved are you?"

She hesitated, looking down at their joined hands. The desire to link fingers was very strong. "I don't know." She met his eyes squarely. "I haven't decided."

"Let me know when you do." He released her hand, and watched her walk away.

"I'm sorry I'm late." Marshall kissed her briefly before he offered Deanna a flute of champagne.

"It's all right." She sipped, surprised that her throat felt so dry.

"It's a little chilly out here, isn't it?" Concerned, he touched her hand. "You're cold. Come inside."

"All right." She glanced back toward Finn as Marshall led her away. "I'm sorry the evening was spoiled yesterday."

"Don't worry about it." After a quick scan of the room, Marshall guided her toward a quiet corner. "We both face emergencies in our work."

"I did call you after I got in."

"Yes, I got the message from my service." His eyes flicked down to his glass before he drank. "I decided to make it an early night."

"Then you didn't see the report."

"Last night? No. But I did catch pieces of it on the morning news. Wasn't that Finn Riley you were dancing with just now?"

"Yes."

"He's had quite a homecoming all in all. I can't imagine being that concise and detached after being so close to death. I suppose he's hardened to it."

Deanna frowned. "I'd say it's more a matter of instinct and training."

"I'm glad your instinct and training haven't made you so cold. Your report from the airport was very passionate, very genuine."

She smiled weakly. "It was supposed to be objective and informative."

"It was very informative." He kissed her again. "And you looked beautiful in the rain." Lingering over the kiss, he missed her wince of annoyance. "Barring news bulletins," he said quietly, "can we plan on slipping away early, having some time alone?"

Twenty-four hours before, she would have said yes, she realized. Now, with the murmur of conversation around them, the music drifting in through the terrace doors, the fizz of champagne on her tongue, she hesitated. Marshall tipped a finger under her chin, a gesture she'd once found endearing.

"Problem?" he asked.

"No. Yes." She let out a breath, impatient with her own wavering. It was time to step back, she thought, and take stock. "I'm sorry, Marshall, Angela's counting on me to see this party through. And to be honest, things are moving a little fast for me."

He didn't remove his hand, but she sensed him drawing in. "I didn't mean to push."

"You weren't. You haven't." She curled her fingers over his wrist in a gesture that was both apologetic and affectionate. "I tend to be cautious—maybe overcautious—in relationships. There are reasons, and I'll explain them to you, when I can."

"No need to rush." He let his hand drop away from her chin. "You know how much I want to be with you, and it's not simply sexual."

"I know that." Rising to her toes, she laid her cheek against his. And remembered, very clearly, the feel of her cheek resting against Finn's as they'd danced.

HE WAS TIRED, AND HE DIDN'T tire easily. Years of snatching sleep on trains and planes and buses, of camping out in jungles and deserts and behind enemy lines had toughened him. He enjoyed the fine linens and mint-bedecked pillows of luxury hotels, but

Finn could sleep just as soundly with his head on a bedroll and the echoes of artillery fire as a lullaby.

Tonight he pined for bed and oblivion. Unfortunately, there was unfinished business. He might have been a man to ignore rules, but he never ignored problems.

"That was the last of them." Angela swept back into the living room looking as fresh and lovely as she had hours earlier. "Everyone was so glad to see you again." She wrapped her arms around him, nestling her head beneath his shoulder.

His hand lifted to stroke her hair in a habitual gesture. She felt soft, and somehow pink, he thought. It was like being tangled in a fragrant, climbing vine. If he didn't nip off the feelers, it would certainly choke him.

"Let's sit down. We need to talk."

"I know it's hard to believe, but I'm about talked out." She skimmed a hand down his shirt, then back up to toy with his top button. "And I've been waiting all evening to be alone with you, to give you your real homecoming." She leaned forward for a kiss. Her eyes flashed like jagged cobalt when he held her off.

"Angela, I'm sorry. I'm not interested in picking up where we left off six months ago." He kept his hands firm on her shoulders. "We ended it badly, and I regret that, but we did end it."

"You're not going to punish me for being overly emotional, for saying things in the heat of the moment. Finn, we meant too much to each other."

"We had an affair," he corrected. "We had sex. It was great sex. And we had a kind of odd friendship. We might be able to salvage the friendship if we put the rest out of the picture."

"You're being cruel."

"I'm being honest."

"You don't want me?" She tossed back her head and laughed. The sound, like her eyes, was glassy. "I know you do. I can feel it." Her skin was glowing as she stepped toward him again. Her lips parted, curved, as she watched his eyes drop to them and linger.

"You know what I can do for you, Finn. What I'll let you do to me. You want as much as I want."

"I don't take everything I want."

"But you took me. Right here, on this floor the first time. Remember?" With her eyes locked on his, she slid her hands up his chest, shivering with triumph when she felt the unsteady thud of his heart under her palm. "I drove you crazy; you tore my clothes off of me. Remember what it was like?" Her voice lowered, sliding through his system like tainted honey.

He remembered, and the memory made him sick with desire. The bite of her fingernails on his back, her teeth at his shoulder. She'd drawn blood and he hadn't given a damn.

"I want you to take me again, Finn." She watched his face as her hand crept downward.

His fingers curled at her back, digging into the silk. He knew what it would be like and, for a moment, desperately craved that moment of violent pleasure. But he remembered much more than the urgent sex and the dazzling fantasies.

"It isn't going to happen again, Angela." He let his hands drop away from her back. She was quick. He should have been prepared, but her vicious backhanded blow knocked him back two steps.

His eyes heated like suns, but he lifted a hand and coolly wiped the blood from his lip. "More than this room hasn't changed, I see."

"It's because I'm older than you, isn't it?" She hurled the words at him as her fury contorted the careful beauty of her face. "You think you can find someone younger, someone you can mold and train and teach to grovel."

"We've played that tune before. I'd say we've played them all." He turned, heading for the door. He was nearly across the foyer when she threw herself at his feet.

"Don't. Don't leave me!" She clung to his legs, sobbing. Rejection sliced at her, bringing as much fear as pain. As it always did. As it always would. "I'm sorry." And she meant it, completely, utterly, at that moment. It only made it worse. "I'm sorry. Please, don't leave me."

"For God's sake, Angela." Pummeled by pity and disgust, he dragged her to her feet. "Don't do this."

"I love you. I love you so much." With her arms twined around his neck, she wept against his shoulder. The love was as true as her earlier fury, as volatile, and as capricious.

"If I thought you meant that, I'd feel sorry for both of us." He jerked her back, gave her a quick shake. Tears. He'd always considered them a woman's most potent and most underhanded weapon. "Turn it off, damn it. Do you think I could have slept with you on and off for three months and not know when you're manipulating me? You don't love me, and you only want me because I walked away."

"That's not true." She lifted her tear-ravaged face. There was such innocent hurt in it, such wretched sincerity, that he nearly faltered. "I do love you, Finn. And I can make you happy."

Furious, with her as well as with his own weakness for her, he pried her arms away. "Do you think I didn't know that you put pressure on James to have me fired just because you didn't want me to take the London assignment?"

"I was desperate." She covered her face with her hands and let the tears leak through her fingers. "I was afraid of losing you."

"You wanted to prove you were in control. And if James hadn't been so solidly behind me, you could have fucked up my career."

"He didn't listen to me." She lowered her hands, and her face was cold. "Neither did you."

"No. I came here tonight because I'd hoped we'd both had enough time to let things settle. Looks like I was wrong."

"Do you think you can walk out on me?" She spoke quietly and with utter calm as Finn moved toward the door. The tears were forgotten. "Do you think it's simple to just turn your back and walk away? I'll ruin you. It may take years, but I swear, I'll ruin you."

Finn paused at the door. She stood in the center of the foyer, her face blotched and puffy with weeping, her eyes swollen and hard as stone. "Thanks for the party, Angela. It was a hell of a show."

DEANNA WOULD HAVE AGREED. As Finn strode toward his car, she was yawning in the elevator as it climbed toward her apartment. She was grateful she had the entire next day off. It would give her time to recover, and time to think through her situation with Marshall.

But the only thing on her schedule now was a long, soothing bath and a good night's sleep.

She had her keys out of her purse before the elevator doors opened. Humming to herself, she unlocked both the standard lock and the dead bolt. Out of habit, she hit the light switch beside the door as she crossed the threshold.

Quiet, she thought. Wonderful, blessed silence. With the door locked again behind her, she crossed automatically to her phone machine to check messages. As she played them back, she slipped out of her black satin pumps and wriggled her cramped toes. She was smiling at the recording of Fran's voice reciting possible baby names when she spotted the envelope near the door.

Odd, she mused. Had that been there when she'd come in? She crossed the room, glancing through the security peephole before bending to scoop up the note.

There was nothing written on the sealed envelope. Puzzled, and fighting off another yawn, she tore it open, unfolded the single sheet of plain white stationery.

There was only one sentence, typed in bold red ink.

Deanna, I adore you.

Chapter Six

"WE'VE GOT THIRTY SECONDS TO AIR."

"We'll make it." Deanna slipped into her chair beside Roger on the news set. Through her earpiece she heard the frantic overlapping voices in the control room. A few feet away, the floor director was shouting demands for information and dancing in place. One of the camera crew was smoking lazily and chatting with a grip.

"Twenty seconds. Jesus." Roger wiped his damp palms on his knees. "Where did Benny get the bright idea to add music to the tape?"

"From me." Deanna gave Roger a brief apologetic smile. "It was just a toss-off idea when I was previewing it. It really will make the piece perfect." Someone was shouting obscenities through her earpiece, and her smile turned a little sickly. Why did she always want perfection? "Honestly, I didn't know he'd grab onto it this way."

"Ten fucking seconds." Roger took a last glimpse in his hand mirror. "If we have to fill, I'm dumping on you, babe."

"We're going to be fine." Her jaw was set stubbornly. She'd make it fine, by God. She'd make it the best damn one-minute-ten the station had ever aired. The swearing in the control room turned to a pandemonium of cheers as the floor director began his count-down. "Got it." She glanced smugly in Roger's direction, then faced the camera.

"Good afternoon, this is *Midday*. I'm Roger Crowell."

"And I'm Deanna Reynolds. The passenger count on flight 1129 from London last Friday was two hundred and sixty-four. Early this morning, that number rose by one. Matthew John Carlyse, son of passengers Alice and Eugene Carlyse, made his first appearance at five-fifteen this morning. Though six weeks premature, Matthew weighed in at a healthy five pounds."

As the tape rolled, to the accompaniment of the crooning "Baby, Baby," Deanna let out a relieved breath and grinned at the monitor. Her idea, she reminded herself. And it *was* perfect. "Great pictures."

"Not bad," Roger agreed, and was forced to smile when the monitor focused on the tiny form squirming and squawling in the incubator. There was a small set of wings pinned to his blanket. "Almost worth the ulcer."

"The Carlyses named their son after Matthew Kirkland, the pilot who landed flight 1129 safely at O'Hare Friday night despite engine failure. Mr. Carlyse said that neither he nor his wife were concerned about making the return flight to London at the end of the month. Young Matthew had no comment."

"In other news . . ." Roger segued into the next segment.

Deanna glanced down at her copy, reviewing her pacing. When she looked up again, she spotted Finn in the rear of the studio. He rocked back on his heels, his thumbs hooked in his front pockets, but he gave her a nod of congratulations.

What the hell was he doing there, watching, evaluating? The man had a full week's free time coming to him. Why wasn't he at the beach, the mountains, somewhere? Even as she turned to the camera again and picked up her cue, she could feel his eyes on her, coolly blue and objective.

By the time they broke for the last commercial before "Deanna's Corner", her nerves had evolved into bubbling temper.

Deanna pushed back from the news desk, descended the step and marched across the snaking cables. Before she could greet her guest for the day, Finn stepped in front of her.

"You're better than I remember."

"Really?" She gave the hem of her jacket a quick tug. "Well, with a compliment like that, I can die happy."

"Just an observation." Curious, he wrapped his fingers around her arm to hold her in place. "I can't make up my mind about you. Am I still on the blacklist because I bumped you off the story the other night?"

"You're not on any list. I just don't like being watched."

He had to grin. "Then you're in the wrong business, Kansas."

He let her go. Impulsively he took one of the folding chairs out of camera range. He hadn't intended to stay, and knew he did so simply to irritate her. He'd come in that afternoon, as he'd come in the evening before, because he enjoyed being back in the Chicago studios.

He didn't have much in his life at the moment other than his career. He preferred it that way. He watched Deanna ease her guest's nerves with off-camera chitchat, and considered. Would she be relieved or annoyed to know he hadn't given her a thought over the remainder of the weekend? Years in the business had made him an expert at compartmentalizing his life. Women didn't interfere with his work, the sculpting of a story or his ambitions.

The months in London had added to his reputation and his credibility, but he was happy to be back.

His thoughts swung back to Deanna as he heard her laugh. A good, smoky sound, he thought. Subtle sex. It suited her looks, he decided. And those eyes. They were warm now, and filled with lively interest as her guest hyped a one-woman art show scheduled for that evening.

At that moment, Finn didn't give a damn about art. But he was interested, very interested, in Deanna. The way she leaned forward, just a little, to add a sense of intimacy to the interview. Not once did he catch her looking at her notes and scrambling for the next question.

Even when they broke, Deanna continued to give her guest her attention. As a result, the artist left the studio with her ego fully pumped. Deanna slipped back behind the news desk with Roger for the close.

"She's good, isn't she?"

Finn glanced behind him. Simon Grimsley was standing just inside the studio doors. He was a thin-shouldered man, with a long, narrow face set in perpetual lines of worry and doubt. Even when he smiled, as he did now, there was a look in his eyes that spoke of inescapable doom. He was losing his hair, though Finn knew him to be on the shy side of thirty. He was dressed, as always, in a dark suit and snugly knotted tie. And, as always, the attire accented his bony frame.

"How's it going, Simon?"

"Don't ask." Simon rolled his dark, pessimistic eyes. "Angela's in one of her moods today. Big time."

"That's not exactly a breaking story, Simon."

"Don't I know it." He lowered his voice as the red light blinked on. "Threw a paperweight at me," he whispered. "Baccarat. Lucky she doesn't have much of an arm."

"Maybe she could get a job with the Cubs."

Simon gave what passed for a chuckle, then guiltily stifled it. "She's under a lot of pressure."

"Yeah, right."

"It isn't easy staying number one." Simon let out a sigh of relief when the "on the air" sign blinked off. Live television kept him in a constant state of turmoil. "Deanna." He signaled to her and nearly hooked his foot in a coil of cable in his hurry to catch up. "Nice show. Really nice."

83

"Thanks." She looked from him to Finn, then back. "How'd this morning's taping go?"

"It went." He grimaced. "Angela asked me to get this message to you." He offered a pale pink envelope. "It seemed important."

"Okay." She resisted the urge to bury the note in her pocket. "Don't worry, I'll get back to her."

"Well, I'd better get upstairs. Come by this afternoon's taping if you get a chance."

"I will."

Finn watched the door swing shut behind Simon. "I'll never understand how anyone so nervous and depressed can deal with the characters *Angela's* books."

"He's organized. I don't know anyone better at sorting things out than Simon."

"That wasn't a criticism," Finn said as he matched her stride out of the studio. "It was a comment."

"You seem to be full of comments today." Out of habit, she turned into the dressing room to redo her makeup.

"Then I've got another one. Your interview with the artist—Myra, was it?—was solid."

Pleasure snuck through her guard. "Thanks. It was an interesting subject."

"It didn't have to be. You kept her grounded when she started to run on about technique and symbolism. You kept it light and friendly."

"I prefer light and friendly." Her eyes met his in the mirror and sizzled. "I'll leave Gorbachev and Hussein to you."

"I appreciate it." He shook his head as she freshened her lipstick. "You're touchy. The observation was meant as a compliment."

He was right, she thought. She was being touchy. "Do you know what I think, Finn?" She smoothed back her hair and turned. "I think there's too much energy in this room. Conflicting energy."

He had felt electricity since the moment he'd scooped her

against him on a rainy runway. "And how does all that conflicting energy make you feel?"

"Crowded." She smiled, in direct response to the amusement in his eyes. "I suppose that's why it always seems you're in my way."

"I guess I'd better move aside then, and give you some room."

"Why don't you?" She picked up the pink envelope she'd set on the counter, but before she could open it, Finn took her hand.

"Question. How do you justify your job as a reporter for CBC with your job with Angela?"

"I don't have a job with Angela. I work the news." In quick, competent moves, she ran a brush through her hair and tied it back. "I occasionally do favors for Angela. She doesn't pay me."

"Just a couple of pals helping each other out?"

She didn't care for the edge in his voice. "I wouldn't say Angela and I were pals. We are friends, and she's been very generous with me. The news division doesn't have a problem with my personal association with Angela, or with the time I give her."

"So I hear. But then the entertainment division wouldn't step back from applying a little pressure when they've got the clout of a top-rated show." He rocked back on his heels, studying her. "It makes me wonder why Angela would go to the trouble just to use you."

Her hackles rose. "She isn't using me. I'm learning from her. And learning is something I find useful."

"Learning what, exactly?"

How to be the best, she thought, but cautiously kept that thought to herself. "She has incredible interviewing skills."

"That she does, but yours seem sharp enough to me." He paused. "At least on soft news."

She nearly snarled, delighting him. "I enjoy what I do, and if I didn't, it still wouldn't be any of your business."

"An accurate statement." He should have dropped the subject, but he knew too well what Angela could do with her claws once they were dug in. Unless he missed his guess, Deanna would bleed fast and copiously. "Would you listen to a friendly warning about Angela?"

"No. I make up my mind about people on my own."

"Suit yourself. I wonder," he continued, searching her face. "Are you as tough as you think you are?"

"I can be tougher."

"You'll need to be." He released her hand and walked away.

Alone, Deanna let out a long, steadying breath. Why was it every time she spent five minutes with Finn, she felt as though she'd run a marathon? Exhausted and exhilarated. Pushing him firmly out of her mind, she tore open Angela's note. The hand-writing was a series of loops and flourishes drawn with a fountain pen.

Deanna darling,
I have something vitally important to discuss with you. My schedule today is maddening, but I can slip away about four. Meet me for tea at the Ritz. Lobby lounge. Believe me, it's urgent.
Love,
Angela

Angela hated to be kept waiting. By four-fifteen, she'd ordered a second champagne cocktail and begun to steam. She was about to offer Deanna the chance of a lifetime, and rather than gratitude, she was greeted with rudeness. As a result, she snapped at the wait-ress when her drink was served, and scowled around the sumptuous lounge.

The fountain behind her tinkled musically. It soothed her a bit, like the frothy sip of champagne. It wasn't really drinking, she thought, pleasing herself. It was like tasting success.

The gilt and glory of the Ritz was a long way from Arkansas, she reminded herself. And she was about to go further yet.

The reminder of her plans softened the frown on her face. The smile bolstered the courage of a matron with blue-tinted hair who approached for an autograph. Angela was all gracious affability. When Deanna hurried in at twenty after four, she saw Angela chatting amiably with a fan.

"Excuse me." Deanna took the seat across from Angela. "I'm sorry I'm late."

"Don't give it a thought." Waving away the apology, Angela smiled. "So nice to have met you, Mrs. Hopkins. I'm glad you enjoy the show."

"I wouldn't miss it. And you're even lovelier in person than you are on TV."

"Isn't that sweet?" Angela said to Deanna when they were alone. "She watches the show every morning. Now she'll be able to brag to her bridge club that she met me in person. Let's get you a drink."

"We'd better make it tea. I'm driving."

"Nonsense." Angela caught the waitress's attention, tapped her glass, then held up two fingers. "I refuse to celebrate with something as passive as tea."

"Then I'd better know what we're celebrating." Deanna slipped out of her jacket. One drink, she estimated, could easily last the entire thirty minutes she'd allowed for the meeting.

"Not until you have your champagne." Angela smiled coyly before sipping her own. "I really need to thank you again for being such a trouper the other night. It turned out to be a wonderful party."

"There wasn't much to do."

"Easy for you to say. You're able to keep a handle on all those little details." With a flutter of her fingers, Angela dismissed them. "They just annoy me." Setting her drink aside again, she took out a cigarette. "And what do you think of Finn?"

"I'd have to say he's one of the best reporters on CBC or any of the networks. Powerful. He has a way of cutting to the heart of an issue, and letting just enough of himself sneak through to intrigue the audience."

"No, no, not professionally." Angela blew out an impatient stream of smoke. "As a man."

"I don't know him as a man."

"Impressions, Deanna." Angela's voice sharpened, putting Deanna on alert. "You're a reporter, aren't you? You're trained to observe. What are your observations?"

Boggy ground, Deanna decided. The station had been ripe with rumors of past history, and the speculation of a current affair between the two stars. "Objectively? He's very attractive, charismatic, and I suppose I'd have to use the word 'powerful' again. He's certainly well liked by the techs, and by the brass."

"Especially the women." Angela began to jiggle her foot, a sign of agitation. Her father had been charismatic, too, hadn't he? she remembered bitterly. And attractive, and certainly powerful—when he was on a winning streak. And he'd left her as well, her and her pathetic, drunken mother for another woman and the siren call of a royal flush. But she'd learned since then, learned a lot about payback. "He can be very charming," she continued. "And very devious. He isn't above using people to get what he wants." She drew deeply on the cigarette, smiled thinly through a mist of smoke. "I noticed him seek you out at the party, and thought I'd give you a friendly warning."

Deanna lifted a brow, wondering how Angela would feel if she knew Finn had used the same phrase just a few hours earlier. "No need."

"I know that you're involved with Marshall at the moment, but Finn can be very persuasive." She tapped out her cigarette, leaning closer. Girl to girl. "I know how news travels at the studio, so there's no need to pretend you don't know about what was between Finn and me before he went to London. I'm afraid since I broke things off, he might try to salve his ego and strike back at me, by making a play for someone I care about. I wouldn't want to see you hurt."

"I won't be." Uncomfortable, Deanna shifted back. "Angela, I really am running thin on time. If this is what you wanted to talk to me about—"

"No, no. Just making small talk. And here we go." She beamed as their drinks were served. "Now we have the proper tools for a toast." She lifted her glass, waited until Deanna had lifted hers. "To New York." The flutes clinked joyfully together.

"New York?"

"All my life I've been working toward it." After a hasty sip, Angela set her glass down. Excitement was shimmering around her in restless waves. Nothing, not even champagne could compete with it. "Now it's reality. What I'm telling you now is in the strictest confidence. Understood?"

"Of course."

"I had an offer from Starmedia, Deanna, an incredible offer." Her voice bubbled like the wine. "I'll be leaving Chicago and CBC in August, when my contract's up. The show will be moving to New York, with the addition of four prime-time specials a year." Her eyes were like blue glass, her fingers running up and down the flute like excited birds searching for a place to land.

"That's wonderful. But I thought you'd already agreed to renew with CBC and the Delacort syndicate."

"Verbally." She shrugged it off. "Starmedia is a much more imaginative syndicate. Delacort's been taking me for granted. I'm going where I'm most appreciated—and most rewarded. I'll be forming my own production company. And we won't just produce *Angela's*. We'll do specials, TV movies, documentaries. I'm going to have access to the best in the business." She paused, always a show-man. "That's why I want you to come with me as my executive producer."

"You want me?" Deanna shook her head as if to clear jumbled thoughts. "I'm not a producer. And Lew—"

"Lew." Angela dismissed her longtime associate with a toss of her head. "I want someone young, fresh, imaginative. No, when I make this move, I won't be taking Lew with me. The job's yours, Deanna. All you have to do is take it."

Deanna took a long, slow sip of champagne. She'd been

expecting the offer of head researcher, and because ambition pointed elsewhere, she was prepared to decline. But this, this was out of nowhere. And it was far more tempting.

"I'm flattered," she began. Flabbergasted, she corrected. "I don't know what to say."

"Then I'll cue you. Say yes."

With a quick laugh, Deanna sat back and studied the woman across from her. Eager, impulsive and, yes, ruthless. Not bad qualities all in all. There was also talent and brains and those edgy nerves Angela thought no one noticed. It was the combination that had pushed her to the top, and was keeping her there.

A top spot on the top show in the market, Deanna calculated. "I wish I could jump at it, Angela. But I need to think this through."

"What is there to think about?" The wine was fizzing in Angela's head. Deanna was just quick enough to save a flute from upending when Angela reached carelessly across the table. "You don't get offers like this every day in this business, Deanna. Take what there is when you can. Do you know the kind of money I'm talking about? The prestige, the power?"

"I have some idea."

"A quarter of a million a year, to start. And all the benefits."

It took Deanna a moment to close her mouth. "No," she said slowly. "Apparently I didn't have any idea."

"Your own office, your own staff, a car and driver at your disposal. Opportunities to travel, to socialize with the cream."

"Why?"

Pleased, Angela sat back. "Because I can trust you. Because I can depend on you, and because I see something of myself when I look at you."

A quick chill danced up Deanna's spine. "It's a very big step."

"Small ones are a waste of time."

"That may be, but I need to think this through. I don't know if I'm suited."

"I think you're suited." Angela's impatience was simmering again. "Why would you doubt it?"

"Angela, one of the reasons I imagine you're offering me this job is because I'm a good detail person. Because I'm thorough and obsessively organized. I wouldn't be any of those things if I didn't take the time to sort this out."

With a nod, Angela took out another cigarette. "You're right. I shouldn't be pushing, but I want you with me on this. How much time do you need?"

"A couple of days. Can I let you know by the end of the week?"

"All right." She flicked on her lighter and studied the flame briefly. "I'll just say one more thing. You don't belong behind a desk on some local noon show reading the news. You were made for bigger things, Deanna. I saw it in you right from the beginning."

"I hope you're right." Deanna let out a long breath. "I really do."

THE LITTLE GALLERY OFF Michigan Avenue was crammed with people. Hardly larger than the average suburban garage, the showroom was brightly lit to suit the bold, splashy paintings arranged nearly frame to frame along the walls. The moment Deanna stepped inside, she was glad she'd followed the impulse to stop in. Not only did it take her mind off Angela's stunning offer that afternoon, but it allowed her to follow up firsthand on her own interview.

The air was ripe with sounds and scents. Cheap champagne and clashing voices. And color, she mused. The blacks and grays of the crowd were a stark contrast to the vibrancy of the paintings. She regretted she hadn't wrangled a camera crew to do a brief update.

"Quite an event," Marshall murmured in her ear.

Deanna turned, smiled. "We won't stay long. I know this isn't exactly your style."

He glanced around at the frantic colors slashed over canvas. "Not exactly."

"Wild stuff." Fran edged her way through, her husband Richard's hand firmly gripped in hers. "Your spot this afternoon had some impact."

"I don't know about that."

"Well, it didn't hurt." Tilting her head up, Fran sniffed the air. "I smell food."

"It's gotten so she can smell a hot dog boiling from three blocks away." Richard shifted in to drape an arm around Fran. He had a pretty, boyish face that smiled easily. His pale blond hair was conservatively cut, but the tiny hole in his left earlobe had once sported a variety of earrings.

"It's heightened sensory awareness," Fran claimed. "And mine tells me there are pigs-in-a-blanket at three o'clock. Catch you later." She dragged Richard away.

"Hungry?" Bumped from behind, Deanna moved comfortably into Marshall's protective arm.

"Not really." Using the advantage of height, he scouted the area and led her away from the heart of the crowd. "You're being a good sport about this."

"Coming here? It's interesting."

She laughed and kissed him again. "A very good sport. I'd just like to make a quick pass through, and congratulate Myra." Deanna looked around. "If I can find her."

"Take your time. Why don't I see if I can find us some canapés."

"Thanks."

Deanna threaded her way through the crowd. She enjoyed the press of bodies, the undertones of excitement, the snippets of overheard conversations. She'd made it halfway around the room when a bold painting stopped her. Sinuous lines and bold splashes against a textured background of midnight blue, it turned the canvas into an explosion of emotion and energy. Fascinated, Deanna moved closer. The label beneath the sleek ebony frame read AWAKENINGS. Perfect, Deanna thought. Absolutely perfect.

The colors were alive and seemed to be fighting their way free of the canvas, away from the night. Even as she studied the work, she felt her pleasure turn to desire, and desire to determination. With a little juggling of her budget . . .

"Like it?"

She felt jolted into awareness. But she didn't bother to turn around to face Finn.

"Yes, very much. Do you spend much time in galleries?"

"Now and then." He stepped up beside her, amused at the way she stared at the painting. Every thought in her head was reflected in her eyes. "Actually, your spot this afternoon convinced me to drop in."

"Really?" She looked at him then. He was dressed much as he'd been when he'd crossed the runway. His expensive leather jacket unsnapped, his jeans comfortably worn, boots well broken in.

"Yes, really. And I owe you one, Kansas."

"Why is that?"

"This." He nodded toward the painting. "I just bought it."

"You—" She looked from him to the painting and back again. Her teeth locked together. "I see."

"It really caught me." He dropped a hand on her shoulder and faced the painting. If he continued to look at her, Finn knew he'd break out in a grin. It was all there in her eyes—the disappointment, the desire, the irritation. "And the price was right. I think they're going to find out very soon that they're underselling her."

It was hers, damn it. She'd already imagined it hanging above her desk at home. She couldn't believe he'd snapped it out from under her. "Why this one?"

"Because it was perfect for me." With the lightest of pressure on her shoulder, he turned her to face him. "I knew the moment I saw it. And when I see something I want . . ." He trailed a finger up the side of her throat, feather light, while his eyes stayed on hers. "I do what I can to have it."

Her pulse jumped like a rabbit, surprising her, annoying her. They were standing toe to toe now, their eyes and mouths lined up.

93

And too close, just an inch too close, so that she could see herself reflected in the dreamy blue of his eyes.

"Sometimes what we want is unavailable."

"Sometimes." He smiled, and she forgot the crowd pressing them together, the coveted painting at her back, the voice in her head telling her to back away. "A good reporter has to know when to move fast and when to be patient. Don't you think?"

"Yes." But she was having a hard time thinking at all. It was his eyes, she realized, the way they focused as if there were nothing and no one else. And she knew, somehow, that he would continue to look at her just that way, even if the ground suddenly fell away beneath her.

"Want me to be patient, Deanna?" His finger roamed over her jawline, lingered.

"I—" The air backed up in her lungs. And for a moment, one startled moment, she felt herself swaying toward him.

"Oh, I see you found refreshments already," Marshall said.

She saw the wry amusement on Finn's face. "Yes, Marshall." Her voice was unsteady. Fighting to level it, she gripped his arm as though he were a rock in the stormy sea. "I ran into Finn. I don't think you've met. Dr. Marshall Pike, Finn Riley."

"Of course. I know your work." Marshall offered a hand. "Welcome back to Chicago."

"Thanks. You're a psychologist, right?"

"Yes. I specialize in domestic counseling."

"Interesting work. The statistics seem to point to the end of the traditional family, yet the overall trend, if you look at advertising, entertainment, seems to be making a move back to just that."

Deanna looked for a barb, but found nothing but genuine interest as Finn drew Marshall into a discussion on American family culture. It was the reporter in him, she imagined, that made it possible for him to talk to anyone at any time on any subject. At the moment, she was grateful.

It comforted her to have her hand tucked into Marshall's, to feel

94

that she could be, if she chose, part of a couple. She preferred, over-whelmingly, Marshall's gentle romancing to Finn's direct assault on the nervous system. If she had to compare the two men, which she assured herself she certainly didn't, she would have given Marshall top points for courtesy, respect and stability.

She smiled up at him even as her eyes were drawn back to the dramatic and passionate painting.

When Fran and Richard joined them, Deanna made introduc-tions. A few minutes of small talk, and they said their goodbyes. Deanna tried to pretend she didn't feel Finn's eyes on her as they nudged their way to the door.

"Be still my heart," Fran muttered in Deanna's ear. "He's even sexier in person than he is on the tube."

"You think so?"

"Honey, if I was unmarried and unpregnant, I'd do a lot more than think." Fran shot one last look over her shoulder. "Yum-yum."

Chuckling, Deanna gave her a light shove out the door. "Get a hold of yourself, Myers."

"Fantasies are harmless, Dee, I keep telling you. And if he'd been looking at me the way he was looking at you, I'd have been a puddle of hormones at his feet."

Deanna combated the jitters in her stomach with a brisk gulp of spring air. "I don't melt that easily."

Not melting easily, Deanna thought later, was part of the prob-lem. When Marshall pulled his car to the curb in front of her building, she knew that he would walk her up. And when he walked her up, he would expect to be invited inside. And then . . .

She simply wasn't ready for the "and then."

The flaw was in her, undoubtedly. She could easily blame her hesitation toward intimacy on the past. And it would be true enough. She didn't want to admit another part of her hesitation was attributable to Finn.

"You don't need to walk me up."

He lifted a hand to toy with her hair. "It's early yet."

"I know. But I have an early call in the morning. I appreciate your going by the gallery with me."

"I enjoyed it. More than I anticipated."

"Good." Smiling, she touched her lips to his. When he deepened the kiss, drawing her in, she yielded. There was warmth there, passion just restrained. A quiet moan of pleasure sounded in her throat as he changed the angle of the kiss. The thud of his heart raced against hers.

"Deanna." He took his mouth on a slow journey of her face. "I want to be with you."

"I know." She turned her lips to his again. Almost, she thought dreamily. She was almost sure. "I need a little more time, Marshall. I'm sorry."

"You know how I feel about you?" He cupped her face in his hand, studying her. "But I understand, it has to be right. Why don't we get away for a few days?"

"Away?"

"From Chicago. We could take a weekend." He tipped her face back and kissed the side of her mouth. "Cancún, St. Thomas, Maui. Wherever you like." And the other side. "Just the two of us. It would let us see how we are together, away from work, all the pressures."

"I'd like that." Her eyes drifted closed. "I'd like to think about that."

"Then think about it." There was a look of dark triumph in his eyes. "Check your schedule, and leave the rest to me."

Chapter Seven

DEANNA HADN'T EXPECTED THE PRICKS OF DISLOYALTY. Television was, after all, a business. And part of the business was to get ahead, to make the best deal. But while the May sweeps consumed the CBC Building, with nightly ratings discussed and analyzed by everyone from top brass to the maintenance crews, she felt like a traitor.

Next year's budgets were being forecasted off the sweeps, and the forecasts were being made on faulty assumptions.

She knew *Angela's* would be gone before the start of the fall season. And with the deal Angela had made, she would compete with CBC's daytime lineup as well as with prime-time specials.

The more celebratory the mood in the newsroom, the more guilt jabbed at Deanna's conscience.

"Got a problem, Kansas?"

Deanna glanced up as Finn made himself comfortable on the corner of her desk. "Why do you ask?"

"You've been staring at that screen for the past five minutes. I'm used to seeing you move."

"I'm thinking."

"That doesn't usually stop you." Leaning forward, he rubbed his thumb between her eyebrows. "Tension."

In defense, she shifted back in her chair to break the contact. "We're in the middle of the May sweeps. Who isn't tense?"

"*Midday's* holding its own."

"It's doing better than that," she snapped back. Pride and loyalty welled together. "We've got a twenty-eight-percent share. We're up three full ratings points since the last sweeps."

"That's better. I'd rather see you fired up than unhappy."

"I wasn't unhappy," she said between her teeth. "I was thinking."

"Whatever." He rose then, and hauled up the garment bag he'd set on the floor.

"Where are you going?"

"New York." In an easy, practiced move, Finn slung the bag over his shoulder. "I'm putting in a few days as substitute host on *Wake Up Call*. Kirk Brooks's allergies are acting up."

Deanna arched a brow. She knew that CBC's *Wake Up Call* was performing poorly, lagging well behind *Good Morning America* and *Today*. "You mean the ratings are acting up."

Finn shrugged and took one of the candy-coated almonds from the bowl on her desk. "That's the bottom line. The brass figures the viewers will think somebody who's been through a few firefights and earthquakes is glamorous." Disgust crossed his face as he swallowed. "So, I'll get up early for a few days and wear a tie."

"It's a little more than that. It's a complicated show. Interviews, breaking stories—"

"Chitchat." The phrase was ripe with contempt.

"There's nothing wrong with chitchat. It involves the viewer, brings them into the picture. And it opens doors."

His lips curved into something between a smile and a sneer. "Right. The next time I interview Qaddafi I'll be sure to ask how he feels about Madonna's new video."

Intrigued, she tilted her head back to study him. She thought she'd pegged him as the reckless rebel who did precisely as he chose and kept the executives groping for the Maalox. "If you hate it so much, why are you doing it?"

"I work here," he said simply, and helped himself to a handful of candy.

Deanna lowered her eyes, toyed with papers on her desk. So did she, she thought miserably. So did she. "Then it's a matter of loyalty."

"First." What was going on inside that head of hers? he wondered. It was a pity he didn't have time to hang around and dig it out. "Then you can expand it. If *Wake Up Call* goes in the sewer, the revenue suffers. What's the first place that feels it?"

"The news department."

"Damn right. You've got the morning show scraping the bottom of the ratings barrel, and the fact that a couple of fat-headed idiots can't seem to program a decent Tuesday night, and before you can say Nielsen, we've got cutbacks."

"Monday and Friday are strong," she murmured. "And we've got *Angela's*."

"It's a little tough knowing that Angela and a handful of sitcoms are saving our ass." Then he smiled, shrugged. "Screwy business. I don't suppose you'd kiss me goodbye."

"I don't suppose I would."

"But you'll miss me." There was enough laughter in his eyes to make her grin back at him.

"You're not going off to war, Finn."

"Easy for you to say. Stay tuned." He sauntered off. Deanna watched him walk up to another woman reporter. The woman laughed, then planted an exaggerated kiss on his mouth. As applause erupted, he turned, grinned at Deanna. With a final salute to the newsroom, he swung through the doors.

Deanna was still chuckling when she returned to her copy. The man might have his flaws, she mused, but at least he could make her laugh.

And, she admitted, he could make her think.

Mentally, she pulled out her list. Two columns, neatly typed, specifying her reasons to accept and decline Angela's offer. There was a hard copy in the top drawer of her desk at home. It was a simple matter to visualize it. With a sigh, she added one word to the "decline" column.

Loyalty.

"Miss Reynolds?"

She blinked and focused. Behind a porcelain pot of lush red hibiscus was a round, cheerful face. It took her a moment to click it in. But when he shoved a pair of wire-rimmed glasses up his pug nose, she remembered.

"Jeff, hi. What's all this?"

"For you." He set it on her desk, then immediately shoved his hands in his pockets. As an editorial assistant, Jeff Hyatt was more comfortable with equipment than with people. He gave Deanna a fleeting smile, then stared at the flowers. "Nice. I ran into the delivery boy, and since I was on my way in . . ."

"Thanks, Jeff."

"No problem."

Deanna had already forgotten him as she reached for the card tucked among the blooms.

How about Hawaii?

Smiling, she reached out to stroke a blossom. One more on the "decline" list, she mused. Marshall.

"MISS REYNOLDS TO see you, Miss Perkins."

"Ask her to wait." With a cigarette smoldering between her fingers, Angela frowned over Beeker's report on Marshall Pike. It was certainly interesting reading, and demanded her full attention. His credentials were well earned—the doctorate from Georgetown, the year studying abroad. And financially, the psychologist did well for himself counseling socialites and politicians on their floundering marriages and dysfunctional families. He offset his lucrative practice by donating three afternoons a week to social services.

Overall, a nice, upstanding profile of a man who had studied well and worked hard and was devoted to preserving family life.

Angela knew all about profiles, and the illusions they fostered.

His own marriage had failed. A quiet, civilized divorce hadn't caused much of a ripple in Chicago society, and certainly hadn't harmed his practice. Still, it was interesting. Interesting because Beeker had discovered that the size of Marshall's settlement with his ex-wife was a whopper, as were the alimony payments. Much more than a brief, childless marriage warranted.

He hadn't contested it, Angela mused. A smile lifted the corners of her mouth as she continued to read. Perhaps he hadn't dared. When a thirty-five-year-old man was caught entertaining his secretary's very lovely, very naked and very young daughter at two A.M., he didn't have a lot of room for negotiations. A minor, however willing, was still a minor. And adultery, particularly with a sixteen-year-old, carried a hefty price tag.

He'd been clever in covering himself, Angela mused, scanning Beeker's file. The secretary had taken a fat lump sum and a glowing reference and moved her family to San Antonio. The wife had taken a great deal more, but barely a whisper about the good doctor had escaped. And when it had—and Angela admired him for his boldness—rumor tied him obliquely with the secretary, not her nubile daughter . . .

So, the elegant Dr. Pike continued his practice as one of Chicago's most eligible bachelors.

The eminent family counselor with a weakness for teenagers. An interesting topic for a show, she decided, and laughed out loud. No, no, they would keep this one private. Some information was worth a great deal more than ratings. Angela closed the file and slipped it into a drawer. She wondered how much Deanna knew.

"Send her in, Cassie."

Angela was all smiles when Deanna walked in. "Sorry I kept you waiting. I had a little something to finish up."

"I know you're busy." Deanna briefly tugged on her earring. "Do you have a few minutes?"

"Of course." She rose, gesturing to a chair. "How about some coffee?"

"No, don't bother." Deanna sat, made herself fold her hands quietly in her lap.

"No trouble. Something cold instead?" Delighted, for the moment, to serve, Angela crossed to the bar and poured them both a mineral water. "If I didn't have a dinner tonight, I'd have Cassie bring in some of those fudge cookies I know she's got in her desk." She laughed lightly. "She doesn't think I know about them. But then, I make it a policy to know everything about my people." After handing Deanna a glass, she dropped into a chair and stretched out her legs. "It's been quite a day so far. And I'm off at dawn for California."

"California? I didn't know you were going on location."

"No, I'm speaking at the commencement exercises at Berkeley." Not bad, Angela thought, for someone who waited tables to get through Arkansas State. "I'll be back for Monday's tapings. You know, Dee, since you stopped by, you might take a look at my speech. You know how I value your input."

"Sure." Miserable, Deanna sipped at the water. "I can't do it until after five, but—"

"No problem. You can fax it back to me at home. I'll give you a copy."

"All right. Angela—" The only way to handle this was straight-forwardly. "I'm here to talk to you about your offer."

"I was hoping you were." Relaxed, satisfied, Angela slipped off her shoes and reached for a cigarette. "I can't tell you how much I'm looking forward to the move to New York, Deanna. That's where the pulse of this business is, you know." She snapped on her lighter, took a quick drag. "That's where the power is. I've already got my agent looking for an apartment."

Her eyes lost their calculating edge and turned dreamy. Inside she was still the girl from Arkansas who wanted to be a princess. "I want something with a view, lots of windows and light, lots of room. A place where I can feel at home, where I can entertain. If I find the right place, we may even shoot some of the specials there. The viewing audience likes to get a peek at our personal lives."

She smiled as she tapped her cigarette. The soft look in her eyes sharpened. "We're going places, Dee. Women have finally gained a solid foothold in broadcasting, and we're going right to the top. You and me." She reached over and gave Deanna's hand a quick squeeze. "You know, your brains, your creativity are only part of the reason I want you with me." Her voice was persuasive and ringing with sincerity. "I can trust you, Dee. I can relax around you. I don't have to tell you what that means to me."

Deanna closed her eyes a moment while guilt churned in her stomach.

"I don't think there's ever been another woman I've felt so close to," Angela concluded.

"Angela, I want—"

"You're going to be more than my executive producer; you're going to be my right hand. In fact, I should have my agent looking for a place for you, too. Nearby," she murmured, envisioning the late-night girl talks she'd never been permitted during her youth. "It's going to be wonderful, for both of us."

"Angela, slow down." With a half laugh, Deanna held up a hand. "I think I understand how much this deal with Starmedia means to you, and I'm thrilled for you. You've been wonderful to me, your help, your friendship, and I wish you all the success in the world." Leaning over, Deanna took Angela's hand. "But I can't take the job."

The gleam in Angela's eyes dimmed. Her mouth tightened. The unexpected rejection nearly stopped her breath. "Are you certain you understand just what I'm offering you?"

"Oh yes, I do. I do," she repeated, squeezing Angela's hand between both of hers before she got up to pace. "And believe me,

I've thought about this carefully. I've had a hard time thinking of anything else." She turned back, gesturing with her hands. "And I just can't do it."

Very slowly, Angela straightened in her chair. She crossed her legs. The simple gesture eradicated all the softness. "Why?"

"A lot of reasons. First, I have a contract."

With a sound caught between disgust and amusement, Angela waved it aside. "You've been around long enough to know how easily that's dealt with."

"That may be, but when I signed I gave my word."

Taking another contemplative drag, Angela narrowed her eyes. "Are you that naive?"

Deanna understood it was meant as an insult. But she merely lifted a shoulder. "There are other factors. Even knowing you don't plan to take Lew, I'd feel guilty stepping into his shoes—particularly since I don't have his experience. I'm not a producer, Angela. And though it's awfully tempting to forget that and jump at the offer— the money, the position, the power. Christ, New York." She blew out a breath that fluttered her bangs. She hadn't fully understood how much she wanted all those things until they had been within reach and she'd had to let them go. "And the chance to work with you. Really work with you, that isn't easy for me to turn my back on."

"But you are." Angela's tone was cool. "That's precisely what you're doing."

"It's just not for me. Other factors just got in the way, no matter how hard I tried to reposition them. My ambitions run in front of the camera. And I'm happy in Chicago. My job, my home, friends are here."

Angela tapped out the cigarette in quick, short bursts, like machine-gun fire. "And Marshall? Did he factor into this decision?"

Deanna thought of the pot of red hibiscus on her desk. "Somewhat. I do have feelings for him. I'd like to give them a chance."

"I have to tell you, you're making a mistake. You're letting details and personal feelings cloud your professional judgment."

"I don't think so." Deanna crossed the room to sit again, leaned forward. It was a tricky business, she thought, turning down an offer without seeming ungrateful. Particularly when the offer had taken on all the connotations of a favor to a friend. "I've looked at this from every angle. That's what I do—occasionally what I overdo. Your offer wasn't easy to turn down, and I don't do it lightly. I'll always be grateful and incredibly flattered that you had enough faith in me to ask."

"So you're going to sit back and read copy?" Now it was Angela who rose. Fury was bubbling so hot within her she could feel it searing under her skin. She'd offered the girl a feast, and she was settling for crumbs. Where was the gratitude? Where was the fucking loyalty? "Your choice," she said coolly as she sat behind her desk. "Why don't you take a few more days—the weekend, while I'm away—in case you have any second thoughts." She shook her head to cut off any comment from Deanna. "We'll talk again Monday," Angela said in dismissal. "Between tapings. Pencil it in for, oh ..." Her mind was working frantically as she flipped through her appointment book. "Eleven-fifteen." Her smile was warm, friendly again when she glanced up. "If you're of the same mind then, I won't give you an argument. Fair enough?"

"All right." It seemed more gracious, and certainly easier to agree. "I'll see you Monday, then. Have a nice trip."

"I will." Deliberately she waited until Deanna was at the door. "Oh, Dee." She smiled and held up a manila envelope. "My speech?"

"Right." Deanna crossed the room again, to take the package.

"Try to get it back to me before nine. I need my beauty sleep."

Angela waited until the door closed before she folded her hands on the desk. Her fingers turned bone-white with the pressure. She took a long moment, staring at the closed door, breathing shallowly. It wouldn't do to rage, she told herself. No, not this time. For Deanna she had to be cool and calm and concise to review the facts.

She'd offered Deanna a position of power, her own unqualified friendship, her trust. And she preferred to read the news at noon because she had a contract, a lease on an apartment and a man.

Could she actually be that artless? Angela wondered. That guileless? That stupid?

She relaxed her hands, forced herself to lean back in her chair and even her breathing. Whatever the answer, Deanna would learn that no one ever turned Angela down.

Calmer now, Angela opened a drawer and took out Marshall's file. The look on her face wasn't hard, nor was it glittery with anger. Her lips trembled into a pout, a child's expression on being denied. Deanna wasn't going to go with her to New York, she mused. And she was going to be very, very sorry.

DEANNA HAD TAKEN ONE STEP into the outer office when her guilty mood vanished into a flood of surprised pleasure.

"Kate. Kate Lowell."

The leggy, doe-eyed woman turned, brushing her glorious mane of flaming hair aside. Her face—the ivory complexion, the delicate bones, the melting eyes and generous mouth—was as stunning as it was famous. The quick, flashing smile was automatic. She was, first and last, an actress.

"Hello."

"Those braces sure as hell did the job." Now Deanna laughed. "Kate, it's Dee. Deanna Reynolds."

"Deanna." The furious nervous tension beneath the smile dissolved. "Oh, God, Deanna." The infectious giggle that turned men to putty rang out. "I can't believe it."

"Imagine how I feel. It has to be fourteen, fifteen years."

For Kate, for one beautiful moment, it felt like yesterday. She could remember all the long talks—the innocence of girlish confidences.

Under Cassie's fascinated eye, the two women crossed the room and embraced. They hung on to each other a moment, tight.

"You look wonderful," they said simultaneously, then laughed.

"It's true." Kate drew back, but kept Deanna's hand in hers. "We do. It's a long way from Topeka."

"Longer for you. What's Hollywood's newest star doing in Chicago?"

"A little business." Kate's smile dimmed. "A little hype. What about you?"

"I work here."

"Here?" The remnants of the warm smile vanished. "For Angela?"

"No, downstairs. In the newsroom. *Midday*, with Roger Crowell and Deanna Reynolds."

"Don't tell me two of my favorite people know each other." Angela stepped out, the gracious hostess. "Kate, dear, I'm sorry you had to wait. Cassie didn't tell me you were here."

"I just got in." The hand still gripping Deanna's stiffened, then relaxed. "My plane was delayed this morning, so I've been running behind all day."

"Awful, isn't it? Even a woman with your talents is subject to the whims of technology. Now tell me . . ." She strolled over to lay a proprietary hand on Deanna's shoulder. "How do you know our Dee?"

"My aunt lived across the street from Deanna's family. I spent a couple of summers in Kansas as a child."

"And you were playmates." Angela's laugh was delighted. "That's charming. And Deanna's been keeping her brush with fame all to herself. Shame on you."

In a subtle move, no less potent for its polish, Kate shifted. The gesture eased Angela out of the circle. "How's your family?"

"They're fine." Baffled by the tension snapping in the air, Deanna tried to find the source of it in Kate's eyes. All she could see—was allowed to see—was the soft, tawny gold. "They never miss one of your movies. Neither do I. I remember how you'd put on plays in your aunt's backyard."

"And you'd write them. Now you're reporting the news."

"And you're making it. You were incredible in *Deception*, Kate. I cried buckets."

"There's Oscar talk." Smoothly, Angela moved forward to drape an arm around Kate's shoulders. "How could there not be when Kate so effectively played the heroic young mother fighting to keep her child." A look passed between them, sharp as a razor. "I attended the premiere. There wasn't a dry eye in the house."

"Oh, I imagine there was one." Kate's smile was brilliant, and curiously feline. "Or two."

"I'd love to give you girls time to catch up." Angela pressed her fingers warningly on Kate's shoulder. "But we're running late."

"I'll let you go." Tucking Angela's speech under her arm, Deanna stepped back. "How long will you be in Chicago?"

"I'm leaving tomorrow." Kate stepped back as well. "It was good to see you."

"And you." Oddly hurt, Deanna turned and walked away.

"Isn't that sweet?" Angela gestured Kate into her office, shut the door. "You running into a childhood friend—who just happens to be my protégée—right in my office. Tell me, Kate, have you kept in touch with Dee? Shared all your secrets with her?"

"Only a fool shares secrets willingly, Angela. Now let's not waste time on small talk. Let's get down to business."

Satisfied, Angela sat behind her desk. "Yes, let's."

TO FINN RILEY, NEW YORK was like a woman: A long-legged, slick-skinned siren who knew her way around the block. She was sexy; she was by turns tacky and chic. And God knew she was dangerous.

Perhaps that was why he preferred Chicago. Finn loved women, and had a weakness for the long-legged, dangerous type. But Chicago was a big, burly man, with sweat on his shirt and a cold brew in his fist. Chicago was a brawler.

Finn trusted an honest fight more than he ever would a seduction.

He knew his way around Manhattan. He'd lived there briefly

with his mother during one of his parents' trial separations. He'd lost track of how many trial separations there had been before the inevitable divorce.

He remembered how reasonable they both had been. How bloodless and civilized. And he remembered being shuffled off to housekeepers, secretaries, prep schools, to spare him, supposedly, from that well-choreographed discord. In reality, he knew neither of his parents had been comfortable with a young boy who had asked direct questions and hadn't been satisfied with logical, gutless answers.

So he had lived in Manhattan, and on Long Island, and in Connecticut and Vermont. He'd summered in Bar Harbor and on Martha's Vineyard. He'd done time in the hallowed halls of three of New England's top prep schools.

Perhaps that was why he still had such restless feet. The minute roots started to dig in, he felt honor-bound to rip them out and move on.

Now he was back in New York. Temporarily. Where he knew the underbelly as well as he knew his mother's elegant penthouse on Central Park West.

He couldn't even say if he preferred one to the other. Any more than he could say that he minded putting in a few days on *Wake Up Call.*

At the moment, Finn put New York out of his mind and concentrated on the ball whizzing toward his nose. It wasn't self-defense nearly as much as it was the spirit of competition. And God knew the exertion of the court was a welcome change from the hours he'd spent sitting on a sofa on the set the last four days.

He sliced out with his racket, letting out a grunt of effort that was lost as the ball caromed off the wall. The power sang up his arm, the echo of the smash reverberated in his head. Adrenaline raced through him as his opponent cracked the ball back.

He met it with a solid backhand. The sweat dribbled satisfactorily down his back, dampening his ragged CBC T-shirt. For the next five minutes, there was only the smash and echo of the ball, the smell of sweat and the sound of labored breathing.

"Son of a bitch." Barlow James sagged against the wall as Finn blew one by him. "You're killing me."

"Shit." Finn didn't bother with the wall. He slid straight down to the floor of the Vertical Club. Every muscle in his body was weeping. "Next time I'll bring a gun. It'll be easier on both of us." He groped for a towel, mopped his soaking face. "When the hell are you going to get old?"

Barlow's laugh barked off the walls of the racquetball court. He was a brawny six-foot-four, flat of stomach, broad of chest, with shoulders like concrete blocks. At sixty-three, he was showing no signs of slowing down. As he crossed toward Finn, he pulled an orange neon sweatband away from his silver mane of hair. Finn had always thought Barlow had a face that belonged on Mount Rushmore. Craggy, huge and powerful.

"Getting soft, kid." Barlow pulled a bottle of Evian out of his gym bag and tossed it underhand to Finn. The second one he kept himself, drinking in deep, greedy gulps. "Almost took you that time."

"I've been playing with Brits." Since he nearly had his breath back, Finn grinned up at him. "They're not as mean as you."

"Well, welcome back to the States." Barlow offered a hand, hauling Finn to his feet. It was like being gripped by a friendly grizzly. "You know, most people would have considered the post in London a promotion, even a coup."

"It's a nice town."

Barlow let out a sigh. "Let's hit the showers."

TWENTY MINUTES LATER, THEY were stretched out on massage tables being pummeled.

"Damn good show this morning," Barlow commented.

"You've got a good crew, solid writers. Give it a little time and you'll be competitive."

110

"Time is shorter than it used to be in this business. I used to hate the goddamn bean counters." He bared his teeth in a grimace. "Now *I'm* a goddamn bean counter."

"At least you're a bean counter with imagination."

Barlow said nothing. Finn held his silence, knowing there was a purpose to this informal meeting.

"Give me an opinion on the Chicago bureau."

"It's tight," Finn said cautiously. "Hell, Barlow, you were bureau chief there for more than ten years, you know what we're working with. You've got a solid combination of experience and fresh blood. It's a good place to work."

"Ratings for the local evening news are weak. What we need is a stronger lead-in. I'd like to see them shift *Angela's* to four, pull her audience along."

Finn shrugged. He didn't ignore ratings, but he did detest their importance. "She's been at nine in Chicago and most of the Midwest for years. You might have a tough time pulling it off."

"Tougher than you think," Barlow murmured. "You and Angela . . . ah, there's nothing going on there anymore?"

Finn opened his eyes, cocked a brow. "Are we going to have a father-son chat, Pop?"

"Wiseass." Barlow chuckled, but his eyes were keen. Finn knew the look. "I wondered if you two had picked up where you left off."

"Where we left off was in the toilet," Finn said dryly. "And no."

"Hmmm. So are relations friendly or strained?"

"Publicly, friendly. Realistically, she hates my guts."

Barlow grunted again. It was good news, he thought, because he was fond of the boy. It was bad news because it meant he might not be able to use him. Making up his mind, he shifted on the table, wrapping the sheet around him and dismissing both masseuses.

"I've got a problem, Finn. A nasty little rumor that came buzzing in my ear a couple of days ago."

Finn pushed himself up. At any other time he would have made a crack about two grown men having an intense conversation while they were half naked and smelling of ginseng. "You want it to buzz in my ear?"

"And stop there."

"All right."

"Word is Angela Perkins is pulling up stakes—in Chicago and with CBC and Delacort."

"I haven't caught wind of that." Considering, Finn pushed the hair away from his face. Like any reporter, he hated getting news secondhand. Even if the news was only a rumor. "Look, it's contract time, right? She probably started the hum herself to get the brass to offer another truckload of money."

"No. Fact is, she's keeping it quiet. Real quiet. What I hear is that her agent's making negotiating noises, but they don't ring true. The leak came from Starmedia. If she leaves, Finn, it'll be a big hole."

"That's the entertainment division's problem."

"Their problem's our problem. You know that."

"Fuck."

"Well said. I only mention it because I thought if you and Angela were still . . ."

"We're not." Finn frowned. "I'll see what I can find out when I get back."

"Appreciate it. Now, let's get some lunch. We'll talk about news magazines."

"I'm not doing a news magazine." It was an old argument, one they continued with perfect amiability as they trailed sheets into the locker room.

"HAWAII SOUNDS PERFECT," Deanna said into the phone.

"I'm glad you think so. How about the second week in June?"

Pleased with the idea, Deanna poured a mug of coffee. She carried it and her portable phone to the table where she'd set up her laptop. "I'll put in for it. I haven't taken any time since I started at the station, so I don't think it'll be a problem."

"Why don't I stop by? We can talk about it, look at some brochures."

She closed her eyes, knowing she couldn't ignore the insistent blip on her computer screen. "I wish we could. I've got work. I had something come in at the last minute that held me up." She didn't mention the hour she'd spent punching up Angela's speech. "Pulling the anchor desk this weekend's really tied me up. How about brunch on Sunday?"

"Say about ten? I could meet you at the Drake. We can look over the brochures and decide on what suits us."

"Perfect. I'll be looking forward to it."

"So will I."

"I'm sorry about tonight."

"Don't be. I've got some work myself. Good night, Deanna."

"Good night."

Marshall hung up. Mozart was playing on the stereo, a quiet fire was burning in the hearth and the scent of lemon oil and fragrant smoke hung in the air.

After polishing off his brandy, he walked up the stairs to his bedroom. There, with the sound of violins lilting through the recessed speakers, he stripped out of his tailored suit. Beneath, he wore silk.

It was a small affectation. He liked soft, expensive things. He liked, admittedly and without shame, women. His wife had often joked about it, he remembered, had even appreciated his admiration for the opposite sex. Until, of course, she'd found him intimately admiring young Annie Gilby.

He winced at the memory of his wife arriving home a full day early from a business trip. The look on her face when she'd walked into the bedroom and discovered him making loud, boisterous love to Annie. It had been a horrible mistake. A tragic one. His argument, perfectly justified, that his wife's preoccupation with her career and her lack of occupation in their bedroom had made him easy game, had fallen on deaf ears.

It hadn't mattered to her that the girl had utterly and deliberately

113

seduced him, had played on his weaknesses, his frustrations. There had been other women, yes. But they had been momentary diversions, discreet sexual releases when his wife was away or involved with her own decorating business. And not worth mentioning.

He would never have hurt Patricia, Marshall assured himself now as he chose dark slacks and a shirt. He had loved her completely, and he missed her miserably.

He was a man who needed to be married, who needed a woman to talk to, to share his life and home with. A bright, intelligent woman, like Patricia. True, he needed the stimulation of beauty. That wasn't a flaw. Patricia had been beautiful, and ambitious; she had a sense of style and taste that was faultless.

In short, she'd been perfect for him. Except for her inability to understand a few very human flaws.

When she had discovered them, she'd been unforgiving as stone. And he had lost her.

Though he still missed her, he understood life continued.

Now he had found someone else. Deanna was beautiful, ambitious, intelligent. She was as perfect a companion as he could want. And he wanted her—had wanted her since he had first seen her face on the television screen. Now she was more than an image, she was reality. He was going to be very careful with her.

Sexually, she was a bit repressed, but he could be patient. The idea of taking her away from Chicago, away from the pressures and distractions, had been brilliant. Once she was relaxed, secure, she would belong to him. Until that time he would harness his needs, his frustrations.

But he hoped it wouldn't be much longer.

Chapter Eight

"MAUI," FRAN SAID OVER A MOUTHFUL OF CHEESEBURGER. "For the weekend. That's so un-Deanna."

"Is it?" Deanna paused over her own meal and considered. "Maybe it is, and I'm going to enjoy every minute of it. We're getting a suite in a hotel right on the beach where the brochure says you can see whales. Binoculars," she said suddenly, and dug in her purse for a pad. "I need a good pair."

Fran craned her neck and read the neat list Deanna had started. "Now, that's our Deanna. Are you going to eat all those fries?"

"No, help yourself." Already engrossed in her list, Deanna pushed her plate toward Fran.

"A weekend in Hawaii sounds pretty serious." Fran doused the fries with ketchup. "Is it?"

"It could be." She glanced up again, and the bloom in her cheeks spoke volumes. "I really think it could be. I feel comfortable with Marshall."

Fran grimaced. "Sweet pea, you feel *comfortable* with an old pair of bunny slippers."

"Not that kind of comfortable. I can relax around him. I know he's not going to pressure me, so that I can ... just let things happen. When it feels right. I can talk to him about anything."

The words came quickly. Too quickly, Fran mused. If she knew Deanna, and she did, she'd have bet a month's pay her best friend was going out of her way to convince herself.

"He has this incredible sense of fairness," Deanna continued. "We're interested in so many of the same things. And he's romantic. I didn't realize how wonderful it would be to have someone send me flowers and arrange candlelight dinners."

"That's because you were always looking for the trapdoor."

"Yeah." Deanna let out a little breath, closed her notebook. "I'm going to tell him about Jamie Thomas."

In an automatic gesture of support, Fran reached out and covered Deanna's hand with hers. "Good. That means you trust him."

"I do." Her eyes darkened with determination. "And I want a normal, healthy relationship with a man. By God, I'm going to have one. I won't be able to do that until I tell him what happened to me. He's coming over for dinner tomorrow."

Fran abandoned the fries to fold her arms on the table between them. "If you need any moral support, you only have to call."

"I'll be fine. I've got to get back," she said after a glance at her watch. "I've got to do a news break at eight-thirty."

"You've got the ten o'clock tonight, too, don't you?" Fran stuffed a last fry in her mouth. "Richard and I'll watch you, while we're all snuggled up in bed. I'll make sure he's naked."

"Thanks." Deanna counted out bills for the tab. "That'll give me a nice visual while I'm reading the news."

IT WAS NEARLY MIDNIGHT WHEN Deanna climbed into bed. As always, she checked her alarm, then made certain there was a pencil and pad on the nightstand beside the phone. The phone rang just as she was reaching for the light. Instinctively, she picked up the receiver with one hand, the pencil with the other.

"Reynolds."

"You were wonderful tonight."

The flutter of pleasure made her smile as she eased back against the pillows. "Marshall. Thanks."

"I just wanted you to know I was watching. It's the next best thing to being with you."

"It's nice to know." It felt glorious, snuggling back in bed, pleasantly sleepy, with the voice of the man she thought she might love in her ear. "I've been thinking about Hawaii all day."

"So have I. And about you." He had her taped image freeze-framed on his set, quietly arousing himself with her image and her voice. "I'm very indebted to Angela Perkins for bringing us together."

"Me too. Sleep well, Marshall."

"I will. Good night, Deanna."

Warm and content, Deanna replaced the receiver. Hugging herself, she laughed and indulged in a dreamy fantasy. She and Marshall walking along the beach while the sun dripped color into the water. Soft breezes. Soft words. The gentle tug low in her stomach pleased her. Normal, she told herself. Certainly that proved she was a normal woman with normal needs. She was ready to take the next step toward fulfilling them. She was eager to.

Only seconds after she switched off the lamp and snuggled down, the phone rang again. Chuckling to herself, she lifted the receiver in the dark.

"Hi," she murmured. "Did you forget something?"

There was only echoing silence in response.

"Marshall?" Her sleepy voice shifted into puzzlement. "Hello? Who's there?" Then into unease as the dull silence continued. "Hello? Is anyone there?" The quiet click brought on a quick shudder.

Wrong number, Deanna assured herself as she hung up. But she was cold. And it was a long time before she warmed again and slept.

*

117

Someone else lay awake in the dark. The ghostly light from the television screen was the only relief. Deanna smiled there, looking out into the room, looking directly into the eyes of her audience of one. Her voice, so smooth, so sweet, so seductive, played over and over on the recorder as it was rewound.

"I'm Deanna Reynolds. Good night. I'm Deanna Reynolds. Good night. I'm Deanna Reynolds. Good night."

"Good night." The answering whisper was soft, no more than a purr of pleasure.

ANGELA HAD PLANNED EVERY detail meticulously. Standing in the center of her office, she turned a slow circle. Everything was ready. There was a faint fragrance of jasmine in the air from the vase of flowers on the table by the love seat. The television set, for once, was blank. The quiet strains of Chopin eased through the speakers of the stereo. Beeker had been very thorough in his report. Marshall Pike preferred classical music, romantic settings and a woman with style. She wore the same trim designer suit she'd worn for that morning's taping, but she'd removed the blouse. The jacket fit with a snug "V," and there was a cunning hint of black lace teasing the cleavage.

At precisely eleven o'clock, she answered the buzzer on her desk. "Yes, Cassie."

"Dr. Pike is here, Miss Perkins."

"Ah, good." A feline smile crossed her face as she walked toward the office door. She liked a man to be prompt. "Marshall." She held out both hands to grip his, easing forward and tilting her head to offer her cheek. And to give him an interesting glimpse of black lace. "I really appreciate your making time for me today."

"You said it was important."

"Oh, and it is. Cassie, would you mind taking those letters right to the post office? Then you can go ahead and take your lunch. I won't need you back here until one." Turning, Angela led Marshall into her office, being certain to leave the door open a few inches.

"What can I get you, Marshall? Something cold?" She trailed a fingertip down her jacket. "Something hot?"

"I'm fine."

"Well then, let's sit down." She took his hand again, steered him toward the love seat. "It's awfully good to see you again."

"It's good to see you, too." Puzzled, he watched her settle back, her skirt riding up on her thigh as she crossed her legs.

"You know how pleased I am with the help you've given me on the show, but I asked you here today to discuss something more personal."

"Oh?"

"You've been seeing a lot of Deanna."

He relaxed and struggled to keep his eyes from roaming down from her face. "Yes, I have. In fact, I've been meaning to call you and thank you for indirectly bringing us together."

"I'm very fond of her. As I'm sure you are," she added, laying a hand lightly on his thigh. "All that energy, that youthful enthusiasm. A beautiful girl."

"Yes, she is."

"And so sweet. Wholesome, really." Angela's fingers stroked lightly along his leg. "Not your usual type."

"I don't know what you mean."

"You're a man who's attracted to experience, to a certain sophistication. Except in one illuminating case."

He stiffened, drew back. "I don't know what you're talking about."

"Yes, you do." Her voice remained pleasant, easy. But her eyes had sharpened like two blue blades. "You see, I know all about you, Marshall. I know about your foolish slip with one Annie Gilby, age sixteen. And all about your previous, I should say pre-Deanna, arrangement with a certain woman who lives on Lake Shore. In fact, I made it my business to know everything there is to know about you."

"You've had me followed?" He struggled for outrage, but panic had already outdistanced everything else. She could ruin him, with one careless announcement on her show. "What right do you have to pry into my personal life?"

"None at all. That's what makes it so exciting. And it *is* exciting." She toyed with the top button of her jacket. When his eyes flicked down to the movement, she glanced at the antique clock behind him. Eleven-ten, she thought, coolheaded, cold-blooded. Perfect.

"If you think you can use some sort of blackmail to ruin my relationship with Deanna, it isn't going to happen." His palms were wet, from fear, and from a terrible arousal. He would resist it. He had to resist it. "She's not a child. She'll understand."

"She may, or she may not. But I do." With her eyes on his, Angela flicked open the first button on her jacket. "I understand. I sent my secretary away, Marshall." Her voice lowered, thickened. "So I could be alone with you. Why do you think I went to all the trouble to find out about you?" She released the second button, toyed with the third and last.

He wasn't sure he could speak. When he forced the words out, they were like grains of sand in his throat. "What kind of game is this, Angela?"

"Any kind you want." She shot forward, quick as a snake, and caught his bottom lip between her teeth. "I want you," she whispered. "I've wanted you for a long time." Straddling him, she pressed his face against the breasts that strained against the hint of black lace. "You want me, don't you?" She felt his mouth open, grope blindly for flesh. There was a flash, razor-edged and hot, that was power. She'd won. "Don't you?" she demanded, gripping his head in both hands.

"Yes." He was already dragging her skirt up to her waist.

Deanna waited impatiently for the elevator to climb to sixteen. She really didn't have time to keep the appointment with

Angela. But she was obligated by that invincible combination of manners and affection. She glanced at her watch again as people shuffled on and off on seven.

Angela was going to be upset, she mused. And there was no preventing it. Deanna hoped the dozen roses she'd brought along would soften the refusal.

She owed Angela much more than a few flowers, she thought. So many people didn't see what a generous and giving person Angela Perkins was, or how vulnerable. All they saw was the power, the ambition, the need for perfection. If Angela had been a man, those traits would have been celebrated. But because she was a woman, they were considered flaws.

As she stepped off the elevator on sixteen, Deanna promised herself that she would follow Angela's example, and the hell with the critics.

"Hi, Simon."

"Dee." He moved past her, double time, then stopped short and rushed back. "It's not her birthday. Tell me it's not her birthday."

"What? Oh." Seeing the horror on his face as he stared at the armload of flowers, she laughed. "No. These are a thank-you gift."

He let out a sigh, pressing his fingers to his eyes. "Thank God. She'd have killed me if I'd forgotten. She was already chewing off heads this morning because her flight was delayed getting in last night."

Deanna's friendly smile faded. "I'm sure she was just tired."

Simon rolled his eyes. "Right, right. And who wouldn't be? I get jet-lagged on the el." To show his complete sympathy with his boss's mood swings, he sniffed deeply at the flowers. "Well, those should brighten her mood."

"I hope so." Deanna continued down the corridor, wondering if Angela was taking Simon to New York. If she wasn't taking Lew . . . just how much of her staff would be laid off? Simon, the perennial bachelor and fussbudget, might be a bit twitchy, but he was loyal.

The twinge of guilt at knowing, when he didn't, that his career was on the line made her wince.

She found the outer office deserted. Puzzled, she looked at her watch again. Cassie must have had an early errand. With a shrug, she approached Angela's door.

She heard the music first, quiet, lovely. The fact that the door was open several inches was rare. Deanna knew that Angela was obsessive about keeping it firmly shut whether she was in or out. Shrugging, she crossed over, knocked lightly.

She heard other sounds now, not as quiet, not as lovely as the music. She knocked again, easing the door open wider.

"Angela?"

The name stuck in her throat as she saw the two forms wrestling on the love seat. She would have stepped back immediately, with embarrassment flaming in her cheeks, but she recognized the man, and the heat drained away into cold shock.

Marshall's hands were on Angela's breasts, his face buried in the valley between them. Even as she watched, those hands, ones she'd admired for their elegance, slid down to tug at the stylish linen skirt.

And as he did, Angela turned her head, slowly, even while her body arched forward. Her eyes met Deanna's.

Even in her haze of shock, Deanna saw the quick smile, the cagey delight before the distress clicked in. "Oh my God." Angela shoved against Marshall's shoulder. "Deanna." Her voice held the horror she couldn't quite bring to her eyes.

He turned his head. His eyes, dark and glassy, fixed on Deanna's. All movement froze, hideously, as if a switch had freeze-framed them. Deanna broke the tableau with a strangled cry. She turned and ran, trampling the roses she'd dropped at her feet.

Her breath was heaving by the time she reached the elevator. There was pain, a terrible pain radiating out from her chest. She stabbed the Down button again and again. Driven, she whirled away and ran for the stairs. She couldn't stand still, couldn't think.

She stumbled down, saving herself from a fall by instinct rather than design. Knowing only that she had to get away, she plunged down, floor after floor, her sobbing breaths echoing behind her.

At street level, she rammed blindly against the door. She battered against it, weeping, until she found the control to depress the handle. Shoving through, she ran straight into Finn.

"Hey." Amusement came and went in a heartbeat. The moment he saw her face, his laughter fled. She was pale as a sheet, her eyes wild and wet. "Are you hurt?" He gripped her by the shoulders, drawing her out into the sunlight. "What happened?"

"Let me go." She twisted, shoving against him. "Goddamn it, leave me alone."

"I don't think so." Instinctively, he wrapped his arms around her. "Okay, baby. I'll just hold on, and you can cut loose."

He rocked, stroking her hair while she wept against his shoulder. She didn't hold back, but let all the shock and hurt pour out with the tears. The surging pressure in her chest eased with them, like a swelling soothed with cool water. When he sensed her calming, Finn shifted his hold. With his arm around her shoulders, he led her across the lot to a low stone wall.

"Let's sit." He dragged a handkerchief out of his pocket and pressed it into her hands. Though he hated a woman's tears, escaping Deanna's would brand him as the worst sort of coward. "You can pull yourself together and tell Uncle Finn all about it."

"Go to hell," she muttered, and blew her nose.

"That's a good start." Gently, he brushed the hair away from her damp cheeks. "What happened, Deanna?"

She looked away from him. There was too much concern, too much willingness to understand in his eyes. "I just found out I'm an idiot. That I have no sense of judgment, and that no one can be trusted."

"Sounds like a résumé for a television news anchor." When she didn't smile, he took her hand. "I haven't got any whiskey on me, and I gave up smoking last year. The best I can offer you is a shoulder."

"I seem to have used that already."

"I have another one."

Instead of leaning on it, she sat up straighter, squeezed her eyes tight a moment. Maybe she was an idiot, but she still had pride. "I just walked in on a woman I considered a friend, and a man I was considering as a lover."

"That's a big one." And he didn't have any clever words to smooth it over. "The psychologist?"

"Marshall, yes." Her lips trembled. With an effort, she firmed them. The tears she'd shed didn't shame her, but they were over. She meant to keep it that way. "And Angela. In her office."

Muttering an oath, he glanced up to the windows on the sixteenth floor. "I don't suppose you could have mistaken the situation."

Her laugh was as dry as dust. "I'm a trained observer. When I see two people, one half naked, pawing each other, I know what they're up to. I don't need corroboration to make the report."

"I guess not." He was silent a moment. The breeze whispered through the plot of grass behind them and waved through the bank of tulips that spelled out CBC in sunny yellow. "I could round up a crew," Finn considered, "go up to sixteen with a camera, lights and a mike, and make his life a living hell."

This time her laugh was less strained. "Interview him at the scene of the crime? It's a nice offer."

"No, really, I'd enjoy it." The more he thought about it, the more he believed it was the perfect solution. "Dr. Pike, as a respected family counselor, how do you explain being caught with your pants down in a place of business before noon? Was this a professional call? A new form of therapy you'd like to share with the public?"

"They weren't down—yet," she said with a sigh. "I interrupted them. And while your offer's tempting, I'd just as soon handle the situation myself." She pushed the used handkerchief back in his hand. "Goddamn it, they made a fool out of me." Springing off the wall, Deanna wrapped her arms tightly around her body.

"She planned it. I don't know why, I don't even know how, but she planned it. I saw it in her eyes."

This news didn't surprise him. Nothing about Angela did. "Have you pissed her off lately?"

"No." She lifted her hand to push back her hair and then stopped. New York, she thought, and nearly laughed again. "Maybe I did," she said softly. "And this is some twisted form of payback for what she sees as ingratitude." Furious now, Deanna turned back toward him. "She knew how I felt about him, and she used it. And what timing. Less than an hour before I have to go on." She looked at her watch, then covered her face with her hands. "Oh God. I've only got twenty minutes."

"Take it easy. I'll go down and tell Benny you're sick. They'll get a sub."

For one indulgent moment, she considered his offer. Then she remembered Angela's crafty, satisfied smile. "No. She'd enjoy that too much. I can do my job."

Finn studied her. Her face was tracked with tears and her eyes were puffy and red-rimmed, but she was determined.

"They grow them tough in Kansas," he said with approval.

Her chin rose another notch. "Damn right they do."

"Let's get you into makeup."

She said nothing until they'd crossed the lot, walked through the door. "Thanks."

"You're welcome. Got any Visine?"

She grimaced as they started up the steps. "That bad?"

"Oh, it's worse."

He kept their conversation light as he steered her into makeup. He brought her ice for her eyes, water for her throat, then stayed to chat while she concealed the worst of the damage with cosmetics. But he was thinking, and his thoughts were anything but light. Anything but kind.

"That's not half bad," he commented. "Try a little more blusher."

He was right. Deanna stroked the brush over her cheek. And saw Marshall's reflection in the mirror. Her hand trembled once before she set the brush aside.

"Deanna, I've been looking for you."

"Oh?" She felt Finn coil beside her, like a big, mean cat about to spring, and laid a hand on his arm. With a jolt she realized the slightest signal from her would have him tearing in. It wasn't as unattractive an image as she wanted to think. "I've been right here," she said coolly. "I have a show to do."

"I know. I . . ." His eyes clung to hers, soft and brown and pleading. "I'll wait."

"There's no need for that." Odd, she thought. She felt powerful. Invincible. There seemed to be no relation between the woman she was at this moment and the one who had run sobbing from Angela's office. "I have a couple minutes to spare." Calmly, she leaned back against the counter and smiled at Finn. There was blood in her eye that had nothing to do with tears. "Would you mind leaving us alone?"

"Sure." He reached over and tipped her chin up another inch with his fingertip. "That's a good look for you, Kansas." With a last, ice-edged stare at Marshall, he strolled out.

"Was it necessary to bring him into our private business?"

Deanna cut him off with a look. "Can you really have the gall to criticize me at a time like this?"

"No." Marshall's shoulders drooped. "No, of course not. You're right. It's just that I find this difficult, and embarrassing enough without the gossip spreading through the newsroom."

"Finn has more interesting things to discuss than your sex life, Marshall. I promise you. Now if you have something to say, you'd better say it. I only have a few minutes."

"Deanna." He stepped forward and would have reached for her, but the flash in her eyes warned him. "I have no excuse for what happened—or nearly happened. But I want you to know there's nothing between me and Angela. It was an impulse," he continued, speaking quickly when Deanna remained silent. "Purely physical and meaningless. It had nothing to do with what I feel for you."

"I'm sure it didn't," she said after a moment. "And I believe you. I believe it was impulsive, meaningless sex."

Relief flooded through him. He hadn't lost her. His eyes brightened as he reached out to her. "I knew you'd understand. I knew the minute I saw you that you were a woman generous enough to accept me, to understand me. That's why I knew we were meant to be together."

Rigid as stone, she stared up at him. "Take your hands off me," she said quietly. "Right now."

"Deanna." When he only tightened his hold, she fought back a bubble of panic, a quick, ugly sensory memory, and shoved.

"I said now." Free, she stepped back and took a deep, steadying breath. "I said I believed you, Marshall, and I do. What you did with Angela had nothing to do with your feelings for me. However, it had everything to do with mine for you. I trusted you, and you betrayed that trust. That makes it impossible for us to part friends. So, we'll just part."

"You're hurt now." A muscle twitched in his cheek. "So you're not being reasonable." It was like Patricia, he thought. So much like Patricia.

"Yes, I'm hurt," she agreed. "But I'm being very reasonable." A ghost of a smile flitted around her mouth, as insulting as a slap. "I make a habit out of being reasonable. I'm not calling you any of the names that occur to me."

"You see this as my fault. As a weakness." Confident in his skills as a mediator, he shifted gears. "What you haven't yet been able to see is your part in it. Your responsibility. I'm sure you'll agree that no successful relationship is the result of one person's efforts. All the weeks we've been together I've been patient, waiting for you to allow our relationship to move to the natural and very human phase of physical pleasure."

She didn't think he could shock her again. But she'd been

wrong. "You're saying because I wouldn't go to bed with you, I forced you to turn to Angela?"

"You're not seeing the grays, Deanna," he said patiently. "I respected your wishes, your need to progress slowly. At the same time, it's necessary for me to satisfy my own needs. Angela was certainly a mistake—"

She nodded slowly. "I see. I'm glad we straightened this out, Marshall, before it went any further. Now I'm going to very reasonably tell you to go to hell."

She started out, her eyes going to smoke when he blocked the doorway. "We haven't finished, Deanna."

"I've finished, and that's all that counts. We both made a mistake, Marshall, a big one. Now get out of my way, and stay out of it before I make another one and embarrass us both by tearing the skin off your face."

Stiffly, he stepped aside. "I'll be ready to discuss this when you've calmed down."

"Oh, I'm calm," she muttered as she headed for the studio. "I'm dead calm, you bastard."

She shoved through the studio doors, strode across the floor and took her place behind the anchor desk.

Finn watched her through the first break. Once he was satisfied she was under control, he slipped out and walked to the elevator.

OVER A CELEBRATORY GLASS of champagne, Angela watched the noon report in her office. She didn't give a damn about the words or images, but she was interested, even fascinated, by Deanna. The girl looked as cool and sweet as an ice-cream soda, Angela thought. Except for the eyes. Angela would have been bitterly disappointed if she hadn't seen the banked fury in Deanna's gaze.

"Direct hit," she murmured, delighted.

I win, she thought again, but couldn't prevent a twinge of admiration.

Curled in the leather chair behind her desk, she sipped and smiled, and finally raised her glass in silent toast to Deanna.

"She's got style, doesn't she?" Finn said from the doorway.

To her credit, Angela didn't jolt. She continued to sip and study the screen. "Absolutely. She could go a long way in the business with the right teacher."

"Is that the role you've carved out for yourself here?" Finn crossed the room, skirted the desk to stand behind Angela's chair. "Going to teach her your way, Angela?"

"My way works. Dee would be the first to tell you how generous I've been with her."

"She scares you, doesn't she?" Finn lowered his hands to Angela's shoulders, holding her firm so that they both faced Deanna's image.

"Why should she?"

"Because she's got more than style. You've got plenty of that yourself. She's got brains, but you have those, too. And guts, and drive. But then she tops you, Angela. Because she's got class. Bred-in-the-bone class." His fingers dug in when she started to shift. He couldn't know just how deeply he'd hit the mark. "That's something you'll never have. You can wear your pearls and your thousand-dollar suits; it doesn't mean a damn. Because you can't wear class. You can't buy it and you can't fake it." He spun her chair around, leaning over her so they were face to face. "And you'll never have it. So she scares the hell out of you, and you had to find a way to show her who was on top."

"Did she come running to you, Finn?" She was shaken, much more than she cared to admit, but she lifted her glass and sipped delicately, even though the drink now seemed a little more like a crutch. "Was she shocked and devastated and crying out for comfort?"

"You're such a bitch, Angela."

"You always liked that about me." Her eyes laughed over the rim of her glass. Then she shrugged. "The truth is, I'm sorry she was hurt that way. There's no denying that Marshall wasn't right for her, but I know she cared for him. The simple fact was he was attracted to me, and I to him." Because she wanted to believe her excuse, she did. Her voice rang with sincerity. "Things got out of hand, and I blame myself entirely. It was thoughtless."

"The hell it was. You don't take a breath without thinking it through."

She smiled again, looking up under her lashes. "Don't be jealous, Finn."

"You're pathetic. Did you think this stunt was going to break her?"

"If she had loved him, it would have." Pursing her lips, she examined her nails. "So, perhaps I did her a favor."

He laughed. "Maybe you did at that. You sure as hell did me one." He turned back to her and grinned. "I want her, and you just cleared the path."

He didn't have to dodge the glass she hurled. It struck the window a full six inches from his head. The crystal shattered. Delighted, Finn stuck his hands in his pockets.

"Your aim still stinks."

There was no laughter now, nor any of the regret she'd convinced herself she felt. There was only rage. "Do you think she'll want you after she hears what I can tell her?"

"Do you think she'll listen to anything you say after this stunt?" There was reckless humor in his eyes. "You overshot your mark this time. She's not going to come whimpering to you. She's going to tough it out. And she's going to get better. And you're going to start looking over your shoulder."

"Do you think I'm worried about some fluffy little news reader?" she demanded. "All I have to do is make a phone call and she'd be gone. Like that." She snapped her fingers. "Who do you think's been keeping this station out of the basement for the last two years? And where do you think it'll go when I pull up stakes?"

"So you *are* leaving." He nodded, rocked back on his heels. "Well, congratulations and bon voyage."

"That's right. When the new season opens I'll be in New York, and *Angela's* will be produced by my own company. CBC's affiliates will come crawling to pay my price to air my show. Within two years, I'll be the most powerful woman in television."

"You might pull it off," he agreed. "For a while."

"I'll still be on top when you're scrounging around for a two-minute spot on the late news." She was trembling now, her temper pricked and pecked by needles of insecurity. "People want me. They admire me. They respect me."

"I certainly did."

Both Finn and Angela turned to the doorway, where Deanna stood, pale under her camera makeup. She noted, with no surprise, that Angela had salvaged most of the rose blooms and had set them prominently on her desk.

"Deanna." Tears swimming in her eyes, Angela started across the room. "I don't know how I can ever apologize."

"Please don't. I think, since it's only the three of us here, we can be honest. I know you planned the whole episode, that you arranged to have me walk in just when I did."

"How could you say such a thing?"

"I saw your face." Her voice hitched, but she steadied herself. She would not lose control. "I saw your face," she repeated. "I'm not sure whether it was because you wanted to prove that I was wrong about Marshall, or if it was because I couldn't accept your offer. Maybe it was a combination of both."

Hurt, every bit as genuine as the pearls at her throat, shuddered through Angela's voice. "You should know me better."

"Yes, I should have known you better. But I wanted to believe in you. I wanted to be flattered that you befriended me, that you saw something in me. So I didn't look past the surface."

"So." Blinking at tears, Angela turned away. "You're going to toss our friendship aside because of a man."

"No, I'm tossing it aside because of me. I wanted you to know that."

"I gave you my time, my help, my affection." Whirling, Angela pounced. "No one turns me down."

"Then I guess I'm the first. Good luck in New York." Good copy, Deanna told herself as she walked out. Damn good copy.

"Don't forget to look over your shoulder," Finn said as he closed the door quietly behind him.

Chapter Nine

ANGELA TRADES WINDY CITY FOR BIG APPLE
TALK SHOW QUEEN TO REIGN IN NEW YORK
MULTIMILLION-DOLLAR DEAL FOR
CHICAGO'S FAVORITE BLONDE

THE HEADLINES GLOATED OVER THE NEWS. EVEN STAUNCH vehicles like the *Chicago Tribune, The New York Times, The Washington Post* carried the banner. For one sunny day in June, stories of Angela's record-breaking deal overshadowed the troubled economy and unrest in the Middle East.

She was in her element.

With the graciousness of royalty, she granted interviews, welcomed a team from *People* into her home, chatted with Liz Smith over the phone. She had a quote for *Variety* and agreed to a layout in *McCall's*.

Finally, through hard work, blind ambition and sheer guts, she had attained what she'd always craved. Undivided attention.

She was canny enough to have nothing but the highest praise for CBC, for Delacort and for Chicago. She even worked up a few tears on *Entertainment Tonight*.

And her clipping service captured every word, every inch of print that revolved around her.

Then, amidst the uproar, she delivered the coup de grace. She would be taking the last six weeks on her contract as vacation.

"She knows how to turn the screws, doesn't she?" Fran rolled a pair of mismatched socks into a ball and tossed them into a laundry basket.

"That's not the worst of it." Deanna paced the tiny living room of Fran's downtown apartment. "Half her staff got pink-slipped. The others have the choice of pulling up stakes and moving to New York or looking for a new job." She hissed through her teeth. "There aren't any damn jobs."

"Obviously you don't read the papers. The administration says we're not in a recession. It's all in our minds."

Unamused, Deanna picked up a book of baby names and slapped it against her palm as she roamed the room. "I saw Lew McNeil's face when he left the building yesterday. God, Fran, he's been with her almost six years, and she cuts him loose without a thought."

Fran chose another pair of socks, one navy, one black. Close enough, she decided, and bundled them together. The heat made her purple tank top stick to her skin. "I'm sorry, Dee, for all of them. Everybody in television knows the game usually stinks. But I'm more concerned about you. Is Marshall still calling?"

"He stopped leaving messages on my machine." She shrugged. "I think he finally figured out I wasn't going to call back. He still sends flowers." With a bitter laugh, she tossed the baby book back onto the coffee table. "Can you believe it? He really thinks if he blankets me in enough posies, I'll forget everything."

"Want to have a men-are-scum session? Richard's playing golf, so he can't be offended."

"No, thanks." For the first time, she focused on her friend. "Fran, you just rolled up a gray sock with a blue one."

"I know. It adds a little excitement to the mornings. I gotta tell you, Dee, Richard's getting staid. You know, Saturday golf dates, three-piece suits. The house in the 'burbs we're buying. Jesus, we used to be rebels. Now we're . . ." She shuddered, lowered her voice. "Mainstream."

Laughing, Deanna sat cross-legged on the floor. "I'll believe that when you buy a Volvo and an espresso machine."

"I almost bought one of those 'Baby On Board' signs the other day. I came to my senses just in time."

"Then you're okay. I haven't even asked how you're feeling."

"Fabulous, really." Fran jabbed a loose pin back into her messy topknot. "All these women at work who've had kids look at me with scorn and envy. They have all these horror stories about pregnancy—morning sickness, fainting, water retention. And I feel like Rocky." She lifted an arm, flexed her muscle and managed to make a couple of freckles ripple. "Like I could go the distance without breaking a sweat." Lips pursed, she held up a checked argyle and a white sweat sock. "What do you think?"

"Why be subtle?" For the next few minutes they worked silently, folding laundry. "Fran, I've been thinking."

"I wondered when you'd get around to it. I could practically see the idea hopping around in your brain."

"It could be impractical," Deanna mused. "Hell, it could be impossible. After I run it by you, I want you to be completely honest."

"All right." Fran shoved the laundry basket away with one bare foot. "Shoot."

"Delacort, Angela's old syndicate, is going to have a big hole in their line-up and in their revenue. I'm sure they can fill it adequately enough, but . . . Did you know Delacort's CEO was Angela's second husband?"

"Sure. Loren Bach." Aside from the occasional grisly mystery, Fran's favorite reading was gossip rags, and she wasn't ashamed of it. If you wanted to know what celebrity was doing what with whom, and where, she was your girl. "They hooked up right after she ditched her first one—the real estate tycoon. Anyway, Loren Bach put a lot of money and muscle behind our girl. Made her a star."

"And though there were a few rumors, and some items in gossip columns to the contrary, they supposedly parted amicably." That much, Deanna had read. "Knowing Angela the way I do now, I really doubt that."

Fran's eyebrows wiggled. Not only did she love gossip, she loved dirty gossip best. "Word was she cost him a cool two million in the settlement, plus the house and furnishings, so I'd make it four mil. I wouldn't think Bach would have too much residual affection for our heroine."

"Exactly. And Bach has a long-standing relationship with Barlow James, the president of CBC's news division." Deanna rubbed her nervous hands on her knees. "And Mr. James likes my work."

Fran cocked her head, her eyes bright as a bird's. "So?"

"So I've got some money saved, I've got some connections." The idea had her heart jittering so that she pressed the heel of her hand against it as if to slow its pace. She wanted this very much, maybe too much. Enough, she realized, to skip several steps of her carefully calculated career plan. "I want to rent a studio, put together a tape. I want to pitch it to Loren Bach."

"Jesus." Fran leaned back against the cushions of the couch and goggled. "Is this you talking?"

"I know how it sounds, but I've thought it through. Bach moved Angela from a small, local show to a national hit. He could do it again. I'm hoping he wants to do it again, not only for his company, but personally. I can put together a series of clips from 'Deanna's Corner' and my news reports. I think I can get Barlow James to back me. And if I had a pilot, something simple and slick, I might have a shot." She rose again, too excited to sit. "The timing's perfect. The syndicate's still reeling from Angela's defection, and they haven't groomed a successor. If I could convince them to give me a chance locally, a handful of markets in the Midwest, I know I could make it work."

Fran blew out a breath, tapped her fingers on her flat belly. "It's off the wall, all right. And I love it." Letting her head fall back, she laughed at the ceiling. "It's just screwy enough to fly."

"I'll make it fly." Deanna came back to crouch in front of Fran and grip her hands. "Especially if I have an experienced producer."

"You can count on me. But the cost of the studio, the techs, even a trimmed-down production staff. It's a lot to risk."

"I'm willing to risk it."

"Richard and I have some put away."

"No." Touched, grateful, Deanna shook her head. "Absolutely not. Not with my godchild on the way. I'll take your brain, your back and your time, but not your money." After patting Fran's belly, she stood again. "Believe me, the first three are more important."

"Okay. So what's your format, what's your topic, where's your audience?"

"I want something simple, comfortable. Nothing issue-oriented. I want to do what I do best, Fran. Talk to people. Get them to talk to me. We get a couple of deep, cozy chairs. God knows I need new furniture anyway. Keep it chummy, intimate."

"Fun," Fran said. "If you're not going for the tears and angst, go for the fun. Something the audience can get involved in."

Deanna pulled at her earlobe. "I thought I might draw on some of the guests I've had on 'Deanna's Corner.' Sort of a woman-in-the-arts thing."

"It's not bad, but it's tame. And it's lofty. I don't think you want talking heads for a demo, especially arty ones." Fran thought over the possibilities. "We did this makeover thing on *Woman Talk* last year. Went over big."

"You mean a before-and-after sort of thing?"

"Yeah. Makeup, hair. It's fun. It's satisfying. But you know what I'd like?" She curled her legs up, leaned forward. "A fashion show sort of thing. What's new for summer? What's hot? What's now? You get, say, Marshall Field's involved. They get to show off some of the summer styles. Career stuff, evening stuff, casual wear."

Eyes half closed, Deanna tried to visualize it. "Right down to shoes and accessories, with a fashion coordinator. Then we choose women out of the audience."

"Exactly. Real women, no perfect bodies."

Warming to the idea, Deanna reached for her purse and took out a notebook. "We'll have to have chosen them earlier. So the fashion coordinator has time to find the right look, the right outfit."

"Then they get, say, a hundred-dollar gift certificate from the department store."

"How to look like a million for a hundred dollars or less."

"Oh, I like it." Fran rocked back. "I really like it."

"I've got to get home." Deanna scrambled up. "Make some calls. We've got to move fast."

"Sweet pea, I've never known you to move any other way."

IT REQUIRED EIGHTEEN-HOUR DAYS, the bulk of Deanna's savings and a surplus of frustration. Because she was able to wrangle only a week off from her duties at CBC, she did without sleep. Fueled on coffee and ambition, she pushed the project forward. Meetings with the promotion people at Marshall Field's, phone calls to union reps, hours of searching for the right set accessories.

The first *Deanna's Hour* might need to be produced on a shoestring, but she didn't intend for it to look that way. Deanna oversaw every step and stage. A loss or a victory, she was determined that it carry her mark.

She bargained. A set of chairs for on-screen credit. She promised. A few hours' labor for a full-time position if the pilot was picked up. She begged and she borrowed. Fifty folding chairs from a local women's group. Floral arrangements, equipment, bodies.

On the morning of the taping, the small studio she had rented was in chaos. Lighting technicians shouted orders and suggestions as they made last-minute adjustments. The models were crammed into a bread box-size dressing room, jockeying for enough space to dress. Deanna's mike shorted out, and the florist delivered a funeral wreath instead of the baskets of summer blossoms.

"'In loving memory of Milo.'" Deanna read the card and let loose with a quick, hysterical laugh. "Oh, Christ, what else?"

"We'll fix it." Firmly, and perhaps frantically, in control, Fran gave her a brisk shove. "I've already sent Richard's nephew Vinnie out for baskets. We'll just pull the flowers out and toss them in. It'll look great," she said desperately. "Natural."

"You bet. We've got less than an hour." She winced at the sound of a crashing folding chair. "If anyone actually shows up for the audience, we're going to look like idiots."

"They're going to show up." Fran attacked the gladiolas. Her hair stood out in corkscrew spikes, like an electric halo. "And we'll be fine. Between the two of us we contacted every women's organization in Cook County. Every one of the fifty tickets is spoken for. We could have managed twice that if we'd had a bigger studio. Don't worry."

"You're worried."

"That's a producer's job. Go change, do your hair. Pretend you're a star."

"Oh, Miss Reynolds? Deanna?" The fashion consultant, a petite, perky woman with a permanent smile, waved from offstage.

"I want to kill her," Deanna said under her breath. "I want it bad."

"Stand in line," Fran suggested. "If she's changed her mind about the running order again, I get first shot."

"Oh, Deanna?"

"Yes, Karyn." Deanna fixed a smile on her face and turned. "What can I do for you?"

"I just have a teeny little problem? The walking shorts in pump-kin?"

"Yes?" Deanna gritted her teeth. Why did the woman have to make a question out of every statement?

"They just don't suit Monica. I don't know what I was thinking of. Do you think we could have someone dash over to the store and pick up the same outfit in eggplant?"

Before Deanna could open her mouth, Fran eased forward. "I'll tell you what, Karyn. Why don't you call the store, have someone dash over here with the outfit."

"Oh." Karyn blinked. "I suppose I could, couldn't I? Goodness, I'd better hurry. It's almost show time."

"Whose idea was it to do a fashion show?"

Fran went back to dismantling the funeral wreath. "It must have been yours. I would never have thought up something this com-plicated. Go put yourself together. You won't make much of a fashion statement in sweats and with curlers in your hair."

"Right. If I'm going to bomb, I might as well look my best doing it."

Deanna's dressing room was the size of a closet, but it boasted a sink, a john and a mirror. She grinned when she saw the big gold star Fran had taped to the door.

Maybe it was just a symbol, she mused as she ran a fingertip over the foil, but it was her symbol. Now she was going to have to earn it.

Even if everything fell apart, she'd have three weeks' worth of incredible memories. The rush and thrill of putting the show together, the fascination and strain of handling all the details. And the knowledge, the absolute certainty that this was exactly what she wanted to do with her life. Added to that, astoundingly, was the fact that so many people believed she could.

There had been tips from the floor director at CBC, advice from Benny and several others on the production end. Joe had agreed to head up the camera crew and had persuaded a few of his pals to help with the sound and lighting end. Jeff Hyatt had arranged for editing and graphics.

Now she would either earn their faith in her—or blow it.

She was fastening on an earring and giving herself a final pep talk when the knock sounded on the door.

"Don't tell me," she called out. "The eggplant won't do either, and we have to dash back for tomato."

"Sorry." Finn pushed open the door. "I didn't bring any food."

"Oh." She dropped the back of her earring and swore. "I thought you were in Moscow."

"I was." He leaned against the jamb as she retrieved the little gold clasp. "And look what happens when I go away for a couple of weeks. You're the top story in the newsroom gossip pool."

"Great." Her stomach sank as she fought the earring into place. "I must have been out of my mind to start this."

"I imagine you were thinking clearly." She looked fabulous, he realized. Nervous, but revved and ready. "You saw an open door and decided you could walk through first."

"It feels like an open window. On the top floor."

"Just land on your feet. So what's your topic?"

"It's a fashion show, with audience participation."

His grin broke out, dimples winking. "A fashion show? That kind of fluff, with your news background?"

"This isn't news." She elbowed past him. "It's entertainment. I hope. Don't you have a war to cover or something?"

"Not at the moment. I figured I'd stick around awhile. Then I could head back to the newsroom with the scoop. Tell me." He put a hand on her shoulder to slow her down. "Are you doing this for yourself, or to irritate Angela?"

"Both." She pressed a fist to her stomach to try to quiet it. "But for me first."

"Okay." He could feel the energy, and the nerves vibrating against his palm. He wondered what it would be like to tap it, when they were alone. "And what's the next step?"

She sent him a sidelong look, hesitated. "Off the record?"

"Off the record," he agreed.

"A meeting with Barlow James. And if I manage to get his endorsement, I'm going to Bach."

"So, you don't intend to pitch in the minors."

"Not for long." She let out a long breath. "A minute ago I was sure I was going to be sick." She tossed her hair back. "Now I feel great. Really great."

"Dee!" Holding her headset in place, Fran rushed down the narrow corridor. "We've got a full house." She snatched Deanna's hand and squeezed. "Every seat. The three women we picked out from the Cook County Historical Society are psyched. They can't wait to start."

"Then let's not."

"Okay." Fran looked sick. "Okay," she said again. "We can go whenever you're ready."

She left the warm-up to Fran, standing just off set and listening to the laughter and applause. The nerves were gone. In their place was a burst of energy so huge she could barely hold still. Pushed by it, she made her entrance, settled into her chair under the lights, in front of the camera.

The theme music, compliments of Vinnie, Richard's nephew and an aspiring musician, danced out. Off camera, Fran signaled for applause. The red light shone steadily.

"Good morning, I'm Deanna Reynolds."

She knew there was chaos off set—the scrambling wardrobe changes, the barking of orders, the inevitable glitches. But she felt completely in control, chatting amiably with the perky, detestable Karyn, then roaming the audience for comments as the models strutted their stuff.

She could almost forget it was a career move instead of a lark as she giggled with an audience member over a pair of polka-dot micro shorts.

She looked like a woman entertaining friends, Finn mused as he

142

loitered at the back of the studio. It was an interesting angle, because it wasn't an angle at all. As a hard newsman with a natural disdain for fluff, he couldn't say he was particularly interested in the topic. But his tastes aside, the audience was enchanted. They cheered and applauded, let out the occasional "ooh" and "aah", then balanced it with cheerful groans over an outfit that didn't hit the mark.

Most of all, they related to Deanna. And she to them, in the way she slipped an arm around an audience member, made eye contact or stepped back to let her guests take the spotlight.

She'd walked through the door, he decided, and smiled to himself. He slipped out thinking it wouldn't hurt to put in a call to Barlow James, and hold that door open a little wider.

ANGELA SWEPT THROUGH THE lofty living room of her new penthouse apartment. Her heels clicked over parquet floors, muffled on carpet, clicked over tile as she stalked from airy window seat to gleaming breakfront. As she paced, she smoked in quick, ragged jerks, struggling with temper, fighting for control.

"All right, Lew." Calmer, she stopped beside a pedestal table, stabbing out the cigarette in a crystal ashtray and tainting the scent of roses with smoke. "Tell me why you think I'd be interested in some little homemade tape of a second-rate newsreader?"

Lew shifted uncomfortably on the velvet settee. "I thought you'd want to know." He heard the whine in his own voice and lowered his eyes. He detested what he was doing: crawling, belly-rolling for scraps. But he had two kids in college, a high-dollar mortgage and the threat of unemployment urging him on. "She rented a studio, hired techs, called in favors. She got some time off from the newsroom and put together a fifty-minute show, plus an audition tape of some of her old stuff." Lew tried to ignore the ulcer burning in his gut. "I hear it's pretty good."

"Pretty good?" Angela's sneer was as sharp as a scalpel. "Why would I have any interest in 'pretty good'? Why would anyone? Amateurs try to push their way into the market all the time. They don't worry me."

"I know—I mean there's talk around the job how the two of you had words."

"Oh?" She smiled frostily. "Did you fly all the way from Chicago to feed me the latest CBC gossip, Lew? Not that I don't appreciate it, but it seems a little extreme."

"I figured . . ." He took a steadying breath, ran a hand through his thinning hair. "I know you offered Deanna my job, Angela."

"Really? Did she tell you that?"

"No." Whatever pride he had left surfaced. He met her eyes squarely. "But it leaked. Just like it leaked that she turned you down." He saw the familiar flash in her eyes. "And I know," he hurried on, "after working with you for so many years, I know you wouldn't like to see her benefit from your generosity."

"How could she?"

"By turning it into a matter of loyalty to the station. By soliciting Barlow James."

He had her interest now. To conceal it, she turned, flipping open an enamel box and taking out a cigarette. Her eyes flicked over toward the bar, where champagne was always chilling. Frightened by the depth of longing for one small swallow, she moistened her lips and looked away again.

"Why should Barlow get involved?"

"He likes her work. He's made a point of calling the station a few times to say so. And when he came to visit the Chicago bureau last week, he made time for a meeting with her."

Angela snapped on her lighter.

"Word is he took a look at the tape. He liked it."

"So he wants to flatter one of his young female reporters?" Angela tossed her head back, but her throat tightened against the smoke. Just one swallow, she thought. One cool, frothy sip.

"She sent the tape to Loren Bach."

144

Very slowly, Angela lowered the cigarette and left it to smolder in the ashtray. "Why, that little bitch," she said softly. "Does she really think she can begin to compete with me?"

"I don't know if she's aiming that high. Yet." He let that idea simmer. "I do know that some of the Midwest affiliates are concerned about the cost of your new show. They might be willing to plug into something cheaper, and closer to home."

"Then let them. I'll bury whatever they put up against me." Giving a bark of a laugh, she strode over to survey her view of New York. She had everything she'd wanted. Needed. At last, at long last, she was the queen overlooking her subjects from her high, impregnable tower. No one could touch her now. Certainly not Deanna. "I'm on top here, Lew, and I'm damn well going to stay there. Whatever it takes."

"I can use my connections, find out what Loren Bach decides."

"That's fine, Lew," she murmured, staring over the tops of the trees of Central Park. "You do that."

"But I want my job back." His voice quavered with emotion, with self-disgust. "I'm fifty-four years old, Angela. At my age, and the way things are out there right now, I can't afford to be sending out résumés. I want a firm, two-year contract. By that time both my kids'll be out of college. I can sell the house in Chicago. Barbara and I can buy a smaller one out here. We don't need the room now. I just need a couple of years to make sure I have something to fall back on. That's not too much to ask."

"You've certainly thought this through." Angela sat on the window seat, lifting her arms and laying them atop the flowered cushion. Her throat had opened again, all on its own. That pleased her. She didn't need a drink when she had the taste of power.

"I've done good work for you," he reminded her. "I can still do good work. Plus, I have plenty of contacts back in Chicago. People who'll pass on inside information, if there's a need for it."

"I can't see that there will be, but . . ." She smiled to herself, considering. "I don't like to ignore possibilities. And I always reward

145

loyalty." She studied him. A drone, she decided. One who would work tirelessly, and one who was afraid enough to bury ethics under necessity. "I'll tell you what, Lew. I can't offer you executive producer. That slot's already filled." She watched him pale. "Assistant producer. I know that technically it's a demotion, but we don't have to look at it that way."

Her smile was bolstering. As easily as a child, she forgot her earlier disgust with him, and her careless betrayal. Now, once again, they were teammates.

"I've always depended on you, and I'm glad I can continue to do so. It's a negligible cut in salary, and it is New York. That makes up for a lot, doesn't it?" She beamed at him, pleased with her own generosity. "And to show you how much I value you, I'll want you on board for the first special. We'll have legal draw up a contract, make it official. In the meantime . . ." She rose, crossed to him to take his hand between both of hers in the warm, affectionate gesture of old friends. "You go back and tidy up your affairs in Chicago. I'll have my real estate agent look for a cozy little place for you and Barbara. Maybe Brooklyn Heights." She rose on her toes to kiss his cheek. "And you keep your ears open, won't you, dear?"

"Sure, Angela," he said dully. "Whatever you say."

Chapter Ten

LOREN BACH'S OFFICE CAPPED THE LOFTY SILVER TOWER THAT was home for Delacort's Chicago base. Its glass walls offered a view that stretched beyond the Monopoly board of downtown. On a clear day, he could see into misted plains of Michigan. Loren liked to say he could stand guard over hundreds of the stations that carried Delacort's programming, and thousands of homes that watched.

The suite of offices reflected his personality. Its main area was a streamlined, masculine room designed for serious work. The deep green walls and dark walnut trim were pleasant to the eye, an uncluttered backdrop for the sleek, modern furnishings and recessed television screens. He knew that it was sometimes necessary to entertain in an office, as well as do business. As a concession and a convenience, there was a semicircular sofa in burgundy leather, a pair of padded chrome chairs and a wide smoked-glass table. The contents of a fully stocked refrigerator catered to his addiction to Classic Coke.

One of his walls was lined with photographs of himself with celebrities. Stars whose sitcoms and dramas had moved into syndication, politicians running for office, network bigwigs. The one telling omission was Angela Perkins.

Adjoining the office was a washroom in dramatic black and white, complete with a whirlpool and sauna. Beyond that was a smaller room that held a Hollywood bed, a big-screen TV and a closet. Loren had never broken the habit of his lean years, and continued to work long hours, often catching a few hours' sleep and a change of clothing right in the workplace.

But his sanctuary was an area that had been converted from office space. It was cluttered with colorful arcade games where he could save worlds or video-damsels in distress, electronic pinball machines that whirled with light and sound, a talking Coke machine.

Every morning he allowed an hour to indulge himself with the bells and whistles and often challenged network executives to beat his top scores. No one did.

Loren Bach was a video wizard, and the love affair had begun in childhood in the bowling alleys his father had owned. Loren had never had any interest in tenpins, but he'd had an interest in business, and in the flash of the silver ball.

In his twenties, with his degree from MIT still hot, he'd expanded the family business into arcades. Then he'd begun to dabble in the king of video: television.

Thirty years later, his work was his play, and his play was his work.

Though he had allowed a few decorative touches in the office area—a Zorach sculpture, a Gris collage—the core of the room was the desk. So it was more of a console than a traditional desk. Loren had designed it himself. He enjoyed the fantasy of sitting in a cockpit, controlling destinies.

Simple and functional, its base was fitted with dozens of cubbyholes rather than drawers. Its work surface was wide and curved, so that when Loren sat behind it, he was surrounded by phones, computer keyboards, monitors.

An adept hacker, Loren could summon up any desired

information skillfully and swiftly, from advertising rates for any of Delacort's—or its competitors'—programs, to the current exchange rate of dollar to yen.

As a hobby, he designed and programmed computer games for a subsidiary of his syndicate's.

At fifty-two, he had the quiet, aesthetic looks of a monk, with a long, bony face and a thin build. His mind was as sharp as a scalpel.

Seated behind his desk, he tapped a button on his remote. One of the four television screens blinked on. Eyes mild and thoughtful, he sipped from a sixteen-ounce bottle of Coke and watched Deanna Reynolds.

He would have viewed the tape without the call from Barlow James—Loren took at least a cursory study of anything that crossed his desk—but it was doubtful that he would have slotted time for it so quickly without the endorsement.

"Attractive," he said into his mini-recorder, in a voice as soft and cool as morning snow. "Good throat. Excellent camera presence. Energy and enthusiasm. Sexy but nonthreatening. Relates well to audience. Scripted questions don't appear scripted. Who does her writing? Let's find out. Production values need improvement, particularly the lighting."

He watched the full fifty minutes, reversing the tape occasionally, freeze-framing, all the while making his brief comments into the recorder.

He took another long sip from the bottle, and he was smiling. He'd lifted Angela from minor local celebrity into a national phenomenon.

And he could do it again.

With one hand he froze Deanna's face on the screen; with the other, he punched his intercom. "Shelly, contact Deanna Reynolds at CBC, Chicago news division. Set up an appointment. I'd like to have her come in as soon as possible."

*

Deanna was used to worrying about her appearance. Working in front of the camera meant that part of the job dealt with looking good. She would often discard a perfectly lovely suit that appealed to her because the cut or the color wasn't quite right for TV.

But she couldn't remember agonizing over the image she projected more than she did when preparing to meet Loren Bach.

She continued to second-guess herself as she sat in the reception area outside his office.

The navy suit she'd chosen was too severe. Leaving her hair down was too frivolous. She should have worn bolder jewelry. Or worn none at all.

It helped somehow to focus on clothes and hairstyles. Twinkie habits, she knew. But it meant she didn't obsess about what this meeting could mean to her future.

Everything, she thought as her stomach clutched. Or nothing.

"Mr. Bach will see you now."

Deanna only nodded. Her throat tightened up like a vise. She was afraid any word that fought its way free would come out as a squeak.

She stepped through the doors the receptionist opened, and into Loren Bach's office.

He was behind his desk, a sloped-shouldered, skinny man with a face that reminded Deanna of an apostle. She'd seen photographs and television clips, and had thought he'd be bigger somehow. Stupid, she thought. She of all people knew how different a media image could be from reality.

"Ms. Reynolds." He rose, extending a hand over the curved Lucite. "It's nice to meet you."

"Thank you." His grip was firm, friendly and brief. "I appreciate your taking the time."

"Time's my business. Want a Coke?"

"I . . ." He was already up and striding across the room to a full-sized, built-in refrigerator. "Sure, thanks."

"Your tape was interesting." With his back to her, Loren popped the caps on two bottles. "A little rough on some of the production values, but interesting."

Interesting? What did that mean? Smiling stiffly, Deanna accepted the bottle he handed her. "I'm glad you think so. We didn't have a great deal of time to put it together."

"You didn't think it necessary to take the time?"

"No. I didn't think I had the time."

"I see." Loren sat behind his desk again, took a long swig from the bottle. His hands were white and spidery, the long, thin fingers rarely still. "Why not?"

Deanna followed his lead and drank. "Because there are plenty of others who'd like to slip into *Angela's* slot, at least locally. I felt it was important to get out of the gate quickly."

He was more interested in how she'd do coming down the stretch. "Just what is it you'd like to do with *Deanna's Hour?*"

"Entertain and inform." Too glib, she thought immediately. Slow down, Dee, she warned herself. Honesty's fine, but put a little thought into it. "Mr. Bach, I've wanted to work in television since I was a child. Since I'm not an actress, I concentrated on journalism. I'm a good reporter. But in the last couple of years, I've realized that doing the news doesn't really satisfy my ambitions. I like to talk to people. I like to listen to them—and I'm good at both."

"It takes more than conversational skills to carry an hour show."

"It takes a knowledge of how television works, how it communicates. How intimate, and how powerful, it can be. And making the subject forget, while the light's on, that he or she is talking to anyone but me. That's my strong point." She shifted, her body edging forward. "I did some summer-interning at a local station in Topeka while I was in high school, and I interned for four years at a station in New Haven during college. I worked as a news writer in Kansas City before my first on-air job. Technically, I've been working in television for ten years."

"I'm aware of that." He was aware of every detail of her

151

professional life, but he preferred getting his own impressions, face to face. He appreciated the fact that she kept her eyes and her voice level. He remembered his first meeting with Angela. All those sexual spikes, that manic energy, that overpowering femininity. Deanna Reynolds was a different matter altogether.

Not weaker, he mused. Certainly not less potent. Simply ... different.

"Tell me, other than fashion shows, what sort of topics did you plan to do?"

"I'd like to concentrate on personal issues rather than front-page ones. And I'd like to avoid shock television."

"No redheaded lesbians and the men who love them?"

She relaxed enough to smile. "No, I'll leave those to someone else. My idea is to balance shows like the demo with more serious ones, but to keep it very personal, involving the audience—studio and the home audience. Topics like step-families, sexual harassment in the workplace, how men and women cope with middle-age dating. Issues that target in on what the average viewer might be experiencing."

"And you see yourself as a spokesperson for the average viewer?"

She smiled again. Here, at least, she could be confident. "I *am* the average viewer. I'm certainly going to watch a special on PBS that interests me, but I'm more than happy to pull up a bar stool with the gang at *Cheers*. I share my first cup of coffee in the morning with the *Chicago Tribune* and Kirk Brooks on *Wake Up Call*. And unless I have an early call, I go to bed with *The Tonight Show*—unless Arsenio looks better that night." Now she grinned and sipped again. "And I'm not ashamed of it."

Loren laughed, then drained his Coke. She'd very nearly described his own viewing habits. "I'm told you moonlighted for Angela."

"Not moonlighting exactly. It wasn't as structured or formal as that. And I was never on her payroll. It was more of an ... apprenticeship." Deanna screened the emotion from her voice. "I learned quite a bit."

"I imagine you did." After a moment, Loren steepled his hands. "It's no secret that Delacort is unhappy about losing *Angela's*. And anyone involved in the business would know that we don't wish her well." His eyes were dark as onyx against his Byronically pale skin. Yes, an apostle, Deanna thought again, but not one who would have gone cheerfully to the Roman lions. "However," he continued, "given her track record, she should continue to dominate the market. We're not ready to go head to head with her, nationally, with another talk-show format."

"You'll counter-program," Deanna said, making Loren stop, raise a brow. "Go against her with game shows, high-rated reruns, soaps, depending on the demographics."

"That would be the idea. I had considered spot-testing a talk-show format, in a handful of CBC affiliates."

"I only need a handful," she said evenly, but gripped the soft-drink bottle with both hands to hold it steady. Sink or swim, she decided. "To start."

Perhaps it was personal, Loren mused. But what of it? If he could use Deanna Reynolds to take a small slice out of Angela, he could afford the cost. If the project failed, he would write it off as experience. But if he could make it work, if he could make Deanna work, the satisfaction would be worth more, much more than advertising revenue.

"Do you have an agent, Ms. Reynolds?"

"No."

"Get one." His dark, mild eyes sharpened. "I'd like to welcome you to Delacort."

"Tell me again," Fran insisted.

"A six-month contract." No matter how many times she said it aloud, the words still echoed gleefully in Deanna's ears. "We'll tape right here at CBC, one show a day, five days a week."

Still dazed even after two weeks of negotiations, she wandered

153

Angela's office. All that was left were the pastel walls and carpet and the steely view of Chicago. "I'll be able to use this office, and two others in accordance with CBC's end of the deal, during the probationary period. We'll be carried by ten affiliates in the Midwest—live in Chicago, Dayton and Indianapolis. We have six weeks to put it together before we premiere in August."

"You're really doing it."

With a half laugh, Deanna turned back. She wasn't smiling like Fran, but her eyes were glowing. "I'm really doing it." She took a deep breath, grateful that none of Angela's signature scent remained in the air. "My agent said the money they're paying me is a slap in the face." Now she grinned. "I told him to turn the other cheek."

"An agent." Fran shook her head and sent her cowbell earrings dancing. "You've got an agent."

Deanna turned toward the window and grinned out at Chicago. She'd chosen a small, local firm, one that could focus on her needs, her goals.

"I've got an agent," she agreed. "And a syndicate—at least for six months. I hope I've got a producer."

"Sweet pea, you know—"

"Before you say anything, let me finish." Deanna turned back. Behind her, the spears and towers of the city shot up into the dull gray sky. "It's a risk, Fran, a big one. If things don't work out, we could be out on our butts in a few months. You've got a solid job at *Woman Talk*, and a baby on the way. I don't want you to jeopardize that for friendship."

"Okay, I won't." Fran shrugged, and because there was no place to sit, settled on the floor, grateful for the give of elastic over her expanding waist. "I'll do it for ego. Fran Myers, Executive Producer. Has a nice ring." She circled her knees with her arms. "When do we start?"

"Yesterday." Laughing, Deanna sat beside her, slung an arm over her shoulders. "We need staff. I might be able to lure in some of Angela's who got pink-slipped or didn't want to relocate. We need story ideas and people to research them. The budget I have to work with is slim, so we'll have to keep it simple." She stared at the bare, pastel walls. "Next contract, it'll be a hell of a lot bigger."

"The first thing you need is a couple of chairs, a desk and a phone. As producer, I'll see what I can beg, borrow or steal." She scrambled to her feet. "But first, I have to go tender my resignation."

Deanna caught her hand. "You're sure?"

"Damn right. I already discussed the possibility with Richard. We looked at it this way: If things go belly-up in six months, I'd be ready for maternity leave anyway." She patted her stomach and grinned. "I'll call you." She paused at the doorway. "Oh, one more thing. Let's paint these damn walls."

Alone, Deanna pulled her knees up to her chest and lowered her head. It was all happening so fast. All the meetings, the negotiations, the paperwork. She didn't mind the long hours; she thrived on them. And the realization of an ambition brought with it a burst of energy that was all but manic. But beneath the excitement was a small, very cold ball of terror.

It was all going in the right direction. Once she adjusted to the new pace, she'd get her bearings. And if she failed, she would simply go back a few steps and start again.

But she wouldn't regret.

"Ms. Reynolds?"

Thoughts scattering, Deanna looked up and saw Angela's secretary in the doorway. "Cassie." With a rueful smile, she glanced around. "Things look a little different these days."

"Yeah." Cassie's own smile came and went. "I was just getting some things out of the outer office. I thought I should let you know."

"That's all right. It won't be my territory officially until next week." She rose and smoothed down her skirt. "I heard you'd decided not to make the move to New York."

"My family's here. And I guess I'm Midwest through and through."

"It's rough." Deanna studied her, the short, tidy curls, the sad eyes. "Do you have something else?"

"Not yet. I've got some interviews lined up, though. Miss Perkins made the announcement, and a week later she's gone. I haven't gotten used to it."

"I'm sure you're not alone there."

"I'll get out of your way. I just had some plants to take home. Good luck with your new show."

"Thanks. Cassie." Deanna stepped forward, hesitated. "Could I ask you something?"

"Sure."

"You worked for Angela for about four years, right?"

"It would have been four years in September. I started as a secretarial assistant straight out of business college."

"Even down in the newsroom we'd hear occasional grumbling from her staff. Some complaints, some gossip. I don't recall ever hearing anything from your direction. I wondered why that was."

"I worked for her," Cassie said simply. "I don't gossip about people I work for."

Deanna lifted a brow, kept her eyes steady. "You don't work for her anymore."

"No." Cassie's voice cooled. "Ms. Reynolds, I know that the two of you had . . . a disagreement before she left. And I understand that you'd feel some hostility. But I'd rather you didn't draw me into a discussion about Miss Perkins, personally or professionally."

"Loyalty or discretion?"

"I'd like to think it's both," Cassie said stiffly.

"Good. You know I'm going to be doing a similar type of program. You may not repeat gossip, but you certainly can't help but hear it around here, so you'd know that my contract is of short term. I may not get beyond the initial six months or ten affiliates."

Cassie thawed a bit. "I've got some friends downstairs. The newsroom pool's running in your favor about three to one."

"That's nice to know, but I imagine that's a matter of loyalty as

well. I need a secretary, Cassie. I'd like to hire someone who understands that kind of loyalty, one who knows how to be discreet as
well as efficient."

Cassie's expression altered from polite interest to surprise. "Are
you offering me a job?"

"I'm sure I won't be able to pay you what Angela did, unless—
no, damn it, *until*—we can make this thing fly. And you'll
probably have to put in some very long, tedious hours initially, but
the job's yours if you want it. I hope you'll think about it."

"Ms. Reynolds, you don't know if I was in on what she did to
you. If I helped set it up."

"No, I don't," Deanna said calmly. "I don't need to know. And
I think, whether we work together or not, you should call me
Deanna. I don't intend to run a less efficient organization than
Angela did, but I hope to run a more personal one."

"I don't have to think about it. I'll take the job."

"Good." Deanna held out a hand. "We'll start Monday morning. I hope I can get you a desk by then. Your first assignment's
going to be to get me a list of who Angela laid off, and who on it
we can use."

"Simon Grimsley would be on top of it. And Margaret Wilson
from Research. And Denny Sprite, the assistant production manager."

"I've got Simon's number," Deanna muttered, dragging out her
address book to note down the other names.

"I can give you the others."

When Deanna saw Cassie take out a thick book and flip it
open, she laughed. "We're going to be fine, Cassie. We're going to
be just fine."

IT WAS DIFFICULT FOR DEANNA to believe that she was leaving
the newsroom behind. Particularly since she was huddled in
Editing reviewing a tape.

"How long is it now?" she asked.

Jeff Hyatt, in the editor's chair, glanced at the digital clock on the console. "Minute fifty-five."

"Hell, we're still long. We need to slice another ten seconds. Run it back, Jeff."

She leaned forward in her swivel chair, like a runner off the mark, and waited for him to cue it up. The report of a missing teenager reunited with her parents had to fit into its allotted time. Intellectually, Deanna knew it. Emotionally, she didn't want to cut a second.

"Here." Jeff tapped the monitor with one blunt, competent finger. "This bit of them walking around the backyard. You could lose it."

"But it shows the emotion of the reunion. The way her parents have her between them, their arms linked."

"It's not news." He shoved up his glasses and smiled apologetically. "It's nice, though."

"Nice," she muttered under her breath.

"Anyway, you've got that together-again business in the interview portion. When they're all sitting on the couch."

"It's good film," Deanna muttered.

"All you need's a rainbow arching around them."

Deanna turned at Finn's voice and scowled. "I didn't have one handy."

Despite her obvious annoyance, he stepped over, dropped his hands on her shoulders and finished watching the tape. "It has more impact without it, Deanna. You soften the interview and the emotion you're after by having them take a stroll together. Besides, it's news, not a movie-of-the-week."

He was right, but it only made it harder to swallow. "Take it out, Jeff."

While he ran tape, editing and marking time, she sat with her arms folded. It was going to be one of the last pieces she did for CBC News. It was a matter of ego, as well as pride, that made her want it perfect.

"I need to do the voice-over," she said with a telling look at Finn.

"Pretend I'm not here," he suggested.

When Jeff was set, she took a moment to study the script. Holding a stopwatch in one hand, she nodded, then began to read.

"A parent's worst nightmare was resolved early this morning when sixteen-year-old Ruthanne Thompson, missing for eight days, returned home to her family in Dayton . . ."

For the next several minutes, she forgot Finn as she and Jeff worked on perfecting the segment. At last, satisfied, she murmured a thanks to the editor and rose.

"Good piece," Finn commented as he walked out of Editing with her. "Spare, solid and touching."

"Touching?" She stopped to angle a look at him. "I didn't think that counted with you."

"It does if it's news. I heard you're moving upstairs next week."

"You heard right." She turned into the newsroom.

"Congratulations."

"Thanks—but you might want to hold off on that until after the first show."

"I've got a feeling you'll pull it off."

"Funny, so do I. Up here." She tapped her head. "It's my stomach that doubts."

"Maybe you're just hungry." Casually, he twined a lock of her hair around his finger. "How about dinner?"

"Dinner?"

"You're off the schedule at six. I looked. I'm clear until eight A.M., when I have to catch a plane for Kuwait."

"Kuwait? What's up there?"

"Rumblings." He gave her hair a little tug. "Always rumblings. So how about a date, Kansas? Some spaghetti, some red wine. A little conversation?"

"I've sort of given up dating for a while."

"Are you going to let that shrink control your life?"

"It has nothing to do with Marshall," she said coolly. But, of course, it did. And because it did, she executed a quick about-face. "Listen, I like to eat, and I like Italian. Why don't we just call it dinner?"

"I won't argue over semantics. Why don't I pick you up at seven? That'll give you time to go home and change. The place I have in mind is casual."

SHE WAS GLAD SHE'D TAKEN him at his word. She'd been tempted to fuss, at least a little, then had settled on a roomy blouse and slacks that suited the midsummer mugginess. Comfort seemed to be the tone of the evening.

The place he'd chosen was a small, smoky café that smelled of garlic and toasting bread. There were cigarette burns in the check-ered tablecloths and hacks in the wooden booth that would have played hell with panty hose.

A stubby candle stuck out of the mouth of the obligatory Chianti bottle. Finn shoved it to the side as they slid into a booth. "Trust me. It's better than it looks."

"It looks fine." The place looked comforting. A woman didn't have to be on her guard in a restaurant that looked like someone's family kitchen.

He could see her relaxing, degree by degree. Perhaps that was why he'd brought her here, he thought. To a place where there was no hovering maître d', no leather-bound wine list.

"Lambrusco okay with you?" he asked as a T-shirt-clad waitress approached their booth.

"That's fine."

"Bring us a bottle, Janey, and some antipasto."

"Sure thing, Finn."

Amused, Deanna rested her chin on her cupped hand. "Come here often?"

"About once a week when I'm in town. Their lasagna's almost as good as mine."

"You cook?"

"When you get tired of eating in restaurants, you learn to cook." His lips curved just a little as he reached across the table to play with her fingers. "I thought about cooking for you tonight, but I didn't think you'd go for it."

"Oh, why?" She moved her hands out of reach.

"Because cooking for a woman, if you do it right, is a surefire seduction, and it's clear you like to take things one cautious, careful step at a time." He tilted his head when the waitress returned with the bottle, filled their glasses. "Am I right?"

"I suppose you are."

He leaned forward, lifting his glass. "So, here's to the first step."

"I'm not sure what I'm drinking to."

Watching her, his eyes dark and focused, he reached out, rubbed his thumb over her cheekbone. "Yes, you do."

Her heart stuttered. Annoyed at herself, she exhaled slowly. "Finn, I should make it clear that I'm not interested in getting involved, with anyone. I have to put all my energies, all my emotions into making the show work."

"You look like a woman with enough emotion to go around to me." He sipped, studying her over the rim. "Why don't we just see what develops?"

The waitress slid the platter of antipasto on the table. "Ready to order?"

"I'm ready." Finn smiled again. "How about you?"

Flustered, Deanna picked up the plastic-coated menu. Odd, she thought, she couldn't seem to comprehend a thing written there. It might as well have been in Greek. "I'll go for the spaghetti."

"Make it two."

"Gotcha." The waitress winked at Finn. "White Sox are up by two in the third."

"White Sox?" Deanna arched a brow as the waitress toddled off. "You're a White Sox fan?"

"Yeah. You into baseball?"

"I played first base in Little League, batted three thirty-nine my best season."

"No shit." Impressed, and pleased, he tapped a thumb to his chest. "Shortstop. Went all-state in high school. Three-fifty my top season."

With deliberate care, she chose an olive. "And you like the Sox. Too bad."

"Why?"

"Seeing as we're in the same profession, I'll overlook it. But if we go out again, I'm wearing my Cubs hat."

"Cubs." He shut his eyes and groaned. "And I was nearly in love. Deanna, I thought you were a practical woman."

"Their day's coming."

"Yeah, right. In the next millennium. Tell you what. When I get back in town, we'll take in a game."

Her eyes narrowed. "At Comiskey or Wrigley?"

"We'll flip for it."

"You're on." She nibbled on a pepperoncini, enjoying the bite. "I'm still ticked about them putting lights in at Wrigley."

"They should have done it years ago."

"It was tradition."

"It was sentiment," he corrected. "And you put sentiment up against ticket sales, sales win every time."

"Cynic." Her smile froze suddenly. "Maybe I could get baseball wives on the show. Cubs and Sox. You'd have viewer interest right off, people taking sides. God knows all you have to do is mention sports or politics in this town to get people going. And we could talk about being married to someone who's on the road weeks at a time during the season. How they deal with slumps, injuries, Baseball Annies."

"Hey." Finn snapped his fingers in front of her face and made her blink.

"Oh, sorry."

"No problem. It's an education to watch you think." It was also, to his surprise, arousing. It made a man wonder—hope—that she would concentrate as fiercely on sex. "And it's a good idea."

Her smile spread inch by inch until her face glowed with it. "It'd be a hell of a kickoff, wouldn't it?"

"Yeah, but you're mixing your sports metaphors."

"I'm going to love this." With her wine in one hand, she settled back against the booth. "I'm really going to love this. The whole process is so fascinating."

"And news wasn't?"

"It was, but this is more—I don't know. Personal and exciting. It's an adventure. Is that how you feel about flying off to one country after another?"

"Most of the time. Different place, different people, different stories. It's hard to get into a rut."

"I can't imagine you worrying about that."

"It happens. You get cozy, lose the edge."

Cozy? In war zones, disaster areas, international summits? She didn't see how. "Is that why you didn't stay in London?"

"Part of it. When I stop feeling like a foreigner, I know it's time to come home. Have you ever been to London?"

"No. What's it like?"

It was easy to tell her, easy for her to listen. They talked over pasta and red wine, over cappuccino and cannoli until the candle in the bottle beside them began to gutter, and the juke fell silent. It was the lack of noise that made Deanna glance around. The restaurant was almost empty.

"It's late," she said, surprised when she glanced at her watch. "You have a plane to catch in less than eight hours."

"I'll manage." But he slid out of the booth as she did.

"You were right about the food. It was fabulous." But her smile faded when he reached out and cupped the nape of her neck in his hand. He held her there, his eyes on hers as he closed the distance between them.

The kiss was slow, deliberate and devastating. She'd expected more of a one-two punch from a man whose eyes could bore a hole in the brain. Perhaps that was why the soft, lazy romance of the kiss disarmed her so completely.

She lifted a hand to his shoulder, but rather than easing him away, as she had intended, her fingers dug in. Held on. Her heart took a long, seamless somersault before it thudded against her ribs.

When her mouth yielded under his, he deepened the kiss. Slowly still, teasing a response from her until her hand slid from his shoulder to cling at his waist.

Dozens of thoughts struggled to form in her head, then skittered away. For here was heat, and pleasure and the undeniable promise, or threat, of much more.

More was what he wanted. Much more desperately than he had anticipated. However simple he'd intended the kiss to be, he was almost undone by it. He eased her away. The small, baffled sound she made as her eyes blinked open had him gritting his teeth against a quick, vicious ache.

It was important to keep steady—though at the moment she couldn't have said why. Instinct alone had her stepping back an inch.

"What was that for?"

"Other than obvious reasons?" He should be amused by the question. "I figured if we got that done here, you wouldn't project what could, should or might happen when I took you home."

"I see." She realized her purse had dropped to the floor, and bent to retrieve it. "I don't plan every aspect of my life out like a feature story."

"Sure you do." He ran a finger down her cheek. It was hot and flushed and made him long for another taste. "But that's okay with me. Just consider that your lead. We'll pick up the rest of the copy when I get back."

Chapter Eleven

By the end of July, Deanna had what could loosely be called a staff. In addition to Fran and Simon, she had a single researcher and a booker, overseen by Cassie. They were still in dire need of bodies and brains—and a budget to pay for them.

The technical end was solid. At one of the endless meetings Deanna attended, it was agreed that Studio B would be fully staffed and carefully lit. Production values would be top-notch.

All she had to do was give them something to produce.

She'd temporarily moved two desks into Angela's old office. One for herself, one for Fran: they divided the work, and brainstormed ideas.

"We've got the first eight shows booked." Fran paced the office, a clipboard in one hand. "Cassie's handling travel and lodging. She's doing a good job, Dee, but she's ridiculously over-worked."

"I know." Deanna rubbed her gritty eyes and struggled to clear her brain. "We need an assistant producer, and another researcher. And a general dogsbody. If we can get the first dozen shows under our belt, we might be able to swing it."

"Meantime, you're not getting enough sleep."

"Even if I had the time, I couldn't." She reached out for the ringing phone. "My stomach's in a constant state of turmoil, and my mind just won't shut off. Reynolds," she said into the receiver. "No, I haven't forgotten," She glanced at her watch. "I have an hour." She blew out a breath as she listened. "All right, tell them to send the wardrobe up. I'll pick what suits and be down for makeup in thirty minutes. Thanks."

"Photo shoot?" Fran remembered.

"And the promos. I can't accuse Delacort of chintzing on the advertising. But damn, I don't have time. We need a staff meeting, and we still have to go through those responses to the eight-hundred number and the write-in."

"I'll schedule it for four." Fran grinned. "Wait until you read some of the stuff from the write-in. Margaret's idea on why ex-husbands should be shot down like a dog is a hoot."

Deanna's smile was strained. "We did tone that down, didn't we?"

"Yeah. It went out 'Why Your Ex-Husband Is Your Ex.' Tame enough, but the responses weren't. We've got everything from serious abuse cases to guys who cleaned engine parts in the kitchen sink. We'll need an expert. I thought a lawyer instead of a counselor. Divorce lawyers have terrific stories, and Richard has plenty of contacts."

"Okay, but—" She broke off as a clothes rack wheeled through the doorway. "Come on, Fran, help me play closet." A head peeked around the suits and dresses. "Oh, hi, Jeff. They've got you making deliveries?"

"I wanted a chance to come up and see the operation." With a shy smile he glanced around. "We're rooting for you downstairs."

"Thanks. How's everybody in the newsroom? I haven't had a chance to stop down for days."

"Pretty good. The heat brings out the loonies, you know? Lots of hot stories breaking." He rocked the rack, loitering as Deanna began to go through the wardrobe. "Deanna, I was kind of wondering, if you—you know—get an opening up here. For somebody to pick up loose ends, answer the phone. You know."

Deanna stopped with her hand on a crimson blazer. "Are you kidding?"

"I know you've got people who've worked this end of things before. But I always wanted to do this kind of television. I just thought . . . you know."

"When can you start?"

He looked startled. "I . . ."

"I mean it. We're desperate. We need someone who can do a little of everything. I know you can from your work downstairs. And your editing skills would be invaluable. The pay's lousy and the hours are miserable. But if you want a shot as an assistant producer—with on-screen credit and all the coffee you can drink—you're hired."

"I'll give my notice," Jeff said through a grin that all but split his face. "I may have to work another week or two, but I can give you all my extra time."

"God, Fran, we've found a hero." Deanna took him by the shoulders and kissed his cheek. "Welcome to bedlam, Jeff. Tell Cassie to fit you for a straitjacket."

"Okay." Flushing, laughing, he backed out of the room. "Okay. Great."

Fran pulled out a plum-colored suit and held it up in front of Deanna. "General dogsbody?"

"One of the best. Jeff can mow down a mountain of paperwork like a beaver taking out a tree. He carries all this stuff in his head. Ask him what won for best picture in 1956, and he knows. What was the lead story on the ten o'clock on Tuesday of last week? He knows. I like the red."

"For the promos," Fran agreed. "Not the stills. What does he do downstairs?"

"Editorial assistant. He also does some writing." She pulled out a sunny yellow dress with turquoise sleeves and round fuchsia buttons. "He's good. Dependable as a sunrise."

"As long as he works long and cheap."

"That's going to change." Her eyes darkened as she held Fran's next selection up in front of her. "I know how much everyone's putting into this. Not just timewise. I'm going to make it work."

TO GIVE THEIR CHANCES A BOOST, Deanna granted interviews—print, radio, television. She appeared on a segment of *Midday* and was interviewed by Roger. She took two days and visited all the affiliates within driving distance, and put in personal phone calls to the rest.

She personally oversaw every detail of her set design, pored over press clippings for program ideas and spent hours reviewing responses to the ads for topic guests.

It left little time for a social life. And it certainly provided a good excuse to avoid Finn. She'd meant what she'd said when she'd told him she didn't want to get involved. She couldn't afford to, she'd decided. Emotionally or professionally. How could she trust her own judgment when she'd been so willing to believe in Marshall?

But Finn Riley wasn't easily avoided. He dropped into her office, stopped by her apartment. Often he carried take-out pizza or white cartons filled with Chinese food. It was hard to argue with his casual comment that she had to eat sometime. In a weak moment, she agreed to go out to the movies with him. And found herself just as charmed, and just as uneasy, as before.

"Loren Bach on one," Cassie told her.

It was still shy of nine o'clock, but Deanna was already at her desk. "Good morning, Loren."

"Countdown, five days," he said cheerfully. "How are you holding up?"

"By my knuckles. The publicity's generated a lot of local interest. I don't think we'll have any problem filling the studio."

"You're getting some interest on the East Coast as well. There's a nice juicy article in the *National Enquirer* about the 'All About Eve' of talk shows. Guess who's playing Margo Channing?"

"Oh hell. How bad is it?"

"I'll fax you the article. They spelled your name right, Eve—ah, Deanna." He chuckled, tickled with his own humor. "From one who knows our heroine well, I can tell you she leaked this little tidbit. Makes it sound as though she all but picked you up out of the street, played big sister and mentor, then was stabbed in the back for her generosity."

"At least they didn't claim I'd been dropped from a spaceship into her front yard."

"Maybe next time. In the meantime, you got some national press. And whether she knows it or not, linked your name with hers in such a way that'll make people curious. I think we can get some play out of this. A tag in *Entertainment Weekly*, maybe another squib in *Variety*."

"Great. I guess."

"Deanna, you can buck the tabloids when you've built the muscle. For now, just consider it free press."

"Courtesy of Angela."

"Word is she's negotiating a contract to write her autobiography. You might be worth a chapter."

"Now I'm excited." Her chair squeaked as she leaned back, reminding her she'd forgotten to oil the springs. That made her lean forward again and add the chore to her growing list on the corner of her desk. "I hope you don't mind if I just concentrate on pulling off the first show. I'll worry about repaying Angela for her generosity later."

"Deanna, you make the show work, that'll be payment enough. Now, let's talk business."

Twenty minutes later, with a headache just beginning to brew behind her eyes, she hung up. What had ever made her think she was good with details? Deanna wondered. What had ever made her think she wanted the responsibility of helming a talk show?

"Deanna?" Cassie entered with a tray. "I thought you'd like some coffee."

"You read my mind." Deanna set aside papers to make room for the pot. "Do you have time for any? We might want to tank up before the rest of the day's schedule hits."

"I brought two cups." She poured both before she took a chair. "Do you want to go over your agenda for today?"

"I don't think so." The first sip of hot black coffee punched its caffeine-laced fist straight into her bloodstream. "It's engraved on my forehead. Have we set up a lunch for the baseball wives after the show?"

"Simon and Fran will play host. Reservations are confirmed. And Jeff thought it might be nice to have roses in the green room when they arrive. I wanted to run it by you."

"Good old Jeff. Very classy idea. Let's put cards on each bunch with a personal thank-you from the staff." After another sip, she pressed a hand to her jittery stomach. "Christ, Cassie, I'm scared to death." Setting the cup aside, she took a deep, calming breath and leaned forward. "I want to ask you something, and I really want you to be brutally honest, okay? No sparing feelings, no false pep talk."

"All right." Cassie laid her steno pad on her lap. "Shoot."

"You worked for Angela a long time. You probably know as much about the ins and outs of this sort of a show as any producer or director. I imagine you have an opinion of why *Angela's* works. And I want to know, candidly, if you believe we have a shot at this."

"You want to know if we can make *Deanna's Hour* competitive?"

"Not even that," Deanna said, shaking her head. "If we can get through the first half a dozen shows without being laughed out of the business."

"That's easy. After next week, people are going to do a lot of talking about *Deanna's Hour*. And more people are going to tune in to see what the deal is. They're going to like it, because they're going to like you." She chuckled at Deanna's expression. "That's not sucking up. The thing is, the average viewer won't see or appreciate the work that's gone into making it all look good and run smoothly. They won't know about the long hours or the sweat. But you know, so you'll work harder. The harder you work, the harder everyone else will. Because you do something Angela didn't. Something I guess she just couldn't. You make us feel important. That makes all the difference. Maybe it won't put you on top of the ratings heap right away, but it puts you on top with us. That counts."

"It counts a lot," Deanna said after a moment. "Thanks."

"In a couple of months, when the show's cruising and the budget opens up, I'm going to come back in here. That's when I'm going to suck up." She grinned. "And hit you for a raise."

"If the damn budget ever opens up, everyone's getting a raise." Deanna blew at her bangs. "In the meantime, I need to see the tapes on the promos for the affiliates."

"You need a promotion manager."

"And a unit manager, and a publicity director, a permanent director and a few production assistants. Until that happy day, I'm wearing those hats, too. Have the newspapers come in yet?"

"I passed them on to Margaret. She's going to screen them for ideas and make clippings."

"Fine. Try to get me the clippings before lunch. We're going to want something really hot for the second week in September. Bach just told me we'll be going up against a new game show in three cities during fall premiere week."

"Will do—oh, and your three o'clock with Captain Queeg is rescheduled for three-thirty."

"Captain—oh, Ryce." Not bothering to hide the smile, Deanna noted it down on her calendar. "I know he's a little eccentric, Cassie."

"And overbearing."

"And overbearing," Deanna agreed. "But he's a good director. We're lucky to have him for the few opening weeks."

"If you say so." She started out, then hesitated and turned back. "Deanna, I didn't know if I should mention it, then I figured it wouldn't be right to start censoring your calls."

"What?"

"Dr. Pike. He called when you were on with Mr. Bach."

Thoughtfully, Deanna set aside her pen. "If he calls back, put him through. I'll take care of it."

"Okay. Oops." She grinned and stepped back to avoid running into Finn. "'Morning, Mr. Riley."

"Hey, Cassie. I need a minute with the boss."

"She's all yours." Cassie closed the door behind her.

"Finn, I'm sorry, I'm swamped." But she wasn't quite quick enough to avoid the kiss when he skirted the desk. She wasn't sure she wanted to.

"I know, I've only got a minute myself."

"What is it?" She could see the excitement in his eyes, feel it in the air sparking around him. "It's big."

"I'm on my way to the airport. Iraq just invaded Kuwait."

"What?" Her reporter's adrenaline made her spring up. "Oh, Jesus."

"Blitzkrieg style. An armored thrust, helicopter-supported. I have a couple of contacts at Green Ramp in North Carolina, a couple of guys I got to know during the fighting at Tocumen airfield in Panama a few months ago. Odds are we'll go with diplomatic and economic pressure first, but there's a damn good chance we'll deploy troops. If my instincts are worth anything, it's going to be big."

"There are blowups over there all the time." Weakly she sat on the arm of her chair.

"It's land, Kansas. And it's oil, and it's honor." He lifted her to her feet, caught her hair in his hand to draw it away from her face. He wanted—needed, he admitted—a long look at her. A good long look. "I may be gone for a while, especially if we send troops."

172

She was pale, struggling to be calm. "They think he has nuclear capabilities, don't they? And certainly access to chemical weapons."

Dimples flashed recklessly. "Worried about me?"

"I was just wondering if you were taking a gas mask as well as a camera crew." Feeling foolish, she stepped back. "I'll watch for your reports."

"Do that. I'm sorry I'll miss your premiere."

"That's okay." She managed a smile. "I'll send you a tape."

"You know." He toyed with a strand of her hair. "Technically, I'm going off to war. The old 'I'm shipping out, babe, and who knows what tomorrow might bring.'" He smiled into her dark, serious eyes. "I don't suppose I could convince you to lock that door over there and give me a memorable send-off."

She was afraid he could. "I don't fall for tired old lines. Besides, everyone knows Finn Riley always brings back the story alive."

"It was worth a shot." But he slipped his arms around her waist. "At least give me something to take into the desert with me. I hear it gets pretty cold at night."

There was a part of her that feared. And a part that yearned. Listening to both, she wrapped her arms around his neck. "All right, Riley. Remember this."

For the first time, she pressed her lips to his without hesitation. There was more than the quick, familiar thrill when her mouth opened to his, more than the slow, grinding ache she'd tried so hard to deny. There was need, yes, to taste, to absorb and, curiously, to comfort.

When the kiss deepened, she let herself forget everything else, and just feel.

She could smell him—soap and light, clean sweat. His hair was soft and full, and seemed to beckon her fingers to comb through and hold on. When his mouth became less patient, when she heard his quiet groan of pleasure, she responded heedlessly, mating her tongue with his, nipping at his lip to add the dark excitement of pain to the pleasure.

She thought he trembled, but could no longer find the will to soothe.

"Deanna." Desperately, he took his mouth over her face, along her throat, where her pulse beat like wings. "Again."

His lips crushed down on hers again, absorbing the flavor, the warmth. Shaken, he drew back just enough to rest his brow against hers, to hold her another moment where he felt so oddly centered, so curiously right.

"Goddamn," he whispered. "I'm going to miss you."

"This wasn't supposed to happen."

"Too late." He lifted his head, brushed his lips over her forehead. "I'll call when I can." As soon as he'd said it, Finn realized he'd never made that promise before. It was the kind of unstated commitment that had him stepping back, tucking his hands safely in his pockets. "Good luck next week."

"Thanks." She took a step back herself so that they took each other's measure like two boxers after a blood-pumping round in the ring. "I know it's a useless thing to say, but be careful."

"I'll be good." His grin was quick and reckless. "That's more important." He walked to the door, then stopped, his hand on the knob. "Listen, Deanna, if that asshole shrink does happen to call back—"

"You were eavesdropping."

"Of course I was, I'm a reporter. Anyway, if he does call back, brush him off, will you? I don't want to have to kill him."

She smiled, but the smile faded quickly. Something in Finn's eyes told her he was serious. "That's a ridiculous thing to say. It happens that I'm not interested in Marshall, but—"

"Lucky for him." He touched a finger to his brow in salute. "Stay tuned, Kansas. I'll be back."

"Arrogant idiot," Deanna muttered. When her eyes began to sting, she turned to stare out at Chicago. There might be a war on the other side of the world, she thought as the first tear spilled over. And a show to produce right here.

So what in the hell was she doing falling in love?

"Okay, Dee, we're nearly ready for you." Fran scooted back into the dressing room. "The studio audience is all in."

"Great." Deanna continued to stare blindly at the mirror as Marcie put the finishing touches on her hair. "Just great."

"They're wearing Cubs hats and White Sox T-shirts. Some people even brought banners, and they're waving them around. I'm telling you, they're revved."

"Great. Just great."

Smiling to herself, Fran glanced down at her clipboard. "All six of the wives are in the green room. They're really chummy. Simon's in there now, going over the setup with them."

"I went in to introduce myself to them earlier." Her voice was a monotone. She could feel the nausea building like a tidal wave. "Oh God, Fran, I really think I'm going to be sick."

"No, you're not. You don't have time. Marcie, her hair looks fabulous. Maybe you can give me some tips on mine later. Come on, champ." Fran gave Deanna a tug that brought her out of the chair. "You need to go out and give the audience a pep talk, get them on your side."

"I should have worn the navy suit," Deanna said as Fran dragged her along. "The orange and kiwi is too much."

"It's gorgeous—and it's bright and young. Just the right combo. You look hip, but not trendy, friendly but not homespun. Now look." Making a little island of intimacy in the midst of backstage chaos, Fran took Deanna by the shoulders. "This is what we've all been slaving for over the last couple of months—what you've been aiming toward for years. Now go out there and make them love you."

"I keep thinking about all this stuff. What if a fight breaks out?

175

You know how rabid Sox and Cubs fans can be. What if I run out of questions? Or can't control the crowd? What if someone asks why the hell I'm doing a silly show about baseball when we're sending troops to the Middle East?"

"Number one, nobody's going to fight because they're going to be having too much fun. Number two, you never run out of questions, and you can control any crowd. And finally, you're doing this show on baseball because people need to be entertained, especially during times like these. Now pull it together, Reynolds, and go do your job."

"Right." She took a deep breath. "You're sure I look okay?"

"Go."

"I'm going."

"Deanna."

She turned, surprised, then infuriated to see Marshall standing an arm's length behind her. Fran's snarl had her stepping forward. "What are you doing here?"

His smile was easy, though his eyes held regret. "I wanted to wish you luck. In person." He held out a bouquet of candy pink roses. "I'm very proud of you."

She didn't reach for the flowers, but she kept her eyes level with his. "I'll accept the wish for luck. Your pride is your business. Now, I'm afraid only staff is allowed back here."

Very slowly, he lowered the flowers. "I didn't know you had it in you to be cruel."

"It seems we were misled. I have a show to do, Marshall, but I'll take a moment to tell you once again that I have no desire to resume any sort of relationship with you. Simon?" She called out without taking her eyes from Marshall's. "Show Dr. Pike out, will you? He seems to have made a wrong turn."

"I know the way," he said between clenched teeth. He let the roses fall to the floor, reminding her how she had dropped a similar bouquet. The scent of them turned her stomach. "I won't always be turned away so easily."

He stalked off with Simon nervously dogging his heels. Deanna allowed herself one long, calming breath.

"Creep," Fran muttered, lifting a hand automatically to soothe the tension in Deanna's shoulders. "Bastard. To come here like this right before a live show. Are you going to be all right?"

"I'm going to be fine." She shook off the fury. There was too much riding on the next hour for her to indulge herself. "I am fine." She headed out, taking the hand mike from Jeff as she passed.

Jeff smiled broadly as he watched her. "Break a leg, Deanna."

She straightened her shoulders. "Hell, I'm going to break two." She stepped onto the set, smiled at the sea of faces. "Hi, everyone, thanks for coming. I'm Deanna. In about five minutes we're going to get this show rolling. I hope you're going to help me out. It's my first day on the job."

"PUT IN THE DAMN TAPE." IN her towering New York office, Angela stubbed out one cigarette and immediately lit another.

"I went out on a limb to get a copy of this," Lew told her as he slipped the tape into the VCR.

"You told me, you told me." And she was sick of hearing it. Sick, too, with fear of what she might see on the monitor in the next few minutes. "Cue it up, damn it."

He hit the Play button and stepped back. Eyes narrowed, Angela listened to the intro music. Too close to rock, she decided with a smirk. The average viewer wouldn't like it. The pan of the audience—people in baseball caps, applauding and waving banners. Middle-class, she decided, and leaned back comfortably.

It was going to be all right after all, she assured herself.

"Welcome to *Deanna's Hour.*" The camera did a close-up of Deanna's face. The slow, warm smile, the hint of nerves in the eyes. "Our guests today, here in Chicago, are six women who know all there is to know about baseball—and not just about squeeze plays and Texas Leaguers."

She's jittery, Angela thought, pleased. She'd be lucky to make it through to commercial. Anticipating the humiliation, Angela allowed herself to feel sorry for Deanna. After all, she thought with a soft, sympathetic sigh, who knew better than she what it was like to face that merciless glass eye?

She'd taken on too much, too soon, Angela realized. It would be a hard lesson, but a good one. And when she failed, as she certainly would, and came knocking on the door looking for help, Angela decided she would be gracious enough, forgiving enough to give her a second chance.

But Deanna made it to commercial, segueing into the break over applause. After the first fifteen minutes, the pleasant flavor of gloating sympathy had turned bitter in her throat.

She watched the show through to the closing credits, saying nothing.

"Turn it off," she snapped, then rose to go to the wet bar. Rather than her usual mineral water, she reached for a split of champagne, spilling it into a flute. "It's nothing," she said, half to herself. "A mediocre show with minimal demographic appeal."

"The response from the affiliates was solid." With his back to her, Lew ejected the tape.

"A handful of stations in the dust bowl of the Midwest?" She drank quickly, her lips tightening on the gulp. "Do you think that worries me? Do you think she could play that in New York? It's what works here that matters. Do you know what my share was last week?"

"Yes." Lew set the tape aside and played the game. "You've got nothing to worry about, Angela. You're the best, and everyone knows it."

"Damn right I'm the best. And when my first prime-time special hits during the November sweeps, I'll start getting the respect I deserve." Grimacing, she drained the champagne. It no longer tasted celebratory, but it thawed all the little ice pockets of fear. "I've already got the money." She turned around, steadier. She could afford to be generous, couldn't she? "We'll let Deanna have her moment, and why not? She won't last. Leave the tape, Lew." Angela went back to her desk, settled down and smiled. "And ask my secretary to come in. I have a job for her."

Alone, Angela swiveled in her chair to study the view of her new home. New York was going to do more than make her a star, she mused. It was going to make her an empire.

"Yes, Miss Perkins."

"Cassie—damn it, Lorraine." Spinning around, she glared at her new secretary. She hated breaking in new employees, being expected to remember their names, their faces. Everyone always expected too much from her. "Get me Beeker on the phone. If he can't be reached, leave a message with his service. I want a call-back ASAP."

"Yes, ma'am."

"That's all." Angela glanced toward the champagne, then shook her head. Oh no, she wasn't going to fall into that trap. She wasn't her mother. She didn't need liquor to get through the day. Never had. What she needed was action. Once she lit a fire under Beeker and had him digging deeper and harder for dirt on Deanna Reynolds, she'd have all the action she could handle.

PART TWO

"All fame is dangerous."

THOMAS FULLER

Chapter Twelve

"COOKED BENEATH A BLAZING SUN, AN ENEMY OF RAINFALL, of plant life, of human beings, are the shifting sands of the Saudi desert." Finn did his best not to squint into the camera as that merciless sun beat down on him. He wore an olive-drab T-shirt, khakis and a faded bush hat. "Sandstorms, unrelenting heat and mirages are common in this hostile environment. Into this world the forces of the United States have come to draw their line in the sand.

"It has been three months since the first men and women of the armed forces were deployed under Desert Shield. With the efficiency and ingenuity of the Yankee, these soldiers are adjusting to their new environment, or in some cases, adjusting their environment to suit them. A wooden box, a liner of Styrofoam and an air-conditioner blower." Finn rested his hand on a wooden crate. "And a few industrious GIs have created a makeshift refrigerator to help combat the one-hundred-and-twenty-degree heat. And with boredom as canny an enemy as the climate, off-duty soldiers spend their time reading mail from home, trading the precious few newspapers that get through the censors and setting up lizard races. But the mails are slow, and the days are long. While parades and picnics back home celebrate Veterans Day, the men and women of Desert Shield work, and wait.

"For CBC this is Finn Riley, in Saudi Arabia."

When the red light blinked off, Finn unhooked his sunglasses from his belt loop and slipped them on. Behind him was an F-15C Eagle and men and women in desert fatigues. "I could go for some potato salad and a brass band, Curt. How about you?"

His cameraman, whose ebony skin gleamed like polished marble with his coat of sweat and sun block, rolled his eyes to heaven. "My mama's homemade lemonade. A gallon of it."

"Cold beer."

"Peach ice cream—and a long, slow kiss from Whitney Houston."

"Stop, you're killing me." Finn took a deep drink of bottled water. It tasted metallic and overwarm, but it washed the grit out of his throat. "Let's see what they'll let us take pictures of, and we'll try for some interviews."

"They ain't going to give us much," Curt grumbled.

"We'll take what we can."

Hours later, in the relative comfort of a Saudi hotel, Finn stripped to the skin. The shower washed away the layers of sand and sweat and grit of two days and nights in the desert. He felt a sweet, almost romantic longing for the yeasty tang of an American brew. He settled for orange juice and stretched out on the bed, coolly naked, quietly exhausted. Eyes closed, he groped for the phone to begin the complicated and often frustrating process of calling the States.

THE PHONE WOKE DEANNA out of a dead sleep. Her first jumbled thought was that it was a wrong number again, probably the same idiot who had dragged her out of a soothing bath earlier, only to hang up without apology. Already cranky, she jiggled the phone off the hook.

"Reynolds."

"Must be, what? Five-thirty in the morning there." Finn kept his eyes closed and smiled at the husky sound of her voice. "Sorry."

"Finn?" Shaking off sleep, Deanna pushed herself up in bed and reached for the light. "Where are you?"

"Enjoying the hospitality of our Saudi hosts. Did you have any watermelon today?"

"Excuse me?"

"Watermelon. The sun's a bitch here, especially about ten in the morning. That's when I started to have this fantasy about watermelon. Curt got me going, then the crew started torturing themselves. Snow cones, mint juleps, cold fried chicken."

"Finn," Deanna said slowly. "Are you all right?"

"Just tired." He rubbed a hand over his face to pull himself back. "We spent a couple of days out in the desert. The food sucks, the heat's worse and the fucking flies . . . I don't want to think about the flies. I've been up for about thirty hours, Kansas. I'm a little punchy."

"You should get some sleep."

"Talk to me."

"I've seen some of your reports," she began. "The one on the hostages Hussein's calling 'guests' was gripping. And the one from the air base in Saudi."

"No, tell me what you've been doing."

"We did a show today on obsessive shoppers. One guest stays up every night watching one of the shopping channels and ordering everything on the screen. His wife finally cut the cable when he bought a dozen electronic flea collars. They don't have a dog."

It made Finn laugh, as she'd hoped it would. "I got the tape you sent. It bounced around a little first, so it took a while. The crew and I watched it. You looked good."

"I felt good. We're getting picked up by another couple of stations in Indiana. Late afternoon. We'll be going up against a monster soap, but who knows?"

"Now tell me you miss me."

She didn't answer right away, and caught herself wrapping the phone cord around and around her hand. "I suppose I do. Now and then."

"How about now?"

"Yes."

"When I get home, I want you to come with me up to my cabin."

"Finn—"

"I want to teach you how to fish."

"Oh?" A smile tugged at her mouth. "Really?"

"I don't think I should get serious about a woman who doesn't know one end of a rod from the other. Keep it in mind. I'll be in touch."

"All right. Finn?"

"Hmmm?"

She could tell he was nearly asleep. "I'll, ah, send you another tape."

"'Kay. See you."

He managed to get the phone back on the hook before he started to snore.

THE REPORTS CONTINUED TO come. The escalation of hostilities, the negotiations for the release of the hostages many feared would be used as human shields. The Paris summit, and the president's Thanksgiving visit to U.S. troops. By the end of November, the UN had voted on Resolution 678. The use of force to expel Iraq from Kuwait was approved, with a deadline for Saddam of January fifteenth.

On the homefront there were yellow ribbons flying—from the tips of car antennae and porch banisters. They were mixed with holly and ivy as America prepared for Christmas, and for war.

"This toy piece will show not only what's hot for kids for

186

Christmas, but what's safe." Deanna looked up from her notes and narrowed her eyes at Fran. "Are you okay?"

"Sure." With a grimace, Fran shifted her now-considerable bulk. "For someone who's got what feels like a small pick-up truck sitting on her bladder, I'm dandy."

"You should go home, put your feet up. You're due in less than two months."

"I'd go crazy at home. Besides, you're the one who should be exhausted, schmoozing half the night at the charity dinner-dance."

"It's part of the job," Deanna said absently. "And, as Loren pointed out, I made a number of contacts, and got some press."

"Mmm. And about five hours' sleep." Fran fiddled with a toy rabbit that wiggled its ears and squeaked when she pressed its belly. "Do you think Big Ed would like this?"

Brow lifted, Deanna studied Fran's belly, where "Big Ed," as the baby was called, seemed to be growing by leaps and bounds. "You already have two dozen stuffed animals in the nursery."

"You started it with that two-foot teddy bear." Setting the bunny aside, Fran reached among the toys scattered on the office floor and chose a combat-fatigued GI Joe. "Why the hell do they always want to play soldier?"

"That's one of the questions we'll ask our expert. Have you heard from Dave?"

Fran tried not to worry about her stepbrother, a National Guard officer who was in the Gulf. "Yeah. He got the box we sent over. The comic books were a big hit. Wow!" With a sound between a gasp and a laugh, she pressed a hand to her stomach. "Big Ed just kicked one through the posts."

"Is Richard really going to buy the baby a Bears helmet?"

"Already has. Which reminds me, I want to make sure we get gender molding into this segment. How society, and parents, continue stereotypes by buying this kind of thing for boys"—she waved the GI Joe—"and this sort of thing for girls." She nudged a Fisher-Price oven with her foot.

"Ballet shoes for girls, football cleats for boys."

"Which leads to girls shaking pom-poms on the sidelines while boys make touchdowns."

"Which," Deanna continued, "leads to men making corporate decisions and women serving coffee."

"God, am I going to screw this kid up?" Fran levered herself out of the chair. The fact that she waddled made her nervous pacing both comic and sweet. "I shouldn't have done this. We should have practiced on a puppy first. I'm going to be responsible for another human being, and I haven't even started a college fund."

Over the past few weeks, Deanna had become used to Fran's outbursts. She sat back and smiled. "Hormones bouncing again?"

"You bet. I'm going to go find Simon and check on last week's ratings—and pretend I'm a normal, sane human being."

"Then go home," Deanna insisted. "Eat a bag of cookies and watch an old movie on cable."

"Okay. I'll send Jeff in to pick up the toys and move them down to the set."

Alone, Deanna sat back and closed her eyes. It wasn't only Fran who was on edge these days. The entire staff was running on nerves. In six weeks, *Deanna's Hour* would either be re-signed with Delacort, or they would all be out of a job.

The ratings had been inching up, but was it enough? She knew she was putting everything she had into the show itself, and everything she could squeeze out into the public relations and press events Loren insisted on. But was that enough?

The trial run was almost over, and if Delacort decided to dump them . . .

Restless, she rose and turned to face the window. She wondered if Angela had ever stood there and worried, agonized over something as basic as a single ratings point. Had she felt the responsibility weigh so heavily on her shoulders—for the show, for the staff, for the advertisers? Is that why she'd become so hard?

Deanna rolled her tensed shoulders. It wouldn't simply be her career crumbling if the show was axed, she thought. There were six other people who had their time and energy and, yes, their egos, invested. Six other people who had families, mortgages, car payments, dentist bills.

"Deanna?"

"Yes, Jeff. We need to get these toys down to the . . ." She trailed off as she turned and spotted a seven-foot plastic spruce. "Where in the world did you get that?"

"I, ah, liberated it from a storeroom." Jeff stepped out from behind the tree. His cheeks were flushed from both nerves and exertion. His glasses slid slowly down the bridge of his nose. His boyishness was endearing. "I thought you might like it."

Laughing, she examined the tree. It was pretty pathetic, with its bent plastic boughs and virulent green color no one would mistake for natural. She looked at Jeff's grinning face, and laughed again. "It's exactly what I need. Let's put it in front of the window."

"It looked kind of lonely down there." Jeff centered it carefully in front of the wide pane. "I figured with some decorations . . ."

"Liberated."

He shrugged. "There's stuff in this building nobody's used—or seen—for years. Some lights, some balls, it'll look fine."

"And plenty of yellow ribbons," she said, thinking of Finn. "Thanks, Jeff."

"Everything's going to be okay, Deanna." He put a hand on her shoulder, gave it a quick, shy squeeze. "Don't worry so much."

"You're right." She pressed her hand on top of his. "Absolutely right. Let's get the rest of the crew in here and decorate this baby."

DEANNA WORKED THROUGHOUT the holidays with the plastic tree glowing behind her. By juggling appointments and putting in three eighteen-hour days, she made time for a frantic, twenty-four-hour trip home over Christmas. She returned to Chicago's bitter cold on the last plane on Boxing Day.

Loaded down with luggage, gifts and tins of cookies from Topeka, she unlocked her apartment. The first thing she saw was the plain white envelope on the rug, just inside. Uneasy, she set her bags aside. It didn't surprise her to find a single sheet in the envelope, or to see the bold red type.

Merry Christmas, Deanna.
I love watching you every day.
I love watching you.
I love you.

Weird, she mused, but harmless considering some of the bizarre mail that had come her way since August. She stuffed the note in her pocket, and she'd barely flipped the lock back in place when a knock sounded on the other side of the door. She tugged off her wool cap with one hand, opened the door with the other.

"Marshall."

His Burberry coat was neatly folded over his arm. "Deanna, hasn't this gone on long enough? You haven't answered any of my calls."

"There's nothing going on at all. Marshall, I just this minute got back into town. I'm tired, I'm hungry, and I'm not in the mood for a civilized discussion."

"If I can swallow my pride enough to come here, the least you can do is ask me in."

"Your pride?" She felt her temper rise. A bad sign, she knew, when only a few words had been exchanged. "Fine. Come in."

He glanced at her bags as he stepped through the door. "You went home for Christmas, then?"

"That's right."

He laid his coat over the back of a chair. "And your family's well?"

"Hale and hearty, Marshall, and I'm not in the mood for small talk. If you have something to say, say it."

"I don't believe this is something we can resolve until we sit down and talk it through." He gestured to the sofa. "Please."

She shrugged out of her coat and took a chair instead. She linked her hands firmly in her lap and waited.

"The fact that you're still angry with me proves that there's an emotional investment between us." He sat, resting his hands on his knees. "I realized that trying to resolve things right after the incident was a mistake."

"The incident? Is that what we're calling it?"

"Because," he continued, calmly, "emotions, on both sides, were running too close to the surface, making it difficult to compromise and vent constructively."

"I rarely vent constructively." She smiled then, but her eyes were hot. "I don't suppose we got to know each other well enough for you to realize that under certain circumstances, I have a nasty temper."

"I understand." He was pleased, very pleased that they were communicating again. "You see, Deanna, I believe part of our difficulties stemmed from the fact that we didn't know each other as well as we should have. We share the blame there, but it's a very human, very natural inclination to show only your best sides when developing a relationship."

She had to take a deep breath, had to school herself to remain seated when the urge to spring up and strike out was churning inside her. "You want to share the blame for that, fine—particularly since I have no intention of ever moving beyond that stage with you."

"Deanna. If you'll be honest, you'll admit that we were creating something special between us." As a good therapist, he kept his eyes steady on hers, his voice mild and soothing. "A meeting of intellects, of tastes."

"Oh, I think our meeting of intellects and tastes took a sharp division when I walked in and found you and Angela groping each other. Tell me, Marshall, did you have the brochures for our proposed Hawaiian tryst in your jacket pocket at the time?"

His color rose. "I have apologized repeatedly for that lapse."

"Now it's a lapse. Before it was an incident. Let me give you my term for it, Marshall. I call it a betrayal, a betrayal by two people I admired and cared for. Deliberate on Angela's side, and pathetic on yours."

The muscle in his jaw began to twitch. "You and I had not fully committed to each other, sexually or emotionally."

"You're saying that if I'd gone to bed with you, it wouldn't have happened? I'm not buying it." She sprang to her feet. "I'm not sharing the blame for this one, pal. You're the one who thought with your glands. So take my advice, doctor, and get the hell out of my house. I want you to stay away from me. I don't want you knocking at my door. I don't want to hear your voice on the phone. And I don't want any more calls in the middle of the damn night where you can't even drum up the guts to speak."

He stood, standing stiffly. "I don't know what you're talking about."

"Don't you?" Her cheeks were flaming.

"I only know that I want to make things right. My eyes have been opened during these months since you cut me out of your life, Deanna. I know you're the only woman who can make me happy."

"Then you're in for a sad life. I'm not available, and I'm not interested."

"There's someone else." He stepped forward, gripping her forearms before she could jerk away. "You can speak of betrayal when you so casually, so easily, move from me to someone else."

"Yes, there's someone else, Marshall. There's me. Now take your hands off me."

"Let me remind you what we had," he murmured, pulling her against him. "Let me show you the way it could be."

The old fear returned, making her tremble as she fought free of his grip. Struggling for air, she braced herself against the chair. Cornered, she was cruel. "You know what would make an

192

interesting topic for my show, Marshall? Try this on. Respected family counselors who harass women they've dated as well as seducing underage girls." She wrapped her arms tight around her body as his color drained. "Yes, I know all about it. A child, Marshall? Can you imagine how that revolts me? The woman you were seeing while you were supposedly developing our relationship is small change compared to that. Angela sent me a little package before she left for New York."

Cold sweat pearled on his brow. "You have no right to publicize my private life."

"And no intention of doing so. Unless you continue to harass me. And if you do—" She trailed off.

"I expected better than threats from you, Deanna."

"Well, looks like you were wrong again." She strode to the door, yanked it open. "Now get out."

Shaken, he picked up his coat. "You owe me the courtesy of giving me the information you have."

"I owe you nothing. And if you're not out this door in five seconds, I'm going to let out a scream that'll raise the roof on this building and bring the neighbors running."

"You're making a mistake," he said as he walked to the door. "A very big mistake."

"Happy holidays," she told him, then slammed the door and turned the bolt.

"GREAT SHOW, DEANNA." MARCIE wiped at her eyes as Deanna walked back into the dressing room. "It was great to have all those families of soldiers over in the Gulf on together. And those tapes from over there."

"Thanks, Marcie." Deanna walked over to the lighted makeup mirror and removed her earrings. "You know, Marcie, it's New Year's Eve."

"I've heard rumors."

193

"It's that time for 'Out with the old, in with the new.'" Pushing a hand through her hair, Deanna turned in front of the mirror, critically studying left profile, right, full face. "And Marcie, my friend, I'm feeling reckless."

"Oh yeah?" Marcie stopped arranging her makeup case in preparation for Bobby Marks. "What kind of reckless? Like going-out-and-picking-up-strange-men-at-cheap-bars reckless?"

"I didn't say I was insane, I said I was reckless. How much time do you have free before Bobby comes in?"

"About twenty minutes."

"Okay, that should do it." Deanna boosted herself into the swivel chair, then spun it away from the mirror. "Change me."

Marcie nearly gave in to the urge to rub her hands together. "You're serious?"

"Deadly. I had a nasty scene with a former relationship a few days ago. I don't know if I'm going to have a job much less a career this time next month. I may just be falling in love with a man who spends more time out of the country than in, and in two weeks we could be at war. Tonight, New Year's Eve, I will not be with the man I think I may be falling in love with, but at a crowded party socializing with strangers because socializing with strangers is now part of my job. So I'm feeling reckless, Marcie, reckless enough to do something drastic."

Marcie clipped the knee-length bib around Deanna's neck. "Maybe you'd better define 'drastic' before I get started."

"Nope." Deanna inhaled deeply, exhaled slowly. "I don't want to know. Surprise me."

"You got it." Marcie picked up her spray bottle and dampened Deanna's hair. "You know, I've been wanting to do this for weeks."

"Now's your chance. Make me a new woman."

Little tangles of nerves formed in Deanna's stomach as Marcie snipped. And snipped. She watched with a faltering heart as tresses of ebony hair hit the tiled floor at her feet.

"You know what you're doing, right?"

194

"Trust me," Marcie told her, as she snipped some more. "You're going to look fabulous. Distinctive."

"Ah, distinctive?" Wary, Deanna tried to turn toward the mirror.

"No peeking." Marcie laid a firm hand on her shoulder. "It's like going into a cold pool," she explained. "If you try to ease it a little at a time, it's a hard, miserable experience. And sometimes you chicken out and back off before you get under. If you do it all at once, you have that one nifty shock, then you love it." She pursed her lips as she wielded the scissors. "You know, maybe it's more like losing your virginity."

"Holy shit!"

Marcie glanced up and grinned at CBC's resident television chef. "Hiya, Bobby. Almost done here."

"Holy shit," he said again, and stepped inside to stare at Deanna. "What'd you do, Dee?"

"I wanted a change." Her voice was weak as she started to lift a hand to her hair. Marcie pushed it away.

"A cold pool," she said darkly.

"It's a change, all right." Bobby stepped back, and shook his head. "Hey, can I have some of this hair?" Stooping, he picked up a handful. "I can have a toupee made. Hell, I could have half a dozen."

"Oh, God, what have I done?" Deanna squeezed her eyes tight.

"Dee? What's keeping you? We need to—oh, Jesus!" Fran stopped in the doorway, one hand covering her gaping mouth, the other pressed to her belly.

"Fran." Desperate, Deanna reached out. "Fran. Fran, I think I had a nervous breakdown. It's New Year's Eve," she babbled. "Bobby's making toupees. I think my life is flashing in front of my eyes."

"You cut it," Fran managed after a moment. "You really cut it."

"But it'll grow back, right?" Deanna snatched a lock of hair from her bib. "Right?"

"In five or ten years," Bobby predicted cheerfully, and arranged some of Deanna's shorn locks atop his bald dome. "Not quite soon enough to honor the clause I imagine you have in your contract restricting appearance changes."

"Oh God." Deanna's already pale cheek went dead white. "I forgot. I just didn't think. I went a little crazy."

"Be sure to have your lawyer use that one with Delacort," Bobby suggested.

"They'll love it," Marcie said grimly. "She'll see for herself in a minute." Marcie fluffed and combed. Unsatisfied, she added a dab of gel, working it in, then styling with the concentration of a woman cutting diamonds. "Now you just take a deep breath, and hold it," Marcie advised, unhooking the bib. "And don't say anything until you take a really good look."

No one spoke as Marcie turned Deanna slowly toward the mirror. Deanna stared at the reflection, her lips parted in shock, her eyes huge. The long mane of hair was gone, replaced by a short, sleek cap with a saucy fringe of bangs. In a daze, she watched the woman in the mirror lift a hand, touch the nape of her neck, where the hair stopped.

"It follows the shape of your face," Marcie said nervously when Deanna only continued to stare. "And it shows off your eyes and eyebrows. You've got these great dark eyebrows with this terrific natural arch. Your eyes are a little almond-shaped and dramatic, but they kind of got lost with all that hair."

"I . . ." Deanna let out a breath, took another. "I love it."

"You do?" As her knees buckled in relief, Marcie dropped into the chair beside her. "Really?"

Deanna watched her own smile bloom. "I love it. Do you realize how many hours a week I had to devote to my hair? Why didn't I think of this before?" She grabbed a hand mirror to view the back. "This is going to save me almost eight hours a week—an entire workday." She picked up the earrings she'd discarded and put them back on. "What do you think?" she asked Fran.

"Not to diminish your time-saving priorities, you look incredible. The hip girl-next-door."

"Bobby?"

"It's sexy. A cross between an Amazon and a pixie. And I'm sure Delacort won't mind reshooting all the promos."

"Oh my God." As the idea took root, Deanna turned to Fran. "Oh my God."

"Don't worry, you'll dazzle Loren with it tonight. Then we'll work it into the next show."

"Post-holiday blues?"

"Sure, sure." Thinking frantically, Fran gnawed on her lip. "Ah—something as simple and frivolous as a new hairstyle can give you that quick lift after the party's over."

"I'll buy it," Bobby decided. "Now, if you ladies don't mind, I need to get into makeup. I have a trout to sauté."

EARLY IN THE FIRST LIGHT OF the new year, with a video of *Deanna's Hour* playing on the TV, a single, lonely figure wandered a small, dark room. On the table where framed pictures of Deanna beamed into the shadowy light, a new treasure was laid: a thick tress of ebony hair wrapped in gold cord.

It was soft to the touch, soft as silk. After a last caress, the fingers wandered away, toward the phone. They dialed slowly, so that the joy could be drawn out. Moments later, Deanna's voice drifted through the receiver, sleepy, a bit uneasy, bringing with it a silver spear of pleasure that lasted long after the receiver was replaced again.

Chapter Thirteen

IT WAS AFTER TWO A.M. IN BAGHDAD WHEN FINN REVIEWED his notes for the scheduled live broadcast on CBC's *Evening News*. He sat on the single chair that wasn't heaped with tapes or cable, dragging on a fresh shirt while his mind honed ideas and observations into a report.

He tuned out his surroundings, the noise of preparation, the smell of cold food and the chatter.

His crew was spread around the suite, checking equipment and tossing jokes. A sense of humor, particularly if it was dark, helped cut the tension. For the past two days, they had hoarded food and bottled water.

It was January sixteenth.

"Maybe we should tie some sheets together," Curt suggested. "Hang them outside the window like a big white flag."

"No, we'll send up my Bears cap." The engineer flicked a finger at its brim. "What red-blooded American boy's going to bomb a football fan?"

"I heard the Pentagon told them to hit the hotels first." Finn glanced up from his notes and grinned. "You know how fed up

Cheney is with the press." Finn picked up the phone that connected him with Chicago and caught the byplay at the news desk between commercials. "Hey, Martin. How'd the Bulls do last night?" As he spoke he moved in front of the window so that Curt could get a video test of him against the night sky. "Yeah, it's quiet here. Nerves are pretty high—so's the anti-American sentiment."

When the director cut in, Finn nodded. "Got it. They're picking up the feed," he told Curt as he moved out onto the balcony. "We'll go on in the next segment. In four minutes."

"Bring up the lights," Curt demanded. "I got a bad shadow here."

Before anyone could move, there was a rattling boom in the distance.

"What the hell was that?" The engineer went pale and swallowed his gum. "Thunder? Was that thunder?"

"Oh, Jesus." Finn turned in time to see the searing glow of tracer rounds split the night sky. "Martin. You still there? Haversham?" He called to the director even as Curt shifted the camera to the sky. "We've got explosions here. The air raid's started. Yes, I'm sure. Get me on the air for God's sake. Get me on the goddamn air."

He heard the curses and cheers from the Chicago control room, then nothing but a statical hiss.

"Lost it. Fuck." Coolly, he eyed the violent light show. He didn't give a thought, at the moment, to one of those deadly lights striking the building. Every thought in his head was focused on transmitting the story. "Keep running that tape."

"You don't have to tell me twice." Curt was all but hanging over the railing. "Look at that!" he shouted in a voice that was tight with nerves and excitement. Air-raid sirens screamed over the crash of exploding shells. "We got ourselves a front-row seat."

In frustration, Finn held his microphone out to record the sounds of battle. "Get Chicago back."

"I'm trying." The engineer worked controls with trembling hands. "I'm trying, goddamn it."

Eyes narrowed, Finn stalked to the balcony rail, then turned to the camera. If they couldn't go live, at least they'd have tape. "Baghdad's night sky erupted at approximately two thirty-five this morning. There are flashes and the answering spears from anti-aircraft. Flames shoot up from the horizon sporadically." When he turned, he saw, with both awe and dull disbelief, the searing comet trail of a tracer flash by at eye level. Its deadly, eerie beauty made his blood pump. What a visual. "Oh, Christ, did you get that? Did you get it?"

He heard his engineer swear thinly as the building shook. Finn shoved his blowing hair out of his face and shouted into his mike. "The city is being rattled by the air raid. The waiting is over. It's started."

He turned back to the engineer. "Any luck?"

"No." Though his color was still gone, he managed a wobbly grin. "I think our friendly hosts are going to be coming along pretty soon to evict us."

Now Finn grinned, a quick, reckless flash as deadly as rifle fire. "They have to find us first."

WHILE FINN TAPED HIS WAR report, Deanna sat, numbed with boredom, through another interminable dinner. Strains of monot-onous piano music wafted through the ballroom of the hotel in Indianapolis. In addition to after-dinner speeches, mediocre wine and rubber chicken, all she had to look forward to was the long trip back to Chicago.

At least, she thought, selfishly, she wasn't suffering alone. She'd dragged Jeff Hyatt with her.

"It's not too bad," he murmured, as he swallowed a bite. "If you put enough salt on it."

She sent him a look that was nearly as bland as the meal. "That's what I love about you, Jeff. Always the optimist. Let's just see if you can smile about the fact that after we finish not eating this, the station manager, the head of sales and two of our advertisers are going to give speeches."

He thought about it a moment, opted for water rather than wine. "Well, it could be worse."

"I'm waiting."

"We could be snowed in."

She shuddered. "Please, don't even joke about that."

"I like these trips, really." Head ducked, he glanced at her, then back to his plate. "Going through the station, meeting everyone, watching them roll out the red carpet for you."

"I like that part myself. Spending time at one of the affiliates and seeing all that enthusiasm for the show. And most of the people are terrific." She sighed and toyed with the lump of rice next to her chicken. She was just tired, she thought. All of her life, she'd had a surplus of energy, and now it seemed she was running on empty. All those demands on time, on her brain, on her body.

Celebrity, she'd discovered, was not all glamour and limos. For every perk there was a price. For every rich-and-famous elbow she rubbed, there were half a dozen corporate dinners or late-night meetings. For every magazine cover, there were canceled social plans. Helming a daily show didn't simply mean having camera presence and good interviewing skills. It meant being on call twenty-four hours a day.

You got what you asked for, Dee, she reminded herself. Now stop whining and get to work. With a determined smile, she turned to the man beside her. Fred Banks, she remembered, station owner, golf enthusiast and hometown boy.

"I can't tell you how much I enjoyed seeing your operation today," she began. "You have a wonderful team."

He puffed up with pride. "I like to think so. We're number two now, but we intend to be number one within the year. Your show's going to help us accomplish that."

"I hope so." She ignored the little ball of tension in her stomach.

201

Her six months was almost up. "I'm told you were born right here in Indianapolis."

"That's right. Born and bred."

While he expounded on the delights of his hometown, Deanna made appropriate comments while her eyes scanned the room. Every table was circled by people who were in some way depending on her to make it. And doing a good show wasn't enough. She'd done so that morning, she thought. Nearly ten hours before—if you didn't count time for makeup, hair, wardrobe and pre-production. Then there'd been an interview, a staff meeting, phone calls to return, mail to screen.

Mail that had included another odd letter from what she was coming to think of as her most persistent fan.

> You look like a sexy angel with your hair short.
> I love the way you look.
> I love you.

She'd tucked the note away and had answered three dozen others. All that before she'd hopped on a plane with Jeff for Indianapolis and the tour of the affiliate, the meetings and handshakes with the local staff, the business lunch, the spot on the news and now this never-ending banquet.

No, a good show wasn't enough. She had to be diplomat, ambassador, boss, business partner and celebrity. And she had to wear each and every hat correctly—while pretending she wasn't lonely, or worried about Finn, or missing those quiet hours when she could curl up with a book for pleasure rather than because she'd be interviewing the author.

This was what she wanted, Deanna told herself, and beamed at the waiter as he served the peach melba.

"You can sleep on the plane going home," Jeff whispered in her ear.

"It shows?"

"Just a little."

She excused herself and pushed back from the table. If she couldn't fix the fatigue, at least she could fix its signs.

She was nearly at the doors when she heard someone tap on the podium mike. Automatically, she looked back and saw Fred Banks standing under the lights. "If I can have your attention. I've just received word that Baghdad is under attack by UN forces."

There was a buzzing in Deanna's ears. Dimly she heard the noise level rise in the ballroom, like a sea at high tide. From somewhere nearby a waiter raised a triumphant fist.

"I hope they kick that bastard's sorry butt."

Slowly, all fatigue washing away, she walked back to the table. She had a job to finish.

FINN SAT ON THE FLOOR OF A hotel bedroom, his laptop on his knees. He hammered out copy as fast as it could pass from his mind to his fingers. It was nearly dawn now, and though his eyes were gritty, he felt no sense of fatigue. Outside, the fire-fight continued. Inside, a game of cat and mouse was under way.

During the past three hours, they had moved twice, hauling equipment and provisions. While Iraqi soldiers swept the building, moving guests and international news crews to the basement of the hotel, Finn and his crew had slipped from room to room. The successful intrigue had his blood pumping.

While he took his round at sentry duty, his two companions sprawled on the bed and snatched sleep.

Satisfied with the copy he'd finished thus far, Finn turned off the computer. He rose, working out the kinks in his back, in his neck, and thinking wistfully of breakfast: blueberry pancakes and gallons of hot coffee. He made do with a handful of Curt's trail mix, then hefted the camera.

At the window he recorded the final images of the first day of war, the lightning flashes of cruise missiles and smart bombs, the streaks of tracers. He speculated on how much devastation they would see when dawn broke. And how much they would get on tape.

"I'm gonna have to report you to the union, pal."

Finn lowered the camera and glanced back at Curt. The cameraman was standing beside the bed, rubbing his tired eyes.

"You're just pissed because I can handle this baby as well as you."

"Shit." Challenged, Curt walked over to take the camera. "You can't do nothing but look pretty on tape."

"Then get ready to prove it. I've got some copy to read."

"You're the boss." He rolled tape in silence as bombs exploded. "Are we going to work on a way to get out of here?"

"I've got some contacts in Baghdad." Finn watched the fires leaping from the horizon. "Maybe."

THE MOMENT THE LAST after-dinner speech was finished, the last hand shaken, the last cheek kissed, Deanna headed for a phone. While Deanna called Fran and Richard, Jeff used the phone beside her to contact the Chicago newsroom.

"What?" Richard answered with a snarl. "What is it?"

"Richard? Richard, it's Deanna. I'm on my way to the airport in Indianapolis. I heard about the air strike, and—"

"Yeah, right. We heard. But we've got our own little crisis right here. Fran's in labor. We're just about to head out to the hospital."

"Now?" Because it felt like her circuits were about to overload, Deanna pressed her fingers hard against her temple. "I thought we had another ten days."

"Tell that to Big Ed. Breathe, Fran, don't forget to breathe."

"Look, I won't hold you up. Just tell me if she's okay."

"She just finished half a pizza—that's why she didn't tell me she was in labor. She already contacted Bach. Looks like you're going to be preempted tomorrow. No, damn it, you're not going to talk to her, Fran, you're going to breathe."

"I'll be there as soon as I can. Tell her . . . Oh, Jesus, just tell her I'll be there."

"I'm counting on it. Hey, we're going to have a baby! See you."

With the line buzzing in her ear, Deanna rested her brow against the wall. "What a day."

"Finn Riley reported the air strike."

"What?" Alert again, she spun around to Jeff. "Finn? He's all right, then?"

"He was on the line with the studio when it hit. He got about five seconds of pictures across before they lost the feed."

"So we don't know," she said slowly.

"Hey, he's been through stuff like this before, right?" He put a hesitant arm around her shoulders as he led her out to their waiting car.

"Yes, of course. Of course he has."

"And look at it this way. We're getting out of here at least an hour early, because everybody wanted to get home and turn on the tube."

She nearly laughed. "You're good for me, Jeff."

He beamed back at her. "Same goes."

IT WAS SIX A.M. WHEN DEANNA finally unlocked the door to her apartment and staggered inside. She'd been up for a full twenty-four hours and was long past fatigue. But, she reminded herself, she'd fulfilled her professional obligations, and she'd seen her god-daughter born.

Aubrey Deanna Myers, she mused, and smiled blearily as she walked to the bedroom. An eight-pound miracle with red hair. After watching that incredibly beautiful life slide into the world, it was hard to believe there was a war raging on the other side of the world.

But as she tugged off her clothes, unspeakably grateful that her show was preempted that morning, she switched on the television and brought that war into her home.

What time was it in Baghdad? she wondered, but her mind

205

simply wouldn't cope with the math. Wearily she sat on the edge of the bed in her underwear and tried to concentrate on the images and reports.

"Be careful, damn you."

It was her last thought as she slid down over the bedspread and tumbled into sleep.

LATE DURING THE SECOND night of the Gulf War, Finn set up at a Saudi base. He was tired and hungry and longed for a bath. He could hear the roar of jets taking off from the airfield to make their way to Iraq. Other news teams, he knew, would be broadcasting reports.

His mood was foul. As a result of the Pentagon's restrictions on the press, he would have to wait his turn in the pool before he could travel to the front—and then he could go only where military officials instructed. For the first time since World War II, all reports would be subject to censorship.

It was one of the few words Finn considered an obscenity.

"Don't you want to take time to shave that pretty face?"

"Cram it, Curt. We're on in ten." He listened to the countdown in his earpiece. "In the predawn hours of day two of Desert Storm ..." he began.

ON HER COUCH IN CHICAGO, Deanna leaned forward and studied Finn's image on-screen. Tired, she thought. He looked terribly tired. But tough and ready. And alive.

She toasted him with her diet soda as she ate the peanut butter sandwich she'd fixed for dinner.

She wondered what he was thinking, what he was feeling, as he spoke of sorties and statistics or answered the scripted questions of the news anchor. The Arabian sky spread at his back, and occasionally he had to raise his voice over the sound of jet engines.

"We're glad that you're safely out of Baghdad, Finn. And we'll stay tuned for further reports."

"Thanks, Martin. For CBC, this is Finn Riley in Saudi Arabia."

"Good seeing you, Finn," Deanna murmured, then sighed and rose to take her dishes into the kitchen. It wasn't until she passed her answering machine that she noticed the rapid blink of the message light.

"Oh, hell, how could I have forgotten?"

Setting the dishes aside, she pushed Rewind. She'd slept a blissful six hours, then had rushed out again. A stop by the hospital, a few hours at the office, where chaos had reigned. That chaos, and the war talk, had driven her out again with a thick file of clippings and a bag of mail. She'd worked the rest of the evening, ignoring the phone. Without checking her messages.

Having a baby and a war was certainly distracting, she thought as she hit Play.

There was a call from her mother. One from Simon. Dutifully, she scribbled the messages on a pad. There were two hang-ups, each with a long pause before the click of the receiver.

"Kansas?" Deanna dropped her pencil as Finn's voice filled the room. "Where the hell are you? It must be five A.M. there. I've only got this line for a minute. We're out of Baghdad. Christ, the place is a mess. I don't know when I'll be able to get through again, so catch me on the news. I'll be thinking about you, Deanna. God, it's hard to think about anything else. Buy yourself a couple of flannel shirts, will you? And some wading boots. It can get cold at the cabin. Write, okay? Send a tape, a smoke signal. And let me know why the hell you're not answering your phone. Later."

And he was gone.

Deanna was reaching down to press Rewind and listen to the message again when Loren Bach's voice flowed out. "Jesus H. Christ, you're a hard woman to get in touch with. I called your office, and your secretary said you were at the hospital. Scared the life out of me until she explained it was Fran having her baby.

Heard it's a girl. Don't know why the hell you're not home yet, but here's the deal: Delacort would like to renew your contract for two years. Our people will be contacting your agent, but I wanted to be the first to tell you. Congratulations, Deanna."

She couldn't have said why, but she sat down on the floor, covered her face with her hands and wept.

THINGS MOVED QUICKLY OVER the next five weeks, at home and away. With the new contract with Delacort signed and sealed, Deanna found both her budget and her hopes expanding. She was able to add to her staff, and furnish a separate office for Fran when she returned from maternity leave.

Best of all, the ratings began a slow, steady climb during the first weeks of the new year.

She had ten cities now, and though she still fell behind *Angela's* whenever the shows were scheduled head to head, the margin had slimmed.

To celebrate the success, she bought a softly patterned Aubusson carpet to replace the flea-market rug in her living room. It went, she thought, perfectly with the desk.

She had a cover on *Woman's Day* scheduled for April, a feature in *People* and, for old time's sake, agreed to appear on a segment of *Woman Talk*. The *Chicago Tribune* did a Sunday spread, calling her a star on the rise.

She turned down, with a combination of amusement and horror, an offer to pose for *Playboy*.

When the red light blinked on, Deanna was seated on set. She smiled, slipping easily, comfortably into thousands of homes.

"Do you remember your first love? That first kiss that made your heart beat faster? The long talks, the secret glances?" She sighed and had the audience sighing with her. "Today, we're going to reunite three couples who remember very well. Janet Hornesby was sweet sixteen when she had her first romance. That was fifty years ago, but she hasn't forgotten the young boy who stole her heart that spring."

The camera began to pan the panel, focusing on giddy, nervous smiles as Deanna continued to speak.

"Robert Seinfield was just eighteen when he left his high school sweetheart and moved two thousand miles away with his family. Though a decade has passed, he still thinks of Rose, the girl who wrote him his first love letter. And twenty-three years ago, college plans and family pressures separated Theresa Jamison from the man she'd thought she'd marry. I think our guests today are wondering, What if? I know I am. We'll find out, after this."

"GOD, GREAT SHOW." FRAN, Aubrey snug in a baby saque at her torso, marched out on the set. "I think Mrs. Hornesby and her fellow might have a second chance."

"What are you doing here?"

"I wanted Aubrey to see where her mother works." Nestling the baby, she looked longingly around the set. "I've missed this place."

"Fran, you've just had a baby."

"Yeah, I heard about that. You know, Dee, you should think about a follow-up show. People love the sentimental stuff. If any of those three couples get together, you could do a kind of anniversary thing."

"I've already thought of that." Deanna stepped back, hands on hips. "Well," she said after a minute. "You look good. Really."

"I feel good. Really. But as much as I love being a mom, I hate being a homebody. I need work or I'm liable to do something drastic. Like take up needlepoint."

"We couldn't let that happen. Let's go up and talk about it."

"I want to say hi to the crew first."

"I'll be up in the office when you're finished." Smiling smugly, Deanna headed to the elevator. She'd won her fifty-dollar bet with Richard. He'd been positive she'd last two full months. On the ride up to the sixteenth floor, she glanced at her watch and calculated time. "Cassie," she began, the minute she stepped into the outer office. "See if you can reschedule my lunch meeting for one-thirty."

"No problem. Great show, by the way. Word is the phones were going crazy."

"We aim to please." With her schedule in mind, she dropped down behind her desk to study the mail Cassie had stacked for her. "Fran stopped by downstairs. She'll be up in a few minutes—with the baby."

"She brought the baby? Oh, I can't wait to see her." She stopped, disturbed by the expression on Deanna's face. "Is something wrong?"

"Wrong?" Baffled, Deanna shook her head. "I don't know. Cassie, do you know how this got here?" She held up a plain white envelope that carried only her name.

"It was already on your desk when I brought the other mail in. Why?"

"It's just weird. I've been getting these notes on and off since last spring." She turned the paper around so Cassie could read it.

"'Deanna, you're so beautiful. Your eyes look into my soul. I'll love you forever.'" Cassie pursed her lips. "I guess it's flattering. And pretty tame compared to some of the letters you get. Are you worried about it?"

"Not worried. Maybe a little uneasy. It doesn't seem quite healthy for someone to keep this up for so long."

"Are you sure they've all been from the same person?"

"Same type of envelope, same type of message in the same type of red print." Distress curled loosely in her stomach. "Maybe it's someone who works in the building."

Someone she saw every day. Spoke with. Worked with.

"Anyone been asking you out, or coming on to you?"

"What? No." With an effort, Deanna shook off the eerie mood, then shrugged. "It's stupid. Harmless," she said, as if to convince herself, then deliberately tore the page in two and tossed it in the trash. "Let's see what business we can clear up before noon, Cassie."

"Okay. Did you happen to catch Angela's special last night?"

"Of course." Deanna grinned. "You didn't think I'd miss my toughest competition's first prime-time program, did you? She did a nice job."

"Not all the reviewers thought so." Cassie tapped the clippings on Deanna's desk. "The one from the *Times* was a killer."

Automatically Deanna reached into the stack and read the first clipped review.

"'Pompous and shallow.'" She winced." 'By turns simpering and sniping.'"

"The ratings weren't what they expected, either," Cassie told her. "They weren't embarrassing, but they were hardly stellar. The *Post* called her self-aggrandizing."

"That's just her style."

"It was a little much, doing that tour of her penthouse for the camera and cooing about New York. And there were more shots of her than her guests." Cassie shrugged, grinned. "I counted."

"I imagine this will be tough for her to take." Deanna set the reviews aside again. "But she'll bounce back." She shot Cassie a warning look. "I've had my problems with her, but I don't wish hatchet reviews on anyone."

"I wouldn't either. I just don't want you to be hurt by her."

"Bullets bounce off me," Deanna said dryly. "Now let's forget about Angela. I'm sure I'm the last thing on her mind this morning."

ANGELA'S INITIAL TANTRUM OVER the reviews had resulted in a snowstorm of shredded newspaper. It littered the floor of her office. She ground newsprint into the pink pile as she paced.

"Those bastards aren't getting away with taking a slice at me."

Dan Gardner, the new executive producer of *Angela's*, wisely waited until the worst of the storm had passed. He was thirty, built like a middleweight with a compact, muscular body. His conservatively styled brown hair suited his boyish face, accented by dark blue eyes and subtly clefted chin.

He had a shrewd mind and a simple goal: to ride to the top on whatever vehicle could get him there the fastest.

"Angela, everyone knows reviews are crap." He poured her a soothing cup of tea. It was a pity, he thought, that their strategy of allowing no previews of the first show had failed. "Those jerks always take cheap shots at whoever's on top. And that's just where you are." He handed her the delicate china cup. "On top."

"Damn right I am." Tea slopped over into the saucer as she whirled away. Fury was better than tears, she knew. No one, absolutely no one would have the satisfaction of seeing how hurt she was. She'd been so proud, showing off her new home, sharing her life with her audience.

They had called it "simpering".

"And the ratings would have proved it," she snapped back, "if it hadn't been for this damn war. The goddamn viewers just can't get enough of the fucking thing. Day and night, night and day, we're bombarded. Why don't we just blow the damn country off the map and be done with it?"

Tears were close, perilously close. She battled them back and sipped the tea like medicine.

She wanted a drink.

"It's not hurting us. Your lead-in to the six o'clock news has come up in five markets. And the viewers loved your remote at Andrews Air Force Base last week."

"Well, I'm sick of it." She hurled the teacup at the wall, sending shards flying and drops splattering over the silk wallpaper. "And I'm sick of that little bitch in Chicago trying to undermine my ratings."

"She's a flash in the pan." He hadn't even jolted at the explosion. He'd been expecting it. Now that it was done, he knew she could begin to calm. And when she'd calmed, she'd be needy.

He'd been seeing to Angela's needs for several months.

"In a year she'll be old news, and you'll still be number one."

She sat behind her desk, leaning back, eyes shut. She was slipping. Nothing seemed to be going the way she'd planned when she'd formed her production company. She was in charge, yes, but there was so much to do. So many demands, so many, many ways to fail.

But she couldn't fail, could never face that. She calmed herself by taking long, slow breaths, just as she did during bouts of stage fright. It was much more productive, she reminded herself, to focus on someone else's failure.

"You're right. Once Deanna bottoms out, she'll be lucky to get a gig on public access." And she had something that might hurry that fine day along.

As the smile curved Angela's lips, Dan walked behind the chair to massage the tension from her shoulders. "You just relax. Let me do all the worrying."

She liked the feel of his hands on her—gentle, competent, sure. They made her feel protected, safe. She so desperately needed that now.

"They love me, don't they, Dan?"

"Of course they do." His hands trailed up to her neck, then brushed down over her breasts. They were soft and heavy and never failed to arouse him. His voice thickened as he felt her nipples harden between the light pinch of his thumb and forefinger. "Everybody loves Angela."

"And they'll keep watching." She sighed, relaxing as his hands molded her.

"Every day. Coast to coast."

"Every day," she murmured, and her smile widened. "Go lock the door, Dan. Tell Lorraine to hold my calls."

"I'd love to."

Chapter Fourteen

DURING THE FRIGID NIGHTS IN THE DESERT, IT WAS HARD TO remember the blazing heat of day. Just as after the first bombs exploded it was difficult to remember the deadly tedium of the long weeks of Desert Shield.

Finn had been through other wars, though he'd never been so hamstrung by military regulations. There were ways, however, for the enterprising reporter to stretch them. He would never have denied that certain sensitive intelligence data couldn't be broadcast without endangering troops. But he wasn't a fool, nor was he blindly ambitious. He saw his job, and his duty, as finding out what was happening, not just what the official reports claimed was happening.

Twice he and Curt climbed into his rented truck with a portable satellite dish bracketed in the bed, and headed out. Over the poorly marked roads and the shifting sand, they managed to link up with U.S. troops. Finn listened to complaints and to hopes, and returned to base to report both.

He watched Scuds fly and Patriots intercept them. He slept in snatches and lived with the possibility of a chemical assault.

When the ground war began, he was ready, eager, to follow it into Kuwait City.

It would be called the Mother of Battles, the hundred hours of fierce fighting to liberate Kuwait. While allied troops took up positions along the Euphrates River, along the highways linking Kuwait to other cities, Iraqis fled. Hustling, as one trooper told Finn, "to get out of Dodge".

There were massive traffic jams, trapped tanks, abandoned possessions. From a dusty truck heading toward the city, Finn observed the wreckage. Mile after mile of shattered vehicles lined the road. Cars, stripped for parts, tilted on crates. Personal possessions littered the roadway, mattresses, blankets, frying pans and ammo clips. Incredibly, a chandelier, its crystals gleaming in the sun, lay on the sand like scattered jewels. And worse, much worse, was the occasional corpse.

"Let's get some tape of this." Finn stepped out of the truck, his boots crunching down on one of the cassette tapes that were blowing across the highway.

"Looks like the garage sale from hell," Curt commented. "Crazy bastards must have been looting on their way out."

"It always comes down to getting your own, doesn't it?" Finn pointed toward a swatch of hot pink flapping from beneath an overturned truck. The evening gown shimmered with sequins. "Where the hell did she expect to wear that?"

Finn prepared for a stand-up as Curt set up his equipment. He hadn't thought anything else could surprise him. Not after seeing the pathetically gaunt Iraqi soldiers wearily surrendering to allied troops. Seeing the fear and fatigue, and the relief, on their faces as they emerged from their foxholes in the desert. He hadn't thought anything else about war could affect him, not the torn bodies, the atrocities of scavengers or the stink of death cooking under the merciless sun.

But that flap of pink silk, rustling seductively in the desert wind, turned his stomach.

It was worse inside the city. The raw nerves, the anger, the devastation, all coated in a layer of oily soot from the fires that depleted Kuwait's lifeblood of oil.

When the wind blew toward the city, the sky would darken with smoke. Midday would become midnight. The seaside was dotted with mines, and explosions rocked the city several times a day. Gunfire continued, not only in celebratory bursts, but in savage drive-by attacks on Kuwaiti soldiers. Survivors searched the cemetery for the remains of loved ones, many of whom had suffered torture and worse.

Through all he observed, through all he reported, Finn continued to think of a sequined evening gown billowing out of the sand.

LIKE THE REST OF THE WORLD, Deanna watched the end of the war on television. She listened to the reports on the liberation of Kuwait, the official cease-fire, the statistics of victory. It became a habit to drop into the newsroom before she left the CBC Building, hoping for a few scraps of information that hadn't yet been aired.

But the reality of day-to-day responsibilities kept her grounded. Whenever she had a free night, she watched the late news, then slipped in a tape of that morning's show. In the privacy of her apartment, she could watch herself critically, searching for ways to improve her on-air skills or to tighten the overall format.

She sat cross-legged on the floor, comfortable in sweatshirt and jeans, a notepad open across her knees. The earrings were wrong, she noted. Every time she moved her head they swung—a distraction for the viewer, she thought, and wrote: No more dangling earrings.

And the hand gestures were too broad. If she didn't watch it, she'd end up being parodied on *Saturday Night Live*. She should be so lucky, she thought with a grin, and scribbled on her pad.

Did she touch people too much? Nibbling her lips, Deanna watched. She always seemed to be laying a hand on a guest's arm or circling an audience member's shoulder. Maybe she should—

The knock on the door had her swearing. Her schedule didn't allow for unexpected visitors after ten. Grudgingly, she switched off the VCR. She glimpsed through the peephole. Then she was tugging at locks, dragging at the chain.

"Finn! I didn't know you were back!"

She didn't know who moved first. In a heartbeat, they were wrapped together, his mouth hard on hers, her hands fisted in his hair. The explosion of need rattled them both, the swell of heat, the blast of power. The bomb detonated inside her, leaving emotions shattered, needs raw. Then he was kicking the door closed as they tumbled to the floor.

She didn't think. Couldn't think. Not with his mouth burning on hers and his hands already urgently possessing. Like tussling children, they rolled over the rug, the only sounds incoherent murmurs and strained breathing.

It wasn't dreamlike, but stark reality. The only reality that mattered. His hands were rough, streaking under the fleece of her shirt to take, digging into her hips to press her fiercely against him.

She seemed to be erupting beneath him, with short, static bursts of energy. Her skin was hot, smooth, unbearably soft. He wanted to taste it, to devour it, to consume the flavor of her flesh and blood and bone. Her mouth wasn't enough—her throat, her shoulder, where he dragged the shirt down. He felt like an animal, rabid and starving, and wanted to glory in it. Yet he knew he could hurt her, would hurt her, if he didn't harness the worst of the need.

"Deanna." He wished he could find some spark of tenderness within the furnace that roared inside him. "Let me . . ." He lifted his head, struggling to clear his vision. He'd barely looked at her, he realized. The moment she'd opened the door and said his name, his control had snapped.

Now she was vibrating like a plucked string beneath him, her eyes huge and dark, her mouth swollen. And her skin . . . He brought his fingertips to her cheek, stroking over the flushed, damp flesh.

Tears. He'd always considered them a woman's greatest weapon. Shaken, he brushed them away and cleared his throat. "Did I knock you down?"

"I don't know." She felt like a jumble of nerve ends and sparks. "I don't care." Slowly, beautifully, her smile bloomed. She framed his face in her hands. "Welcome home." She let their slow, quiet kiss soothe them both.

"I've been told I have considerable finesse with women." Taking her hand, he closed it into a loose fist and pressed it to his lips. "Though it might be hard for you to believe at the moment."

"I'd rather not ask for corroboration."

His grin flashed. "Look, why don't we . . ." He trailed off as he stroked a hand over her hair. Confused, he pulled back, eyes narrowed, and studied her. "What in the hell did you do to your hair?"

In automatic defense, she combed her fingers through it. "I cut it. New Year's Eve." Her smile wavered. "The viewers like it—three to one. We did a poll."

"It's shorter than mine." With a half laugh, he moved back to squat on his haunches. "Come here, let me get a good look." Without waiting for assent, he hauled her to a sitting position.

She sat, pouting a little, her eyes daring him, and the lamplight glowing over the glistening cap. "I was tired of dealing with it," she muttered when he only continued his silent study. "This saves me hours a week, and it suits the shape of my face. It looks good on camera."

"Um-hmm." Fascinated, he reached out to toy with her earlobe, then skimmed his finger down the side of her throat. "Either several months of celibacy is playing hell with my libido, or you're the sexiest woman alive."

Delighted, flustered, she hugged her knees. "You look pretty good yourself. You know they're calling you the Desert Hunk."

He winced. After the ribbing he'd taken from his associates, he was hard-pressed to find the humor in it. "It'll pass."

"I don't know. There's already a fan club here in Chicago."

Seeing that he could be embarrassed only amused her. "You did look pretty hunky with Scuds flying in the sky behind you, or with tanks rolling across the sand at your back. Especially since you didn't shave for a couple of days."

"Once the ground war started, water was at a premium."

Her amusement faded. "Was it bad?"

"Bad enough." He took her hand, gently now, remembering to appreciate the elegance. That was what he needed, the warm reality of her. Maybe, in a day or two, the things he'd seen, the things he'd heard would fade a little.

"Do you want to talk about it?"

"No."

"You look tired." She could see now how drawn he was beneath the desert tan. "When did you get back?"

"About an hour ago. I came straight here."

Even as her heart picked up rhythm, she responded to the weariness in his eyes. "Why don't I fix you something to eat? You can get your bearings."

He kept her hand in his, wishing he could explain to her, to himself, how much steadier he felt being here. Being close. "I wouldn't turn down a sandwich, especially if it came with a beer."

"I can probably handle that." She got to her feet, gave his hand a tug. "Come on, stretch out on the couch, relax with Carson. While you're eating, I'll fill you in on all the news and gossip from CBC."

He rose, waiting until she'd punched the remote. "Are you going to let me stay tonight, Deanna?"

She looked back at him, her eyes huge, but steady. "Yes."

Turning quickly, she walked into the kitchen. Her hands were trembling, she realized. And it was wonderful. Her whole body was quivering in response to that long, last look he'd given her before she'd rushed away. She didn't know what it would be like, but she knew that she'd never wanted anyone more. The months of separation hadn't stunted the emotions that had begun growing inside her.

And that first greedy kiss as they'd tumbled heedless to the floor had been more stunning, more erotic than any fantasy she'd woven while she'd waited for him to come back.

He'd come to her. She pressed a hand to her stomach. Nerves were jittering, she thought. But they were good nerves, hot and strong, not cold, cowardly ones.

Tonight, she would take the step. She would reclaim herself. Because she wanted, Deanna thought. Because she chose.

Putting a sandwich of cold ham and cheese on a platter, she added a pilsner of beer. She lifted the tray and smiled to herself. Desire was as basic and human as hunger. Once they had satisfied the latter, she would take him to her bed, into her body.

"I could put together something hot," she said as she carried the tray back into the living room. "There's a can of soup in the—" Deanna broke off and stared.

Carnac the Magnificent was on a roll. Ed was hooting in response. And Finn Riley, the Desert Hunk, was sleeping like a baby.

He'd pried off his battered hightops, but hadn't bothered to remove his jacket. Unrelenting work, travel and jet lag had finally taken their toll. He lay flat on his stomach, his face smashed into one of Deanna's satin pillows, his arm dangling limply over the edge of the couch.

"Finn?" Deanna set the tray aside and put a hand on his shoulder. When she shook him, he didn't stir, a hundred and sixty pounds of exhausted male.

Resigned, she went for a spare blanket and tucked it around him. She locked the front door, secured the chain. Switching the lamp to low, she sat down on the floor in front of him. "Our timing," she said quietly and kissed his cheek, "continues to suck." With a sigh, she picked up the sandwich and tried to fill the void of sexual frustration with food and television.

*

FINN PULLED OUT OF THE dream, chilled with sweat. The fading vision behind his eyes was horrid—the body riddled with bullets at his feet, blood and gore staining the pink silk and sequins of the tattered evening gown. In the quiet light of morning, he struggled to sit up, rubbing his hands over his face.

Disoriented, he tried to get his bearings. Hotel room? What city? What country? A plane? A taxi?

Deanna. Remembering, Finn let his head fall back against the cushions and moaned. First he'd tossed her to the floor, then he'd passed out. A rousing segment in the frustrating journal of their romance.

He was surprised she hadn't dragged him out of the apartment by the feet and left him snoring in the hall. Fighting free of the blanket, he staggered up. He swayed a moment, his body still floating with fatigue. He'd have killed for coffee. He supposed that was why he thought he smelled some brewing. After months in the desert, he knew that mirages weren't only the result of heat, but of desperate human desires.

He rolled his stiff shoulders and swore. Christ, he didn't want to think about desires.

But maybe it wasn't too late. A quick injection of instant coffee, and he could slip into bed with Deanna and make up for his neglect the night before.

Bleary-eyed, he stumbled toward the kitchen.

She was no mirage, standing there in a beam of sunlight, looking fresh and lovely in slacks and a sweater, pouring gloriously scented coffee into a red ceramic mug.

"Deanna."

"Oh!" She jolted, nearly upending the mug. "You startled me. I was concentrating on some mental notes for the show." She set the pot down, brushed suddenly damp hands down her hips. "How'd you sleep?"

"Like a rock. I don't know whether to be embarrassed or apologetic, but if you share that coffee, I'll be anything you want."

"There's nothing to be embarrassed or apologetic about." But she couldn't meet his eyes as she reached for the mug. "You were exhausted."

He lightly stroked a hand over her hair. "How angry are you?"

"I'm not." But her gaze cut away from his when she pushed the mug into his hand. "Do you want cream or sugar?"

"No. If not angry, what?"

"It's hard to explain." There wasn't enough room in the kitchen, she realized. And he was blocking the way out. "I've really got to go, Finn. My driver will be here in a few minutes."

He stood his ground. "Try to explain."

"This isn't easy for me." Unnerved, she snapped out the words and turned away. "I'm not experienced in morning-after conversation."

"Nothing happened."

"That's not the point, not really. I wasn't thinking last night. I couldn't. When I saw you, I was overwhelmed by what was happening, what I was feeling. No one's ever wanted me the way you did last night."

"And I blew it." No longer interested in coffee, he set the mug carefully on the counter. "I'm sorry. Maybe I shouldn't have stopped that first mad rush, but I was afraid I'd hurt you."

She turned slowly, her eyes reflecting her confusion. "You weren't hurting me."

"I would have. Christ, Deanna, I could have eaten you alive. And tearing into you on the floor, it was . . ." He thought bitterly of Angela. "It was too careless."

"That's my point. Not on your side, Finn, on mine. I was careless, and that's not like me." There seemed to be nothing she could do with her hands. She lifted them, let them fall as he continued to stand and study her. "The feelings you've stirred up aren't like me. And the way things turned out . . ." She tugged at her earlobe. "It gave me time to think."

"Great." He snatched up the mug again and took a long drink. "Terrific."

"I haven't changed my mind," she said as she watched his eyes darken. "But we need to talk, before this goes any further. Once I explain, once you understand, I hope we can keep going."

There was a plea in her eyes, something she needed from him. He didn't have to know what it was to respond. Crossing to her, he cupped her chin in his hands and kissed her lightly. "Okay. We'll talk. Tonight?"

Nerves vanished in relief. "Yes, tonight. Fate must be looking out for me. It's the first free weekend I've had in two months."

"Come to my place." As her body softened beautifully against his, he kissed her again, lingering, persuasive. "There's something I very much want to do." He nipped at her lip until her eyes fluttered closed.

"Yes."

"I very, mmm, very much ..." He traced her lips with his tongue, dipped slowly inside to savor. "Want to cook for you."

"So, what's he going to cook?"

"I didn't ask." Briskly, Deanna checked over her wardrobe list, noting the dates that certain skirts, blazers, blouses and accessories had been worn. She had a production assistant who dated and tagged each piece, listing not only when it had been worn, but in combination with what other items.

"It's pretty serious when a man cooks for you—especially on a Friday night." Fran kept one eye on Aubrey, who was taking a peaceful nap in the Portacrib. "Very high-powered wooing."

"Maybe." Deanna smiled at the idea. Meticulously, she began to arrange her choices for the following week's line-up of shows. "I plan on enjoying it."

"My instincts tell me he's good for you. I'd like a little more time to check him out personally, but the look on your face when you came in this morning was almost enough."

"What kind of look?"

"Happiness. Strictly feminine happiness. Different from the gleam in your eye when Delacort renewed us, or when we got picked up by six new stations."

"How about when we moved into first place in Columbus?"

"Even different from that. This is all-important. The show, what you're able to do with it. The way you've shifted things around so I can bring Aubrey to work."

"I want her here, too," Deanna reminded her. "Nobody on staff is going to have to make the choice between parenthood and career. Which brings up a topic idea I had."

Fran picked up her clipboard. "Shoot."

"Finding ways to incorporate day care into the workplace. Right in office buildings and factories. I read an article about this restaurant, family-run. They have what amounts to a preschool right off the kitchen. I've already given Margaret the clipping."

"I'll check it out."

"Good. Now let me tell you my idea about Jeff."

"Jeff? What about him?"

"He's doing a good job, wouldn't you say?"

"I'd say he's doing a great one." Fran glanced over as Aubrey sighed in her sleep. "He's totally devoted to you and the show, and he's a wizard at cutting through the fat."

"He wants to direct." Pleased that she'd been able to surprise Fran, Deanna sat back. "He hasn't said anything to me, to anyone. He wouldn't. But I've watched him. You can see it by the way he hangs around the studio, talking to the cameramen, the techs. Every time we get a new director, Jeff all but interrogates him."

"He's an editor."

"I was a reporter," Deanna pointed out. "I want to give him a shot. God knows we need a permanent director, somebody who can slide into the groove, who understands my rhythm. I think he'll fit the bill. What, as executive producer, do you think?"

"I'll talk to him," Fran said after a moment. "If he's interested, we've got a show scheduled for next week on video dating. It's light. We could test him out on it."

"Good."

"Deanna." Cassie stood in the doorway, a newspaper rolled tight in her hand.

"Don't tell me. I've only got twenty minutes before shooting the new promo, and after that I've got to get across town and charm the Chicago chapter of NOW. I swear, warden, I wasn't trying to make a break for it."

"Deanna," Cassie repeated. There was no humor in her eyes. Only distress. "I think you should see this."

"What is it? Oh, not the tabloids again." Prepared to be mildly irked, she took the paper from Cassie, unfolded it and glanced at the screaming headline. "Oh my God." Her knees went to jelly as she groped behind her for a chair. "Oh, Fran."

"Take it easy, honey. Let me see." Fran eased Deanna down into a chair and took the paper.

SECRET LIFE OF AMERICA'S GIRL NEXT DOOR
Midwest's Darling a Party-Hardy College Girl
Deanna's Former Lover Tells All!

There was a big red EXCLUSIVE! bannering the corner, and a sidebar hinting at WILD NIGHTS! DRUNKEN ORGIES! SEX ON THE FIFTY-YARD LINE! beneath a recent photo of Deanna. Beside her was a grainy photograph of a man she'd tried to forget.

"That son of a bitch!" Fran exploded. "That lying bastard. Why the hell did he go to the tabs with this? He's dripping with money."

"Who knows why anyone does anything." Sickened, Deanna stared at the bold headlines. The frightened, broken girl she had been resurfaced. "He got his picture in the paper, didn't he?"

"Honey." Fran quickly turned the paper over. "Nobody's going to believe that trash."

"Of course they are, Fran." Her eyes were bright and hard.

"They'll believe it because it makes titillating copy. And most people won't get past the headlines anyway. They'll scan them when they're checking out in the supermarket. Maybe they'll read the copy on the front page, even flip through to the inside. Then they'll go home and chat about the story with their neighbors."

"It's crap. Exploitive crap, and anybody with a working brain knows it."

"I just thought you should know." Cassie handed Deanna a cup of water. "I didn't want you finding out from someone else."

"You were right."

Cassie pressed her lips together. "You've gotten some calls on it." Including one, which she would not pass on, from Marshall Pike.

"I'll handle them later. Let me see, Fran."

"I'm going to fucking burn this rag."

"Let me see," Deanna repeated. "I can't deal with it if I don't know what it says."

Fran reluctantly handed the paper to her. As with the worst of tabloid press, there was just enough truth mixed in with the lies to have impact. She had indeed gone to Yale. And she had dated Jamie Thomas, a star tackle. Yes, she had attended a postgame party with him in the autumn of her junior year. She'd danced, she'd flirted. She'd consumed more alcohol than might have been wise.

She certainly had taken a walk to the playing field with him on that cool, clear night. And she had laughed as he'd rushed over the grass, tackling invisible opponents. She'd even laughed when he'd tackled her. But the story didn't say that she'd stopped laughing very quickly. There was no mention of fear, of outrage, of sobbing.

In Jamie's recollection she hadn't fought. She hadn't screamed. In his version he hadn't left her alone, her clothes torn, her body bruised. He didn't say how she'd wept on that chilly grass, her spirit shattered and her innocence violently stolen.

"Well." Deanna brushed a tear from her cheek. "He hasn't changed his story over the years. Maybe he's embellished it a little more, but that's to be expected."

"I think we should contact Legal." It took all of Fran's control to speak calmly. "You should sue Jamie Thomas and the paper for libel, Dee. You're not going to let him get away with it."

"I let him get away with a lot worse, didn't I?" Very neatly, very deliberately, she folded the paper, then tucked it into her purse. "Cassie, please clear my schedule after the NOW meeting. I know it may cause some problems."

"No problem," Cassie said instantly. "I'll take care of it."

"Cancel everything," Fran told her.

"No, I can do what I have to do." Deanna picked up her sweater. However steady her voice, her movements, her eyes were devastated.

"Then I'll go with you. You're not going home alone."

"I'm not going home at all. There's someone I need to talk to. I'll be fine." She squeezed Fran's arm. "Really. I'll see you Monday."

"Damn it, Dee, let me help."

"You always have. I really have to do this one thing alone. I'll call you."

SHE DIDN'T EXPECT THE explanation to be easy. But she hadn't known she would find herself sitting in the driveway beside Finn's beautiful old house, fighting for the courage to walk up and knock on the door.

She sat watching the bare limbs of the spreading maples tremble in the high March wind. She wanted to watch the strong, white sunlight flash and gleam off the tall, graceful windows, and glint off the tiny flecks of mica in the weathered stone.

Such a sturdy old house, she thought, with its curving gables and arrow-straight chimneys. It looked like a dependable place, a haven against storms and wind. She wondered if he'd chosen to give himself some personal calm away from the chaos of his work.

She wondered if it would offer her any.

Bracing herself, she stepped from the car, walked along the

walkway of stones and stepped up onto the covered porch he'd had painted a deep, glossy blue.

There was a brass knocker in the shape of an Irish harp. She stared at it a long time before she knocked.

"Deanna." He smiled, holding out a hand in welcome. "It's a little early for dinner, but I can fix you a late lunch."

"I need to talk to you."

"So you said." He let his hand drop when she didn't take it, then closed the door. "You look pale." Hell, he thought, she looked as fragile as glass. "Why don't you sit down?"

"I'd like to sit." She followed him into the first room off the hallway.

Her first distracted glimpse of the room simply registered man. No frills, no flounces, just sturdy, dignified old pieces that murmured of easy wealth and masculine taste. She chose a high-backed chair in front of the fire that burned low. The warmth was comforting.

Without asking, he walked to a curved cabinet and chose a decanter of brandy. Whatever was preying on her mind went deep enough to make her withdraw.

"Drink this first, then tell me what's on your mind."

She sipped, then started to speak.

"Finish it," he interrupted impatiently. "I've seen wounded soldiers with more color than you have right now."

She sipped again, more deeply, and felt the heat fight with the ice shivering in her stomach. "There's something I want to show you." She opened her bag, took out the paper. "You should read this first."

He glanced down. "I've already seen it." In a gesture of disdain, he tossed it aside. "You've got more sense than to let that kind of tripe get to you."

"Did you read it?"

"I stopped reading poorly written fiction when I was ten."

"Read it now," Deanna insisted. "Please."

He studied her another minute, concerned and confused. "All right."

She couldn't sit after all. While he read, Deanna got up to wander around the room, her hands reaching nervously for mementos and knickknacks. She heard the paper rattle in his hands, heard him swear quietly, viciously under his breath, but she didn't look back.

"You know," Finn said at length, "at least they could hire people who can write a decent sentence." A glance at her rigid back made him sigh. He tossed the paper aside again. He rose, crossing to lay his hands on her shoulders. "Deanna—"

"Don't." She stepped away quickly, shaking her head.

"For Christ's sake, you've got too much sense to let some sloppy journalism turn you inside out." He couldn't stem the impatience, or the vague disappointment in her reaction. "You're in the spotlight. You chose to be. Toughen up, Kansas, or go back and stick with the noon news."

"Did you believe it?" She whirled around, her arms folded tight across her chest.

For the life of him he couldn't figure out how to handle her. He tried for mild amusement. "That you were some sort of nubile nymphomaniac? If you were, how could you have resisted me for so long?"

He was hoping for a laugh, and would have settled for an angry retort. He got nothing but frozen silence. "It's not all a lie," she said at length.

"You mean you actually went to a couple of parties in college? You popped the top on a few beers and had a fling with a jock?" He shook his head. "Well, I'm shocked and disillusioned. I'm glad I found this out before I asked you to marry me and have my children."

Again, his joke didn't make her laugh. Her eyes went from blank to devastated. And she burst into terrible tears.

"Oh, Christ. Don't, baby. Come on, Deanna, don't do this."

Nothing could have unmanned him more. Awkward, cursing himself, he gathered her close, determined to hold her tight, even when she resisted. "I'm sorry." For what, he couldn't say. "I'm sorry, baby."

"He raped me!" she shouted, jerking away when his arms went limp. "He raped me," she repeated, covering her face with her hands as the tears fell hot and burning. "And I didn't do anything about it. I won't do anything now. Because it hurts." Her voice broke on a sob as she rocked back and forth. "It never, never stops hurting."

He couldn't have been more shocked, more horrified. For a moment, everything in him froze and he could only stand and stare as she wept uncontrollably into her hands with the sun at her back and the fire crackling cheerfully beside her.

Then the ice inside him broke, exploded with a burst of fury so ripe, so raw that his vision hazed. His hands curled into fists, as if there were something tangible he could pummel.

But there was nothing but Deanna, weeping.

His arms dropped to his sides again, leaving him feeling helpless and miserable. Relying on instinct, he scooped her up, carried her to the couch, where he could sit, cradled her in his lap until the worst of the tears were spent.

"I was going to tell you," she managed. "I spent last night thinking about it. I wanted you to know before we tried—to be together."

He had to get past the anger, somehow. But his jaw was clenched and his words sharp. "Did you think it would change anything I feel for you?"

"I don't know. But I know it scars you, and no matter how many ways you're able to go on with your life, it's always in there. Since it happened . . ." She took the handkerchief he offered and mopped at her face. "I haven't been able to put it aside far enough, or deep enough, to feel able to make love with a man."

The hand that was stroking her hair faltered only a moment. He remembered vividly the way he had plunged in the night before.

And the way he would have initiated the physical end of their relationship if something hadn't restrained him.

"I'm not cold," she said in a tight, bitter voice. "I'm not."

"Deanna." He eased her head back so that she would meet his eyes. "You're the warmest woman I know."

"Last night there was nothing there but you; I had no time to think. This morning it didn't seem fair for you not to know first. Because if things didn't work, physically, it would be my fault. Not yours."

"I think that's the first really stupid thing I've ever heard you say. But we'll put it aside for now. If you want to talk this through, I'll listen."

"I do." But she shifted away so that she could sit on her own. "Everyone on campus knew Jamie Thomas. He was a year ahead of me, and like most of the other women in college, I had a crush on him. So when he made a move in my direction at the beginning of my junior year, I was flattered and dazzled. He was a football star, and a track star, and he had a three-point-oh average. I admired that, and his plans to go into the family firm. He had brains and ambition, a good sense of humor. Everybody liked him. So did I."

She took a steadying breath, let herself remember. "We saw a lot of each other during the first couple months of that semester. We studied together, and went for long walks and had all those deep, philosophical discussions college students can be so smug about. I sat in the stands at football games and cheered him on."

She paused. "We went to a party after the biggest game of the season. He'd had a terrific game. Everybody was celebrating, and we got a little drunk. We went back to the field, just he and I, and he started to run through all these football moves. Clowning around. Then he stopped clowning, and he was on top of me. It seemed all right at first. But he got really rough, and he frightened me. I told him to stop. But he wouldn't stop."

Cut the act, Dee. You know you want it. You've been begging for it all night.

She shuddered, gripping her hands tight. "And I started crying, begging him. And he was so strong, and I couldn't get away. He was tearing my clothes. He was hurting me."

Goddamn tease.

"I called for help, but there was no one. I screamed. He put his hand over my mouth when I screamed. He had big hands. And I could only see his face."

You're going to love it, babe.

"His eyes were glazed—like glass. And he was inside me. It hurt so much I thought he would kill me. But he didn't stop. He didn't stop until he'd finished. After a while—it seemed like such a long time—he rolled off me, and he laughed."

Come on, Dee, you know you had fun. Ask around. Nobody makes the women happy like good old Jamie.

"Then he stopped laughing, and he got angry because I was crying. I couldn't stop crying."

Don't pull that shit with me. We both wanted it. You say anything different and half the football team will say you made it with them, right here. Right on the fucking fifty-yard line.

"He yanked me up, stuck his face in mine. And he warned me that if I tried to pretend I hadn't been willing, no one would believe me. Because he was Jamie Thomas. And everyone liked Jamie. So he left me there, and I didn't do anything. Because I was ashamed."

The grainy newspaper photo swam into Finn's mind, and he struggled against the violence that rose in him. But he kept his tone even. "Didn't you have anyone to go to?"

"I told Fran." Her nails were biting into her palm and slowly, deliberately she relaxed her hand. "After a couple of weeks, I couldn't hide it from her. She wanted to go to the dean, but I wouldn't." She stared down at her own hands and felt the hot shame wash over her again. "She finally bullied me into counseling. After a while, I got over the worst of it. I don't want it to control my life, Finn." She looked at him then, eyes swollen and full of grief. "I don't want it to spoil what we may be able to have."

232

He was afraid any words he tried might be the wrong ones. "Deanna, I can't tell you it doesn't matter, because it does." When she dropped her gaze, he touched her cheek, urging her eyes back up to his. "Because I can't stand the thought of you being hurt that way. And because you may not be able to trust me."

"It isn't that," she said quickly. "It's me."

"Then let me do something for you." Gently, he kissed her forehead. "Come to the cabin with me. Now. Today. Just a weekend alone where we can relax."

"Finn, I don't know if I can give you what you want."

"I don't care about what you can give me. I'm more interested in what we can give each other."

Chapter Fifteen

SHE SUPPOSED HE CALLED THE PLACE A CABIN BECAUSE IT was built of wood. Far from the primitive box she'd imagined, the trim, two-story structure had upper and lower covered decks joined by open stairs. Outside, the cedar shingles had silvered with weather and time and were accented by deep blue shutters. Tall, spreading yews tucked the house into its own private reserve.

Instead of a lawn, rocks, low evergreens, flowering bushes, herbs and hardy perennials covered the ground. A few brave crocuses were already peeking through.

"You garden. How did you learn?"

"I read a lot of books." Finn hauled their suitcases from the trunk while Deanna stood at the head of the gravel drive and looked around. "I never know how long I'll be away, so grass wasn't practical. I didn't like the idea of hiring a lawn service. It's mine." Faintly embarrassed by the statement, he shrugged. "So I spent a few weeks putting in stuff that wouldn't need a lot of attention."

"It's beautiful."

He'd wanted her to think so, he realized. "It'll look better in another month or two. Let's go inside. I'll start a fire, then show you around."

She followed him up to the porch, ran her hand along the arm of a rocking chair. "It's hard to picture you sitting here, looking out over a rockery and doing nothing."

"It'll get easier," he promised, and led her inside.

The cabin opened up into a large room, topped by a loft and a quartet of skylights. One wall was dominated by a fireplace fashioned of river rock; another was crowded with books on built-in shelves. The paneling was the color of honey, as was the flooring, over which he'd scattered rugs—Orientals, French, English, Indian. And, incredibly, the lush black sheen of a bear rug, complete with snarling head and claws.

Catching her eye, Finn grinned. "It was a gift—some of the guys from the station."

"Is it real?"

"Afraid so." He crossed to the hearth, where the bear spread like a wide black pool. "I call him Bruno. Since I'm not the one who shot him, we get along pretty well."

"I guess he's ... good company."

"And he doesn't eat much." He sensed her nerves, shivering along the chilled air. And he understood them. He'd rushed her out of Chicago before she'd been able to think things through. Now she was alone with him. "Colder in here than it is outside."

"Yes." She rubbed her hands as she wandered to one of the windows to study his view. There was no other house to disturb the panorama, only those lush yews and trees not yet greening. "It doesn't seem that we could be only an hour or so out of the city."

"I wanted somewhere I could get away." He built a fire competently, quickly. "And where I could get back quickly if a story broke. There's a TV, radio and fax machine in the other room."

"Oh, I see. You can take the boy out of the newsroom ... That's nice," she said, and walked over to where the wood was beginning to crackle and spark.

"There's another fireplace upstairs." He took her bag and gestured toward the steps that led to the loft.

The second floor held one large bedroom that echoed the simple furnishings of the main room. A sitting area in front of a window contained a love seat in deep hunter green, another rocker, a low pine table and a three-footed stool. The gleaming brass bed was covered with burgundy corduroy and faced a small stone fireplace. There was a pine dresser and a roomy armoire.

"Bath's through there." Finn indicated the door with a nod of his head as he crouched to set the fire.

Curious, Deanna nudged the door open. Staring, she stood on the threshold unsure whether to laugh or applaud. Although the rest of the cabin might have reflected rustic elegance, in the bathroom, Finn had gone for dramatic.

The ebony, oversized tub was fitted with jets and surrounded by a ledge that snugged against a wide window. The separate shower was constructed of glass block and white tile. The wall over the sink was mirrored and hugged by a long counter of black-and-white tiles, as neat as a chessboard. A portable television sat on it, facing the tub.

"Some bathroom."

"If you're going to relax," Finn commented as he rose, "you might as well relax."

"No TV in the bedroom?"

Finn opened one door of the armoire. There, atop a trio of drawers, was the blank eye of a television screen. "There's a shortwave in the drawer of the nightstand." When she laughed, he held out a hand. "Come down and keep me company while I cook dinner."

"You, ah, didn't bring your bags up," she said as they started down.

"There's another bedroom downstairs."

"Oh." She felt the tension dissolve, even as she was pricked by regret.

He stopped at the base of the steps, turned, put his hands on her shoulders and kissed her lightly. "Okay?"

She rested her brow against his a moment. "Yes," she said. "Okay."

And it was, sitting at the breakfast bar putting a salad together while Finn sliced potatoes into thin strips for frying, listening to the high March wind blow through the evergreens and tap at the windows. It was easy, relaxing in the country kitchen while potatoes fried and chicken grilled and laughing at his stories of adventures in the marketplaces in Casablanca.

All the while the kitchen TV murmured, keeping the world in the background, and somehow making the atmosphere they shared more intimate.

The room was warm and cozy, with dark curtaining the windows and candles flickering on the kitchen table. "It's wonderful," she told him after another bite of chicken. "You're as good as Bobby Marks."

"And I'm cuter."

"Well, you've got more hair. I suppose I should offer to cook tomorrow."

"That depends." He curled his fingers around hers, grazed his teeth over her knuckles. "How are you at broiling fresh fish?"

"Is that what's on the menu?"

"If our luck holds. We should be able to pull a couple out of the lake in the morning."

"In the morning?" She blinked. "We're going fishing in the morning?"

"Sure. What do you think I brought you up here for?" When she laughed he shook his head. "Kansas, you don't understand the master plan. After we've dropped line together for a couple of hours, pulled in trout together, cleaned them—"

"Cleaned them?"

"Sure. After all that, you won't be able to resist me. The excitement, the passion, the elemental sexuality of fishing will have overwhelmed you."

"Or will have bored me senseless."

"Have a little faith. There's nothing like man—or woman— against nature to stir up the juices."

"That's quite a plan." She tipped back in her chair, amazingly relaxed. "Have you had much success with it?"

He only grinned and topped off their wine. "Want to look at my lures?"

"I don't think so. You can surprise me tomorrow."

"I'll wake you up at five."

The glass froze an inch from her lips. "At five? A.M.?"

"Dress warm," he warned her.

DEANNA HAD BEEN CERTAIN she'd be restless, had been sure her nerves would resurface the moment the house was quiet around her. But the instant she'd snuggled under the blankets, she'd dropped into a deep, dreamless sleep. A sleep that was rudely disturbed by a hand shaking her shoulder.

She opened her eyes, blinked into the dark and closed them again.

"Come on, Kansas, rise and shine."

"Is there a war?" she mumbled into the pillow.

"There's a fish with your name on it," Finn told her. "Coffee'll be ready in ten minutes."

She sat up, blinked again and was able to make out his silhouette beside the bed. And she could smell him—soap and damp skin. "How come you have to catch fish at dawn?"

"Some traditions are sacred." He leaned down, unerringly finding her warm, sleepy mouth with his. Her sigh of response had his muscles tightening, and his mind skidding toward an entirely different morning activity. "You'll want that long underwear I told you to pack." He cleared his throat, forced himself to step back before he gave up and crawled under the blankets with her. "It'll be cold out on the lake."

He left her huddled in bed. He hadn't slept well. Big surprise,

238

Finn thought wryly. She needed time, he reminded himself. And care. And patience. What she didn't need was for him to unstrap the desire that was clawing inside of him. It would frighten her, he was sure, if she understood just how much he wanted.

It very nearly frightened him.

THERE WAS FOG ON THE LAKE. Light fingers of it tore like cotton in the breeze and muffled the sound of the boat's motor. In the east the sky was struggling to light, and the silver sun glanced off the mist, hinting at rainbows. She could smell water and pine, and the soap from Finn's shower. Deanna sat at the bow of the small boat, her hands resting on her knees, the collar of her jacket turned up against the chill.

"It's beautiful." Her breath puffed out in smoke. "Like we're the only ones around for miles."

"The Senachwine gets plenty of campers and hikers." He cut the engine and let the boat drift on water as calm as glass. "We've probably got company on the lake already."

"It's so quiet." But she did hear, in the distance, the putt of another engine, the call of a bird and the faint lap of water against the hull.

"That's the best thing about fishing." After dropping anchor, he handed her a rod. "You can't rush it. You can't crowd it. All you have to do is sit in one spot and let your mind rest."

"Let your mind rest," she repeated.

"What we're doing here is float fishing," he began. "It takes more finesse than bait fishing."

"Right."

"No sarcasm, please. It's an art."

"Art? Really."

"The art," Finn continued, "is to lay the float gently on the surface so that it entices the fish as you skillfully reel it back."

Deanna glanced up from her study of the pretty lures and looked out over the water. "I don't see any fish."

"You will. Trust me. Now you're going to cast the line out. It's all in the wrist."

"That's what my father always says about horseshoes."

"This is every bit as serious." He moved surefootedly to her end of the boat.

"Horseshoes are serious?"

"Christ, Deanna, don't you know anything? When a man needs to relax, to unwind, it doesn't mean he doesn't want competition."

She grinned when he shifted her hands on the rod. "My father would like you."

"Sounds like a sensible man. Now keep your hands firm, wrists supple." He steadied her, casting the line out so that it landed with a quiet plop in the still waters. Ripples ringed magically around the lure, spreading, delighting her.

"I did it!" Beaming, she looked over her shoulder at Finn. "Okay, *you* did it, but I helped."

"Not bad. You have potential." He took up his own rod, chose a lure. He cast off soundlessly, with barely a ripple on the lake. Through Deanna's pleasure came the hot spirit of competition.

"I want to do it again."

"You're supposed to do it again. But you have to reel it in first." Her brow arched. "I knew that."

"Slow," he said, with a hint of a smile as he demonstrated. "Smooth. Patience is as much an art as casting."

"So we just sit here, and keep tossing the line out and bringing it back in?"

"That's the idea. I get to sit here and look at you. Which is a pretty good way to spend the morning. Now if you were a man, we'd liven things up by telling lies—about fish and women."

Her brow was knitted in concentration as she cast off again. Her lure did not land soundlessly, but she enjoyed its celebratory plop. "In that order, I imagine."

"Generally, you mix it up. Barlow James and I once spent six hours out here. I don't think we told each other a single truth."

"I can lie."

"Nope. Not with those eyes. I'll make it easy for you; tell me about your family."

"I've got three brothers." She stared at the lure, looking for action. "Two older and one younger. The older two are married, and the youngest is still in college. Should I, like, move this around or anything?"

"No, just relax. Are they all still in Kansas?"

"Yeah. My father owns a hardware business, and my oldest brother went in with him. My mother keeps the books. What are you doing?"

"Playing this one out," he said calmly as he reeled in. "He's hooked."

"You've got one." She leaned forward in the boat, jerking her line. "Already?"

"Did you grow up in the city or the suburbs?"

"The 'burbs," she said impatiently. "How come you've got one already? Oh, look!" She stared, fascinated, as he drew the fish out of the lake. It wriggled, the strengthening sun flashing off its fins. The fascination remained as he netted it and plopped it onto the bottom of the boat. "You must have used a better lure than mine," she said as Finn removed it and laid the fish on ice.

"Want to trade?"

The stubborn line creased her brow. "No." She studied him as he cast off again. Determined, she reeled in, shifted positions, then cast off the opposite side of the boat with more enthusiasm than style.

When Finn only grinned at her, she put her nose in the air. "What about your family?"

"I don't have any to speak of. My parents divorced when I was fifteen. I was the only child. They're both lawyers." He braced his rod so that he could uncap the thermos of coffee and pour for both of them. "They buried each other under a very civilized mountain of papers, and agreed to split everything fifty-fifty. Including me."

241

"I'm sorry."

"What for?" It wasn't a bitter question, but a simple one. "Family ties don't run strong in the Rileys. We each have our own life, and prefer it that way."

"I don't mean to criticize, but that sounds awfully cold."

"It is cold." He sipped coffee and absorbed the quiet pleasure of the chilly morning with the sun breaking over the water. "It's also practical. We don't have anything in common but blood. Why pretend otherwise?"

She didn't know how to respond. She was far away from her family, but the connection was there, always there. "They must be proud of you."

"I'm sure they're pleased that the money they spent on my education wasn't wasted. Don't look like that." He reached out and patted her ankle. "I wasn't traumatized or scarred. The fact is, it's been a plus careerwise. If you don't have roots, you don't have to keep ripping them out every time you get an assignment."

Perhaps there was no need to feel sympathy for the man, but she couldn't prevent it spreading in her for the boy he'd been. "Roots don't have to hold you back," she said quietly. "Not if you know how to transplant them."

"Kansas?"

"Yes?"

"You've got a bite."

"I've got—oh!" Her line tugged again. If Finn hadn't reached out and held her still, she would have leaped up and capsized them. "What do I do? I forgot. Wait, wait," she said, before he could reply. "I want to do it myself."

Brow puckered in concentration, she turned the reel, feeling the resistance as the fish fought back. There was a moment when she felt an urge to release it. Then the line went taut, and the spirit of competition overwhelmed everything else.

When she finally dropped the catch awkwardly in the bottom of the boat, she shouted with laughter. "He's bigger than yours."

"Maybe."

She slapped Finn's hand aside before he could remove the lure. "I'll do it."

With the sun rising higher in the east, they grinned at each other over a five-pound trout.

THEY CARRIED FOUR FISH back to the cabin with them. Two apiece. Deanna had argued hotly for a tie breaker, but Finn had started the motor. You didn't catch more than you could eat, he'd told her as he cleaned them.

"That was great." Still revved, Deanna spun around the kitchen. "Really great. I feel like a pioneer. Are we going to have fish for lunch?"

"Sure. We'll fry some up. Let me beef up the fire in the living room first."

"I really thought it would be boring," she said, following him in. "I mean that in a good way." Laughing, she combed a hand through her hair. "But it was exciting, too. I don't know. Satisfying." She laughed again.

"You've got a knack for it." Finn added another log, sat back on his heels. "We can go out for a couple hours tomorrow morning before we head back."

"I'd like that." She watched the firelight dance over his forearm as he prodded the quiet flames into a roar. His profile was to her, relaxed, his eyes dark as they stared into the fire. His hair fell over his brow, curled above the collar of his shirt. "I'm glad you brought me here."

He looked over his shoulder, smiled. "So am I."

"Not just for the fishing lesson."

His smile faded, but his eyes stayed on hers. "I know."

"You brought me here to get me away from the papers, and the talk, and the ugliness." She looked past him, into the fire, where the flames were rising. "You haven't asked me any more questions."

He laid down the poker and turned to face her. "Did you want me to?"

"I don't know." She tried for a smile. "What question would you ask?"

He asked the one that had kept him restless through the night. "Are you afraid of me?"

She hesitated. "A little," she heard herself say. "More afraid of what you can make me feel."

He glanced back at the fire. "I won't pressure you, Deanna. Nothing happens between us that you don't want." He looked back at her now, his eyes dark, intense. "I promise."

Rather than relaxing, the tension coiled in her stomach; his words, and her certainty that he would keep them, balled it tighter. "It's not that kind of fear, Finn. It's . . . seductive."

The look in his eyes made her body yearn. She turned away quickly so that she could say it all, say it quickly. "Because of what happened, I've never been able to get back what I lost. Until you." She turned back slowly. The nerves were vicious. She could feel her heart pounding strong and hard in her breast. "I think, until you. And I'm afraid of that. And afraid that I might spoil it."

Though he stood, he didn't approach her. "Whatever happens between us happens to and because of both of us. It'll wait until you're ready."

She looked down at her hands, linked tight in front of her. "I'd like to ask you a question."

"All right."

"Are you afraid of me?"

She stood there, lashes concealing her eyes, slim and fragile-looking in the oversized shirt. A log shifted lazily behind him and sent out a short, small burst of sparks.

"Deanna, I've never been so afraid of anything in my life as I am of you, and what you can make me feel."

Her lashes lifted then. And she was no longer so fragile, not with her eyes huge and smoky, her lips softly curved. The first step toward him was the hardest. Then it was easy, to walk to him, to slip her arms around him, to rest her head on his shoulder.

"I couldn't have asked for a better answer. Finn, I don't want to lose what I'm feeling right now." When he didn't move, she looked up, lifted her hands to his chest. "I don't think I will if you make love with me."

Of all the emotions he'd expected to feel, alarm was the last. Yet it was alarm that came first, swiftly, overpoweringly, as she looked up at him with trust and doubt warring in her eyes. "There's no pressure here, Deanna."

"There is. Not from you. In me." Was that his heart racing under her palm? she wondered. How could it be beating so fast when he was watching her so calmly, when his hands were so light on her shoulders. "I need you."

It wasn't merely desire that stabbed through him at the words. There was something sharper and hotter fused with it. His hands slid from her shoulders to her face, cupping it as he lowered his mouth to hers.

"I won't hurt you."

"I know," she said, but trembled nonetheless. "I'm not afraid of that."

"Yes, you are." And he regretted that, bitterly. "But you won't be." He promised that, fiercely. "You only have to tell me to stop."

"I won't." There was determination in her eyes again. He swore to himself he would change it to pleasure.

Her mouth went dry when he unbuttoned her shirt. Slowly, his eyes on hers, he peeled away the first layer, cast it aside. Then smiled. "This is going to take a while."

Her laugh bubbled out, nervous and shaky. "I've got plenty of time."

Her eyes closed, her mouth lifted to his. It was right, so simply, so easily right to press her body to his, to lift her arms and take him to her. She shivered again when he tugged the turtleneck away. But it wasn't from cold. Nor was it from fear. Still her breath caught when he lifted her into his arms and laid her on the thick pelt of the hearthrug.

"I don't want you to think of anything but me." He kissed her again, lingered over it before sitting back to tug off her boots. "No one but me."

"No, I'm not. I can't."

Sun and firelight danced over her closed lids. She listened to it hiss and spark, heard the rustle as he removed his own shirt, pried off his boots. Then he was beside her, gently stroking her face until she opened her eyes and looked at him.

"I wanted you from the first moment I saw you."

She smiled, willing herself to relax, to beat back those little frissons of doubt. "Almost a year ago."

"Longer." His lips toyed with hers, warmed them, waited for hers to respond. "You came running into the newsroom. You headed straight for your desk, then you pulled back your hair with this red ribbon and started beating out copy. It was a few days before I left for London." He skimmed a hand over the insulating silk covering her torso, barely touching her, hinting only of what could be. "I watched you for a while. It was like someone had hit me with a hammer. All those months later, I saw you standing on the tarmac in the rain."

"And you kissed me."

"I'd saved it up for six months."

"Then you stole my story."

"Yeah." He grinned, then lowered his mouth to her curved lips. "And now I've got you."

She stiffened instinctively when his hand slipped under the silk. But he didn't grope, didn't rush. In moments, the easy caress of his fingers on her skin had her muscles loosening. When they slid up to circle her breast, her body curved to welcome them.

Like warm rain, this pleasure was soft and quiet and soothing. She accepted it, absorbed it, then ached for it, as he slowly undressed her.

The heat from the fire radiated out, but she felt only his hands, molding gently, exploring, arousing. His touch lingered, then moved on, lighting flames in which those tiny raindrops of pleasure began to sizzle. When she trembled now, she trembled from the heat. And her breath strangled in her throat.

He no longer felt the beast clawing at him. There was a sweetness here, and a power. He knew as his lips roamed from hers down to the swell of her breasts that she was his, as completely, as absolutely as if they had been lovers for years.

Her body was like water in his hands, rising and falling with the tide of pleasure they brought to each other. He heard the wind scraping at the windows, the spit of the fire in the hearth. And the sound of his name whispering from her lips.

He knew he could make her float, as she was floating now, her eyes like smoke and her muscles like warmed wax. And he knew he had only to inch her higher, just a bit higher, to watch her break through those clouds into the storm.

She felt his teeth scrape over her hip, and the hand she was stroking through his hair went taut. Heat coiled hot in her belly as his tongue streaked over her. She shook her head to refuse it, to will away the sudden, uncontrollable quivering. Then the furnace of pressure built so quickly. She writhed, struggling toward it, struggling away. She tried to call out, to tell him to wait, to give her a moment to prepare. But the pleasure geysered through her, spurting molten through her system.

He watched the instant of frantic denial, the stunned panic, the mindless pleasure. Everything she felt echoed inside him. As breathless as she, he levered himself over her, raining kisses over her glowing face until she was wrapped around him, until her movements grew frantic and his own churning need demanded release.

"Look at me." He fought the words out of his burning throat. "Look at me."

And when she did, when their eyes met, held, he slipped inside her. Slowly, his hands fisted in the rug as if he could grip control there, he lowered to her, felt her rise to meet him until they moved together silkily.

When her lips curved, he pressed his face to her throat and took them both over the edge.

Chapter Sixteen

STILL DREAMING, SHE TURNED TO HIM, AND HE WAS THERE. Arms moving to enfold her, body ready to possess her. As the warm light of dawn slid lazily into the room, they joined again. Rhythm fluid, flesh warm, passions met. It was so easy, so effortless, to glide together, without hurry, without thought, while the air throbbed as steady as a pulse.

The ebb and flow of their bodies, the movement of sex as simple as breathing, had her lips curving before they met his in a long, deep, dusky kiss.

When their needs peaked, as gentle as the morning, she sighed out his name and drifted from dream to reality to find him still pulsing inside her, a second heartbeat.

"Finn." She spoke again, smiling into the quiet morning light. The cross he wore pressed against her skin, just below her heart.

"Hmmm?"

"This is an even better way to start the day than fishing."

He chuckled, nuzzling at her neck. "Yesterday morning all I could think about was crawling into this bed with you."

Her smile spread. "Well, you're here now."

"It seems I am." He lifted his head, studying her as he toyed with the hair at her temple. Her eyes were big and sleepy, her skin glowing with that translucent polish that was the afterflush of good sex. "We overslept."

"No." Delighted with how easy it was, she ran her hands down his back to the taut skin of his buttocks. "We slept perfect. Absolutely perfect."

"You know . . ." He cupped her breast, rubbing his thumb over the nipple and watching her lips part on an unsteady breath. "I was going to teach you how to fly-fish this morning."

At his gentle tug, fresh arousal settled in her belly. "Were you?"

"A dry fly-fisherman is the aristocrat of angling. It takes . . . a master's touch."

She turned her head when he lowered his mouth to her throat. "I could learn."

"I think you could." He scraped his teeth over the pulse that fluttered like bird wings. There was nothing, he decided, more erotic than feeling a woman open herself to pleasure. "I believe you have unlimited potential."

She sighed, tightening in response as he hardened inside her. "I always want to be the best. It's probably a flaw."

"I don't think so," he murmured. She arched to meet him, already shuddering over the first peak. "It's definitely a virtue."

"DEANNA, WHY WOULD A sharp woman like you continue this sentimental attachment to a loser?"

"It's not sentimental." Deanna sniffed as she unlocked the door to her apartment. "It's a very practical, very logical loyalty. The Cubs are going to surprise everyone this year."

"Yeah, right." After indulging in a snort, Finn followed her inside. "It would be a surprise if they managed to crawl out of the basement. When's the last time the Cubs came close?"

That stung. "That's not the point." Her voice, despite her best intentions, was very prim. "They have heart."

"Too bad they don't have bats."

She stuck her nose in the air and turned to her answering machine. "Excuse me. I have to check my messages."

"No problem." Grinning, he dropped down on the couch. "We can finish this later. I probably didn't mention that I was captain of the debate team in college. And this is one I can't lose."

To show her disdain, she stabbed the Play button.

"Deanna, Cassie. Sorry to bother you at home—even if you're not there. We've got a couple of changes in Monday's schedule. I'll just fax them to you. If you have any questions, you know where to reach me. And, oh hell, we've had a lot of calls on the tabloid article. I've screened a lot of them out, but if you want to respond, I have a list of reporters you may want to agree to speak with. I'll be in most of the weekend. Call if you want me to set something up."

"She never asked any questions," Deanna murmured. "No one at the office asked any questions at all."

"They know you."

She nodded, switching off the machine for a moment. "You know, Finn, as hard as the job can be, as much energy as it demands, I wake up some mornings with the feeling that I've fallen into clover."

"If you ask me, making a living out of chatting for an hour a day smells more like gravy."

That made her smile a little. "You handle the earthquakes. I'll handle the heartaches."

He tugged off his jacket. "It's a shame to waste all those brains."

"I'm not wasting them," she began hotly. "I'm—" But she caught the glint in his eye and stopped. He was only trying to draw her in again. "No thanks, captain. I'm not going to debate you." She turned back to the answering machine, stopped again. "Do you ever worry that someone's going to take it all away from you? Tell you one day that it's over, that there'll be no more cameras?"

"No." His confidence, the easy arrogance of it, made her smile widen. "And neither should you." He tipped her chin up, kissed her. "You're terrific at fluff."

"Shut up, Finn." She stabbed the Play button again, then scribbled down the brief message from Simon on a potential hitch on tomorrow's show, another from Fran telling her the hitch had been diverted. She waited through the blank tape on a delayed hang-up, then gritted her teeth over three calls from reporters who'd managed to wangle her unlisted number.

"You all right?" Finn came up behind her to rub the tension from her shoulders.

"Yes." She indulged herself a moment by leaning back against him. "I'm fine. I have to decide whether to refuse to comment or to draft a statement. I guess I don't want to think about it yet."

"Then don't."

"Playing ostrich won't make it go away." She straightened, stepped aside to stand on her own. "I want to make the right decision. I hate making mistakes."

"Then you've got two choices. You react emotionally, or you react like a reporter."

Her brow creased as she thought it through. "Or I combine the two," she said softly. "I've been thinking about doing a show on date rape. I kept pulling back because I thought I was too close. But maybe I'm just close enough."

"Why would you put yourself through that, Deanna?"

"Because I've *been* through it. Because men like Jamie walk away from it. And because . . ." She let out a long breath that threatened to catch in her throat. "I'm tired of being ashamed that I didn't do anything about it. I've got a chance to make up for that now."

"It'll hurt you."

"Not the way it once did." She reached for him then. "Not anymore."

His grip on her tightened. Damn it, he needed to protect her. And she needed to stand on her own. The one thing he could do

252

was track down Jamie Thomas and have a nice, long . . . chat. "If you decide to do the show, let me know. I want to be there if I can."

"Okay." She tilted her head back to kiss him before drawing away. "Why don't I open some wine? Let's forget about all this for a while."

She needed to. He could see the tension creeping back, like a thief, into her eyes. "As long as you're going to let me stay. And this time I won't fall asleep on the couch."

"I won't give you the chance," she told him, and walked into the kitchen.

Out of habit, he moved to the television first, switching it on just as the late news began. He turned toward the couch, intending to take his boots off and put his feet up. He spotted the envelope lying on the rug just inside the door.

"I've got some chips." Deanna carried out a tray and set it on the coffee table. "The drive gave me an appetite." Her smile froze when she spotted the envelope in his hand. "Where did you get that?"

"It was inside the door." He'd started to hold it out to her, but drew it back now. She'd gone pale. "What's the problem?"

"It's nothing." Annoyed with herself, she shook off the vague, niggling fear. "It's silly, that's all." Trying to convince them both she was unconcerned, she took the envelope and split it open.

Deanna,
nothing they say would ever change my feelings.
I know it's all a lie.
I'll always believe you.
I'll always love you.

"A shy fan," she said with a shrug that came off as more of a defensive jerk. "Who needs to get a life."

Finn took the sheet from her, scanned it. "Response to the tabloids, I'd say."

"Looks like." But the anonymous faith didn't cheer her.

"I take it you've gotten one of these before."

"I'd have a whole collection if I'd kept them." She picked up her glass of wine. "They've been coming on and off for a year."

"A year?" He looked at her, his eyes intense. "Like this?"

"Here, at the newsroom, at my office." She moved her shoulders again, restless. "Always the same format and same type of message."

"Have you reported it?"

"To whom? The police?" Whatever unease she'd felt vanished in a laugh. "Why? What could I tell them? Officer, I've been receiving anonymous love letters. Call out the dogs."

"A year makes it more than harmless love letters. It makes it obsession. Obsessions are not healthy."

"I don't think a dozen or so sappy notes over a year constitutes an obsession. It's just someone who watches me on TV, Finn, or who works in the building. Someone who's attracted to the image but too shy to approach me in person for an autograph." She thought about the calls, those silent messages in the middle of the night. And that he had been able to slip a note under her door. "It's a little spooky, but it's not threatening."

"I don't like it."

She took his hand to draw him down on the couch with her. "It's just your reporter's instinct working on overdrive." Because his mouth was much more intoxicating, she set the wine aside. "Of course, if you want to be a little jealous . . ."

Her eyes were laughing at him. Finn smiled back, letting her set the mood. But he thought about the single sheet of paper lying open on the coffee table, its message of devotion as red as blood.

"NOT ONE STATEMENT." ANGELA chuckled to herself and stretched on her stomach over the pink satin sheets of her big bed. The television was on, and newspapers and magazines littered the floor around her.

It was a beautiful room, majestic and museum-like with its curved and gilded antiques and fussy, feminine flounces. One of the maids had griped to a friend that she was surprised there wasn't a velvet rope across the door and a charge for admission.

There were mirrors on every wall, oval and square and oblong, reflecting both the taste she'd purchased and her own image.

The only colors other than the gold and wood tones were pink and white, a candy cane she could savor in long, greedy licks.

There were banks of roses, dewy fresh, so that she never had to breathe without drawing in the rich, satisfying scent she equated with success. At the head of the giltwood bed was a mountain of pillows, all slick silks and frothy lace. She tapped her pink-tipped toes against them, and gloated.

Near the bed was a fauteuil, where she had carelessly tossed one of her many negligees.

Once, long ago, she had envied others their beautiful possessions. She had, as a child, as a young woman, stared through shop windows and wished. Now she owned, or could own, whatever she desired.

Whomever.

Naked, his subtle muscles gleaming, Dan Gardner straddled her hips and rubbed fragrant oil into her back and shoulders.

"It's been over a week," she reminded him, "and she hasn't made a peep."

"Do you want me to contact Jamie Thomas?"

"Hmmm." Angela stretched luxuriously under his hands. She was feeling pampered and victorious. And calm, beautifully calm. "Go ahead, and tell him to keep talking to reporters, maybe expand on the story a bit. Remind him that if he doesn't make enough trouble for our little Dee, we'll have to leak the story about his love affair with China White."

"That should do it." Dan admired the body under his as much, or nearly as much, as he admired Angela's mind. "If it comes out he's earmarking business funds for cocaine, his career will bottom out. Even if it is in Daddy's firm."

"Remind him of that if he balks. Rich boy's going to pay," she murmured. She would have hated him for being born into wealth and privilege and squandering it all on a weakness like drugs. But the pathetic way he'd folded after her first threat made her despise him.

"Oh, and send a case of Dom Perignon to Beeker." Angela examined her nails, scowling at a minute flaw in the candy-pink polish. "He did a good job. But keep him on the case. If we find enough of the dirt our little Dee's brushed under the rug, we can bury her in it."

"I love your mind, Angela." And aroused by it, he bit her sharply on the shoulder. "It's so beautifully twisted."

"I don't give a damn what you think of my mind." With a low chuckle, she levered herself so that he could slip his oil-slicked hands over her breasts. "And in this case it's focused straight and true. However it happened, she's sneaking up in the ratings. I'm not going to allow that, Dan, not after she betrayed my friendship. So you just keep—" She scrambled suddenly to her knees, letting out a howl of protest as a clip of Deanna and Finn rolled over the screen.

"In other entertainment news," the announcer continued, "talk-show star Deanna Reynolds accompanied CBC foreign correspondent Finn Riley to a National Press Club banquet in Chicago, where Riley was honored for his work during the Gulf War. The inside word is that Riley, America's Desert Hunk, is considering an offer to head a weekly news magazine for CBC. Riley had no comment about the project, or his personal relationship with Chicago's darling Deanna."

"No!" Angela exploded from the bed, a compact, golden missile detonating. "I took her in. I offered her opportunities, gave her my affection. And she moves in on me."

She stalked naked to an open bottle of champagne and poured lavishly. There were tears, as genuine and as painful as her bitterness, stinging her eyes.

"And that son of a bitch turned on me, too." In one violent gesture, she tossed the sparkling wine back. Its heat burst into her stomach like love. "He turned on me, and he turned to her. To *her*. Because she's younger." Enraged, and suddenly frightened when she saw the glass was empty, she hurled it toward the television. It slapped the corner of the cabinet and sliced delicately in two. "She's nothing. Less than nothing. A pretty face and a tight body. Anybody can have those. She won't keep Finn. He'll shake her off, and so will the viewers." She dashed the tears aside with a vicious hand, but her mouth continued to tremble. "They'll want me. They always want me."

"She can't come close to you, Angela." Dan approached her slowly, making sure his eyes were filled with understanding and desire. "You're the best there is. In public." Gently, he turned her so that they faced the full-length mirror. "In private," he murmured, watching her watching his hands caress. "You're so beautiful. She's built like a boy, but you ... You're a woman."

Desperate for reassurance, she clasped her hands over his, tightening her grip until he squeezed her breasts painfully. "I need to be wanted, Dan. I need to know people want me. I can't survive without that."

"They do. I do." He was used to her outbursts, accustomed to her neediness. And he knew how to use both to his advantage. "When I see you on the set, so cool, so controlled, you dazzle me." He slipped his hand between her thighs, patiently stroking until she was damp, until she quivered. Until he did. "And I can hardly wait until I can get you alone, like this."

Her breath grew shallow, but her vision was clear, focused hard on the glass as his busy hands worked over her. The flavor of champagne was still on her tongue, making her yearn for more. Crave more. She swallowed it and concentrated on what she saw in the glass.

"You'd do anything for me."

"Anything."

"And to me."

He laughed. He knew where the power was. The more she needed, the more she plotted, the more she placed in his hands. And the truth was, sex with Angela was like a dark, violent ride into an irresistible hell.

"What do you want me to do, Angela?"

"Take me here, right here, so I can watch."

He laughed again. She was quivering like a bitch in heat, her eyes riveted on her own body. Her vanity, the pathetic insecurity of it, was one more hold he had on her. But when he started to shift, she shoved him back.

"No." She could barely breathe now. Her full white breasts still carried the angry red marks from his hands. She wanted them there, wanted them as proof that she was desired. "From behind. Like an animal."

His mouth watered at the image. His erection ached like a wound. Desperate to take, he shoved her roughly to her knees. Eyes feral, teeth bared, she watched him crouch over her. He jerked her head back by the hair, hissing when she growled low in her throat.

"I won't stop. Even if you beg."

"Fuck me." Her smile glinted like a sword already bloodied. "And when you're done, we're going to find a new way to make her pay."

"Watch." He held her head still with one hand. "I want you to watch."

He drove himself into her viciously, the blood all but bursting in his veins when she cried out in pain and shock and greedy pleasure. His fingers dug hard into her hips while he rammed inside her again and again until the sweat ran off both of them like rain, and his vision dimmed.

But hers stayed clear. She saw the blood on her lip where her teeth had dug in, the sheen of sweat and tears on her face. And as the horrible, loveless orgasm slammed through the agony and need,

Dan's face dissolved into Finn's. And she smiled as he cried out her name and shuddered, shuddered, shuddered.

She was wanted. She was desired. She was the best.

"DEANNA, ARE YOU SURE you want to do this?" Fran nibbled on her thumbnail, a habit she'd broken years before, as she stood beside Deanna's desk.

"Absolutely sure." She continued to sign the outgoing mail. Her signature was quick and neat and automatic. "It's a show I want to do. How many carts did we get back?"

Fran frowned down at the forms in her hand, the carts they passed to the audience after each program. These had been typed simply: Do you know of anyone who has experienced date rape? Is this a topic you would be willing to discuss on *Deanna's Hour*?

There was room for comments, for names and phone numbers. Out of the two hundred carts Fran had surveyed, she had chosen only two.

"These are the ones I thought you should see." Reluctantly, Fran laid them on the desk. "It's going to be painful for you, Deanna."

"I can handle it."

She skimmed the first cart, then went back and read each word again.

He said I asked for it. I didn't. He said it was my own fault. I'm not sure. I'd like to try to talk about it, but I don't know if I can.

Setting the cart aside, she reached for the second.

It was my first date after my divorce. It was three years ago, and I haven't been with a man since. I'm still afraid, but I trust you.

"Two women," Deanna murmured. Yes, it was painful. There was a tight, angry fist lodged in her chest. "Right out of the studio audience. How many more, Fran? How many more are out there wondering if it was their fault? How many more are afraid?"

"I can't stand to see you hurt this way. You know if you do this, you're going to have to bring up Jamie Thomas."

"I know that. I've already run it by Legal."

"And if he sues?"

Deanna sighed, barely refrained from rubbing her eyes and smearing makeup. She hadn't slept well—and with Finn in Moscow, she'd slept alone. But it hadn't been doubt keeping her wakeful. It had been anticipation.

"Then he sues. To encapsulate what I got from Legal, he's already gone public with his version. Since it's a matter of his word against mine, I'm going public with my version. I could have done so in a dozen interviews since the tabloids hit. Two dozen," she corrected, with a grim smile. "I prefer to do it this way, my way, on my own show."

"You know the press will jump all over it."

"I know." She was calm now, dead calm. "That's why we're going to schedule it during the May sweeps."

"Jesus, Dee—"

"I'm going public with this, Fran, and I hope to God even one woman who watches is helped by what I'm doing." She used the heels of her hands to rub the dampness from her cheek. "And by Christ, I'm going to kill the competition in the ratings while I'm at it."

DEANNA'S NERVES WERE steady as stone before the show. In her precise manner, she had gone over her scripted question cards while Marcie put the finishing touches on her makeup. Prepared, even eager, she swiveled in her chair toward Loren Bach.

"Now, are you here to observe, Loren, or to offer advice?"

"Some of both." He folded his long, white fingers together. "As you know, I don't make it a habit to interfere with the content of the show."

"I do know that, and I appreciate it."

"But I do make a habit out of protecting my people." He sat silently a moment, gathering his thoughts while he studied the

260

orderly room filled with stacks of newspapers, magazines, all current, a shelf of neatly marked videos that could be slipped into the VCR for viewing. The room smelled lightly of cosmetics and lotions. Feminine, yes, he mused, but also tools of the trade. The dressing room was as much a work space as her office.

"It's possible for you to do this show, and do an excellent job, without bringing your personal experience into it."

"Possible, yes." She rose then to close the door Marcie had left open. "Are you asking me to do that, Loren?"

"No. I'm reminding you of it."

"Then I'll remind you that I'm part of the show, not just a host. An intimate part; that's what makes it work for me and, I think, for the viewing audience."

He smiled, and his eyes remained keen. She looked polished and poised, he mused. "I wouldn't argue with that. But Deanna, if you have any doubts about what you're doing, there is no need to go ahead."

"I don't have doubts, Loren. I have fears. I think, at least I hope, that facing them is the answer. You may have concerns that Jamie Thomas will try some sort of legal retribution, but—"

Loren waved that away. "I have lawyers to deal with that. In any case, it seems the brunt of the publicity backfired on him. He is, at the moment, on an extended vacation in Europe."

"Oh, I see." She took a deep breath. "Well then."

"You don't mind if I stay to watch the show?" He rose as she did.

"I'd appreciate it." On impulse she leaned forward and kissed his cheek. When he blinked in surprise, she smiled. "That wasn't for my business associate. It was for your support."

When she opened the door, she found herself instantly scooped up into Finn's arms.

"You're supposed to be in Moscow."

"I'm back." He'd pulled every string he could grab to arrive in Chicago in time for the show. "You look good, Kansas. How do you feel?"

"Shaky." She pressed a hand to her stomach. "Ready."

"You'll be fine." He kept an arm around her shoulders and nodded to Loren. "Good to see you."

"And you. You can keep me company while Deanna goes to work."

"Fine." Finn walked Deanna toward the set. "Working tonight?"

"I have a network dinner at seven. But I think I can get out by ten."

"Want to come by my place?"

"Yes." She gripped his hand, hard. The closer she got to the set, the more her stomach twisted. She shot one look at Fran, braced herself. "Like diving into a cold pool."

"What?"

She forced a smile as she glanced up at Finn. "Just some advice I got once. See you in an hour, huh?"

"I'll be here."

Deanna took her place with the three women already fidgeting onstage. She spoke quietly to each one of them, then miked, waited for her cue.

Music. Applause. The objective red eye of the camera.

"Welcome to *Deanna's Hour*. Our show today deals with a painful subject. Rape in any form is tragic and horrible. It takes on a different dimension when the victim knows and trusts her attacker. Every woman on this stage has been a victim of what is called date, or acquaintance, rape: And we all have a story to tell. When it happened to me nearly ten years ago, I did nothing. I hope I'm doing something now."

Chapter Seventeen

To celebrate Deanna's first year on the air, Loren Bach threw a party in his penthouse overlooking Lake Michigan. Over the low music and chink of glasses, voices buzzed. Faintly, from the adjoining game room, came the beeps and bells of video games.

In addition to the staff of the show and CBC and Delacort executives, he had invited a handful of carefully selected columnists and reporters. The publicity on Deanna since the May sweeps showed no sign of abating. Loren had no intention of allowing it to.

While the ratings climbed, so did the advertising revenue. As Chicago's darling rapidly became America's darling, Deanna's growing celebrity opened the doors to booking stellar names who breezed on the show to hype their hot summer movies and concert tours. She continued to mix the famous with segments on dealing with jealous spouses, choosing the right swimwear and computer dating.

The result was a carefully crafted show with an appealing, casual, homey look. Deanna was at the core, as awestruck as her audience by the appearance of a glamorous movie star, as amused as they by the notion of choosing a mate with a machine, as wary and unnerved as any woman of stripping down to a bikini on a public beach.

The girl-next-door image drew the audience. The sharp, practical mind behind it structured the vision.

"Looks like you made it, kid."

Deanna smiled at Roger as she kissed his cheek. "Through the first year, anyway."

"Hey, in this business that's a minor miracle." He chose a baby carrot from his buffet plate and bit in with a sigh. He'd put on a few pounds over the past months. The camera gleefully advertised every ounce. "Too bad Finn couldn't be here."

"The Soviets would pick my anniversary to stage a coup." She tried not to worry about Finn, back in Moscow.

"Have you heard from him?"

"Not for a couple of days. I saw him on the news. Speaking of which, I caught your new promo. Very sharp."

"Our news team is your news team," Roger said in his announcer's voice. "Keeping Chicago informed."

"You and your new partner have a nice rhythm."

"She's all right." He switched to celery, found it just as bland. "Good voice, good face. But she doesn't get my jokes."

"Rog, nobody gets your jokes."

"You did."

"No." She patted his cheek. "I pretended I did, because I love you."

There was a quick pinch around his heart. "We still miss you around the newsroom."

"I miss you too, Roger. I'm sorry about you and Debbie."

He shrugged, but the wounds of his recent divorce were still tender. "You know what they say, Dee. Shit happens. Maybe I'll be looking into that computer dating."

She gave a snort of laughter and squeezed his hand. "I have one word of advice on that. Don't."

"Well, since Finn's busy hopping all over the globe, maybe you'd be interested in a stable, slightly older man."

She would have laughed again, but she wasn't entirely sure he was joking. "There happens to be this stable, slightly older man whose friendship means a lot to me."

"Hi, Dee."

"Jeff."

"I saw you didn't have a glass, and thought you might like some champagne."

"Thanks. You never miss a detail. I pulled a coup of my own when I stole Jeff away from the news department," she told Roger. "We'd never get *Deanna's Hour* on the air without him."

He beamed with pleasure. "I just pick up the loose ends."

"And tie them up in a bow."

"Excuse me." Barlow James slipped behind Deanna and circled her waist with his arm. "I need to steal the star for a moment, gentlemen. You're looking fit, Roger."

"Thanks, Mr. James." With a wan smile, Roger held up another carrot. "I'm working on it."

"I won't keep her long," Barlow promised, and led Deanna toward the open terrace doors. "You look more than fit," he commented. "You look luminous."

She laughed. "I'm working on it."

"I believe I have something that might add to the glow. Finn contacted me this morning."

Relief came one heartbeat before pleasure. "How is he?"

"In his element."

"Yes." She looked out at the lake, where pale fingers of moonlight nudged past clouds to brush the water. The silhouettes of boats rocked gently in the current. "I suppose he is."

"You know, between the two of us, we might be able to apply enough pressure to convince him to do that news magazine and keep his butt in Chicago."

"I can't." Though she wished she could. "He has to do what suits him best."

"Don't we all," Barlow said with a sigh. "Now, I've dulled some of that glow. This should bring it back." He took a long slim box from his inside jacket pocket. "Finn asked me to pick this up for you. Something he had made before he was called away. I'm to tell you he's sorry he can't give it to you himself."

She said nothing as she stared at its contents. The bracelet was delicately fashioned of oval gold links, cut to catch the light and joined together by the rainbow hue of multicolored gems. Emerald, sapphire, ruby, tourmaline fired and flashed in the moonlight. At the center a filigreed *D* and *R* flanked a brilliant array of sizzling diamonds that shaped a star.

"The star's self-explanatory, I believe," Barlow told her. "It's to commemorate your first year. We're confident there'll be many more."

"It's beautiful."

"Like the woman it was made for," Barlow said, slipping it from the box to clasp it around her wrist. "The boy certainly has taste. You know, Deanna, we need a strong hour on Tuesday nights. You may not feel comfortable using your influence to persuade him to fill it. But I do." He winked and, patting her shoulder, left her alone.

"You're too damn far away," she said quietly, rubbing a fingertip over the bracelet.

She had so much that she wanted, she reminded herself. So much that she'd worked toward. So why was she still so unsettled? Very much like the boats on the water below, she mused. Anchored, yes, but still shifting, still tugging against the tide.

Her show was rapidly becoming national. But she had yet to select a new apartment. She was enjoying national exposure in the media, most of it flattering. And she was standing alone at a party thrown in her honor, feeling lost and discontented.

For the first time in her life her professional goals and personal ones seemed out of balance. She knew exactly what she wanted for her career, and could see the steps toward achieving it so clearly. She felt capable and confident when she thought of pushing *Deanna's Hour* to the top of the market. And whenever she stood in front of the audience, the camera on and focused, she felt incredibly alive, completely in control, with just enough giddy pleasure thrown in to make it all a continual thrill.

She wasn't taking success for granted, for she knew too well the caprices of television. But she knew that if the show was canceled tomorrow, she would pick up, go on and start over.

Her personal needs weren't so clear-cut, nor was the route she wanted to take. Did she want the traditional home and marriage and family? If it was possible to mix that kind of ideal with a high-powered and demanding career, she would find a way.

Or did she want what she had now? A place of her own, a satisfying yet strangely independent relationship with a fascinating man. A man she was madly in love with, she admitted. And who, though the words hadn't been said, she was certain loved her as deeply.

If they changed what they had, she might lose this breathless, stirring excitement. Or she might discover something more soothing and equally thrilling to replace it.

And because she couldn't see the answer, because the confusion in her heart blinded her vision, she struggled all the harder to separate intellect from emotion.

"There you are." Loren Bach strode out on the balcony, a bottle of champagne in one hand, a glass in the other. "The guest of honor shouldn't be hiding in the shadows." He topped off her glass before setting the bottle aside on the glass table beside him. "Particularly when the media is in attendance."

"I was just admiring your view," she countered. "And giving that media a chance to miss me."

"You're a sharp woman, Deanna." He clicked his glass against hers. "I'm taking this evening to feel very smug about going with my instincts and signing you."

"I'm feeling pretty smug about that myself."

"As long as you don't let it show. That wide-eyed enthusiasm is what sells, Dee. That's what the audience relates to."

She grimaced. "I am wide-eyed and enthusiastic, Loren. It's not an act."

"I know." He couldn't have been happier. "That's why it's so perfect. What did I read about you recently—" He tapped a finger against his temple as if to shake the memory loose. "'Midwest sensibilities, an Ivy-League brain, a face that makes a man yearn for his high school sweetheart, all coated with a quiet sheen of class.'"

"You left out my quick, sexy laugh," she said dryly.

"Complaining, Deanna?"

"No." She leaned comfortably against the railing to face him. The scent of hibiscus from the bold red blooms in the patio pots mixed exotically with the fragrance of champagne and lake water. "Not for a minute. I love every bit of it. The spread in *Premiere*, the cover on *McCall's*, the People's Choice nomination—"

"You should have won that," he muttered.

"I'll beat Angela next time." She smiled at him, her bangs fluttering in the light breeze, the diamonds at her wrist glinting in the starlight. "I wanted that Chicago Emmy, and I've got it. I intend to win a national one, when the time comes. I'm not in a hurry, Loren, because I'm enjoying the ride. A lot."

"You make it look easy, Dee, and fun." He winked. "That's the way I sell computer games. And that's the way you slip right through the television screen into the viewer's living room. That's the way you up the ratings." His smile hardened, glinted in the shadowy light. "And that's the way you're going to knock Angela out of first place."

Because the gleam in Loren's eye made her uneasy, Deanna chose her response carefully. "That's not my primary goal. As naive as it may sound, Loren, all I want is to do a good job and provide a good show."

"You keep doing that, and I'll handle the rest." It was odd, he thought, that he hadn't realized just how much revenge against Angela burned in him. Until Deanna. "I'm not going to claim that I made Angela number one, because it's more complex than that.

But I speeded the process along. My mistake was to be deluded enough by the screen image and marry someone who didn't exist off camera."

"Loren, you don't have to tell me this."

"No, no one has to tell you anything, but they do. That's part of your charm, Deanna. I can tell you that Angela shed me as carelessly as a snake sheds its skin when she'd decided she'd outgrown me. It's going to give me a lot of satisfaction to help you gun her down, Deanna." He drank again, with relish. "A great deal of deep satisfaction."

"Loren, I don't want to go to war with Angela."

"That's all right." He touched his glass to hers again. "I do."

LEW MCNEIL WAS AS obsessed with Angela's success as Loren Bach was with her failure. His future depended on it. He had hopes to retire in another decade, with his nest egg securely in place. He had no hopes of remaining with *Angela's* for that long. His best chance was to work out his contract while the show remained a number-one hit, then slide gently into another producing slot.

He had some reason to worry. While *Angela's* was still in command of the top rung, and the show had added another Emmy to its collection, its star was fraying at the edges. In Chicago she had managed to command her staff using her iron will and her penchant for perfection, and leavening them with doses of considerable charm.

Since the move to New York, a great deal of the charm had been shaken by stress, and the stress was doused with French champagne.

He knew—had made it his business to know—that she had poured a great deal of her own money into the fledgling A.P. Productions. The veteran show kept the company out of the red, but Angela's dabbling in television movies had been disastrous thus far. Her last special had received lukewarm reviews, but the ratings had put the show into the top ten of the week.

That was fortunate, but her daily ratings had plummeted in August, when she had insisted on running repeats while she took an extended vacation in the Caribbean.

No one could deny that she deserved the break. Just as no one could deny that the timing had been poor with *Deanna's Hour* steadily closing the distance in points.

There were other mistakes, other errors in judgment, the largest being Dan Gardner. As the power shifted gradually from Angela's hands to those of her lover and executive producer, the tone of the show altered subtly.

"More complaints, Lew?"

"It's not a complaint, Angela." He wondered how many hours of his life he'd spent standing beside her chair in her dressing room. "I only wanted to say again that I think it's a mistake to have a homeless family on the program with a man like Trent Walker. He's a shark, Angela."

"Really?" She took a slow drag on her cigarette. "I found him quite charming."

"Sure, he's charming. He was real charming when he bought that shelter then turned the building into high-priced condos."

"It's called urban renewal, Lew. In any case, it should be fascinating to see him debate with a family of four who are currently living in their station wagon. Not only topical"—she crushed out the cigarette—"but excellent TV. I hope he wears the gold cuff links."

"If it goes the wrong way, it may look as though you're unsympathetic to the plight of the homeless."

"And what if I am?" Her voice cracked like a whip. "There are jobs out there. Too many of these people would rather take a handout than earn an honest living." She thought of the way she'd waited tables and cleaned up slop to pay for her education. The humiliation of it. "Not all of us were born to the good life, Lew. When my book comes out next month, you can read along with everyone else how I overcame my modest beginnings and worked my way to the top." With a sigh, she dismissed the hairdresser. "That's fine, dear, run along. Lew, let me say first that I don't appreciate your second-guessing me in front of members of my staff."

"Angela, I wasn't—"

"And second," she interrupted, still frigidly pleasant. "There's no need for concern. I have no intention of letting anything go wrong, or of giving the soft-hearted public an unflattering opinion on my stand. Dan's already seeing to it that it leaks that I, personally, will sponsor the family we're highlighting on the show. I will at first modestly decline to comment, then, reluctantly, will agree that I have found employment for both parents, along with six months' rent and a stipend for food and clothing. Now . . ." She gave her hair one last fluff as she rose. "I'd like to look them over before we go on the air."

"They're in the green room," Lew murmured. "I decided to put Walker elsewhere for the time being."

"Fine." She swept by him and into the corridor. All graciousness and warm support, she greeted the family of four who sat nervously huddled together on the sofa in front of the television. Waving away their thanks, she pressed food and drink on them, patted the little boy on the head and tickled the toddler under the chin.

Her smile snapped off like a light when she started back to her dressing room. "They don't look like they've been living on the street for six weeks to me. Why are their clothes so neat? Why are they so clean?"

"I—they knew they were going on national TV, Angela. They put themselves together as best they could. They've got pride."

"Well, dirty them up," she snapped. She had a headache coming on like a freight train and wanted her pills. "I want them to look destitute, for Christ's sake, not like some middle-class family down on their luck."

"But that's what they are," Lew began.

She stopped, turned, freezing him with eyes as cold as a doll's.

"I don't care if the four of them have fucking MBA's from Harvard. Do you understand me? Television is a visual medium. Perhaps you've forgotten that. I want them to look like they just got swept off the street. Put some dirt on those kids. I want to see holes in their clothes."

"Angela, we can't do that. It's staging. It crosses the line."

"Don't tell me what you can't do." She jabbed one frosty pink nail into his chest. "I'm telling you what's going to be done. It's my show, remember. *Mine*. You've got ten minutes. Now get out of here and do something to earn your salary." She shoved him out, slamming the door behind him.

The panic attack had nearly overtaken her in the hall. Chills raced over her skin; she leaned back against the door shuddering. She would have to go out there soon. Go out and face the audience. They would be waiting for her to make the wrong move, to say the wrong words. If she did, if she made one mistake, they would leap at her like wild dogs.

And she would lose everything. Everything.

On wobbly legs, she lunged across the room. Her hands shook as she poured the champagne. It would help, she knew. She'd discovered after years of denial that just one small glass before a show could chase away those cold, clammy chills. Two could ease all those gnawing fears.

She swallowed greedily, draining the glass, then poured the second with a steadier hand. A third glass wouldn't hurt, she assured herself. Just smoothing out the rough edges. Where had she heard that before? she wondered as she brought the crystal to her lips.

Her mother. Good God, her mother.

Just smoothing out the rough edges, Angle. A couple sips of gin smooths them all right out.

Horrified, she dropped the full glass, spilling bubbling wine over the rug. She watched it spread, like blood, and turned away shivering.

She didn't need it. She wasn't like her mother. She was Angela Perkins. And she was the best.

There would be no mistakes. She promised herself that as she turned to the mirror so that her image, glossy and elegant, could calm her. She would go out and do what she did best. And she would keep those wild dogs at bay yet again. She would tame them, and make them love her.

"Satisfied, Lew?" Still riding on the echoes of applause, Angela dropped into the chair behind her desk. "I told you it would work."

"You were great, Angela." He said it because it was expected.

"No, she was fabulous." Dan sat on the edge of her desk and leaned over to kiss her. "Having that kid sit on your lap was inspired."

"I like kids," she lied. "And that one seemed to have some brains. We'll see to it that he gets in school. Now . . ." She sat back, letting the family slip from her mind as casually as she slipped out of her shoes. "Let's get down to business. Who is *she* looking to book next month?"

Resigned, Lew passed Angela a list. He didn't have to be told they were discussing Deanna. "The names with the asterisks have already booked."

"She's going after some heavy hitters, isn't she?" Angela mused. "Movies, fashion. Still steering clear of politics."

"Fluff over substance," Dan said, knowing that comment would please her.

"Fluff or not, we wouldn't want her to get lucky. She's already snagged too much press. That damn Jamie Thomas affair." Her mouth tightened into a thin line of disgust as she thought of him hiding out in Rome.

"We still have the data on him," Dan reminded her. "Easy enough to leak his drug problem to the press."

"Leaking that gains us nothing, and would only drum up more sympathetic press for Deanna. Let it go." She scanned the sheet of paper. "Let's see who we know well enough on here to persuade to give Deanna a pass." She glanced up and gave Lew a bland smile. "You can go. I won't need you."

When Lew closed the door quietly behind him, Dan lighted Angela's cigarette. "That hangdog face of his gets old fast," he commented.

"But he has his uses." Pleased, she tapped the list with one lacquered nail. "It's very satisfying to know what our little Dee is planning almost before she does." Angela checked two names on the list. "I can take care of both of these with a casual phone call. It's so gratifying to have important people owe you. Ah, now, look here. Kate Lowell."

"Very hot." Dan rose to pour them both a Perrier. "One of those rarities that makes the term, 'actress-model' a compliment."

"Yes, she's very beautiful, very talented. And very hot right now with her new movie burning up the box office." Angela's smile was slow and surprisingly sweet. "It so happens Deanna knows Kate. They summered in Topeka together. And it so happens I know an interesting little secret of Kate's. A little secret that will make certain she won't be chatting to her old pal on the air. In fact, I think we'll just book her ourselves. I'll take care of this one. Personally."

"I JUST DON'T UNDERSTAND IT, Finn." Deanna snuggled down on the couch beside him, resting her head against his chest. "One minute we were making the travel arrangements, the next we get a line from her publicist about unexpected scheduling conflicts."

"It happens." He was more interested in nibbling on her fingers than talking shop.

"Not like this. We tried to reschedule, gave them an open date, and got the same response. I really wanted her on in November, but

I didn't contact her personally because I didn't want it to seem like calling in a favor from a friend." She shook her head, remembering how warm, then how distant Kate had been when they'd seen each other in Angela's office. "Damn it, we used to be friends."

"Friendships are often one of the first casualties of this business. Don't let it get you down, Kansas."

"I'm trying not to. I know we'll get someone else. I guess I feel snubbed, personally and professionally." She made an effort to push it out of her mind. Their time was too precious to waste. "This is nice."

"What is?"

"Just sitting here, doing nothing. With you."

"I like it myself. Kind of habit-forming." He stroked a finger over the bracelet she wore. Since his return from Moscow, he hadn't seen her without it. "Barlow James is in town."

"Mmm. I heard. Do you want something to eat?"

"No."

"Good." She sighed lustily. "Neither do I. I don't want to move all day. All wonderful Sunday."

An absolutely free Sunday for both of them, she mused. And she didn't want to spoil it by mentioning the latest note she'd found mixed with her viewer mail.

> **I know you don't really love him, Deanna.**
> **Finn Riley can't mean as much to you as I will.**
> **I can wait for you.**
> **I'll wait forever.**

Of course, that note had been nothing compared to the one from the Alabamian truck driver who wanted her to see the country from the bed in his sixteen-wheeler. Or the self-ordained minister who claimed to have had a vision of her naked—a sign from God that she, and her checkbook, were meant to join him in his work.

So it was nothing to worry about. Really, nothing at all.

"I had a meeting with him yesterday."

She blinked. "Who?"

"Barlow James." Because he could see she was clicking into her think mode, Finn tugged at her ear. "Keep up, will you?"

"Sorry. Where's he sending you now?"

"I have to leave for Paris in a few days. I thought you might like to fly out there next weekend."

"Fly out to Paris?" She turned to look at him. "For the weekend?"

"You take the Concorde. We eat French food, see French sights and make love in a French hotel. I might even be able to fly back with you."

The idea made her sit upright. "I can't imagine flying off to Paris for a weekend."

"You're a celebrity," he reminded her. "You're supposed to do things like that. Don't you ever read fan magazines?"

Her eyes were alight with the possibilities. "I've never been to Europe."

"You've got a passport, don't you?"

"Sure. I even renewed it recently, a habit from my reporting days, when I nursed the vague hope of copping some exciting foreign assignment."

"So, I'll be your exciting foreign assignment."

"If I could clear my schedule . . . I *will* clear my schedule." She twisted around to throw her arms around him.

"Where are you going?" he demanded, tightening his grip when she started to wriggle away.

"I have to make a list. I have to get a Berlitz tape and a guidebook, and—"

"Later." He laughed his way into the kiss. "God, you're predictable, Kansas. Whatever I toss at you, you make a list."

"I'm organized." She thumped a fist against his chest. "That doesn't mean I'm predictable."

"You can write up six lists later. I haven't told you about my meeting with Barlow."

But she wasn't listening. She'd need one of those mini video recorders, she decided. Like Cassie had. And a phrase book. "What?" She blinked when Finn tugged on her hair. "The meeting with Barlow," she said, tucking her mental list aside. "You just said he was sending you to Paris."

"That's not what the meeting was about. It was a continuation of discussions we've been having on and off for about a year."

"The news magazine." She grinned. "He won't give up, will he?"

"I'm going to do it."

"I think it's—you're what!" She jerked upright again. "You're going to do it?"

He'd expected her to be surprised. Now he was hoping she'd be pleased. "It's taken us a while to agree on terms and format."

"But I didn't think you were interested at all. You like being able to plug into any story that comes along. Toss your garment bag over your shoulder, pick up your laptop and go."

"The paladin of newscasters." He toyed with her earring. "I'd still do that, to an extent. When something breaks, I'd go, but I'd be covering it for the show. We'd do remotes whenever they were called for, but we'd base here in Chicago." That had been a sticking point, since Barlow had wanted him in New York. "I'd be able to take a story and explore all the angles instead of fitting it into a three-minute piece on the news. And I'd spend more time here. With you."

"I don't want you to do this for me." She got to her feet quickly. "I won't deny that it's hard for me to say goodbye so often, but—"

"You've never said so."

"It wouldn't have been fair. God, Finn." She dragged both hands through her hair. "What could I have said? Don't go. I know there are world-altering events taking place, but I'd rather you stay home with me?"

He rose as well, brushed a knuckle down her cheek. "It wouldn't have hurt my ego to hear it."

277

His quiet words shivered through her. "It wouldn't have been fair to either of us. And you changing the thrust of your career because of me won't be fair either."

"I'm not just doing this for you. I'm doing it for myself, too."

"You said you didn't want to put down roots." She was distressed, because she realized she was near tears. She wouldn't have been able to explain them to him, or to herself. "I remember that. Finn, we're professionals, and we both understand the demands of the career. I don't want to make you feel pressured."

"You don't get it, do you?" His impatience was back. "There's nothing I wouldn't do for you, Deanna. Things have changed for me in this past year. It's not as easy for me to pick up and go. It's not a snap for me to fall asleep in some hotel halfway around the world. I miss you."

"I miss you too," she said. "Does that make you happy?"

"Damn straight it does." He eased her forward, kissed her softly, gently, until her mouth grew greedy and hot under his. "I want you to miss me. I want it to kill you every time I go away. And I want you to feel as baffled and uncomfortable and as frustrated as I am with this whole mess we've gotten ourselves into."

"Well, I do, so that's just fine for both of us."

"Fine and dandy." He released her. If she wanted to fight with reason, he'd give her plenty of it. Objective words were, after all, his stock-in-trade. "I'll still have to go. I'll have more control over where and when, but I'll have to go. And I want you to suffer whenever I do."

"You," she said precisely, "can go to hell."

"Not without you." He caught her face in his hand, holding tight when she would have jerked away. "Goddamn it, Deanna. I love you."

When his hand went limp, she stepped back on shaky legs. Her eyes were huge and fixed on his face. It took her a moment before she could breathe again. Another moment before she could form coherent words. "You've never said that before."

Her reaction wasn't precisely what he'd hoped for. Then again, he had to admit that his declaration hadn't been exactly polished. "I'm saying it now. You have a problem with it?"

"Do you?"

"I asked you first."

She only shook her head. "I don't suppose I do. It makes it kind of handy, because I love you too." She let out a quick, catchy sigh. "I didn't realize how much I needed the words."

"You're not the only one who has to take things in stages." He reached out, touched her cheek. "Pretty scary, huh?"

"Yeah." She took his wrist, held tight while the first flood of pleasure poured through her. "I don't mind being scared. In fact, I like it, so if you'd like to tell me again, it's okay."

"I love you." He scooped her up, making her laugh as they tumbled onto the couch. "You'd better hold on to me," he warned her, and tugged her sweater over her head. "I'm about to scare you to death."

Chapter Eighteen

IN DEPTH WITH FINN RILEY PREMIERED IN JANUARY, A mid-season replacement for a disastrous hospital drama. The network had high hopes that a weekly news magazine featuring a recognizable face could drag the time slot out of the ratings basement. Finn had experience and credibility, and most important, he was wildly popular with women, particularly in the coveted eighteen-to-forty category.

CBC ushered the show onto the air with plenty of hype. Promos were run, ads were designed, theme music was composed. By the time the set, with its three-dimensional world map and sleek glass counter, was constructed, Finn and the three reporters on his team were already hard at work.

His vision of the project was much simpler than jazzy promotion spots or expensive props. He was, as he told Deanna, doing something he'd always fantasized about. He was coming in as relief pitcher after the seventh-inning stretch. All he had to do was throw strikes.

With his first program, he managed to strike out the competition with a thirty-percent share. Around water coolers the next morning, Americans chatted about the U.S. chances for Olympic gold, and Finn Riley's cagey interview with Boris Yeltsin.

In the spirit of friendly competition, Deanna scheduled a program featuring Rob Winters, a veteran film actor whose directorial debut was winning critical and popular acclaim.

Charming, handsome and cozily at home in front of the camera, Rob kept both the studio and viewing audiences entertained. His final anecdote, involving the filming of a steamy love scene and an unexpected invasion of sea gulls, closed the show with a roar of laughter.

"I can't thank you enough for doing the show." Deanna clasped his hand warmly after he'd finished signing autographs for lingering members of the audience.

"I nearly didn't." While security ushered the last of the audience from the studio, he studied Deanna carefully. "To be frank, the only reason I agreed to come on was because I was pressured not to." He flashed his famous grin. "That's why I have a reputation for being difficult."

"I'm not sure I understand. Your agent advised you against doing this?"

"Among others." Deanna studied him, confused. "Got a minute?" he asked.

"Of course. Would you like to go upstairs to my office?"

"Fine. I could use a drink." His quick smile was back. "You'd last about twenty minutes in Hollywood with eyes like that." He put a friendly hand on her arm as they walked on set toward the elevator. "If you let enough people see what you're thinking, you'll be gobbled up and swallowed whole."

Deanna stepped inside the elevator, pushed the button for the sixteenth floor. "And what am I thinking?"

"That it's barely ten o'clock in the morning and I'm going to start knocking back doubles." His grin was as fast and potent as a jigger of whiskey. "You're thinking I should have stayed at Betty Ford a little longer."

"You did tell me during the show that you didn't drink any longer."

"I don't—alcohol. My newest addiction is Diet Pepsi with a twist of lime. A little embarrassing, but I'm man enough to handle it."

"Deanna—" Cassie turned from her workstation. When she saw the man beside Deanna, her eyes popped wide open.

"Did you need me for something, Cassie?"

"What?" She blinked, flushed, but didn't take her eyes off Rob's face. "No—no, it's nothing."

"Rob, this is Cassie, my secretary and sergeant at arms."

"Nice to meet you." Rob took her limp hand in both of his.

"I enjoy your work, Mr. Winters. We're all thrilled you could do the show today."

"My pleasure."

"Cassie, hold my calls, please. I'll fix you that drink," she told Rob as she led him into her office.

The room had changed considerably from the early days. The walls were painted a bold teal, and the carpet had been replaced by oak flooring and geometric rugs. The furniture was streamlined and built for comfort. Gesturing Rob to a chair, she opened a compact refrigerator.

"I haven't been up here in four or five years, I guess." He stretched out his long legs and glanced around. "It's an improvement." He looked back at Deanna. "But then, pastel pinks probably aren't your style."

"I suppose not." She sliced lime and added it to two iced soft drinks. "I'm curious why your agent advised you against doing the show." Curious wasn't the word, but she kept her voice mild. "We do our best to make our guests comfortable."

"It probably had something to do with a call from New York." He accepted the glass, waited until Deanna took a seat. "From Angela Perkins."

"Angela?" Baffled, she shook her head. "Angela called your agent about your coming on my show?"

"The day after your people contacted him." Rob took a long sip. "She said a little bird had told her that I was considering a stop in Chicago."

"Sounds like her," Deanna muttered. "But I don't know how she could have found out so quickly."

"She didn't say." Watching Deanna's face, he rattled the ice in his glass. "And she didn't bring it up when she spoke to me, either. Two days later. With my agent she used charm, reminding him that she'd booked me on *Angela's* when my career was floundering, and that if I agreed to go on with you, she wouldn't be able to welcome me to New York as she'd hoped to. She wanted me for her next special, and guaranteed that she would use her influence to add weight to my Oscar nomination. Which meant talking the film up in public and in private and contributing to the ad campaign."

"Some not-so-subtle bribery." Her voice tightened with anger held under strict control. "But you're here."

"I might not have been if she'd stayed with bribery. I want that award, Deanna. A lot of people, including me, thought I was washed up when I went into rehab. I had to beg for money to make this film. I made deals and promises, told lies. Whatever it took. Halfway through production, the press was saying that the public was going to stay away in droves because nobody gave a shit about an epic love story. I want that award."

He paused, drank again. "I'd just about made up my mind to take my agent's advice and give you a pass. Then Angela called me. She didn't use charm, she threatened me. And that was her mistake."

Deanna rose to refill his glass. "She threatened not to support the film if you came on my show?"

"She did better than that." He took out a cigarette, shrugged. "Do you mind? I haven't kicked this vice yet."

"Go ahead."

"I came here because I was pissed." He struck a match, blew out smoke. "My little way of telling Angela to get fucked. I wasn't going to bring any of it up, but there's something about the way

283

you handle yourself." He narrowed his eyes. "You've just got to trust that face of yours."

"So I'm told." She managed a smile, though bitterness was bubbling in her throat. "Whatever the reason you came on, I'm glad you did."

"You're not going to ask me what else she threatened me with?"

Her smile fluttered again, more easily. "I'm trying not to."

He gave a short laugh and set the Pepsi aside. "She told me you were a manipulative, scheming monster who'd use any means necessary to stay in the spotlight. That you'd abused her friendship and trust, and that the only reason you were on the air was that you were screwing Loren Bach."

Deanna merely lifted a brow. "I'm sure Loren would be surprised to hear it."

"It sounded more like a self-portrait to me." He took another drag, tapped his cigarette restlessly in the ashtray. "I know what it is to have enemies, Deanna, and since it seems we now have a mutual one, I'm going to tell you what Angela held over my head. I'll need you to keep it to yourself for twenty-four hours, until I get back to the coast and arrange a press conference."

Something cold skittered up her spine. "All right."

"About six months ago I went in for a routine exam. I was worn out, but then I'd been working pretty much around the clock for more than a year, doing the film, overseeing the editing, gearing up for promotion. I'd been a pretty regular customer of the medical profession during my drinking days, and my doctor is very discreet. Discretion aside, Angela managed to get wind of the test results." He took one last drag on the cigarette, crushed it out. "I'm HIV-positive."

"Oh, I'm sorry." Instantly she reached out and gripped his hand hard in hers. "I'm so sorry."

"I always figured the booze would get me. Never figured it would be sex."

He lifted the glass. The ice rattled musically when his hand

284

shook. "Then again, I spent enough time drunk that I didn't know how many women there were, much less who they were."

"We're finding out more every day—" She cut herself off. It was so trite, she thought, so pathetically useless. "You're entitled to your privacy, Rob."

"An odd statement from an ex-reporter."

"Even if Angela leaks this, you don't have to confirm."

He sat back again, looking amused. "Now you're pissed."

"Of course I am. She used me to get to you. It's just television, for God's sake. It's *television*. We're talking about ratings points here, not world-altering events. What kind of business is this that someone would use your tragedy to shake down the competition?"

In a lighter mood, he sipped at his drink. "It's show business, babe. Nothing's closer to life and death than life and death." He smiled wryly. "I ought to know."

"I'm sorry." She closed her eyes and fought for control. "A temper tantrum isn't going to help you. What can I do?"

"Got any friends who are voting members of the Academy?"

She smiled back. "Maybe a couple."

"You might give them a call, use that sexy, persuasive voice to influence their vote. And after that, you can go back in front of the camera and beat the pants off *Angela's*."

Her eyes kindled. "You're damn right I will."

SHE CALLED A STAFF MEETING that afternoon in her own office and sat behind her desk to project the image of authority. The anger was still with her, simmering deep. As a result, her voice was clipped, cool and formal.

"We have a problem, a serious one, that just recently came to my attention." She scanned the room as she spoke, noting the puzzled faces. Staff meetings were often tiresome, sometimes heated, but always informal and essentially good-natured.

"Margaret," she continued. "You contacted Kate Lowell's people, didn't you?"

"That's right." Unnerved by the chill in the air, Margaret nibbled on the earpiece of her reading glasses. "They were very interested in having her come on. We had the hook that she'd lived in Chicago for a few years when she was a teenager. Then they switched off. Scheduling conflicts."

"How many other times has that happened in the last six months?"

Margaret blinked. "It's hard to say right off. A lot of the topic ideas don't pan out."

"I mean specifically celebrity-oriented shows."

"Oh, well." Margaret shifted in her seat. "We don't do a lot of those because the format generally runs to civilian guests, the everyday people you do so well. But I'd guess that five or six times in the last six months we've had somebody wiggle off the hook."

"And how do we handle the projected guest list. Simon?"

He flushed. "Same as always, Dee. We toss around ideas, brainstorm. When we come up with some workable topics and guests, we do the research and make some calls."

"And the guest list is confidential until it's confirmed?"

"Sure it is." He nervously slicked a hand over his hair. "Standard operating procedure. We don't want any of the competitors to horn in on our work."

Deanna picked up a pencil from the glass surface of her counter, tapped it idly. "I learned today that Angela Perkins knew we were interested in booking Rob Winters within hours of our contacting his agent." There was a general murmuring among the staff. "And I suspect," Deanna continued, "from what I learned, that she was also aware of several others. Kate Lowell appeared on *Angela's* two weeks after her people claimed a scheduling conflict. She wasn't the only one. I have a list here of people we tried to book who guested on *Angela's* within two weeks of our initial contact."

"We've got a leak." The muscles in Fran's jaw twitched. "Son of a bitch."

"Come on, Fran." Jeff cast worried glances around the room. He shoved at his glasses. "Most of us have been here from the first day. We're like family." He tugged at the collar of his T-shirt, cutting his eyes back to Deanna. "Man, Dee, you can't believe any of us would do anything to hurt you or the show."

"No, I can't." She pushed a hand through her hair. "So I need ideas, suggestions."

"Jesus. Jesus Christ," Simon mumbled under his breath as he pressed his fingers to his eyes. "It's my fault." Dropping his hands, he gave Deanna a shattered look. "Lew McNeil. We've kept in touch all along. Hell, we've been friends for ten years. I never thought . . . I'm sick," he said. "I swear to God it makes me sick."

"What are you talking about?" Deanna asked quietly, but she thought she knew.

"We talk once, twice a month." He shoved back from the table, crossing the room to pour a glass of water. "Usual stuff— shop talk." Taking out a bottle, he shook two pills into his hand. "He'd bitch about Angela. He knew he could to me, that it wouldn't go any further. He'd tell me some of the wilder ideas her team had come up with for segments. Maybe he'd ask who we were lining up. And I'd tell him." He swallowed the pills audibly. "I'd tell him, because we were just two old friends talking shop. I never put it together until this minute, Dee. I swear to Christ."

"All right, Simon. So we know how, we know why. What are we going to do about it?"

"Hire somebody to go to New York and break all of Lew McNeil's fingers," Fran suggested as she rose to go stand beside the clearly distressed Simon.

"I'll give that some thought. In the meantime, the new policy is not to discuss any guests, any topic ideas or *any* of the developmental stages of the show outside of the office. Agreed?"

There was a general murmuring. No one made eye contact.

"And we have a new goal. One we're all going to concentrate on." She paused, waiting until she could skim her gaze over each face. "We're going to knock *Angela's* out of the number-one spot within a year." She held up a hand to stop the spontaneous applause. "I want everyone to start thinking about ideas for remotes. We need to start taking this show on the road. I want sexy locations, funny locations. I want the exotic, and I want Main Street, USA."

"Disney World," Fran suggested.

"New Orleans, for Mardi Gras," Cassie put in, and lifted her shoulders. "I always wanted to go."

"Check it out," Deanna ordered. "I want six doable locations. I want all the topic ideas we have cooking on my desk by the end of the day. Cassie, make a list of all the personal appearance requests I've got and accept them."

"How many?"

"All of them. Fit them into my schedule. And put in a call to Loren Bach." She sat back and rested her palms on the surface of the desk. "Let's get to work."

"Deanna." Simon stepped forward as the others filed out. "Can I have a minute?"

"Just," she said, and smiled. "I want to get started on this campaign."

He stood stiffly in front of her desk. "I know it might take you a little time to replace me, and that you'd like a smooth transition. I'll hand in my resignation whenever you want."

Deanna was already drawing a list on a legal pad in front of her. "I don't want your resignation, Simon. I want you to use that wily brain of yours to put me on top."

"I screwed up, Dee. Big time."

"You trusted a friend."

"A competitor," he corrected. "God knows how many shows I sabotaged by opening my big mouth. Shit, Dee, I was bragging, playing 'My job's bigger than your job.' I wanted to needle him because it was the only way I could stick it to Angela."

"I'm giving you another way." She leaned forward, eyes keen. She felt the power in her now, and she would use it, she knew, to finish what Angela had begun. "Help me knock her out of the top slot, Simon. You can't do that if you resign."

"I can't figure why you'd trust me."

"I had a pretty good idea where the leak had come from. Simon, I spent enough time around here to know you and Lew were tight." She spread her fingers. "If you hadn't told me, you wouldn't have had to offer to resign. I'd have fired you."

He rubbed a hand over his face. "So I admit to being a jerk and I keep my job."

"That about sums it up. And I expect, because you're feeling like one, you'll work even harder to put me on top."

More than a little dazed, he shook his head. "You picked up a few things from Angela after all."

"I got what I needed," she said shortly. She snatched up her phone when it buzzed. "Yes, Cassie?"

"Loren Bach on one, Deanna."

"Thanks." She let her finger hover over the button as she glanced back at Simon. "Are we straight on this?"

"As an arrow."

She waited until the door shut behind Simon, then drew in a deep breath. "Loren," she said when she made the connection. "I'm ready to go to war."

IN THE COLD, GLOOMY HOURS of a February morning, Lew kissed his wife goodbye. She stirred sleepily, and gave his cheek a pat before snuggling under the down quilt for another thirty-minute nap.

"Chicken stew tonight," she mumbled. "I'll be home by three to put it on."

Since their children had grown, each had fallen into a comfortable morning routine. Lew left his wife sleeping and went downstairs alone to eat breakfast with the early news. He winced over the weather report, though a glance out the window had already told him it wasn't promising. The drive from Brooklyn Heights to the studio in Manhattan was going to be a study in frustration. He bundled into a coat, pulled on gloves, put on the Russian-style fur hat his youngest son had given him for Christmas.

The wind was up, tossing the nasty wet snow into his face, letting it sneak under the collar of his coat. It was still shy of seven, dreary enough that the streetlights still glowed. The snow muffled sound and seemed to smother the air.

He saw no one out in the tidy neighborhood but an unhappy cat scratching pitifully on his owner's front door.

Too used to Chicago winters to complain about a February storm, Lew trudged to his car and began to clean the windshield.

He paid no attention to the fairy-tale world forming behind him. The low evergreens with their frosting of white, the pristine carpet that coated winter grass and pavement, the dancing flakes that swirled in the dull glow of the street-lamps.

He thought only of the drudgery of scraping his windshield clean, of the discomfort of snow on his collar, of the nip of the wind at his ears. Of the traffic he had yet to face.

He heard his name called, softly, and turned to peer through the driving snow.

For a moment he saw nothing but white and the snow-smothered beam of light from the streetlamp.

And then he saw. For just an instant, he saw.

The shotgun blast struck him full in the face, cartwheeling his body over the hood of his car. From down the block a dog began to bark in high, excited yips. The cat streaked away to hide in a snow-coated juniper.

The echo of the shot died quickly, almost as quickly as Lew McNeil.

"That was for Deanna," the killer whispered, and drove slowly away.

WHEN DEANNA HEARD the news a few hours later, the shock of it overshadowed the envelope she'd found on her desk. It said simply:

Deanna, I'll always be there for you.

Chapter Nineteen

DEANNA LOUNGED IN FINN'S BIG TUB WITH STEAMING WATER whirling and pulsing around her, her eyes half closed and a frothy mimosa in her hand. It was the middle of a Saturday morning, and she had more than an hour before Tim O'Malley, her driver, would be by to pick her up for an appearance in Merrillville, Indiana.

She felt as lazy and smug as a cat curled in a sunbeam.

"What are we celebrating?"

"You're in town; I'm in town. And not counting your afternoon across the state line today, it looks like it could stay that way for a week."

From the opposite end of the tub, Finn watched her tension ease, degree by degree. She'd been wound tight as a spring for weeks. Longer, he thought, sipping the icy drink. Even before Lew McNeil's random and senseless murder, she'd been a bundle of nerves. In the weeks following Lew's death her feelings had shifted from remorse to anger to guilt to frustration over a man who had done his best to sabotage her show for his own ends.

Or Angela's ends, Finn theorized.

But now she smiled, and her eyes were heavy with pleasure. "Things have been a little chaotic lately."

"You flying off to Florida, me chasing presidential candidates from state to state. Both of us trying to put together a show with press and paparazzi dogging our heels." He shrugged, rubbing his foot up and down her slick, slippery leg.

It hadn't been easy for anyone on her staff, or his, to work with the continued and pesky attention the media had focused on their relationship. For reasons neither of them could fathom, they had become the couple of the year. Just that morning, Deanna had read about her wedding plans in a tabloid some helpful soul had tucked under the front doormat.

All in all it made her uneasy, unsure and far too distracted.

"Do you call that chaotic?" Finn asked, and drew her attention back.

"You're right, just another day in the simple life." Her sigh was long and sumptuous. "And at least we're getting things done. I really liked your show on Chicago's decaying infrastructure, even if it did make me start to worry that the streets are going to crumble under my car."

"Everything was there—panic, comedy, half-crazed city officials. Still, it wasn't as gripping as your interview with Mickey and Minnie Mouse."

One eye opened. "Watch it, pal."

"No, really." His grin was wicked. "You've got America talking. What kind of relationship do they have, and what part does Goofy play in it? These burning questions need to be answered—and who knows, it might help take some of the heat off us?"

"We were dealing with American traditions," she shot back. "On the need for entertainment and fantasy, and the enormous industry that fuels it. Which is every bit as relevant as watching politicians sling insults at each other. More," she said, gesturing with her glass. "People need some mode of escape, particularly during a recession. You do your shows on global warming and the socioeconomic troubles in the former Soviet Union, Riley. I'll stick with the everyday issues that affect the average person."

He was still grinning at her. Deanna took a sip of her mimosa and scowled at him. "You're riding me on purpose."

"I like the way your eyes get dark and edgy." He set his glass aside so that he could slide forward and lay his body over hers. Water sloshed lazily over the lip of the tub. "And you get this line right here"—he rubbed his thumb between her brows—"that I get to smooth away."

His free hand was busy smoothing something else. "Some might say you're a sneaky bastard, Finn."

"Some have." He nipped at her lips. "Others will. And speaking of Mickey and Minnie." His hands cruised over her hot, soft skin.

"Were we?"

"I was wondering if we can compare our relationship to theirs. Undefined and long-term."

While the jets of water frothed around them and between them, she stroked a hand through his damp hair. It felt so good to be here, to know that at any moment the comforting heat could erupt into explosive heat. "I can define it: We're two people who love each other, who enjoy each other, who want to be with each other."

"We could be with each other more if you'd move in with me."

It was a subject they'd discussed before. And one they had been unable to resolve. Deanna pressed her lips to his shoulder. "It's easier for me to have my own place when you're away."

"I'm here more than I'm gone these days."

"I know." Her lips slid up his throat as she tried to distract him. "Give me some time to work it out in my head."

"Sometimes you've got to trust your impulses, Deanna, your instincts." His mouth met hers, tasting of frustration and desire.

He knew if he pushed, she'd agree, but his instinct warned him not to rush her. "I can wait. Just don't make me wait too long."

"We can give it a trial run." Her blood was pulsing as frantically as the bubbling water. "I'll move some things in, stay here through next week."

"I'll make it hard for you to leave again."

"I bet you will." She smiled, pushing his hair back, framing his face. "I'm so in love with you, Finn. You can believe that. And I swear, the rumors about me and Goofy are all lies. We're just friends."

He tipped her head back so that her body slipped farther into the water. "I don't trust the long-eared son of a bitch."

"I just used him to make you jealous—though he does have a certain guileless charm I find strangely appealing."

"You want charm? Why don't I—damn." Finn tossed his wet hair back and reached for the tubside phone. "Hold that thought," he told her. "Yeah, Riley."

Deanna was considering several interesting ways to distract him when she saw the change in his face. The water shifted and slopped over as he climbed from the tub to reach for a towel.

"Get Curt," he said, dripping as he slung the towel around his waist. "And contact Barlow James. I want a full crew, a mobile unit on the spot five minutes ago. I'll be at the site in twenty minutes." He swore, not so lightly, under his breath. "You can if I tell you that you can."

"What is it?" Deanna turned off the tub and rose. Water streamed from her as she shook out a towel. She already knew he was leaving.

"There's a hostage situation over in Greektown." With a quick flick of the wrist, he turned on the television even as he headed into the bedroom to drag on clothes. "It's bad. Three people are already dead."

She shivered once. Then as quick, as brisk as he, she reached for her robe. She wanted to tell him she'd go with him. But of course she couldn't. There were several hundred people waiting for her in the ballroom of an Indiana hotel.

Why was she so cold? she wondered as she bundled hurriedly into her robe. He was already tucking a shirt into his slacks, as calmly as a man going to his office to work on tax forms. He'd survived air raids and earthquakes. Surely a skirmish in Greektown was nothing to worry about.

"You'll be careful."

He grabbed a tie, a jacket. "I'll be good." As she reached into the closet for the suit she'd chosen for her afternoon appearance, he spun her around for a kiss. "I'll probably be back before you."

THE WORST KIND OF WAR was one with no front lines or battle plans. It was fueled on anger and fear and the blind need to destroy. The once-tidy restaurant with its pretty, striped awning and sidewalk tables was destroyed. Shards from the broken window sparkled like scattered gems over the sidewalk. The flap of the awning in the raw spring wind was smothered by the static-filled drone of police radios. Reporters held back by barricades swarmed like hungry wolves.

There was another volley of gunshots from inside. And a long, terrified scream.

"Jesus." Sweat popped out on Curt's brow as he held the camera steady. "He's killing them."

"Get a shot of that cop there," Finn ordered. "The one with the bullhorn."

"You're the boss." Curt focused in on a cop in a neon orange trench coat with a hangdog face and graying hair. Amid the screams and shouts, the weeping, the bitter threats and curses from inside the restaurant, the steely-eyed cop continued to talk in a soothing monotone.

"Pretty cool customer," Curt observed, then at a signal from Finn shifted, crouched to get a shot of the SWAT team taking position.

"Cool enough," Finn agreed. "If he keeps at it, they might not need the sharpshooters. Keep rolling. I'm going to see if I can work my way over and find out who he is."

THE BALLROOM WAS FILLED TO capacity. From where Deanna sat on the raised dais, she could see all three hundred and fifty people who had come to hear her talk about women in broadcasting. She was going to give them their money's worth. She'd gone over her notes thoroughly once again on the drive from Chicago, letting her concentration lapse only when she caught a glimpse of Finn on the limo's television.

He was, as Barlow James would say, in his element. And, it seemed, she was in hers.

She waited through the flattering introduction, through the applause that followed it, then rose and walked to the podium. She scanned the room, smiled.

"Good afternoon. One of the first things we learn in broadcasting is that we work weekends. Since we are, I hope to make the next hour as entertaining as it is informative. That, to me, is television, and I've found it a very satisfying way to make a living. It occurred to me that as you are professionals, you wouldn't have much opportunity to watch daytime TV, so I'm hoping to convince you to set your VCRs Monday morning. We're on at nine here in Merrillville."

That earned Deanna her first chuckle, and set the tone for the next twenty minutes, until her speech segued into a question-and-answer period.

One of the first questioners asked if Finn Riley had accompanied her.

"I'm afraid not. As we all know, one of the boons, and the curses, of this business is the breaking story. Finn's reporting on one right now, but you can catch him on *In Depth* Tuesday nights. I always do."

"Miss Reynolds, how do you feel about the fact that looks have become as much a part of the criteria for on-air jobs as credentials?"

"I would certainly agree with network executives that television is a visual medium. To a point. I can tell you this: If in thirty years Finn Riley is still reporting, and considered a statesman, I'd not only expect but demand, as a woman, to be given the same respect."

FINN WASN'T THINKING ABOUT the future. He was too involved in the present. Using wile, guile and arrogance, he'd managed to gain a position beside the hostage negotiator, Lieutenant Arnold Jenner. Jenner still held the bullhorn but had taken a short break in his appeal to his quarry to release the hostages.

"Lieutenant, the word I've gotten here is that Johnson—that's his name, isn't it, Elmer Johnson?"

"It's the one he answers to," Jenner said mildly.

"He has a history of depression. His VA records—"

"You wouldn't have access to his medical records, Mr. Riley."

"Not directly." But he had contacts, and he'd used them. "My take on this is that Johnson served in the military and has been troubled since his discharge in March of last year. Last week he lost his wife and his job."

"You're well informed."

"I get paid to be. He went into this restaurant at just past ten this morning—that's about three hours ago—armed with a forty-four Magnum, a Bushmaster, a gas mask and a carbine. He shot and killed two waiters and a bystander, then took five hostages, including two women and a twelve-year-old girl, the owner's daughter."

"Ten," Jenner said wearily. "The kid's ten. Mr. Riley, you do good work, and usually I enjoy it. But my job right now is to get those people out of there alive."

298

Finn glanced over, noting the position of the sharpshooters. They wouldn't wait much longer. "What are his demands? Can you tell me that?"

It hardly mattered, Jenner decided. There had been only one, and he hadn't been able to meet it. "He wants his wife, Mr. Riley. She left Chicago four days ago. We're trying to locate her, but we haven't had any luck."

"I can get it on the air. If she catches a bulletin, she may make contact. Let me talk to him. I might be able to get him to bargain if I tell him I'll put all my people on it."

"You that desperate for a story?"

Insults were too common in his line of work for Finn to take offense. "I'm always ready to bargain for a story, Lieutenant." His eyes narrowed as he measured the man beside him. "Look, the kid's ten. Let me try."

Jenner believed in instinct, and he also knew, without a doubt, that he couldn't hold the situation from flash point much longer. After a moment, he handed Finn the bullhorn. "Don't promise what you can't deliver."

"Mr. Johnson. Elmer. This is Finn Riley. I'm a reporter."

"I know who you are." The voice came out, a high-pitched shriek through the broken glass. "Do you think I'm stupid?"

"You were in the Gulf, right? I was too."

"Shit. You figure that makes us buddies?"

"I figure anybody who did time over there's already been to hell." The awning flapped, reminding him of the road to Kuwait, and the sparkle of pink sequins. "I thought maybe we could make a deal."

"There ain't no deal. My wife gets here, I let them go. She doesn't, we're all going to hell. For real."

"The cops have been trying to reach her, but I thought we could put a new spin on it. I've got a lot of contacts. I can get your story national, put your wife's picture on television screens from coast to coast. Even if she isn't watching, someone who knows her is bound to be. We'll put a number on, a special number where she can call in. You can talk to her, Elmer."

That was good, Jenner decided, even as he braced to rip the bullhorn from Finn's hands if the need arose. Using his first name, offering him not only hope but a few minutes of fame. His superiors might not approve, but Jenner thought it could work.

"Then do it!" Johnson shouted out. "Just fucking do it."

"I'll be glad to, but I can't unless you give something back. Just let the little girl come out, Elmer, and I'll plug your story across the country within ten minutes. I can even fix it so you can get a message to your wife. In your own words."

"I'm not letting anybody out, except in a body bag."

"She's just a kid, Elmer. Your wife probably likes kids." Christ, he hoped so. "If you let her go, she'll hear about it, and she'll want to talk to you."

"It's a trick."

"I've got a camera right here." He glanced toward Curt. "Is there a TV in the bar in there?" he called out.

"What if there is?"

"You can watch everything I do. Everything I say. I'll have them put me on live."

"Then do it. Do it in five minutes, fucking five minutes, or you're going to have another body in here."

"Call the desk," Finn shouted. "Patch me in. Set up for live now." Then he turned back to Jenner.

"You'd make a pretty good cop—for a reporter."

"Thanks." He handed Jenner the bullhorn. "Tell him to send her out while I'm on the air, or I go to black."

IN PRECISELY FIVE MINUTES, Finn faced the camera. Whatever his inner turmoil, his delivery was calm and well paced, his eyes cool. Behind him was the shattered exterior of the restaurant.

"This morning in Chicago's Greektown, this family-run

restaurant erupted with violence. Three people are known dead in the standoff between police and Elmer Johnson, a former mechanic who chose this spot to take his stand. Johnson's only demand is contact with his estranged wife, Arlene."

Though he sensed activity behind him, Finn's eyes stayed fixed on the camera's light.

"Johnson, well armed, is holding five hostages. In his appeal to—"

There was a scream from behind him. Finn shifted instantly to give Curt room to tape.

It happened quickly, as if all the waiting hours had been focused on this one moment. The child, trembling and weeping, stepped outside. Even as the shadow of the awning fell over her face, a wild-eyed man sprinted out, screaming as he hurtled toward escape. The rash of gunfire from the restaurant propelled the man forward, off his feet. It was Jenner, Finn saw, who scooped the child aside even as Johnson stumbled to the door.

The sniper's bullet plowed through Johnson's forehead.

"Oh man." Curt kept repeating the words over and over under his breath as he held the camera steady. "Man, oh man, oh man."

Finn only shook his head. The burning in his left arm made him glance down curiously. Brows knit, he touched the hole in his sleeve. His fingers came away sticky with blood.

"Well, hell," he murmured. "I got this coat in Milan."

"Shit, Riley." Curt's eyes bulged. "Shit. You're hit."

"Yeah." He didn't feel any pain yet, only dull annoyance. "You just can't patch leather, either."

ON MONDAY, AS SOON AS THE morning show was taped, Deanna stood in the center of her office, her eyes glued to the TV screen. It seemed unbelievable that she could hear Finn's voice supplying the details over the special report.

She saw the scene as he had, the shattered glass, the bloodied body. The camera bobbled and swung as the sniper fired. Her heart jerked as she heard the pop and ping of bullets.

Through it all, Finn's voice remained calm, cool, with an underpinning of fury she doubted any of his viewers were aware of. She stood, a fist pressed to her heart as the camera zoomed in on the child, weeping in the arms of a rumpled man with graying hair.

"Deanna." Jeff hesitated in the doorway, then crossed the room to stand beside her.

"It's horrible," she murmured. "Unbelievable. If that man hadn't panicked and run out that way, if he hadn't done that, it might have turned out differently. That little girl, she could have been caught in the cross fire. And Finn . . ."

"He's okay. Hey, he's right downstairs. Back on the job."

"Back on the job."

"Deanna," he said again, and laid a hand on her shoulder. "I know it must be tough for you. Not only knowing it happened, but actually watching it." He walked over and switched off the set. "But he's okay."

"He was shot." She whirled away from the blank screen and struggled for composure. "And I was in Indiana. You can't imagine how horrible it was to have Tim come into the ballroom and tell me he'd seen it on the limo's set. And to be helpless. Not to be there when they took him to the hospital."

"If it upsets you this much, and you asked him, he could get a desk job."

For the first time all morning she gave him a genuine smile. "Things don't work that way. I wouldn't want them to. We'd better get back to work." She gave his hand a quick squeeze before rounding her desk. "Thanks for listening."

"Hey. That's what I'm here for."

*

"EVERYBODY STAYS LATE TONIGHT," Angela announced at an emergency staff meeting. "Nobody leaves until we lock in this show. I want a panel, and I want it hard-line. Three from this white supremacist group, three from the NAACP. I want radicals." She sat behind her desk, her fingers drumming on the surface. "Make sure each side gets at least a dozen tickets, so they can seed the audience. I want to blow the roof off."

She stabbed a finger at her head researcher. "We've got some statistics here in New York. Get me some of the relatives."

"Some of them might not be easy to persuade."

"Then pay them," she snapped. "Money always turns the tide. And I want some tape, as graphic as possible, from rallies. Some witnesses to racially motivated crimes, perpetrators would be better. Promise that we'll protect their identities. Promise them anything, just get them."

When she fell into silence, Dan gave a nod that signaled the end of the meeting. He waited until the door was closed again.

"You know, Angela, you could be walking on thin ice here."

Her head snapped up. "You sound like Lew."

"I'm not advising you against doing it. I'm just suggesting that you watch out for the cross fire."

"I know what I'm doing." She'd seen Finn's report, as had nearly every other American with a television set. Now she was going to outdo him as well as Deanna. "We need something hot, and the timing couldn't be better. The country's in an uproar about race, and the city's a mess."

"You're not worried about Deanna Reynolds." He smiled, knowing he had to defuse the tantrum he saw building in her eyes.

"She's climbing up my back, isn't she?"

"She'll slip off." He took her rigid hands in his. "What you need now is a boost in publicity. Something that will focus the public's attention on you." He lifted her hand, admiring the way the sun dashed off the diamonds in her watch. "And I've got an idea how to do it."

"It better be good."

"It's more than good, it's inspired." He kissed her hand, watching her over her knuckles. "The American public loves one thing more than they love hearing about graft and sex and violence. Weddings," he said as he drew her gently to her feet. "Big, splashy weddings—private weddings dotted with celebrities. Marry me, Angela." His eyes were soft. "I'll not only make you happy, I'll see to it that your picture's on every major newspaper and magazine in the country."

The flutter of her heart was quick. "And what would you get out of it, Dan?"

"You." Reading her clearly, he lowered his head to kiss her. "All I want is you."

ON THE SECOND SATURDAY in June, Angela donned a Vera Wang shell-pink gown of silk, encrusted with tiny pearls. Its sweetheart neckline framed a flattering hint of her rounded breasts, its full, elaborate skirt accented her tiny waist. She wore a wide-brimmed hat with a fingertip veil and carried a bouquet of white orchids.

The ceremony took place in the country home she'd purchased in Connecticut, and was attended by a stellar guest list. Some were pleased to be there, drawn either by sentiment or the notion of having their name and photo included in the press releases. Others came because it was easier to accept than to face Angela's fury later.

Elaborate gifts crowded the large parlor and, under uniformed guard, were on display for the select members of the press. No one seeing all this, Angela thought, would doubt how much she was loved.

The reception spilled out into the rose garden, where a champagne fountain bubbled and white doves cooed.

When the event was buzzed incessantly by helicopters crammed with paparazzi, she knew it was a success.

Like any new bride, she glowed. The sun glinted off the five-carat diamond gracing her left hand as she posed with Dan for photos.

She told the reporters, regretfully, that her mother, her only living relative, was too ill to attend. In reality she was tucked in a private clinic, drying out.

Kate Lowell, looking young and fresh in a billowing sundress, kissed Angela's cheek for the benefit of the cameras. Her long red-gold hair flowed down her bare back, melted copper over sun-kissed peaches. She had a face the camera worshiped, ice-edged cheekbones, full lips, huge gold eyes. The image was completed by a sinuous body, killer legs and a rich infectious giggle.

Kate Lowell could have become a star on the sole basis of her glorious physical attributes. She certainly had done her share of commercial endorsements. But she had something more: talent and charm that burned every bit as hot as her box-office appeal. And ambition that seared through both.

She enchanted the photographer by shooting him a dazzling smile, then turned the other cheek for Angela. "I hate your guts," she said softly.

"I know, darling." Beaming, Angela slipped her arm around Kate's waist, fingers digging ruthlessly into flesh as she turned her best side to the camera. "Smile pretty now, show why you're the number-one female box-office draw."

Kate did, with a smile that could have melted steel at five paces. "I wish you were dead."

"You and so many others." She hooked her arm through Kate's and strolled off, two bosom friends stealing a private moment. "Now, is it true that you and Rob Winters are considering scripts for a TV movie?"

"No comment."

"Now, now, darling." Angela's voice was a purr, deadly feline. "Didn't we agree to scratch each other's backs?"

"I'd like to scratch your eyes." But she knew she couldn't. There was much too much at stake for her to indulge herself quite that blatantly. Still, there were other weapons. Tilting her head, Kate studied Angela's face. "That's an excellent tuck, by the way. Barely noticeable." Her smile was quick and sincere when Angela bristled. "Don't worry, *darling*, it'll be our secret. After all, a girl's got to do everything necessary to maintain the illusion of youth. Especially when she's married to a younger man."

Behind the flirty little veil, Angela's eyes were as hard as marbles. It was her day, by God. Hers. And nothing and no one would spoil it. "A script's come my way, Katie dear. I think you'll find it fascinating. And I think you'll be able to pique Rob's interest as well. The two of you have been pals for years, and it would be a friendly boost if you persuaded him to do it. After all, he doesn't have a great deal of time left to pick and choose, does he?"

"You bitch."

Angela gave a trilling laugh. Nothing could have pleased her more than seeing Kate's smug smile fade. "The trouble with actors is they need someone to write that clever dialogue. You'll have the script by Monday, darling. I really would consider it a favor if you'd read it quickly."

"I'm getting tired of your favors, Angela. Other people might call it blackmail."

"I'm not other people. It's simply a matter of my having certain information that I'm more than happy to keep to myself. A favor to you, dear. In return, you do one for me. That's called cooperation."

"One day you're going to cooperate yourself right into hell."

"It's just business." With a sigh, Angela patted Kate's flushed cheeks. "You've been around long enough to know better than to take everything so personally. We'll discuss terms when I get back from my honeymoon. Now, you'll have to excuse me. I can't ignore my guests."

Although Kate's imagination didn't run to dialogue, she had no trouble with visuals. As Angela glided away, Kate saw the frothy silk splattered with blood.

"One day," she whispered, yanking a rose from a bush and crushing it in her hand. "One day, someone's finally going to get the guts and do it."

"SHE LOOKS WONDERFUL." Lolling on the couch in the cabin, Deanna studied the front cover of *People*. "Radiant."

Finn drummed up the energy to glance over. They had finally been able to synchronize a full three days off, together. If the phone didn't ring, the fax didn't shrill and the world didn't collapse within the next twenty-four hours, they would have made it through.

"She looks like one of those prop wedding cakes. All fancy fake icing over the inedible."

"Your vision's skewed by malice."

"Yours should be, too."

She only sighed and flipped through to the cover story. "I don't have to like her to admit she's lovely. And she looks happy, really happy. Maybe marriage will mellow her."

He only snorted. "Since this is her third time at bat, that's doubtful."

"Not if this is the right one. I don't wish her bad luck, personally or professionally." She peered over the top of the magazine. "I want to whip her butt on merit."

"You are whipping her butt."

"In Chicago, and a few other markets. But this wedding's bound to shift the tide at least for a time."

He stretched his arms over his head, muscles rippling. Deanna could see the faint scar where the bullet had sliced through.

"Why do you think she did it?"

"Oh come on, Finn, give her some credit. A woman doesn't get married so that she can get her picture on a few covers."

"Kansas." Amazed that she could still be so naive, he took the

307

magazine from her. "When you're slipping down the ladder, you grab hold of any handy rope."

"I think that's a mixed metaphor."

"You think this is for love?" Laughing, he sent the magazine sailing. Angela, the happy bride, landed facedown. "She's had six weeks of free publicity since the day her secret engagement mysteriously leaked."

"It could have leaked." She gave him a friendly shove with her stockinged foot. "And even if she planted it, it doesn't change the bottom line. She's a beautiful, vibrant woman who fell for a gorgeous, magnetic man."

"Gorgeous?" Finn snagged her foot by the ankle. "You think he's gorgeous?"

"Yes, he's—" She shrieked, twisting as he tickled her foot. "Stop that."

"And magnetic?"

"Sexy." Giggling helplessly, she reared up to try to free herself. "Sinfully attractive." She tried biting when he wrestled her down.

"You fight like a girl."

She blew her hair out of her eyes and tried to buck him off. "So what?"

"I like it. And I'm now honor-bound to erase Dan What's-his-name from your mind."

"Dan Gardner," she said primly. "And I don't know if you can. I mean, he's so elegant, so polished, so . . ." She gave a mock shiver. "So romantic."

"We'll shoot for a contrast."

With one swipe, he dragged his hand down her breezy cotton blouse and sent buttons flying.

"Finn!" Caught between shock and amusement, she started to shove him back. The laughing protest ended on a strangled gasp as he fastened his mouth to her breast.

Instant heat. Instant need. It burst through her like light, blindingly bright. The hands that had playfully pressed against his shoulders tightened like vises, short, neat nails digging crescents into his flesh. Her heart stuttered beneath his greedy mouth, losing its pace, then racing ahead in a wild sprint.

His hands were already tugging aside the remains of her blouse, then streaking over bared skin to arouse and demand. The strong summer sun streamed through the windows, fell over her in hot white light. Her skin was moist from it, from his rough, impatient touch. With his mouth still feasting on her, he slid his hand under the baggy leg of her shorts and drove her ruthlessly to a fast, violent climax.

"Again." Driven himself, he fixed his mouth on hers, swallowing her cry as he pushed her higher.

He wanted her like this. So often he was content to let them take each other slowly, savoring each touch, each taste on the long, lazy journey toward fulfillment. He loved the way her body grew sinuous and soft, the way his own pleasures built layer by layer.

But now he wanted only the fast, molten ride, the mindlessness of hurried, urgent sex. He wanted to possess her, to brand her, to feel her body rock fitfully under his, until he was sunk deep.

He tore at her clothes even as she tugged and yanked at his. Her breath was hot on his flesh, her mouth streaking hungrily over him, sounds of desperate excitement humming in her throat.

He shifted, gripping her hips and lifting her up so that the muscles in his arms quivered. Then he was sheathed in her. Their twin cries of triumph shivered on the sultry air.

With her head thrown back, her long, slim body glistening with sweat, she took him deeper, drove him as he had driven her. Ruthlessly, relentlessly. She gripped his hands, guiding them over her damp body, urging him to claim more while her heart galloped in a mad race of its own.

The orgasm struck, a sweaty fist that pummeled and pummeled and left her body a mass of indescribably exquisite aches. The air was clogged and burning in her lungs. She sobbed to release it, sobbed to gulp it back in.

She felt his body lunge, vaulting her over that final, keen edge. Like wax melted in the sun, she slid down to him and lay limp.

His own mind cleared gradually, the static from the storm dying to a steady quiet that was her breathing. The dark haze that had covered his vision lifted so that he closed his eyes against the hard sunlight.

"I guess I protected my honor," he murmured. She gave a strangled laugh.

"I didn't know—God, I can't breathe." She tried again. "I didn't know tweaking your ego would be so . . . rewarding."

"Relaxed?"

She sighed. "Very."

"Happy?"

"Completely."

"Then this is probably a good time to ask you to think about something."

"Hmmm. I don't think I *can* think just now."

"Put this in the back of your mind." His hand gently massaged her back. "Let it stew there for a while."

"What am I supposed to stew about?"

"Marrying me."

She jerked back. "Marrying you?"

"Is looking shocked another way to tweak my ego?"

"No." Staggered, she pressed a hand to her cheek. "God, Finn, you know how to toss one in from left field."

"We'll talk baseball later—since the Cubs are in the basement." Goddamn nerves, he thought, while his stomach clenched. It was ridiculous for him to feel these tugs of panic, but all he could imagine was her saying no. Absolutely not.

For the first time in his life he wanted something and someone he wasn't sure he could have.

He levered himself up so that they sat, naked, facing each other, both still achy and sated with sex. The plan was, he reminded himself, to keep it light, natural.

310

"It shouldn't be such a surprise, Deanna. We've been lovers for more than a year."

"Yes, but . . . we haven't even resolved living together yet—"

"One of my points. My strategy in getting you to live with me; then easing you into marriage just isn't panning out."

"Your strategy?"

He didn't mind the edge in her voice. It matched the one in his own. "Kansas, the only way to handle you is like a chess game. A man has to think a half dozen moves ahead and outflank you."

"I don't think I care for that analogy."

"It's an accurate one." He pinched her chin lightly between his fingers. "You spend so much time thinking things through, trying to avoid making the wrong move. I have to give you a shove."

"Is that what this proposal is?" She batted his hand away. "A shove?"

"We'll call it more of a nudge, since I'm willing to let you think it over."

"That's generous of you," she said between her clenched teeth.

"Actually," he continued, "I'm giving us both time. I can't say I'm completely sold on the idea myself."

She blinked. "Excuse me?"

It was inspired, he realized. Absolutely inspired. Two could play tweak-the-ego. "We're coming from opposite fields here on this subject. You from a big, happy family, all those traditional trappings, where 'till death do us part' means something. For me, marriage has always meant 'till divorce do us part.'"

Incensed, she snatched up her blouse, swore, then tossed it aside. "For someone so cynical, I'm surprised you'd consider it."

His mouth quivered as she dragged on his T-shirt. "I'm not cynical, I'm realistic. Marriage has become like newspapers. You toss them out when you're through, and not a hell of a lot of people bother to recycle."

"Then what's the point?" She yanked on her shorts.

"I'm in love with you." He said it quietly, simply, and stopped

311

her from storming out of the room. "I'd like to think about the idea of starting a life with you, having children, giving some of those traditional trappings a shot."

His words deflated her anger. "Damn you, Finn," she said helplessly.

He grinned up at her. "Then you'll think about it."

Chapter Twenty

DAN GARDNER DIDN'T MARRY ANGELA FOR HER MONEY. NOT entirely. Some people were unkind enough to think he had—even to say he had. During the first few weeks of their marriage there was considerable speculation in the tabloid press about the matter, as well as the disparity in their ages: ten years almost to the day. A firm believer in publicity, Dan had planted the articles himself.

But there were other reasons he had married her. He admired her skills. He understood her flaws and, most important to him, how to exploit them. It was he, recognizing her insecurities and her suspicions, who had insisted on signing a prenuptial agreement. Divorce would not benefit him. But Dan wasn't planning on divorce—unless it benefited him. It was he—knowing her weakness for romance and her need to be the center of love— who arranged for candlelit dinners for two, quiet weekends in the country. When she needed attention beyond what he could provide, he arranged for that as well. As Angela became more and more obsessed with eroding ratings, he picked up the threads of several A. P. Production projects and deftly increased the profits.

He might not have married her for her money, but he intended to enjoy it.

"Look at this!" Angela heaved a copy of *TV Guide* across the room. It landed with Deanna's picture faceup. "Just look! 'Daytime's new princess,' my ass." Her silk robe billowed out like a sail as she paced the snowy carpet of her penthouse. "'Warm and accessible, sexy and sharp.' They fawned over her, Dan. Goddamn it, they gave her the cover and two full pages."

"Don't let it spook you." Because they were staying in for the evening, Dan poured her a full flute of champagne. She was easier to handle when she was drunk and weepy. And when she was needy, the sex was simply stupendous. "She's just got a longer way to fall now, that's all."

"That's not all." Angela snatched the glass away from him. She didn't want to need a drink, but she did and she was in no mood to fight the longing. "You saw the ratings. She's had a twenty-percent share for the last three weeks."

"And you ended up the year as number one," he reminded her.

"It's a new year," she snapped back. "Yesterday doesn't count." She drank deeply, then planted the dainty heel of her feathered mule in Deanna's left eye. "Not so pretty now, are you?" Fueled on envy, she kicked the magazine aside. "No matter what I do she keeps moving up. Now she's getting my press." After draining the glass, she thrust it back at Dan.

"*Angela's* isn't your only interest." Dutifully he refilled the glass for her. "You have the specials, the projects A. P. Productions is involved with. Your interests and your impact are more diverse than hers." He watched her eyes consider as she drank. "She's got one note, Angela. She plays it well, but it's just one note."

The description steadied her quaking heart. "She was always limited, with her little timetables and note cards." But as her fury drained, despair crept into the void. "I don't want her cutting me out, Dan." Her eyes filled, swimming with hot tears as she gulped down champagne. "I don't think I could stand it. Not from her of all people."

"You're making it too personal." Sympathetically, he filled her glass again, knowing that after the third drink she'd be as pliant as a baby with a full tummy.

"It is personal." The tears spilled over, but she let Dan lead her to the couch. She cuddled there on his lap with tangled threads of contentment and unease working through her. It had been the same cuddling on her father's lap on the rare occasions when he had been home and sober. "She wants to hurt me, Dan. She and that bastard Loren Bach. They'd do anything to hurt me."

"No one's going to hurt you." He tipped the glass to her lips the way a mother might urge medicine on a whiny child.

"They know I'm the best."

"Of course they do." Her neediness aroused him. As long as her neuroses bloomed, he was in charge. Setting her glass aside, he parted her robe to nuzzle her breasts. "Just leave everything to me," he murmured. "I'll take care of it."

"Do arguments with your mate end up as war zones, with flying accusations and flying dishes? 'How to Fight Fair', tomorrow on *Deanna's Hour*."

"Okay, Dee, we need some bumpers for the affiliates."

She rolled her eyes at the assistant director, but dutifully scanned the cue cards. "View the best on Tulsa's best. KJAB-TV, channel nine. Okay, let's run through them."

For the next hour she taped promos for affiliates across the country, a tedious chore at best, but one she always agreed to.

When it was done, Fran walked on set with a chilled sixteen-ounce bottle of Pepsi. She waddled a little, heavily pregnant with her second child. "The price of fame," she said.

"I can pay it." Grateful, Deanna took a long, cool drink. "Didn't I tell you to go home early?"

"Didn't I tell you I'm fine? I've got three weeks yet."

"Three more weeks and you won't fit through the doorway."

"What was that?"

"Nothing." Deanna drank again before heading off set. She paused by the large mirror, hooking an arm through Fran's so that they stood side by side. "Don't you think you're a bit bigger than you were when you were carrying Aubrey?"

Fran snuck an M&M into her mouth. "Water weight."

Deanna caught the whiff of candy and lifted a brow. "Sure it couldn't have anything to do with all those chocolate doughnuts you've been scarfing down?"

"The kid has a yen for them. What am I supposed to do? The cravings have to be filtered through me first." Tilting her head, Fran studied her reflection. The new chin-length hair bob might have been flattering, she thought. If her face hadn't looked like an inflated balloon. "Jeez, why did I buy this brown suit? I look like a woolly mammoth."

"You said it, I didn't." Deanna turned toward the elevators, eyeing Fran owlishly as she pressed the button.

"No cracks about weight restrictions, pal." With what dignity she could muster, Fran waddled in and stabbed sixteen. "I can't wait until it's your turn. If you'd just give in and marry Finn, you could start a family. You, too, could experience the joys of motherhood. Swollen feet, indigestion, stretch marks and the ever-popular weak bladder."

"You're making it so appealing."

"The trouble—and the reason I am once again approaching the size of a small planet—is that it *is* appealing." She pressed a hand to her side as the baby—once again dubbed Big Ed—tried out a one-two punch. "There's nothing quite like it," she murmured. The doors opened. "So, are you going to marry the guy or what?"

"I'm thinking about it."

"You've been thinking about it for weeks." Fran braced a hand on her spine as they walked to Deanna's office.

"He's thinking, too." She knew it sounded defensive. Annoyed, she sailed through the empty outer office into her own. "And things are complicated right now."

"Things are always complicated. People who wait for the perfect moment usually die first."

"That's comforting."

"I wouldn't want to push you."

"Wouldn't you?" Deanna smiled again.

"Nudge, sweetie pie, not push. What's this?" Fran picked up the single white rose that lay across Deanna's desk. "Classy," she said, giving it a sniff. "Romantic. Sweet." She glanced at the plain white envelope still resting on the blotter. "Finn?"

No, Deanna thought, her skin chilled. Not Finn. She struggled for casualness and picked up a pile of correspondence Cassie had typed. "Could be."

"Aren't you going to open the note?"

"Later. I want to make sure Cassie gets these letters out before the end of the day."

"God, you're a tough sell, Dee. If a guy sent me a single rose, I'd be putty."

"I'm busy."

Fran's head jerked up at the change in her tone. "I can see that. I'll get out of your way."

"I'm sorry." Instantly contrite, Deanna reached out. "Really, Fran, I didn't mean to bite your head off. I guess I'm a little wired. The Daytime Emmy business is coming up. That stupid tabloid story about my secret affair with Loren Bach hit last week."

"Oh, honey, you're not letting that get to you. Come on. I think Loren got a kick out of it."

"He can afford to. It didn't make him sound as though he was sleeping his way to a thirty-percent share."

"Nobody believes those things." She huffed at Deanna's

317

expression. "Well, nobody with an IQ in the triple digits. As far as the Emmys go, you've got nothing to worry about there either. You're going to win."

"That's what they keep telling Susan Lucci." But she laughed and waved Fran away. "Get out of here—and go home this time. It's nearly five anyway."

"Talked me into it." Fran laid the rose back on the desk, not noticing Deanna's instinctive recoil. "See you tomorrow."

"Yeah." Alone, Deanna reached cautiously for the envelope. She took the ebony-handled letter opener from her desk set and slit it cleanly open.

> DEANNA, I'D DO ANYTHING FOR YOU.
> IF ONLY YOU'D LOOK AT ME, REALLY LOOK.
> I'D GIVE YOU ANYTHING. EVERYTHING.
> I'VE BEEN WAITING SO LONG.

She was beginning to believe the writer meant every word. She slipped the note neatly back into the envelope, opened her bottom desk drawer to place it on the mounting stack of similar messages. Determined to handle the matter practically, she picked up the rose, studying its pale, fragile petals as if they held a clue to the identity of the sender.

Obsession. A frightening word, she thought, yet surely some forms of obsession were harmless enough. Still, the flower was a change in habit. There'd been no tokens before, only the messages in deep red. Surely a rose was a sign of affection, esteem, fragrant and sweet. Yet the thorns marching up the slender stem could draw blood.

Now she was being foolish, she told herself. Rising, she filled a water glass and stuck the rose inside. She couldn't stand to see a beautiful flower wither and die. Still, she set it on a table across the room before she went back to her desk.

For the next twenty minutes, she signed correspondence. She still had the pen in her hand when her intercom buzzed.

"Yes, Cassie."

"It's Finn Riley on two."

"Thanks. I've finished these letters. Can you mail them on your way home?"

"Sure thing."

"Finn? Are you downstairs? I'm sorry, we had a couple of glitches here and I'm running behind." She glanced at her watch, grimaced. "I'll never make dinner at seven."

"Just as well. I'm across town, stuck at a meeting. Looks like I won't make it either."

"I'll cancel, then. We'll eat later." She glanced up at Cassie as the woman slipped the signed correspondence from Deanna's desk. "Cassie, cancel my seven o'clock, will you?"

"All right. Is there anything else you need before I go? You know I can stay to go over those tapes with you."

"No, thanks. See you tomorrow. Finn?"

"Still here."

"I've got some tapes I need to review. Why don't you swing by here and pick me up on the way home? I'll cancel my driver."

"Looks like it'll be about eight, maybe later."

"Later's better. I'll need at least three hours to finish here. I get more done when everyone's gone home anyway. I'll raid Fran's food stash and burrow in until I hear from you."

"If I can't make it, I'll let you know."

"I'll be here. 'Bye."

Deanna replaced the receiver, then swiveled in her chair to face the window. The sun was already setting, dimming the sky, making the skyline gloomy. She could see lights blinking on, pinpoints against the encroaching dusk.

She imagined buildings emptying out, the freeway filling. At home, people would be switching on the evening news and thinking about dinner.

If she married Finn, they would go home. To their home, not his, not hers.

If she married Finn ... Deanna toyed with the bracelet she always wore, as much a talisman to her as the cross Finn wore was to him. She would be making a promise of forever if she married him.

She believed in keeping promises.

They would begin to plan a family.

She believed, deeply, in family.

And she would have to find ways, good, solid, clever ways to make it all work. To make all the elements balance.

That was what stopped her.

No matter how often she tried to stop and reason everything out, or how often she struggled to list her priorities and plan of attack, she skittered back like a spooked doe.

She wasn't sure she could make it work.

There wasn't any hurry, she reminded herself. And right now her priority had to be managing that next rung on the ladder.

She glanced at her watch, calculating the time she needed against the time she had. Long enough, she thought, to let herself relax briefly before getting back to work.

Trying one of the stress-reduction techniques she'd learned from a guest on her show, she shut her eyes, drawing long, easy breaths. She was supposed to imagine a door, closed and blank. When she was ready, she was to open that door and step into a scene she found relaxing, peaceful, pleasant.

As always, she opened the door quickly, too quickly, impatient to see what was on the other side.

The porch of Finn's cabin. Spring. Butterflies flitted around the blooming herbs and flowering ground cover of his rock garden. She could hear the sleepy droning of bees hovering around the salmon-colored azalea she had helped him plant. The sky was a clear, dazzling blue so perfect for dreams.

She sighed, beautifully content. There was music, all strings. A flood of weeping violins flowing through the open windows behind her.

Then she was lying on that soft, blooming lawn, lifting her arms to Finn. The sun haloed around his hair, casting shadows over his face, deepening his eyes until they were so blue she might have drowned in them. Wanted to. And he was in her arms, his body warm and hard, his mouth sure and clever. She could feel her body tighten with need, her skin hum with it. They were moving together, slowly, fluidly, as graceful as dancers, with the blue bowl of the sky above them and the drone of bees throbbing like a pulse.

She heard her name, a whisper twining through the music of the dream. And she smiled and opened her eyes to look at him.

But it wasn't Finn. Clouds had crept over the sun, darkening the sky to ink so that she couldn't see his face. But it wasn't Finn. Even as her body recoiled, he said her name again.

"I'm thinking of you. Always."

She jerked awake, skin clammy, heart thumping. In automatic defense, she wrapped her arms tight around herself to ward off a sudden, violent chill. The hell with meditation, she thought, struggling to shake off the last vestige of the dream. She'd take work-related stress any day. She tried to laugh at herself, but the sound came out more like a sob.

Just groggy, she thought. A little groggy from an unscheduled catnap. But her eyes widened as she stared at her watch. She'd been asleep for nearly an hour.

A ridiculous waste of time, she told herself, and rose from the chair to work out kinks. Work, she told herself firmly, and started to shrug out of her suit jacket as she turned back to her desk.

And there were roses. Two perfectly matched blooms speared up from the water glass in the center of her desk. In instant denial, she stepped forward, her eyes cutting across the room to where she had set the single flower earlier. It was no longer there. No longer there, she thought dully, because it was now on her desk, joined by its mate.

She rubbed the heel of her hand against her breastbone as she stared at the roses. Cassie might have done it, she thought. Or

Simon or Jeff or Margaret. Anyone who'd been working late. One of them had found the second rose somewhere and had brought it in, slipped it in with the first. And seeing her sleeping, had simply left them on her desk.

Seeing her sleeping. A shudder ran through her, weakening her legs. She'd been asleep. Alone, defenseless. As she sagged against the arm of the chair, she saw the tape resting on her blotter. She could tell from the manufacturer's label it wasn't the type they used on the show.

No note this time. Perhaps a note wasn't necessary. She thought about running, rushing pell-mell out of the office. There would be people in the newsroom. Plenty of people working the swing between the evening and the late news.

She wasn't alone.

A telephone call would summon security. An elevator ride would take her into the bustle of activity a few floors below.

No, she wasn't alone, and there was no reason to be afraid. There was every reason to play the tape.

She wiped her damp palms on her hips before taking the tape from its sleeve and sliding it into the VCR slot.

The first few seconds after she hit Play were a blank, blue screen. When Deanna watched the picture flicker on, her forehead creased in concentration. She recognized her building, heard the whoosh of traffic through the audio. A few people breezed by on the sidewalk, in shirtsleeves, indicating warm weather.

She watched herself come through the outside door, her hair flowing around her shoulders. Dazed, she lifted a hand, combing her fingers through the short cap. She watched herself check her watch. The camera zoomed in on her face, her eyes smoky with impatience. She could hear, hideously, the sound of the camera operator's unsteady breathing.

A CBC van streaked up to the curb. The picture faded out.

And faded in. She was strolling along Michigan with Fran. Her arms were loaded with shopping bags. She wore a thick sweater and a suede jacket. As she turned her head to laugh at Fran, the picture froze, holding steady on her laughing face until dissolve.

There were more than a dozen clips, snippets of her life. A trip to the market, her arrival at a charity function, a stroll through Water Tower Place, playing with Aubrey in the park, signing autographs at a mall. Her hair short now, her wardrobe indicating the change of seasons.

Through it all, the mood-setting soundtrack of quiet breathing.

The last clip was of her sleeping, curled in her office chair.

She continued to stare after the screen sizzled with snow. Fear had crept back, chilling her blood so that she stood shivering in the slanted light of the desk lamp.

For years he'd been watching her, she thought. Stalking her. Invading small personal moments of her life and making them his. And she'd never noticed.

Now he wanted her to know. He wanted her to understand how close he was. How much closer he could be.

Leaping forward, she fumbled with the Eject button, finally pounded it with her fist. She grabbed her bag, stuffing the tape inside as she dashed from the office. The corridor was dark, shadowy from the backwash of light from her office. A pulse beat in the base of her neck as she dashed to the elevator.

Her breath was sobbing when she pushed the button. She whirled around and pressed her back to the wall, scanning the shadows wildly for movement.

"Hurry, hurry." She pressed a hand to her mouth as her voice echoed mockingly down the empty corridor.

The rumble of the elevator made her jump. Nearly crying out in relief, she spun toward the doors, then fell back when she saw a form move away from the corner of the car and step toward her.

"Hey, Dee. Did I give you a jolt?" Roger stepped closer as the doors slithered closed at his back. "Hey, kid, you're white as a sheet."

"Don't." She cringed back; her eyes flashed toward the fire door leading to the stairs. She would have to get past him. She would get past him.

"Hey, what's going on?" The concern in Roger's voice had her gaze sliding cautiously back to him. "You're shaking. Maybe you'd better sit down."

"I'm fine. I'm leaving now."

"You'd better catch your breath first. Come on. Let's—"

She jerked back, avoiding his hand. "What do you want?"

"Cassie stopped downstairs on her way out." He spoke slowly, letting his hand fall back to his side. "She said you were working late, so I thought I'd come up and see if you wanted to catch some dinner."

"Finn's coming." She moistened her lips. "He'll be here any minute."

"It was just a thought. Dee, is everything okay? Your folks all right?"

A new fear gripped her throat, digging in like talons. "Why? Why do you ask that?"

"You're rattled. I thought you'd gotten some bad news."

"No." Giddy with panic, she edged away. "I've got a lot on my mind." She barely muffled a scream as the elevator rumbled again.

"Jesus, Dee, take it easy." In reflex, he grabbed her arm as she started to race by him toward the stairs. She swung back to fight, and the elevator doors opened.

"What the hell's going on?"

"Oh, God." Tearing free from Roger, Deanna fell into Finn's arms. "Thank God you're here."

His grip tightened protectively as his eyes bored into Roger's. "I said, what the hell's going on?"

"You tell me." Shaken, Roger dragged a hand through his hair. "I came up a minute ago, and she was ready to jump out of her skin. I was trying to find out what happened."

"Did he hurt you?" Finn demanded of Deanna and earned a curse of outrage from Roger.

"No." She kept her face buried against his shoulder. The shaking, the horrible shaking wouldn't stop. She thought she could hear her own bones rattling together. "I was so scared. I can't think. Just take me home."

FINN MANAGED TO PRY A disjointed explanation from her on the drive home, then, pushing a brandy on her, had watched the tape himself.

She offered no protest when he strode to the phone and called the police. She was calmer when she related the story again. She understood the value of details, of timetables, of clear-cut facts. The detective who interviewed her in Finn's living room sat patiently, jotting in his notepad.

She recognized the gray-haired man from the tape from Greektown—he had snatched the little girl out of the line of fire.

Arnold Jenner was a quiet, meticulous cop. His square face was offset by a nose that had been broken, not on the job but by a line drive during a precinct softball game. He wore a dark brown suit that strained only slightly over the beginnings of a paunch. His hair was caught somewhere between brown and gray and trimmed ruthlessly short. There were lines around his mouth and eyes that indicated he either laughed or frowned easily. His eyes, a pale, sleepy green, should have been as nondescript as the rest of him. But as Deanna stared into them, she was comforted by a sense of trust.

"I'd like to have the letters."

"I didn't save all of them," she told him, and felt ashamed by the tired acceptance in his eyes. "The first few—well, it seemed harmless. On-air reporters get a lot of mail, some of it on the odd side."

"Whatever you have, then."

"I have some at the office, some at my apartment."

"You don't live here?"

"No." She shot a look at Finn. "Not exactly."

"Mmm-hmmm." Jenner made another note. "Miss Reynolds, you said that last portion of tape would have been taken this evening, between five-thirty and six-twenty."

"Yes. I told you, I'd fallen asleep. I was tense, so I thought I'd try this routine a guest on the show had suggested. An imagery, meditation thing." She shrugged, feeling foolish. "I guess it's not my style. I'm either awake or I'm asleep. When I woke up, I saw the second rose on the desk. And the tape."

He made noises in his throat. Like a doctor, Deanna thought.

"Who would have access to your offices at that hour?"

"All manner of people. My own staff, anyone working downstairs."

"So the building would be closed to all but CBC personnel?"

"Not necessarily. The rear door wouldn't be locked at that hour. You'd have people going off shift, others coming on, people picking them up or dropping them off. Sometimes even tours."

"Busy place."

"Yes."

His eyes lifted to hers again, and she realized why they weren't nondescript. He wasn't simply looking at her: he was looking in. Finn had that ability, that same quick, scalpel gaze that cut right through into your thoughts. Perhaps that was why she found him reassuring.

"Is there anyone you can think of? Someone you've rebuffed? Someone who's shown a more than casual or friendly interest in you?"

"No. Really, there's no one I know who would keep doing something like this. I'm sure it's a stranger—a viewer, probably. Otherwise I'd probably have noticed them taping me."

"Well, the way your show's been going, that doesn't narrow the possible suspects." In an old habit, he doodled on his pad. The doodle became Deanna's face, the frightened eyes and the mouth that struggled to curve up. "You do a lot of public appearances. Have you noticed any particular face that keeps showing up?"

"No. I thought of that."

"I'll take the tape with me." He rose then, tucking his notebook neatly in his pocket. "Someone will come by for the notes."

"There's nothing else, is there?" She rose as well. "There's really nothing else."

"You never know what we might pick up from the tape. Sophistication of equipment or some small identifying sound. In the meantime, try not to worry. This kind of thing happens more often than you think." And because she kept trying to smile, he wanted to reassure her. "You hear about the big ones, like that woman who keeps breaking into Letterman's house, but the truth is, it's not just celebrities who have to deal with obsessions. Not too long ago we had this woman focused on this stockbroker. Nice-looking guy, but no Adonis. Anyhow, she called him at work, at home, sent telegrams, left love notes under the windshield wiper of his car. She even had pictures of herself in a wedding dress that she had doctored with one of him in a tux. Showed it to his neighbors to prove they were married."

"What happened?"

"He took out a peace bond on her, and she broke it by camping on his doorstep. She went in for a psychiatric evaluation. When she got out, she decided she wasn't in love with the stockbroker anymore. Claims she divorced him."

"So the moral is, sometimes these things run their course."

"Could be. Thing is, some people don't have as firm a grip on reality as they might. You'd probably feel better if you tightened up your security a little."

"I'll do that. Thank you, Detective Jenner."

"I'll be in touch. A real pleasure meeting you, Miss Reynolds, and you, Mr. Riley. I've spent a lot of time with the two of you in my living room."

"So, that's that," she said as she closed the door behind Jenner.

"Not by a long shot." Finn took her firmly by the shoulders. He hadn't interrupted her interview with Jenner. But now it was his turn. "You're not working late alone anymore."

"Really, Finn—"

"That's not negotiable, so don't give me grief on this. Do you know what went through me when I saw you standing in the hall, terrified, fighting off Crowell?"

"He was trying to help," she began, then closed her eyes and sighed. "Yes, yes, I think I do know. I'm sorry. I'll bring work home when I have to."

"Until this thing is resolved, you need twenty-four-hour protection."

"A bodyguard?" She would have laughed if she wasn't afraid he'd take a chunk out of her. "Finn, I won't work late in the building. I'll even make sure I have a buddy when I go on any remotes or appearances. But I'm not hiring some thug named Reno to lurk over me."

"It's not unusual for a woman in your position to hire private security."

"Whatever my position, I'm still Deanna Reynolds from Topeka, and I refuse to have some big-shouldered hulk frighten off the people I'm trying to reach. I couldn't stand it, Finn. That's just too Hollywood for me. I'm not taking this lightly," she continued. "Believe me, I'm going to take very serious care of myself. But I haven't been threatened."

"You've been spied on, followed, taped, harassed by anonymous notes and phone calls."

"And it frightens me, I admit it. You were right about the police. I should have called them before. Now that you have, I feel like the whole situation has been put in the right compartment. Let's give them a chance to do what we pay them for."

Frustrated, he stalked down the hall and back. "A compromise," he said at length. "Christ, I'm always digging up compromises for you."

Judging the storm was blowing over, she moved in to wrap her arms around him. "That's why our relationship is so healthy. What's the compromise—a bodyguard named Sheila?"

"You move in here. I'm not budging on this, Deanna. Keep your place; I don't care. But you live here, with me."

"Funny." In a subtle peace treaty, she pressed a kiss to his cheek. "I was going to suggest the same solution."

He tipped her face up to his. He wanted to ask, badly, if she was agreeing because she was frightened or because she needed him. But he didn't ask. "What about when I'm out of town?"

"I've been thinking about asking you how you felt about dogs." Her lips curved against his. "We could go by the pound this weekend. With so many abandoned animals, it seems the right route."

Chapter Twenty-one

AWARDS WERE NOT IMPORTANT. QUALITY WORK AND THE satisfaction of a job well done were their own reward. Statues and speeches were nothing more than industry hype.

Deanna didn't believe any of it.

For a girl from Kansas whose first on-the-air job had been reporting on a dog show, alighting from a limo in Los Angeles as an Emmy nominee was a thrill. And she didn't mind admitting it.

The day was perfect. There was bound to be smog, but she didn't see it. The sky was the deep, dreamy blue of a watercolor painting, dazzled by the brilliant white sun. A balmy breeze teased the elegant gowns and carefully coiffed hair of the attendees and wafted the scents of perfume and flowers over the enthusiastic crowd.

"I can't believe I'm here." It took all of her willpower not to bounce on the seat of the limo like a kid at the circus. Then she gave up and bounced anyway.

"You've earned it." Charmed by her, Finn took her hand and brought it to his lips.

"I know that, up here." She tapped her temple. "But in here"—

she laid her hand on her heart—"I'm afraid someone's going to pinch me and I'll wake up and realize it's only a dream. Ouch."

"See, you're awake." He grinned as she rubbed her forearm. "And you're still here."

However giddy she felt, she slid gracefully from the limo, tossing her head up as she straightened and scanned the crowd. The sun glinted off her short, beaded gown and scattered light.

Finn thought she'd chosen well; the strapless column of glittery scarlet made her look young and fresh and every inch the star. Several people in the crowd recognized her instantly and shouted her name.

Their reaction obviously surprised her, he realized with a hint of a smile. She looked dazed, then dazzled, then delighted. She waved back, not with the careless insouciance of a seasoned veteran, but with genuine pleasure and enthusiasm.

"I feel like I'm walking into a movie." She chuckled as she linked hands with Finn. "No, like I'm walking out of the last reel, and I've got the hero."

He pleased her, and the crowd, by kissing her. Not just a friendly peck but a deep, lingering embrace that gave the paparazzi plenty of fuel. They stood a moment in the flashing sun, a picture-perfect couple in evening dress. "That was because you're beautiful." He kissed her again to the eruption of cheers. "And that's for luck."

"Thanks. On both counts."

They started toward the building, where fans and onlookers had been parted like the Red Sea by police barricades. Celebrities and press were mingling, creating quick bites that would be shown on the evening news segments.

She knew some of these people, Deanna thought. Some had come on her show, had sat beside her and chatted like old friends. Others she had met during the benefits and events that became part of the job. She exchanged greetings and good wishes, cheek busses and handclasps as they wandered toward the lobby.

Mikes slashed out at them, cameras wheeled in their direction, impeding progress.

"Deanna, how does it feel to be here tonight?"

"Who designed your dress?"

"Finn, what's it like to have a hit show when so many news magazines have failed?"

"Any marriage plans?"

"Christ, it's like an obstacle course," Finn muttered as they worked their way through the gaggle of reporters.

"I'm loving every minute of it." She eased closer, eyes dancing. "Don't you know when they ask about your dress designer, you've made it?"

"They didn't ask me."

She turned, fussing with his tie. "And you look so nice, too. Very *GQ*."

He grimaced. "Please. I can't believe I got talked into doing that photo layout."

"It was smashing."

"I'm a newscaster, not a model."

"But you have such cute dimples."

They didn't flash. They didn't so much as wink as he cornered her with one steely-eyed glare. "Keep that up and I'll leak the news that you changed your underwear three times before getting into that dress tonight."

"Okay, they're not cute. No matter what Mary Hart said last week on *ET*."

"She said—never mind." No way was he going to get pulled into that one. "Let's get a drink before we go in."

"Considering the occasion, it'll have to be champagne. Just one," she added, pressing a hand to her middle. "I don't think my system can handle any more."

"Wait here. I'll fight the horde."

"I told you you were my hero."

She turned, and would have scooted off into a corner, where she could stand and observe, but she found herself face to face with Kate Lowell.

"Hello, Dee."

"Hello, Kate." Deanna offered a hand and they shook like strangers. "It's good to see you."

"It doesn't feel as though you mean it," she said as she straightened her shoulders. "You look terrific, ready to win."

"I hope so."

"I'd like to wish you luck. Really excellent luck, considering your competition."

"Thanks."

"Don't. It's purely selfish on my part. By the way, Rob Winters said to send his best if I ran into you."

Deanna's stiff smile softened. "How is he?"

"Dying," Kate said shortly, then let out a breath between her teeth. "Sorry. We've been friends for a long time, and it's hard to watch."

"You don't have to apologize. I understand about friendships and loyalties."

Kate dropped her gaze. "Direct hit, Dee."

"Cheap shot," she corrected. Instinctively she took Kate's hand again. There was none of the mannered politeness this time. Just support, basic and unstudied. "I can't even imagine what it must be like for you."

Kate studied their joined hands, remembered how easy it had once been. "Dee, why didn't you announce Rob's condition when he told you about it?"

"Because he asked me not to."

Kate shook her head. "That was always enough for you. I'd wondered if you'd changed."

"I have, but that hasn't."

"I really hope you win tonight. I hope you cut her off at the knees." With this, she turned and walked away.

As Deanna watched the other woman walk through the crowd,

she thought she understood the tears she'd seen in Kate's eyes, but not the venom in her voice.

"Well, we have come up in the world." Angela glided into Deanna's line of vision, a frothy dream of candy-pink silk and icy diamonds. "Smile for the camera, dear," she whispered as she leaned forward to air-kiss both of Deanna's cheeks. "Surely you haven't forgotten everything I taught you."

"I haven't forgotten a thing." Deanna let her lips curve up. She hated the fact that her stomach jittered with nerves. Hated more the fact that they were bound to show. "It's been a long time."

"It certainly has. I don't believe you've met my husband. Dan, this is Deanna Reynolds."

"A pleasure." As polished as a fine gem, Dan took Deanna's hand in his. "You're every bit as charming as Angela told me."

"I'm sure she told you nothing of the kind, but thanks. I saw your pre-Emmy special last night, Angela. I enjoyed it."

"Did you?" Angela held up a cigarette for Dan to light. "I have so little time to watch television myself these days."

"That's interesting. I'd think that would insulate you from your audience. I love to watch. I suppose I'm really the average viewer."

"Average isn't something I'd settle for." Angela's gaze shifted over Deanna's shoulder, smoldered. "Hello, Finn. Isn't it interesting that we'd all have to come to Los Angeles to have a reunion?"

"Angela." Smoothly, he passed Deanna her glass of champagne, then slipped an arm around her waist. "You're looking well."

"He used to be much more clever with his compliments," Angela told Dan. She made the rest of the introductions and, spotting a camera out of the corner of her eye, angled herself into a prominent position. "I really must powder my nose before we go in. Deanna, come along with me. No woman goes to the ladies' room alone."

Though Finn tightened his grip, Deanna eased away. "Sure." Better to face whatever unpleasantness Angela had in mind now,

334

she decided, than wait for it to be played out in public. "Finn, I'll meet you inside in a minute."

To offer the camera a friendly tableau, Angela hooked her arm through Deanna's. "We haven't had one of our private talks for ages, have we?"

"It would be a little tough, since we haven't seen each other in two years."

"Always so literal." With a light laugh, Angela swung into the ladies' lounge. It was nearly empty, as she'd hoped. Later it would be full, but now people were eager to be seated. She walked to the mirrored counter, pulled out a chair and did exactly what she'd said she would do. She powdered her nose. "You've chewed off most of your lipstick," she said dryly. "Nervous?"

"Excited." Deanna remained standing, but set her glass aside to dig a lipstick out of her evening bag. "I imagine that's a natural reaction to being nominated."

"It becomes routine after a while. I have several awards, you know. Interesting that you've been nominated for that show on date rape. I'd considered that more of a self-confessional hour, not a mix of views." Angela patted her hair, searching for any out-of-place strands as she turned her face side to side. "I imagine Finn will cop one of the prime-time statues himself when they come out. He's well liked in the industry, and he's been able to create a show that appeals to the news buffs as well as the viewer looking for entertainment."

"I thought you didn't watch television."

Angela's eyes sharpened. It surprised Deanna that their reflection didn't leave slices on the glass. "I glance at something now and then, if I think it might interest me. Of course, Finn has always interested me." Slowly, with relish, she glided her tongue over her lips. "Tell me, do his eyes still go that wicked cobalt shade when he's aroused?" She dabbed perfume at her wrists. "You do manage to arouse him occasionally, don't you?"

"Why don't you ask him?"

"I may do that—if I get him alone. Then again, if I get him

alone, he might forget all about you." Smiling, she twirled up a spiral of hot pink lipstick. "So what would be the point?"

Deanna wasn't nervous any longer, she was simply irked. "The point might be that you're married, and that Finn stopped being interested in you a long time ago."

"Do you really believe that?" Angela's laugh was as brisk and chilly as a puff of December air. "Darling, if I decided to have an affair with Finn—and Dan's a very understanding man, so my marriage is no obstacle—he'd not only be willing, he'd be grateful."

Moving beyond irked, Deanna felt little knots of tension twine in her stomach, but her smile came easily. "Angela." There was a laugh in her voice. "Trying to make me jealous is a waste of time. You had sex with Finn. I know that. And I'm not naïve enough to imagine he didn't find you tremendously attractive and alluring. But what I have with him now is on an entirely different level. You're only embarrassing yourself by trying to convince me he's like some trained mutt who'll come running if you snap your fingers."

Angela slapped the lid on the lipstick. "You're very cool, aren't you?"

"No, not really. I'm just happy." She sat then, hoping they could bury at least the sharpest edge of the hatchet. "Angela, we were friends once—or at least friendly. I'm grateful for the opportunity you gave me to learn and observe. Maybe the time's passed where we can be friendly, but I don't see why we have to snipe at each other. We're competitors, but there's more than enough room for both of us."

"Do you think you can compete with me?" Angela began to shake, from her shoulders down to her spine. "Do you really think you can come close to what I've achieved, to what I have, to what I'm going to have?"

"Yes," Deanna said, and rose. "Yes, I do. And I don't have to resort to planting lies in the tabloids or low-level espionage to do it. You've been in the business long enough to tolerate a little heat, Angela."

"You cocky bitch. I'll bury you."

"No, you won't." Her pulse was drumming now, a primitive

tom-tom rhythm that pumped through her blood in anticipation of a fight. "You're going to have a hell of a time keeping up with me."

On a cry of outrage, Angela snatched the champagne flute and tossed the contents in Deanna's face. Two women who entered the room froze like statues as Angela followed up with a vicious slap.

"You're nothing," Angela shrieked, her face as pink as the silk she wore. "Less than nothing. I'm the best. The fucking best."

She lunged, fingers curled and extended like claws. With a haze of fury misting her vision, Deanna struck out, her open palm cracking Angela's flushed cheek. In an instant all movement froze. For once at least, they were both on equal terms. Horrified, the two women in the doorway gasped in unison and stared.

"Ladies, excuse us." Kate Lowell stepped out from the stalls to the lounge, and motioned to the women. They flew out again, obviously in a hurry to bear tidings. "Well, well, and I thought all the competition was going to be out there."

Dazed, Deanna stared down at her hand, which was still burning from the blow it had delivered. She blinked against the champagne stinging her eyes. "Oh hell."

Kate nodded to the outside door, still swinging from the exit of the other women. "It's going to make an interesting sidebar in tomorrow's Daytime Emmy coverage." She smiled suddenly, a brilliant flash of perfect teeth. "Would you like me to referee?"

"Stay out of this." Teeth clenched, Angela took a step toward Deanna. She'd been humiliated now, publicly. That, above all, was intolerable. "And you stay out of my way. You've crossed the line."

"I didn't turn the other cheek," Deanna returned, "and I don't intend to. So why don't we try to stay out of each other's way?"

"You won't win tonight." With a hand that continued to tremble, Angela picked up her bag. "Or ever."

"Lousy exit line," Kate mused as the door swung shut behind Angela.

"I don't know. It had potential." Deanna closed her stinging eyes. "What now?"

"Clean yourself up." Kate moved forward briskly to run cold water on a snowy washcloth. "Put yourself back together and get out there."

"I lost my temper," she began, then caught sight of herself in the mirror. "Oh Jesus." Her cheeks were suffused with heat, dripping with wine. Her eyes were smoldering and smudged with mascara.

"Put the image back on," Kate advised, handing her the damp cloth. "And when you walk out, walk out with a smile."

"I think I should—" Braced for the worst, she spun toward the door as it swung open. Her already hot cheeks fired further as Finn strolled in.

"I beg your pardon, ladies, but as a reporter it's my duty to ask what the hell's going on in here. Somebody said—" He broke off, taking in the scene with one pithy glance. "Christ, Kansas, I can't leave you alone for a minute." He sighed, picked up one of the dry, fluffy hand towels on the counter and offered it. "I didn't think that was a maidenly blush I noticed on Angela's cheek. Which one of you slugged her?"

"The pleasure was Deanna's."

He leaned over to kiss her damp cheek. "Nice going, champ." He touched his tongue to her lip. "You're supposed to drink the champagne, baby, not wear it."

Deanna set her shoulders and turned back to the mirror to deal with the damage. She would not be cowed, she promised herself. She simply would not be. "Just keep everyone out for five minutes, will you?"

"Your category's coming up," he said casually as he headed for the door.

"I'll be there."

SHE WAS, MAKEUP FRESHENED, hair fluffed, nerves raw. She sat beside Finn, her hand clenched spasmodically over his. Out of camera range, she hoped.

Her mind was as keen as a sword as she watched the presenters breeze or fumble their way through scripted jokes and into lists of nominees. She applauded politely, or occasionally with enthusiasm, as winners were announced and made their way to the stage.

She filed every instant, every gesture, every word in her memory. Because it mattered now, horribly. She'd lost a good deal of the sweet excitement she'd felt when they'd rolled up in the limo. No, she thought, she wasn't just the kid from Kansas now, dazzled by the lights and the luminaries. She was Deanna Reynolds, and she belonged.

It wasn't simply an award any longer, a pat on the back for a job well done.

Now it was a symbol. The culmination of what had started so long ago. It was a symbol of triumph over the deceit, the manipulations, the ugly intrigue that had flashed into pathetic spite in a ladies' washroom.

The camera was on her. She could feel that cool, objective eye focus in. She could only hope that for once her emotions weren't so clearly mirrored on her face. She heard Angela's name announced, then her own.

She couldn't catch her breath. Then Finn lifted their joined hands to his lips and the sharpest edge of tension smoothed.

"And the Emmy goes to . . ."

God, how could it take so long to open one envelope?

"Deanna Reynolds, for *Deanna's Hour*, 'When You Know Him.'"

"Oh." All the breath that had backed up in her lungs came out in that one long sound. Before she could take another, Finn's mouth was over hers.

"I never had a doubt."

"Me neither," she lied, and was laughing as she rose out of the chair to walk through the applause to the stage.

The award was cool and smooth in her hands. And solid as stone. She was afraid if she looked at it, she'd weep. Instead she looked out into the lights.

"I want to thank my team, every one of them. They're the best. And I want to thank the women who appeared on the show, who battled back their fears to bring a painful subject out of the dark. I can't think of any show I've done, or will do, that could be as difficult or as rewarding for me. Thank you for giving me something to remind me. Now I'm going backstage to stare at this beautiful lady."

AFTER THE SPEECHES, THE applause, the interviews and the parties, Deanna lay propped up in bed, resting in the curve of Finn's shoulder. Casually, she crossed her feet at the ankles.

"I think mine's prettier than your National Press Award," she said.

"Mine's more professional."

She pursed her lips, studying the gold statue standing on the bureau. "Mine's shinier."

"Deanna." He turned his head to kiss her temple. "You're gloating."

"Yep. And I'm going to keep right on gloating. You've won all sorts of awards, Overseas Press Club, the George Polk. You can afford to be jaded."

"Who says I'm jaded? And when I win my Emmy it'll be every bit as shiny as your Emmy."

With a delighted laugh, she rolled over to lie on top of him. "I won. I didn't want to admit how badly I wanted that statue. After that scene with Angela, I felt I had to win. For me, yes, but also for everybody who works with me. When they called my name, I was flying. Really flying. It was great."

"An interesting evening all around." He ran a hand down her spine, enjoying the way her body curved to his touch. "Tell me again how you demolished her."

Deanna's lashes fluttered down. "I did not demolish her. It was a particularly effective but ladylike slap."

"Like hell." Grinning, he tipped her face up, then laughed out loud at the unholy glee in her eyes.

"I shouldn't be proud of it." She chuckled and sat up to straddle him, her body pale and naked. "But for just an instant, before I was horrified, I felt wonderful. Then I was numb, then I was furious all over again." She linked her fingers, lifting her arms up high. "Besides, she started it."

"And you finished it. You can count on her coming after you with both barrels now."

"Let her. I feel invulnerable. Impervious." She stretched high. "Incredible. It just can't get any better than this."

"Yes, it can." To prove it, he reared up, running a line of kisses up her torso. Her soft sigh glided through him. Her hands fluttered down to cradle his head.

"You might be right."

The sky was pearling with dawn, chasing the shadows from the room. Her body arched back, already fluid and ready for his. They had loved once in delirious haste, and now moved together slowly, letting the needs smolder and the air spark.

Gliding fingertips, whispering sighs, quiet urgings for more. Torso to torso they pressed together, tangled sheets pooled around them and morning sliding softly into the room. A touch, a taste, a subtle shift in rhythm. They lowered together to roll lazily over the bed, length to length.

No rush, no hurry. Quiet explosions shuddered through her blood, then streamed away like silk until others built. Her mouth sought his, sighs merging, tongues dancing. Even when he slipped into her, filling her, the flash of heat was as comforting as a sunbeam.

ACROSS TOWN THERE WAS another hotel room bed that hadn't been slept in, or loved in. Angela sat on the edge of it, her robe held protectively over her breasts. The dress she had worn was a tattered heap of silk on the floor, a victim of her temper.

Most of that temper was spent now, and she huddled like a child on the big bed, fighting back tears.

"It doesn't mean anything, honey." Dan urged champagne on her, the equivalent to a kiss where it hurt. "Everybody knows the fucking awards are a sham."

"People watch." She stared straight ahead, sipping the wine she'd ordered chilled for celebration and now served as commiseration. "Thousands of people, Dan. They saw her walk up there, when it should have been me. They saw her pick up my award. *My* award, goddamn her."

"And they'll forget about it tomorrow." He stifled both impatience and disgust. The only way to handle Angela, and to keep them both riding high, was to cajole, flatter and lie. "Nobody remembers who got what when the glitter fades."

"I remember." She tossed up her head, and her face was icy again, eerily controlled. "I remember. She's not getting away with it. With any of it. I'm going to do whatever it takes to make her pay. For the slap, for the award. Everything."

"We'll talk about it later." He'd already gotten word on the incident in the lounge. Too many people—people who couldn't be easily bought off—had heard that Angela struck first. "Now you've got to relax. You have to look your best when we fly home later today."

"Relax?" she spat at him. "Relax? Deanna Reynolds is getting my press, my ratings, now my awards." And there was Finn. Oh, no, she wouldn't forget Finn. "How the hell can you tell me to relax?"

"Because you can't win if you look like a resentful has-been." He watched her eyes flare with fury, then chill to an icy gleam.

"How dare you speak to me that way? And tonight of all nights."

"I'm telling you this for your own good," he continued, assured he had the upper hand when her lips trembled. "You need to project dignity, maturity, confidence."

"She's ruining my life. It's just like when I was a kid. Someone was always taking what I wanted."

"You're not a kid anymore, Angela. And there'll be other awards."

She wanted *this* award. But she held the words back. He'd only become more remote and disgusted. She needed him beside her, supporting her, believing in her. "You're right. Absolutely right. Tomorrow, in public, I will be gracious, humble and dignified. And believe me, Deanna Reynolds is not going to win another award that should be mine." Forcing a smile, she reached out a hand and drew him down beside her. "I'm just so disappointed, Dan. For both of us. You worked just as hard as I did for that Emmy."

"We'll work harder for the next one." Relieved, he kissed the top of her head.

"Sometimes it takes more than work. God knows I've had plenty of experience there." She sighed and drank again. She'd drink all she wanted tonight, she promised herself. At least she deserved that much. "When I was a kid I did all the chores around the house. Otherwise we would have lived in a pigsty. I've always liked things to look right, to look pretty. To look the best they can. I started doing cleaning for other people. Did I ever tell you that?"

"No." Surprised that she had now, he rose to fetch the bottle. He topped off her glass. "You don't like to talk about your childhood. I understand that."

"I'm in the mood for it." She sipped again, gesturing toward her cigarettes. Obligingly, Dan picked them up, lighted one for her. "I earned extra money that way, so I could buy things. My own things. But I earned more than money. You know ..." She took a contemplative drag. "It's amazing what people leave lying around their homes, tucked into drawers, closed in boxes. I was always curious about people. That's why I ended up in this business, I suppose. And I found out a lot about the people I worked for. Things they preferred to be kept private. I might mention to a certain married woman the name of a man not her husband. Then I might admire some earrings, or a bracelet, or a dress." Through the haze of smoke, she smiled at the memory. "It was magical how quickly what I admired became mine. Just for doing the small favor of keeping information to myself."

"You started young," Dan observed. Her voice was only a little slurred, so he added more wine to her glass.

"I had to. Nobody was going to fight for me. Nobody was going to lift me out of that hellhole I lived in but me. Mama drunk; Daddy off gambling or whoring."

"It was tough on you."

"It made me tough," she corrected. "I watched the way people lived, and I saw what I wanted. I found ways to get what I wanted. I improved myself and I broke my back to be the best. No one's going to take me off the top of the heap, Dan. Certainly not Deanna Reynolds."

He tipped her face back for a kiss. "That's the Angela I know and love."

She smiled. Her head felt light, dizzy, her body free. Why, she wondered, had she been so afraid of relaxing with a bottle or two? "Prove it," she invited, and slipped the robe off her shoulders.

Chapter Twenty-two

THE SNOW OUTSIDE THE CABIN WAS FAIRY-TALE WHITE. Rocks and shrubs caused the white covering to heave into mounds and bumps so that it resembled a blanket under which dozens of elves might burrow, waiting for spring. No cloud marred the eerie, icy blue of the sky, and the sun glinted off the glossy bark of trees.

From the window, Deanna watched Finn and Richard help Aubrey build a snowman. In her bright blue snowsuit, the toddler looked like a little exotic bird who'd lost her way going south. Curling tendrils of hair, as red as a cardinal's wing, escaped from her cap.

Beside her the men were giants, bulky in their heavy coats and boots. She watched as Richard showed Aubrey how to pat and mold a snowball. He pointed at Finn, and with a giggle that carried through the glass, Aubrey bounced it lightly off Finn's knee, but he crumpled convincingly to the ground as if hit by a boulder.

The dog, the mop-haired mongrel Finn and Deanna had dubbed Cronkite, sent up a din of barks and a shower of snow in his desperation to join the game.

"Sounds like quite a snowman." Fran shifted her infant

daughter from her right to her left breast. Kelsey latched on, suckling happily.

"They've started a small war," Deanna reported. "Casualties are light, but it looks to be an extended battle."

"You can go out and spend some of that nervous energy. You don't have to stay in here with me."

"No, I like watching. I'm so glad all of you could come up for the weekend."

"Since it's the first free one you've had in six weeks, I'm amazed you'd share it."

"Getting away with friends is one of those luxuries I've had to do without too much." She sighed a little. There was no use thinking about all the weekends, the holidays, the quiet evenings at home she'd missed. She had what she'd asked for. "I've discovered I need things like this to keep me centered."

"Glad to help. Richard found the idea of fishing in this weather just primitive and macho enough to pique his interest. As for me"—she stroked her daughter's cheek as she rocked gently in the chair Finn had hauled in from the porch and scrubbed down for just that purpose—"I was ready to go anywhere. When we get snow this early in November, it's going to be a long winter."

"And not a particularly pleasant one." Fran was right about the nervous energy, Deanna realized. She could feel it swirling inside— white water in the bloodstream. Deanna turned away from the window to sit on the hearth, where the fire crackled hot and brightly behind her. "I feel like I've been under siege, Fran. All this—this tabloid crap about Angela and me brawling in the ladies' lounge at the Emmys."

"Honey, most of that's died down, and everyone knew it was crap to begin with."

"Most everyone." Restless, she rose again, prowling. "All those sly allegations in the press about her bearing up stoically after I supposedly refused her offer of friendship. Friendship, my butt." She shoved her hands in her pockets, dragged them out again to gesture. "And that nasty undertone of glee in some of the stories. 'Talk show divas in cat fight'. 'Claws bared in ladies' room'. And it was just close enough to the truth to make us both look like idiots. Of course, Loren couldn't be happier. The ratings have sky-rocketed since the Emmys, and there's no sign of a downswing. People who couldn't care less about the content of the show are tuning in to see if I lose it and punch out a guest."

Fran snickered, then caught Deanna's quick glare. "Sorry."

"I wish I could think it was funny." Grabbing the poker, she stabbed viciously at the flaming logs. "I did think it was funny, until I started getting letters."

"Oh, Dee, the majority of the mail has been supportive, even flattering."

"So I'm perverse." Her shoulders jerked. Oh, she hated the fact that she was being a fool. Hated more that she couldn't seem to stop thinking about the whole ugly incident. "I keep remembering the ones that weren't. The ones that ranged from 'You should be ashamed of yourself', to 'You should be horsewhipped for your lack of gratitude to a fragile little flower like Angela Perkins'." Her narrowed eyes were as hot as the flames. "Belladonna probably looks like a fragile little flower."

"I wouldn't know." Fran shifted the baby to her shoulder. "Most of that's blown over. Why don't you tell me what's really eating at you?"

Deanna gave the fire one last poke. "I'm scared." She said it quietly, as a fresh frisson of ice skated up her spine. "I got another note."

"Oh God. When?"

"Friday, right after I spoke to the literacy group at the Drake."

"Cassie was with you."

"Yes." Deanna rubbed at the dull ache at the back of her neck. "I don't seem to go anywhere alone anymore. Always an entourage."

"Cassie's hardly an entourage." But Fran recognized the twist of topic as avoidance. "Tell me about the note, Dee."

"We ran a little long with the photo session afterward. Cassie left—she had a few things she wanted to finish up at the office before the weekend."

She flashed back to it, the scene as clear in her mind as a film loop. Another handshake, another snick of the camera shutter. People crowding around for a word, for a look.

"Just one more picture, Deanna, please. You and the mayor's wife."

"*Just* one more." Cassie spoke up, her smile amiable, her voice firm. "Miss Reynolds is already running late for her next appointment."

Deanna remembered feeling amusement. Her next appointment, thankfully, was throwing a few sweaters into her suitcase and heading out of the city.

She posed again, with the mayor's wife and the plaque for her work for literacy, then eased her way along, with Cassie running interference.

"Good job, Dee. Here, let me take that." Cassie slipped the plaque into her briefcase while Deanna bundled into her coat.

"It didn't feel like a job. They were great."

"They were—you were." Cassie cast a leery eye over her shoulder. The elegant lobby of the Drake was still crowded with people. "But take my word on this. Just keep walking and don't look back or you won't get out of here until midnight." To hurry her along, Cassie took her arm and led Deanna out of the lobby and onto the sidewalk. "Listen, I'm going to take a cab back to the office."

"Don't be silly. Tim can drop you off."

"Then you'll think of something you just have to do while you're there. Go home," Cassie ordered. "Pack, leave. Don't show your face in this town until Sunday night."

It sounded too good to argue. "Yes, ma'am."

Laughing, Cassie kissed her cheek. "Have a great weekend."

"You too."

They parted there, heading in opposite directions through the snapping wind and swirling snow.

"Sorry I'm late, Tim."

"No problem, Miss Reynolds." With his long black coat flapping around his knees, Tim opened the door of the limo. "How'd it go?"

"Fine. Really fine, thanks."

Still glowing with the energy of a job well done, she slipped inside the cushy warmth.

And there it was. Just that plain envelope, a square of white against the burgundy leather seat . . .

"I asked Tim if someone had come up to the car," Deanna continued, "but he hadn't seen anyone. It was cold and he'd gone inside the building for a while. He said the car was locked, and I know how conscientious Tim is, so I'm sure it was."

Too many notes, Fran thought, as her stomach muscles jiggled. And they were coming too often in the last couple of months. "Did you call the police?"

"I called Lieutenant Jenner from the car phone. I don't have any control over this." Her voice rose as much in frustration as fear. And it helped, she realized, to have something, anything other than fear coursing through her. "I can't analyze it and put it in a slot. I can't tidy it up or toss it away." Determined to calm herself, she rubbed her hands over her face as if she could massage away the panic. "I can't even discuss this rationally. Every time I remind myself that I haven't been threatened, I haven't been hurt, I feel this little bubble of hysteria building up. He finds me everywhere. I want to beg him to leave me alone. To just leave me alone. Fran," she said helplessly, "I'm a mess."

Fran got up to lay Kelsey in the playpen. She crossed to take Deanna's hands in hers. There was more than comfort in the contact—anger simmered just beneath. "Why haven't you told me this

349

before? Why haven't you let me know how much this is upsetting you?"

"You've got enough to handle. Aubrey, the new baby."

"So you took pity on the new mother and pretended that you were shrugging this whole business off as a by-product of fame?" Suddenly furious, Fran slapped both hands on her hips. "That's crap, Dee. Insulting crap."

"I didn't see the point in worrying you," Deanna shot back. "There's so much stuff going on right now—the show, the backlash from Angela; Margaret's teenager wrecked the car, Simon's mother died." Despising the need to defend herself, she turned back to the window. "Finn's going off to Haiti next week." Outside the dog leaped at flying snowballs. Deanna wanted to weep. Resting her head on the cool glass, she waited until her system leveled. "I thought I could handle it myself. I wanted to handle it myself."

"What about Finn?" Fran walked over to rub her hand over Deanna's stiff back. "Does he have a clue what's going on inside you right now?"

"He has a lot on his mind."

Fran didn't bother to repress a disgusted snort. "Which means you've been playing the same game with him. Did you tell him about this last note?"

"It seemed best to wait until he got back from this next trip."

"It's selfish."

"Selfish?" Her voice cracked in surprised hurt. "How can you say that? I don't want him worried about me when he's thousands of miles away."

"He *wants* to worry about you. Jesus, Dee, how can anyone so sensitive, so compassionate, be so obstinate? You've got a man out there who loves you. Who wants to share everything with you, good and bad. He deserves to know what you're feeling. If you love him half as much as he loves you, you've got no right to keep things from him."

"That wasn't what I meant to do."

"It's what you are doing. It's unfair to him, Dee. Just like—" She cut herself off, swearing. "I'm sorry." But her voice was stiff and cool. "It's none of my business how you and Finn deal with your relationship."

"No, don't stop now," Deanna said, equally cool. "Finish it. Just like what?"

"All right, then." Fran took a deep breath. Their friendship had lasted more than ten years. She hoped it would weather one more storm. "It's unfair for you to ask him to put his own needs on hold."

"I don't know what you mean."

"For God's sake, look at him, Dee. Look at him with Aubrey." She clamped her hand on Deanna's arm and pushed her back to the window. "Take a good look."

She did, watching Finn spin Aubrey around and around, snow spewing up at his feet. The child's delighted shrieks echoed like a song.

"That man wants a family. He wants you. You're denying him both because you haven't got everything neatly stacked in place. That's not just selfish, Dee. It's not just unfair. It's sad." When Deanna said nothing, she turned away. "I've got to change the baby." Gathering Kelsey up, she left the room.

Deanna stood where she was for a long time. She could see Finn wrestling with the dog as Aubrey leaped into her father's arms to slide a ragged cap onto the top of the big-bellied snowman.

But she could see more. Finn crossing the tarmac in a torrent of rain, a cocky grin on his face and a swagger in his step. Finn exhausted and asleep on her couch, or laughing as she reeled in her first fat fish. Gentle and sweet as he took her to bed. Gritty-eyed and grim as he returned from observing some fresh disaster.

He was always there, she realized. Always.

SHE WENT THROUGH THE motions that evening, serving up big bowls of beef stew, laughing at Richard's jokes. If someone had peeked in the kitchen window, they would have seen a jolly group of friends sharing a meal. Attractive people, comfortable with one another. It would have been difficult to spot any tension, any discord.

But Finn was a trained observer. Even had that not been the case, he could judge Deanna's moods by the flick of an eyelash.

He hadn't questioned her about the tension he sensed, hoping she would tell him on her own. As the evening wore on, he accepted, impatiently, that he would have to push. Perhaps he would always have to push.

He watched her settle down in the living room, a smile on her face. Unhappiness in her eyes.

God, the woman frustrated him. Fascinated him. For almost two years they had been lovers, as physically intimate as it was possible to be. Yet no matter how open she was, how honest, she managed to tuck away little pieces. Closing them off from him, locking them tight and hoarding them.

She was doing it now, he realized.

Her hand might reach for his, holding it with comfortable familiarity. But her mind was elsewhere, methodically working through a problem she refused to share.

Her problem, she would say in that reasonable tone that by turns infuriated and amused him. Nothing she couldn't handle on her own. Nothing she needed him to deal with.

Hurt, Finn set his glass aside and slipped upstairs.

He built up the fire in the bedroom, brooding over it. He wondered how long he could wait for Deanna to take the next step. Forever, he thought, with an oath. She was as much a part of him as his muscle and bone.

The need that had been growing in him for family, for a steady, rooted life, was nothing compared with his need for her.

What was much worse, as well as totally unexpected, was that he wanted, quite desperately, for her to need him.

A new one for Riley, he mused, and wished he could see the

humor in this realization. The need to be needed, to be tied down, to be . . . settled, he realized, wasn't a particularly comfortable sensation, and after several months, he understood it wasn't going to go away.

And he was beginning to hate the status quo.

She found him crouched at the hearth, staring into the flames. After closing the door quietly at her back, she crossed over, brushed a hand through his hair.

"What the hell is going on, Deanna?" He continued to stare into the fire. "You've been edgy since we got here last night, and pretending not to be. When I came in before dinner, you'd been crying. And you and Fran are circling each other like a couple of boxers in the tenth round."

"Fran's angry with me." She sat on the hassock and folded her hands in her lap. She could feel his tension in the air. "I guess you will be, too." Lowering her eyes, she told him about the note, answering his terse questions and waiting for his reaction.

She didn't wait long.

He stood where he was, with the fire snapping at his back. His gaze never left her face and was calm, entirely too calm.

"Why didn't you tell me right away?"

"I thought it was best to wait until I'd sorted through it a bit."

"You thought." He nodded, slipped his hands into his pockets. "You thought it was none of my concern."

"No, of course not." She hated the fact that his cool interviewing skills always put her on the defensive. "I just didn't want to spoil the weekend. There's nothing you can do anyway."

His eyes darkened at that—the wicked cobalt Angela had described. It was a sure sign of passion. Yet his voice, when he responded, didn't alter so much as a degree in tone. That was control.

"Goddamn you, Deanna, you sit there and make me treat this like a hostile interview where I have to drag the facts out of you." Fear and fury burned through him. "I'm not tolerating this. I'm fed up with your tucking things away and filing them under 'For Deanna Only.'" He stepped forward then and, with a speed that had her blinking, pulled her to her feet. She'd expected him to be angry, but she hadn't expected the rage she saw on his face.

"Finn," she said carefully. "You're hurting me."

"What do you think you're doing to me?" He released her so quickly she staggered back a step. He spun away, shoving fisted hands in his pockets. "You don't have a clue. Don't you know how badly I want to get my hands on this creep? That I want to break him in half for causing you one minute of fear? How useless I feel when you get one of those goddamn notes and the color drains out of your face? And how much worse it is, how much harder it is, because after all this time you don't trust me?"

"It isn't a matter of trust." The violence in his eyes had her heart jumping into her throat. In all the time they'd been together, she'd never seen him so close to the edge. "It's not, Finn. It's pride. I didn't want to admit that I couldn't handle it alone."

He was silent for a long time, the only sound the spit of flames eating steadily at dry logs. "Damn your pride, Deanna," he said quietly. "I'm tired of beating my head against it."

Panic welled up inside her like a geyser. His words were a closing statement, a segment ender. With an involuntary cry of alarm, she grabbed his arm before he could stalk out. "Finn, please."

"I'm going for a walk." He stepped back, holding palms up, afraid he might cause them both irreparable damage if he touched her. "There are ways of working off this kind of mad. The most constructive one is to walk it off."

"I didn't mean to hurt you. I love you."

"That's handy, because I love you, too." And at the moment, his love felt as though it were killing him. "It just doesn't seem to be enough."

"I don't care if you're mad." She reached out again and clung. "You should be mad. You should shout and rage."

Gently, while he could still manage it, he loosened her grip.

"You're the shouter, Deanna. It's in the genes, I'd say. And I come from a long line of negotiators. It just so happens I'm out of compromises."

"I'm not asking you to compromise. I only want you to listen to what else I have to say."

"Fine." But he moved away from her, to the window seat in the shadows. "Talk's your forte, after all. Go ahead, Deanna, be reasonable, objective, sympathetic. I'll be the audience."

Rather than rise to the bait, she sat again. "I had no idea you were this angry with me. It's not just about me not telling you about this last note, is it?"

"What do you think?"

She'd interviewed dozens of hostile guests over the years. She doubted if any would be tougher than Finn Riley with his Irish up. "I've taken you for granted, and I've been unfair. And you've let me."

"That's good," he said dryly. "Start out with a self-deprecating statement, then circle around. It's no wonder you're on top."

"Don't." She threw her head back, the firelight glinting in her eyes. "Let me finish. At least let me finish before you tell me it's over."

There was silence again. Though she couldn't see his face when he spoke, she heard the weariness in his voice. "Do you think I could?"

"I don't know." A tear spilled over, glimmering in the shifting light. "I haven't let myself think about it until recently."

"Christ, don't cry."

She heard him shift, but he didn't move toward her.

"I won't." She brushed the tear away, swallowed the others that threatened. She knew she could weaken him with tears. And that she would despise herself for it. "I've always thought that I could make everything come out in order, if I just worked at it diligently enough. If I planned it all carefully enough. So I wrote lists, adhered to timetables. I've cheated us both by treating our relationship as if it were a task—a wonderful task—but a task to be handled." She was talking too fast, but couldn't stop, the words

355

tumbling over each other in their hurry to be said. "And I suppose I was feeling pretty smug about the job I was doing. We fit so well together, and I loved being your lover. And then today, I watched you outside, and I realized for the first time how badly I've botched it all." God, she wished she could see his face, his eyes. "You know how I hate to make mistakes."

"Yes, I do." He had to take a moment. It wasn't only her pride on the line. "It sounds as though you're the one doing the ending, Deanna."

"No." She sprang up. "No, I'm trying to ask you to marry me."

A log collapsed in the grate, shooting sparks and hissing fire. When it settled again, the only sound she heard was her own unsteady breathing. He rose, crossed from shadow into light. His eyes were as guarded and enigmatic as an ace gambler calling a bluff. "Are you afraid I'll walk if you don't do this?"

"I imagine the hole there would be in my life if you did, and I'm terrified. And because I'm terrified I wonder why I've waited so long. Maybe I'm wrong and you don't want marriage anymore. If that's the way you feel, I'll wait." She thought if he continued to stare at her with that mild curiosity, she'd scream. "Say something, damn it. Yes, no, go to hell. Something."

"Why? Why now, Deanna?"

"Don't make this an interview."

"Why?" he repeated. When he grabbed her arms she realized there was nothing mild about his mood.

"Because everything's so complicated now." Her voice rose, trembled, broke. "Because life doesn't fit into any of my neat scheduling plans, and I don't want being married to you to be neat and orderly. Because with the November sweeps raging, and all this crazy publicity with Angela, and you going off to Haiti, it's probably the worst possible time to think about getting married. So that makes it the best time."

Despite his tangled emotions, he laughed. "For once your logic totally eludes me."

"I don't need life to be perfect, Finn. For once, I don't need that. It just has to be right. And we're so absolutely right." She blinked back more tears, then gave up and let them fall. "Will you marry me?"

He tipped her head back so that he could study her face. And he smiled, slowly, as all those tangled emotions smoothed out into one silky sheet. "Well, you know, Kansas, this is awfully sudden."

NEWS OF THE ENGAGEMENT spread quickly. Within twenty-four hours of the official announcement, Deanna's office was deluged with calls. Requests for interviews, offers from designers, caterers, chefs, congratulatory calls from friends. Curiosity calls from other reporters.

Cassie fielded them, batting the few back to Deanna that required the personal touch.

Oddly there had been no calls, no notes, no contact at all from the one person who had been hounding her for years. No matter how often Deanna told herself she should be relieved at the respite, it frightened her more than seeing one of those neat, white envelopes on her desk or tucked under her door.

BUT NONE CAME, BECAUSE none were written. In the shadowy little room where pictures of Deanna beamed contentedly from walls and tabletops, there was little sound but weeping. Hot, bitter tears fell on the newspaper print that announced the engagement of two of television's most popular stars.

Alone, alone for so long. Waiting, waiting so patiently. So sure that Finn would never settle down. That Deanna could still be had. Now the hope that fueled patience was smashed, a delicate cup of fragile glass tossed aside and discovered to have been empty all along.

There was no sweet wine of triumph to be shared. And no Deanna to fill those empty hours.

But even as the tears dried, the planning began. She merely had to be shown—surely that was all—that no one could love her more completely. She needed to be shown, to be shocked into awareness. And, she needed to be punished. Just a little.

There was a way to arrange it all.

DEANNA HAD VOTED FOR a small, simple wedding. A private ceremony, she told Finn as he'd finished up the last of his packing for Haiti. Just family and close friends.

And it had been he who'd tossed her the curve.

"Nope. We're shooting the works on this one, Kansas." He'd zipped up his garment bag and slung it over his shoulder. "A church wedding, organ music, acres of flowers and several weeping relatives neither one of us remembers. Followed by a reception of mammoth proportions where some of those same relatives will drink too much and embarrass their respective spouses."

She chased down the steps after him. "Do you know how long it would take to plan something like that?"

"Yeah. You've got five months." He dragged her close for a hard, deep kiss. "You've got an April deadline, Deanna. We'll look over your list when I get back."

"But, Finn." She was forced to scoot down and grab the dog by the collar before he joyfully rushed out of the door Finn opened.

"This time *I* want it perfect. I'll call as soon as I can." He started down to where his driver waited, swinging around and walking backward with a grin teasing his dimples. "Stay tuned."

So she was now planning a full-scale wedding. Which, of course, prompted the topic idea of wedding preparations and related stress.

"We could book couples who'd broken up because the fighting and spats during the wedding plans undermined their relationship."

From her seat at the head of the conference table, Deanna eyed Simon owlishly. "Thanks, I needed that."

"No, really." He turned his chuckle into a cough. "I have this niece . . ."

Margaret groaned and pushed her purple-framed glasses up her pug nose. "He's always got a niece, or a nephew, or a cousin."

"Can I help it if I've got a big family?"

"Children, children." Hoping to restore order, Fran shook Kelsey's rattle. "Let's try to pretend we're a dignified, organized group with a number-one show."

"We're number one," Jeff chanted, grinning as others picked up the rhythm. "We're number one."

"And we want to stay there." Laughing, Deanna held up both hands. "Okay, though it doesn't do anything for my peace of mind, Simon's got a good idea. How many couples do you figure break up sometime between the *Will you* and the *I do*?"

"Plenty," Simon said with relish. "Take my niece—" He ignored the paper airplane Margaret sailed in his direction. "Really, they'd booked the church, the hall, found the caterer. All this time, according to my sister, they fought like tigers. The big blowup came over the bridesmaids' dresses. They couldn't agree on the color."

"They called off the wedding because of the bridesmaids' dresses?" Deanna narrowed her eyes. "You're making this up."

"Swear to God." To prove it, Simon placed a hand on his heart. "She wanted seafoam, he wanted lavender. Of course, the flowers were a contributing cause. If you can't agree on that, how can you agree on where to send your kids to college? Hey." He brightened. "Maybe we can get them."

"We'll keep it in mind." Deanna jotted down notes. Among them was a warning to be flexible over colors. "I think the point here is that wedding preparations are stressful, and there are ways of lessening the tension. We'll want an expert. Not a psychologist," she said quickly, thinking of Marshall.

"A wedding coordinator," Jeff suggested, watching Deanna's face for signs of approval or dismissal. "Somebody who orchestrates the

359

whole business professionally. It *is* like a business," he said, glancing around for confirmation. "Marriage."

"You betcha." Fran tapped the rattle against the table. "A coordinator's good. We could talk about staying within your means and expectations. How not to let your fantasies about perfection cloud the real issue."

"Cheap shot," Deanna tossed back. "We could use the mother and father of the bride. Traditionally they're in charge of the checkbook. What kind of strain is it personally and financially? And how do we decide, reasonably and happily, on invitations, the reception, the music, the flowers, the photographer? Do we have a buffet or a sit-down meal? What about centerpieces? The wedding party, decorations, the guest list?" The faintest hint of desperation crept into her voice. "Where the hell do you put out-of-town guests, and how is anyone supposed to put all this together in five months?"

She lowered her head on her arms. "I think," she said slowly, "we should elope."

"Hey, that's good," Simon piped up. "Alternatives to wedding stress. I had this cousin . . ."

This time Margaret's airplane hit him right between the eyes.

WITHIN WEEKS, DEANNA'S organized desk was jumbled with sketches of bridal gowns, from the elaborately traditional to the funkily futuristic.

Behind her, the same homely plastic tree Jeff had hauled into her office that first Christmas leaned precariously to starboard, overweighted by balls and garlands.

Someone—Cassie, she assumed—had spritzed some pine-scented air freshener around. The cheery aroma made the fading dyed plastic boughs even more pathetic. And Deanna loved it.

It was a tradition now, a superstition. She wouldn't have replaced the ugly tree with the richest blue spruce in the city.

"I can't quite see saying 'I do' in something like this." She held up a sketch for Fran's perusal. The short, skinny dress was topped with a headpiece that resembled helicopter blades.

"Well, after, Finn could give you a spin and the two of you could glide down the aisle. Now this one's hot." She held up a drawing; the elongated model was spread-legged in a bare-midriff mini with spike-heeled boots.

"Only if I carry a whip instead of a bouquet."

"You'd get great press." She tossed it aside. "You don't have a lot of time to decide before April comes busting out all over."

"Don't remind me." She shuffled another sketch on top, her twin-diamond engagement ring flashing. A diamond for each year it had taken him to wear her down, he'd told her as he'd slipped it on her finger. "This one's nice."

Fran peeked over her shoulder. "That one's gorgeous." She oohed a bit over the billowing skirts and full sleeves. The bodice was snug, trimmed in pearls and lace with the design repeating on the flowing train. The headpiece was a simple circlet from which the frothy veil flowed.

"It's really stunning. Almost medieval. A real once-in-a-lifetime dress."

"You think so?"

Recognizing her interest, Fran narrowed her eyes. "You've already decided on it."

"I want a completely unbiased opinion. And yes," she admitted with a laugh. "I knew the minute I saw it." She tidied the pile, laying her choice on top. "I wish the rest of it were so simple. The photographer—"

"I'm in charge of that."

"The caterer."

"Cassie's department."

"Music, napkins, flowers, invitations," she said before Fran could interrupt her again. "Let me at least pretend this is driving me crazy."

"Tough, when you've never looked happier in your life."

"I really have you to thank for it. You gave me the kick in the butt I needed."

"Glad to oblige. Now, we're going to get out of here while you've got a free evening and go down to Michigan Avenue for some trousseau shopping. With Finn on a shoot across town, this is the only chance I've got. There's not a minute to waste."

"I'm ready." She grabbed her purse as the phone rang. "Almost." Because Cassie was already gone for the day, Deanna answered herself. "Reynolds," she said out of habit, and her brilliant smile withered. "Angela." She glanced up and caught the interest in Fran's eye. "That's very nice of you. I'm sure Finn and I will be very happy."

"Of course you are," Angela cooed into the receiver as she continued to slice through a cover photo of Finn and Deanna with a letter opener. "You always were the confident one, Deanna."

To keep herself calm, Deanna shifted to study the teetering Christmas tree. "Is there something I can do for you?"

"No, not at all. There's something I want to do for you, dear. Let's call it an engagement gift. A little tidbit of information you might be interested in, about your fiancé."

"There's nothing you can tell me about Finn I'd be interested in, Angela. I appreciate your best wishes, and now I'm afraid I'm just on my way out."

"Don't be in such a rush. I recall your having a healthy sense of curiosity. I doubt you've changed so much. It really would be very wise, for you and for Finn, if you listened to what I have to say."

"All right." Setting her teeth, Deanna sat down again. "I'm listening."

"Oh, no, dear, not over the phone. It so happens I'm in Chicago. A little business, a little pleasure."

"Yes, your luncheon with the League of Women Voters tomorrow. I read about it."

"There's that, and another little matter. But I'll be free for a chat, say, at midnight."

"The witching hour? Angela, that's so obvious, even for you."

"Watch your tone, or I won't give you the opportunity of hearing what I have to say before I go to the press. You can consider my generosity a combination engagement and Christmas gift, darling. Midnight," she repeated. "At the studio. My old studio."

"I don't—damn it." Echoing Angela's response, Deanna slammed down the phone.

"What's she up to?"

"I'm not sure." With her celebratory mood in tatters, Deanna stared into space. "She wants to meet with me. Claims she has some information I need to hear."

"She only wants to cause trouble, Dee." The worry was in Fran's voice, in her eyes. "*She's* in trouble. In the past six months, her show's gone dramatically downhill with rumors about her drinking, about her staging shows, bribing guests. It's hardly a surprise that she'd want to fly out on her broomstick and hand you a poisoned apple."

"I'm not worried about it." Deanna shook off the mood and rose again. "I'm not. It's time the two of us had it out once and for all. In private. There's nothing she can say or do that can hurt me."

PART THREE

"All power of fancy over reason is a degree of insanity."

SAMUEL JOHNSON

Chapter Twenty-three

BUT SOMEONE HAD HURT ANGELA.

Someone had killed her.

Deanna continued to scream, high, piercing cries that burned her throat like acid. Even when her vision grayed, Deanna couldn't take her eyes off the horror beside her. And she could smell the blood, hot and coppery and thick.

She had to escape before Angela reached out with that delicate, dead hand and squeezed it around her throat.

With little mewling sounds of panic, she crawled out of the chair, afraid to move too fast, afraid to take her eyes off of what had been Angela Perkins. Every move, every sound was echoed by the monitor while the camera objectively recorded, its round, dark eye staring. Something tugged her back. On a soundless gasping scream, Deanna lifted her hands to fight what she couldn't see, and tangled her fingers in the wires of a lapel mike.

"Oh God. Oh God." She tore herself free, hurling the mike aside and fleeing the set in a blind panic.

She stumbled, caught a horrified glimpse of herself in the wide wall mirror. A hot laugh bubbled in her throat. She looked insane, she thought wildly. And she bit down on her hysteria, afraid it would slide from her throat in a mad chuckle. She nearly fell, tripping over her own feet as she ran down the dark corridor. Someone was breathing down her neck. She could feel it, she knew it, hot, greedy breath whispering behind her.

Sobbing, she hurtled into her dressing room, slammed the door, threw the lock, then stood in the dark with her heart pounding like a rabbit's.

She fumbled for the light, then screamed again when her own reflection jumped at her. A glittery gold garland ringed the mirror. Like a noose, she thought. Like a spangled noose. Boneless with terror, she slid down against the door. Everything was spinning, spinning, and her stomach heaved in response. Clammy with nausea, she crawled to the phone. The sound of her own whimpering iced her skin as she punched the number for emergency.

"Please, please help." Dizzy and sick, she lay on the floor, cradling the receiver. "Her face is gone. I need help. The CBC Building, Studio B. Please hurry," she said, and let the darkness swallow her.

IT WAS JUST PAST ONE A.M. when Finn arrived home. His first thoughts were for a hot shower and a warm brandy. He expected Deanna home within the hour, after whatever emergency meeting she had. She'd been vague about the details when she'd caught him between shoots, and he hadn't had the time or the inclination to press. They'd both been in the business too long to question midnight meetings.

He sent his driver off and started up the walk, both amused and embarrassed that the dog was setting up a din that would wake the neighbors for blocks.

"Okay, okay, Cronkite. Try for a little dignity." He reached for his keys as he climbed onto the porch, wondering why Deanna had forgotten to leave on the porch light. Little details like that never escaped her.

Wedding plans were rattling her brain, he thought, pleased at the idea.

Something crunched under his foot. He glanced down and saw the faint glitter of broken glass. His initial puzzlement turned to fury when he saw the jagged shards of the beveled glass panels beside the door.

Then his mouth went dry. What if her meeting had been canceled? What if she'd come home? He burst through the door in thoughtless fear, shouting her name.

Something crashed at the back of the house, and the dog's frantic barking turned into a desperate howl. Thinking only of Deanna, Finn hit the lights before he sprinted toward the source of the crash.

He found nothing but destruction, a mindless and brutal attack on their possessions. Lamps and tables were overturned, glassware shattered. When he reached the kitchen, his mind was cold as ice. He thought he saw a form running across the lawn. Even as he tore aside the shattered door to give chase, the dog howled again, scratching pitifully against the locked utility room door.

He wanted to give chase. It burned in him to hunt down whoever had done this and throttle him. But the possibility that Deanna was somewhere in the house, hurt, stopped him.

"Okay, Cronkite." He unlocked the door and staggered back as the dog leaped joyously at him. His thick body was shivering. "Scared you, did he? Me too. Let's find Deanna."

He searched every room, growing colder with every moment. The devastation was as total as tornado damage, both the priceless and the trivial capriciously destroyed.

But the worst, the most terrifying, was the message scrawled in Deanna's lipstick on the wall above the bed they shared.

I loved you
I killed for you
I hate you

"Thank God she wasn't here. Thank God." Grimly he picked up the phone and called the police.

"TAKE IT EASY." LIEUTENANT Jenner helped Deanna steady a glass of water.

"I'm all right now." But her teeth chattered on the rim of the glass. "I'm sorry. I know I was incoherent before."

"Understandable." He'd had a good long look at Angela Perkins's body and found Deanna's condition understandable indeed. He didn't blame her for huddling inside the locked room, needing to be gently persuaded to open the door to admit him. "You're going to want to have a doctor take a look at you."

"I'm fine, really."

Shock, he imagined. It was nature's way of closing down the system and offering the illusion of comfort. But her eyes were still glassy, and even though he'd thrown his overcoat over her shoulders, she was shivering.

"Can you tell me what happened?"

"I found her. I came in and found her."

"What were you doing at the studio after midnight?"

"She asked me to meet her. She called—she ..." She sipped again. "She called."

"So you arranged to meet her here."

"She wanted to—to talk to me. She said she had information about ..." Defenses clicked in. "About something I needed to know. I wasn't going to come, then I thought it might be best if we had it out."

"What time did you get here?"

"It was midnight. I looked at my watch in the parking lot." The colored lights in the distance, the haze of Christmas cheer. "It was midnight. I thought maybe she hadn't arrived yet, but she could have had her driver drop her off. So I let myself into the studio. And it was dark, so I thought she wasn't here, and that was good. I wanted to be first. Then, when I started to turn on the lights, something hit me. When I woke up I was on the set, and I couldn't think. The camera was on. Oh, God, the camera was on, and I saw, in the monitor, I saw her." She pressed a hand to her mouth to hold back the whimpers.

"Take a minute." Jenner leaned back.

"I don't know anything else. I ran in here and locked the door. I called the police, and I passed out."

"Did you see anybody on your way to the studio?"

"No. No one. The cleaning crews would have gone by now. There would be a few people in the newsroom, manning the desk overnight, but after the last broadcast, the building clears out."

"You need a card to get into the building, don't you?"

"Yes. They put in a new security system about a year ago."

"Is this your purse, Miss Reynolds?" He held out a generous shoulder bag in smooth black leather.

"Yes, that's mine. I must have dropped it when I—when I came in."

"And this card." He held up a clear plastic bag. Inside was a slim, laminated card with her initials in the corner.

"Yes, that's mine."

He set the bag aside and continued to take notes. "What time did Miss Perkins contact you about this meeting?"

"About five. She called my office."

"Your secretary took the call?"

"No, she'd already gone home. I took it myself." Something trembled through the shield of shock. "You think I killed her? You think I did that to her? Why?" She lurched to her feet, swaying like a drunk as the overcoat slid to the floor. "How could I? Why would

I? Do you think I lured her here, and murdered her, then taped it all so I could show it to all my loyal viewers in the morning?"

"Calm down, Miss Reynolds." Jenner got cautiously to his feet. She looked as though she might dissolve if he touched her. "No one's accusing you of anything. I'm just trying to get the facts."

"I'll give the facts. Someone killed her. Someone blew her face away and propped her up on the set. Oh God." She pressed a hand to her head. "This can't be real."

"Sit down and catch your breath." Jenner took her by the arm. There was a commotion in the corridor behind him and he turned to the door.

"Goddamn it, I want to see her." Finn shoved his way clear of the cop trying to detain him and burst through the doorway. "Deanna." He sprinted forward as she swayed toward him. "You're all right." He vised his arms around her, burying his face in her hair. "You're all right."

"Finn." She pressed against him, desperate for the feel of his flesh, his warmth, his comfort. "Someone killed Angela. I found her. Finn, I found her."

But he was already drawing her away, appalled by the swelling and matted blood on the back of her head. Relief twisted into a dark, keen thirst for revenge. "Who hurt you?"

"I don't know." She burrowed back into his arms. "I didn't see. They think I did it. Finn, they think I killed her."

Over her trembling shoulder he stared stonily at Jenner. "Are you out of your mind?"

"Miss Reynolds is mistaken. We have no intention of charging her at this time. Nor, in my opinion, in the future."

"Then she's free to go."

Jenner rubbed his chin. "Yes. We'll need her to sign a statement, but we can do it tomorrow. Miss Reynolds, I know you've had a shock, and I apologize for having to put you through the questioning. I advise you to go by the hospital, have someone take a look at you."

"I'll take her. Deanna." Gently Finn eased her back to the chair. "I want you to wait here a minute. I need to talk to Lieutenant Jenner."

She clung to his hand. "Don't leave."

"No, just outside the door. Just for a minute. Detective."

Jenner followed Finn into the corridor, nodding to a uniform to back off. "She's had a rough night, Mr. Riley."

"I'm aware of that. I don't want you to add to it."

"Neither do I. But certain wheels have to turn. I've got a nasty murder, and as far as I can tell, she's the only witness. You wouldn't mind telling me where you were tonight?"

Finn's eyes cooled. "No, I wouldn't. I was taping a segment on the South Side. I'd guess I'd have about a dozen witnesses to place me there until about midnight. My driver took me home, dropped me off just after one. I put in a call to 911 at one-twenty."

"Why?"

"Because my house had been trashed. You want to verify that, contact your superior."

"I don't doubt your word, Mr. Riley." Jenner rubbed his chin again, toying with the timetable. "You said one-twenty?"

"Give or take a minute. Whoever broke in left a message for Deanna on the bedroom wall. You can check with your associates for details. I'm getting Deanna out of here."

"I'll do that." Jenner made another note. "Mr. Riley, I'd take her out another way. I wouldn't want her going through the studio."

"Hey, Arnie!" Another plainclothes cop signaled from the studio end of the corridor. "M.E.'s finished here."

"Tell him to hang on a minute. We'll be in touch, Mr. Riley."

Saying nothing, Finn turned back into the dressing room. He took off his own coat, pushing Deanna's limp arms through the sleeves. He didn't want to waste time looking for hers. "Come on, baby, let's get out of here."

"I want to go home." She leaned heavily against him as he led her out.

"No way. I'm taking you to E.R."

"Don't leave me there."

"I'm not leaving you."

He took the long way around, circumventing the studio, choosing the angled stairs that led to the parking lot. Because he knew what to expect before he opened the door, he kissed her brow, held her by the shoulders.

"The place is going to be swarming with reporters and Minicams."

She squeezed her eyes tight, shivered. "I know. It's okay."

"Just hold on tight to me."

"I already am."

When he shoved the door open, the flash of klieg lights blinded her. She shielded her eyes and saw nothing but eager bodies rushing toward her, microphones stabbing out like lances and the wide, demanding eye of the camera.

Questions hurtled at her, making her hunch her shoulders in defense as Finn propelled her through the surging sea of reporters.

She knew most of them, she realized. Liked most of those she knew. Once upon a time they had competed for stories. Once upon a time she would have been among them, pressing forward, scurrying for that one telling picture, that one mumbled comment.

Then flying to the news desk to get the item—she was an item now—on the air minutes, even seconds, before the competition.

But she was no longer the observer. She was the observed. How could she tell them how she felt? How could she tell them what she knew? Her mind was like glass, throbbing from some deadly, high-pitched whine. She thought if she couldn't have silence, she would explode and shatter.

"Christ, Dee."

A hand reached for her, hesitating as she cringed away. And she saw Joe, the Minicam on his shoulder, his baseball cap askew.

"I'm sorry," he said, and swore again. "I'm really sorry."

"It's all right. I've been there, remember? It's just the job." She climbed gratefully into Finn's car and closed her eyes. Tuned out.

JENNER TURNED THE STUDIO over to the forensic team. Since he'd already had two men question the occupants of the building, he decided to wait until morning before doing a follow-up there. Instead, he left the CBC Building and drove to Finn Riley's home.

He wasn't surprised, or displeased, when Finn pulled into the driveway behind him.

"How's Miss Reynolds?"

"She's got a concussion," Finn said tersely. "They're keeping her overnight for observation. I had a feeling I'd find you here."

Jenner nodded as they started up the walk. "Chilly night," he said conversationally. "Dispatch showed your call came in at one twenty-three. First unit arrived at one twenty-eight."

"It was a quick response." Though it hadn't seemed quick as he'd spent that endless five minutes looking over the destruction of his home. "Are you handling B and Es, too, Lieutenant?"

"I like to diversify. And the truth is"—he paused just outside the door—"I figure I've got an interest in this. Between the business in Greektown and the investigation on those letters Miss Reynolds has been getting, I figure I've got an interest. Does that bother you?"

Finn studied Jenner in the starlight. The man looked tired, yet completely alert. It was a combination Finn understood perfectly. "No."

"Well then." Jenner sliced through the police tape over the damaged door. "Maybe you'll take me on the grand tour."

Riley was a pretty snappy dresser, Jenner mused as they moved inside. The kind who leaned toward leather jackets and faded jeans. Jenner had tried on a leather jacket once. He'd looked like a cop. He always did.

"Did you mention the trouble here to Miss Reynolds?"

"No."

375

"Can't blame you. She's had a rough night." He glanced around. The place looked as if it had been bombed. "So have you."

"You could say that. Almost every room was trashed." Finn gestured toward the living area off the main hall. "I didn't take a lot of time going through it."

Jenner grunted. Word was the minute Finn had learned of the trouble at CBC, he'd sprinted out, leaving the destruction behind.

"You must be pretty steamed." That was putting it mildly, Jenner mused. What he saw on Finn's face was cold rage. If he'd run across the perp, he'd have sliced him into little pieces. Though it was unprofessional, Jenner would have given a great deal to see it.

"I can replace the things," Finn said as they started upstairs.

"Yeah." Jenner stepped inside the bedroom, nodded toward the wall. "So our friend's taken to writing on walls." Taking out his pad, Jenner copied the writing style onto a blank page. This was the first time the writer had exposed himself this way. "Makes a statement." One quick scan and he'd taken in the devastation of the room. "Forensics are going to have a hell of a time sorting through this mess." He toed a broken perfume bottle with his foot. "Tiffany," he commented. "A hundred fifty an ounce. My wife, she likes that scent. I bought her the cologne for her birthday. And those sheets. Irish linen. My grandmother had a tablecloth. I used to rub my face over it when I was a kid."

Nearly amused, Finn leaned on the doorjamb and studied Jenner. "Is this how you conduct an investigation, Lieutenant? Or do you moonlight for an insurance company?"

"Always was a sucker for quality." He slipped his pad back in his pocket, just above the snug weight of his weapon. "So, Mr. Riley, I'd have to say we have a connection."

"So, Lieutenant, I'd have to agree with you."

"Murder happened by midnight." He scratched the back of his

376

neck. "The drive from CBC to here takes fourteen minutes, at the speed limit. He spends, say, ten minutes setting the stage, turning on the equipment. Another ten to get over here. You get home about twenty after one. Yeah, I'd say that's enough time."

"You're not telling me anything I don't know, Lieutenant. What's next?"

"We'll canvass the neighborhood tomorrow. Somebody might have seen something."

"You haven't had time to interview Dan Gardner."

"No." A ghost of a smile moved Jenner's lips. "My next stop."

"Mine too."

"Mr. Riley, you'd be better off going back to the hospital, watching over your lady. Leave this to me."

"I'll watch out for Deanna," Finn returned. "And I'm going to talk to Gardner. I'm going to use everything and everyone I know to get to the root of this. I can go with you, Lieutenant, or I can go around you."

"That's not friendly, Mr. Riley."

"I'm not feeling friendly, Lieutenant Jenner."

"Don't imagine you are, but this is police business."

"So was Greektown."

Jenner's brows lifted as he studied Finn. The man knew which buttons to push, he mused.

"I like you," Jenner said after a moment. "I liked the way you handled yourself in Greektown. Saw you take that hit." He scratched his chin, considered. "You just kept right on reporting."

"That's my job."

"Yeah, and I got mine. I'm willing to bend the rules a bit, Mr. Riley, for a couple reasons. One, I really admire your lady, and two . . . I figure there's a ten-year-old girl out there who just might owe you her life. I might not have mentioned, I have a grand-daughter that age."

"No, you didn't mention it."

"Well." Jenner simply nodded again. "You can follow me in your car."

WHEN DEANNA SURFACED, IT was midmorning. Yet it wasn't necessary to orient herself; she remembered everything too clearly. She was in the hospital under observation. She wished she could laugh at the term. She understood that she would remain under all manner of observation for a long time.

She turned her head, mindful of the dull ache swimming inside, and studied Finn. He was dozing in the chair beside the bed, his hand covering hers. Unshaven, exhausted and pale, he was the most comforting sight she could imagine.

Not wanting to disturb him, she shifted slowly. But her slight movement woke him.

"Are you hurting?"

"No." Her voice was weak; she put an effort into strengthening it. "You shouldn't have sat up all night. They'd have found somewhere for you to stretch out."

"I can sleep anywhere. I'm a reporter, remember?" He scrubbed his hands over his face, then stretched out the kinks in his back. "You should try to get some more sleep."

"I want to go home. A mild concussion isn't enough to keep me in the hospital." She sat up, but cautiously, knowing if she so much as sneezed he'd run for a nurse. "No double vision, no memory lapses, no nausea."

"You're pale as wax, Deanna."

"You're not looking so hale and hearty yourself. Want to crawl in here with me?"

"Later." He scooted over to sit on the side of the bed and touched his hand to her cheek. "I love you."

"I know. I don't think I could have gotten through last night without you."

"You don't have to get through anything without me."

She smiled, but her eyes strayed from his to the television bracketed to the wall at the foot of the bed. "I don't suppose you've heard the morning news?"

"No." He turned, looked at her intently. "No," he repeated. "We'll deal with it later."

Yes, she thought. Later was better. "It was horrible the way she died. Horrible the way it was all so perfectly staged. I need to think about it, but I can't seem to."

"Then don't. Don't push it, Deanna." He looked over as he heard Fran's voice, lifted high in indignant rage as she argued with the guard outside the door. "I'll tell her you're resting."

"No, please. I want to see her."

Finn had just gone to the door to have a word with the guard when Fran burst in. She bulleted toward the bed and snatched Deanna into her arms. "Oh God, I've been sick ever since I heard. Are you all right? How bad are you hurt?"

"Just a bump on the head." She returned the embrace, squeezing hard. "I was just about to get up and get dressed."

"Are you sure?" Fran drew her back; she might have been examining one of her children for symptoms. "You're so pale. Finn, go get the doctor. I think he should take another look at her."

"No." She took Fran's hands firmly in hers. "They just wanted me overnight for observation. I've been observed. The office? What's going on?"

Something flickered in Fran's eyes, then she shrugged. "Chaos. What else? The cops are taking statements from everyone."

"I should go in, do something."

"No." The protest came quickly, fiercely. "I mean it, Dee. There's nothing you can do, and if you came in at this point, you'd only add to the confusion. As soon as I go back and tell everyone you're okay, it should calm down a little." Her lips trembled before she wrapped her arms around Deanna again. "You really are okay? It must have been horrible for you. Every time I think of what could have happened—"

"I know." Comforted, Deanna cradled her head on Fran's shoulder. "Angela. God, Fran, I still can't believe it. Who could have hated her that much?"

Pick a number, Fran thought. "I don't want you to worry about the show or the office. We ran a re-broadcast today. Cassie's canceling and rescheduling guests we'd booked for the next week."

"That's not necessary."

"I'm the producer, and I say it is." After a last squeeze, Fran pulled back and turned to Finn for support. "Are you going to throw your weight in with me?"

"It doesn't appear to be necessary, but sure. I'm taking her up to the cabin for a while."

"I can't just leave. Jenner's bound to want to talk to me again. And I have to talk to Loren, to my staff."

Finn studied her a moment. There was pain in her eyes as well as the dregs of terror and shock. "Here's the way I see it," he said mildly. "I can spring you out of here later today and take you to the cabin. Or I can arrange for them to keep you in that bed for another couple of days."

"That's absurd." Deanna wanted to be angry, but she was too tired. "Just because we're getting married doesn't mean you can arrange my life."

"It does when you're too stubborn to do what's best for you."

"Well." Fran gave a satisfied nod and kissed Finn's cheek. "Now that I know she's in capable hands, I'm going to go find that doctor. I need to talk to you," she said under her breath, then turned back to Deanna. It was a relief to see the sulky turn of her friend's mouth. "Don't worry about the details," she told her. "The gang and I can handle everything. I'll be back in a few minutes."

"Fine. Great." Deanna plopped back on the pillows, wincing when the sudden movement made her head pound. "Just tell everyone I decided to go fishing."

"Good idea." Finn walked to the door to open it for Fran. "I'll

380

see if I can round up someone to put through the release papers. Stay in bed," he ordered, and walked outside. "What is it you don't want her to know?"

"There are cops swarming all over the sixteenth floor." Fran cast one last, worried glance over her shoulder as they walked to the elevators. "Her office has been torn apart, like someone went through it in an insane rage. Chairs hurled around, broken glass. All the lists she'd put together for the wedding and the sketches of the dresses were ripped up. Somebody had written all over the walls in red ink." As Finn watched, her cheeks drained of color so that her freckles stood out in stark relief. "It just said 'I love you', again and again and again. I don't want her to see it, Finn."

"She won't. I'm going to take care of her."

"I know that." Fran pressed her fingers to her eyes. "But I'm scared. Whoever killed Angela is so focused on Dee. I don't think he'll ever leave her alone."

Finn's eyes were sharp as a sword. "He won't get near her. There's someone I have to meet. You stay with her until I get back."

AFTER A TWO-HOUR CATNAP, Jenner rapped on the door of Dan Gardner's hotel suite. Beside him Finn was running through a mental list of questions he wanted answered.

"He'd better be in the mood to talk this time."

Jenner only shrugged. He didn't mind taking the long route, as long as it ended in the right place. "Hard to talk when you're sedated."

"Conveniently," Finn murmured.

"Guy's wife gets snuffed, he's entitled to break down."

"Wouldn't you think he'd want some details before he went under, Lieutenant? The way I see it, the longer he delays talking to you, the longer he has to formulate an alibi. Angela Perkins was a wealthy woman. Care to guess who's the chief beneficiary?"

"Then if he killed her, he'd have been stupid not to have an alibi to begin with. I've got a feeling you're a man used to being in charge of things."

"And?"

"You're going to have to take a backseat here. I've got an instinct about you, Mr. Riley, so I'm letting you tag along—that way I can pick your brain. But you're going to have to remember who's running this investigation."

"Cops and reporters have a lot in common, Lieutenant. We won't be the first who've used each other."

"Nope." Jenner heard the rattle of the chain. "But that doesn't change the pecking order."

Finn nodded grudgingly as the door opened. Dan Gardner looked like a man who'd been on a wild, two-day bender. His face was gray, his eyes sunken, and his hair stood out in tufts. His black silk robe and pajamas added an elegance that only accented his unkempt appearance, like fresh gilt on a tattered painting.

"Mr. Gardner?"

"Yeah." Dan brought a cigarette to his lips, gulping in smoke like water.

"I'm Detective Jenner." He held up his badge.

Dan glanced at it, then spotted Finn. "Hold it. What's he doing here?"

"Research," Finn said.

"I'm not talking to any reporters, especially this one."

"That's funny, coming from someone who woos the press like a lovesick suitor." Finn put a hand on the door before Dan could shut it. "I'll keep it off the record. But I can tell you, you're better off speaking with me when you've got a cop around. I'm in a real bad mood."

"I'm not well."

"I sympathize, Mr. Gardner," Jenner put in before Finn could comment. "You're certainly not obliged to speak in Mr. Riley's presence, but I have a feeling he'll just come back. Why don't we try it this way, and keep this as short as possible? It would be easier on you to do this here than to come to the station."

Dan stared at them both a moment, then with a shrug, he turned around, leaving the door open.

The drapes were still drawn, giving the parlor of the suite a gloomy air. The smell of cigarettes was strong, mixing uneasily with the fragrance from the two huge vases of roses flanking the sofa.

Dan sat between them, blinking when Jenner switched on a lamp.

"I'm sorry to have to disturb you at this time, Mr. Gardner," Jenner began. "But I need your cooperation."

Dan said nothing, only took another greedy drag from the cigarette. Angela's brand, he thought, and felt the smoke sting bitterly in his throat.

"Can you tell us what you know about your wife's activities yesterday?"

"Besides getting murdered?" With a humorless laugh, he roused himself to go to the bar and pour a generous portion of whiskey.

Finn only lifted a brow as Dan drank it down, poured again. It was barely ten A.M.

"It would help," Jenner continued, "if we had a clear sense of her movements throughout the day. Where she went, who she had contact with."

"She got up about ten." Dan came back to the sofa. The whiskey helped, he realized. He felt as though he were gliding an inch above the floor. "She had a massage, had her hair and makeup done, a manicure. All here in the suite." He drank with one hand, smoked with the other, his movements mechanical and strangely rhythmic. "She did a print interview, *Chicago Tribune*, then went downstairs to the ballroom for the luncheon. She had several other appointments through the day—interviews, meetings. Most of them here in the suite."

He crushed out the cigarette, sat back with the blue haze of smoke hovering over his head like a dirty halo.

"Were you with her?" Finn demanded.

Dan shot him one resentful glance, then shrugged. "I was in

and out. Mostly out. Angela didn't like distractions when she was dealing with the press. She had a dinner interview with *Premiere* magazine to hype her next special." In a jerky movement, he reached over to yank another cigarette from the pack on the coffee table. "She told me she didn't know how long it would run, and that she had a later meeting afterward, that I should go out to a blues bar and amuse myself."

"And did you?" Jenner asked.

"I had a steak, a couple of drinks, listened to some piano at the Pump Room."

Jenner noted it down. "Did you have any company?"

"I wasn't in the mood for company. We haven't had a lot of time to relax in the past few months, so I took advantage of it." His bloodshot eyes narrowed. "Are you looking for Angela's schedule, or mine?"

"Both," Jenner said pleasantly. He doodled a bit, a quick sketch of the room, of Dan Gardner's face. "It helps if we have a clear sense of things. When did you last see your wife, Mr. Gardner?"

"Just before seven, when she was getting ready for dinner."

"And did she tell you she planned to meet Deanna Reynolds at CBC later that night?"

"No." He bit the word off. "If she had, I would have discouraged it." He leaned forward now, enough of a showman to know which lines to punch. "He knows it, too," he added, jerking his head toward Finn. "That's why he wants in on the investigation, to try to head it off. It's no secret Deanna Reynolds hated my wife, was envious and driven to destroy her. I have no doubt that she killed Angela, or had her killed."

"That's an interesting theory," Finn mused. "Is that the line you're going to feed through your publicist?"

Jenner cleared his throat. "Did Miss Reynolds make any threats against your wife that you're aware of?"

Dan's eyes cut back to Jenner, bored in. "I told you, she attacked her physically once before. Christ knows she attacked her emotionally dozens of times over the years. She wanted Angela out of the way. Now she is. That should be clear enough. What are you doing about it?"

"We're looking into it," Jenner said mildly. "Mr. Gardner, what time did you return to the hotel last night?"

"Twelve-thirty, one o'clock."

"Did you meet anyone, speak with anyone who could verify that?"

"I resent the implication, Lieutenant. My wife is dead." He stabbed out the cigarette, breaking it in two. "And from what I've been told, there was only one person with her." He stared at Finn, secure that he could say whatever he chose with impunity. "A person who had every reason to hurt her. I don't appreciate being asked to supply an alibi."

"But can you?" Finn countered.

His teeth snapped together. "You're really reaching, aren't you, Riley? Do you really think you can throw the police off Deanna and onto me?"

Finn lifted a brow. "I don't believe you answered the question."

"It's possible one of the night clerks saw me come in. It's also possible that the waitress at the club would remember serving me, and what time I left. What kind of alibi does Deanna Reynolds have?"

Was it rage? Jenner wondered. Or was it fear that simmered in Gardner's voice? "I'm afraid I can't discuss that at this time. Do you have any idea how your wife might have gained access to the CBC Building and Studio B?"

"She worked there for some time," Dan said dryly. "I imagine she walked in. She'd know the way."

"There's a security system that wasn't in operation during the time your wife was based in the building."

"Then I'd imagine Deanna let her in. Then she killed her." He shifted forward, resting one hand on the black silk covering his knee. "Imagine what this will do for her ratings, Lieutenant Jenner.

He knows." Dan jabbed a finger toward Finn. "How many Nielsen homes will tune in to watch a cold-blooded killer, Riley? She'll murder the competition." He laughed, rubbing a hand over and over his face. "Just like she murdered Angela."

"Whoever killed your wife won't benefit from it." Jenner glanced at Finn, pleased to see he was maintaining an outward calm. Jenner decided he liked the pattern of their work together. Not something as clichéd as good cop—bad cop. Just teamwork. "Did Miss Perkins have an appointment book, a calendar?"

"Her secretary kept her calendar, but Angela always carried a small date book in her purse."

"Would you mind if we took a look in her room?"

Dan pressed the heels of his hands to his eyes. "Fuck, do what you want."

"You ought to order up some breakfast, Mr. Gardner," Jenner said as he rose.

"Yeah. I ought to do that."

Jenner took out a card and left it on the coffee table beside the ashtray of smoldering butts. "I'd appreciate it if you'd contact me if you think of anything else. We'll be out of your way in just a few minutes."

The first thing Finn did in the bedroom of the suite was open the drapes. Light spilled relentlessly into the room. The bureau top was crowded with bottles and pots, the expensive toys of a vain woman who could afford the best. A champagne flute with a pale pink outline of lipstick at the rim stood in the center. A floral silk robe flowed gracefully over the arm of a chair, its hem brushing matching ballet-style slippers.

The only evidence that a man shared the room was the suit hung on the valet.

"You didn't mention an appointment book in her purse, Lieutenant."

"There wasn't one." He glanced around the room like a hound sniffing the air. "Cosmetics, hotel key, cigarettes, lighter, a silk hankie, a roll of Certs, an eelskin wallet with ID, credit cards and better than three hundred cash. But no date book."

"Interesting." Finn nodded toward the champagne flute. "I'd say that was hers, wouldn't you, sitting there with her perfumes and skin creams."

"More than likely."

"There's another out in the parlor, over by the wet bar. Lipstick on that, too. Dark, hot-red lipstick."

"Good eye, Mr. Riley. Why don't we see if room service knows who Angela's drinking partner was?"

CARLA MENDEZ HAD NEVER had much excitement in her life. She'd been the oldest of five children born to a shoe salesman and a waitress and had lived a simple, uninspired life. At thirty-three, she had three children and a husband who was slavishly faithful and usually out of work.

Carla didn't mind her job as a hotel maid. She didn't like it particularly, but she did her job well if mechanically and tucked away tiny bottles of shampoo and skin cream as religiously as she tucked away her tips.

She was a small, sturdy woman, built like a fireplug, with tightly permed black hair and tiny dark eyes that were nearly lost in a network of worry lines. But her eyes were bright now, flitting from cop to reporter.

She didn't like cops. If Jenner had approached her alone, she would have closed up like a clam, on principle. But she couldn't resist Finn Riley. The way his dimples deepened when he smiled at her, the gentlemanly way he'd taken her hand.

And he wanted to interview her.

It was, for Carla, the biggest moment of her life.

Sensing her mood, Jenner hung back and let Finn take the ball.

"What time did you come into Miss Perkins's room to turn down the bed, Mrs. Mendez?"

"Ten o'clock. Usually I'd turn down much earlier, but she told me not to come in, not to disturb her before ten. She had appointments." Primly, she tugged on the hem of her uniform. "I don't like to work so late, but she was very nice." The twenty-dollar tip had been even nicer. "I've seen her on TV, too. But she wasn't stuck-up or anything. She was real polite. Messy, though," she added. "She and her husband used about six bath towels between them every day. And she had cigarette butts in every single ashtray. Dishes everywhere." She glanced around the parlor. "Cleaning up after people gives you insight," she said, and left it at that.

"I'm sure it does." Finn gave her an encouraging smile. "Was Miss Perkins with her husband when you were turning down the bed in their suite?"

"Can't say. Didn't see him. Didn't hear him. But I heard her, and the other one."

"The other one?"

"The other woman. They were scratching at each other like cats." Carla tugged on her hem again, examined her shoes. "Not that I listened. I mind my own business. I've been working in this hotel for seven years. You can't do that if you poke into people's private lives. But when I heard how she'd been murdered—Miss Perkins—I said to Gino, that's my husband, I said to Gino that I'd heard Miss Perkins going at it with this woman in her suite only a couple hours before she was dead. He said I should maybe tell my supervisor, but I thought it might cause trouble."

"So you haven't told anyone about it?" Finn prompted.

"No. And when you came in and said you wanted to talk to me about the people in 2403, I figured you already knew." Her eyes flashed back up. "Maybe you didn't."

"What can you tell us about the woman who was with Miss Perkins, Mrs. Mendez?"

"I didn't see her, but I heard her all right. Heard both of them. The woman said, 'I'm sick and tired of playing your games, Angela. And one way or the other they're going to stop.' Then Miss Perkins laughed. I knew it was her 'cause like I said, I've seen her on TV. And she laughed the way people do when they're feeling mean. And she said something like, 'Oh, you'll keep playing, darling. The stakes ...'" Carla screwed up her nose as she concentrated. "'The stakes are too high,' she said, 'for you to do anything else.' They called each other names for a while. Then the other woman said, 'I could kill you, Angela. But maybe I'll do something even better than that.' Then I heard the door slam, and Miss Perkins was laughing again. I finished up real quick and went out in the hall."

"You know, Mrs. Mendez, I think you should try my line of work." She preened and tugged on her hem again. "You're very observant," he added.

"It comes natural, I guess. You see a lot of funny things working in a hotel."

"I'm sure you do. I wonder ... Did you see the woman who'd left?"

"No. There wasn't anybody out there, but it took me a couple of minutes to finish stacking fresh towels, so she could have gotten on the elevator. That was my last room, so I went home after that. The next morning I heard that Miss Perkins had been killed. At first I thought maybe that woman had come back and killed her right there in my suite. But I found out it didn't happen in the hotel at all. It happened at the TV station where Deanna Reynolds has her show. I like her show better," she added guilelessly. "She has such a nice smile."

DEANNA TRIED TO USE THAT smile as Finn hesitated at the front door of the cabin. "I'm fine," she told him. She'd told him that repeatedly since she'd been released from the hospital three days before. "Finn, you're going to pick up a few things at the store; you're not leaving me to defend the fort against marauding hostiles. Besides"— she bent down to scratch the dog's ears—"I have a champion."

"Champion wimp." He cupped Deanna's face in his hands. "Let

me worry, okay? It's still a new experience for me to fret." He grinned. "I like fretting over you, Deanna."

"As long as you're not fretting so much you forget to buy me that candy bar."

"Hershey's Big Block, no almonds." He kissed her, relieved when her lips curved gently, sweetly under his. The day he'd had her to himself at the cabin had dulled the edge of her horror, he knew, but she still slept poorly and jolted at unexpected sounds. "Why don't you take a nap, Kansas?"

"Why don't you go get me that candy bar?" She drew back, her smile securely in place. "Then you can take a nap with me."

"Sounds like a pretty good deal. I won't be long."

No, she thought as she watched him walk to the car. He wouldn't be long. He hated leaving her alone. Though what he expected her to do was beyond her. Collapse in a hysterical heap? she wondered, lifting her hand in a wave as he headed down the lane. Run screaming from the house?

With a sigh, she crouched down again to rub the dog while he whined and scratched at the door. He loved to go for rides, she thought now. But Finn had left him behind, a canine sentry.

Not that she could blame Finn for being overprotective at this point. She'd been alone with a murderer, after all. A murderer who could have taken her life as quickly, as cruelly as he had taken Angela's. Everyone was worried about poor Deanna, she thought. Her parents, Fran. Simon, Jeff, Margaret, Cassie. Roger and Joe and plenty of others from the newsroom. Even Loren and Barlow had called to express concern, to offer help.

"Take all the time you need," Loren had told her, without a single mention of ratings or expenses. "Don't even think about coming back until you're stronger."

But she wasn't weak, Deanna decided. She was alive.

No one had tried to kill her. Surely everyone must understand that one simple point. Yes, she had been alone with a murderer, but she was alive.

Straightening, she wandered around the cabin, tidying what was already competently neat. She brewed some tea she didn't want, then wandered more with the cup warming her hands. She poked at the cheerfully blazing fire.

She stared out the window. She sat on the couch.

She needed, desperately needed, to work.

This wasn't one of their stolen weekends filled to the brim with laughter and lovemaking and arguments over newspaper editorials. There wasn't a newspaper in the house, she thought in frustration. And Finn said there was some trouble with the cable, so television was out as well.

He was doing his best to keep the outside world at bay, she knew. To put her in a protective bubble, where nothing and no one could cause her distress.

And she'd let him, because what had happened in Chicago had seemed too horrible to think about; she'd let Finn push it all to the side for her.

But now she needed to take some action.

"We're going back to Chicago," she told the dog, who responded with a thud of his tail on the floor. She turned to the steps, intending to pack, when she heard the sound of a car on the drive. "He couldn't even have gotten to the store yet," she muttered, heading to the door behind the happily barking dog. "Look, Cronkite, I love him, too, but he hasn't been gone ten minutes." Deanna pushed open the screen, laughing as the dog bulleted through. But when she looked up and saw the car, the laughter died.

She didn't recognize the car, a dull brown sedan with dings in both fenders. But she recognized Jenner and found herself tugging the collar of her flannel shirt around her throat. She should have felt relieved to see him, to know he was trying to solve the case. Instead she felt only a tightening of the nerves that trapped her somewhere between fear and resignation.

Jenner grinned, obviously charmed by Cronkite's yapping and

dancing around his legs. He bent down, unerringly finding the spot between Cronkite's ears that sent the dog into spasms of pleasure.

"Hey there, boy. There's a good dog." He chuckled when Cronkite plopped down on his rump and extended a paw to shake. "Know your manners, do you?" With the dog's dusty paw in his hand, he glanced up when Deanna stepped out on the porch. "This is quite a watchdog you've got here, Miss Reynolds."

"I'm afraid that's as fierce as he gets." The brisk December breeze invaded her bones. "You're a long way from Chicago, Lieutenant."

"Nice drive." Leaving his hand extended for the dog to sniff, he glanced around. The snow had melted, and the evergreens were glossily green. The breeze hummed through denuded trees and threatened to pick up and get mean. "Pretty place. Must feel good to get out of the city now and then."

"Yes, it does."

"Miss Reynolds, I'm sorry to disturb you, but I have some questions on the Perkins homicide."

"Please, come in. I've just made tea, but I can put on coffee if you'd prefer." How could they talk about murder without a nice, sociable cup? Deanna thought as her stomach turned.

"Tea's fine." Jenner walked toward the door with the dog prancing behind him.

"Sit down." She gestured him inside, toward the great room. "I'll just be a minute."

"Mr. Riley's not with you?" Jenner took a turn around the room, interested in the getaway lives of the rich.

"He went to the store. He'll be back shortly."

Hepplewhite. Jenner noted a side table and ladder-back chair. The rug was Native American. Navajo, he imagined. The glassware was Irish. Waterford.

"You have a good eye, Lieutenant." Her face bland, Deanna carried the tea tray into the room.

He didn't realize he'd spoken aloud, and smiled a little. It didn't bother him to be caught snooping. He got paid for it. "I like quality stuff. Even when I can't afford it." He nodded to the vase on the mantel, stuffed with early spring blooms. "Staffordshire?"

"Dresden." Annoyed, Deanna set the tray down with a snap. "I'm sure you didn't drive all the way out here to admire the bric-a-brac. Have you found out who killed Angela?"

"No." Jenner settled himself on the sofa with the dog at his feet. "We're beginning to put things together."

"That's comforting. Sugar, lemon?"

She was playing it tough, Jenner thought. "Black, thanks." He might have believed Deanna's act, if it hadn't been for the shadows under her eyes. "With sugar. Lots of it."

His grin apologetic, Jenner began to spoon sugar into the cup Deanna poured for him. "Sweet tooth. Miss Reynolds, I don't want to make you go through your whole statement again—"

"And I appreciate it." Deanna caught herself snapping the words, and sighed. "I want to cooperate, Lieutenant. I just don't see what more I can tell you. I had an appointment with Angela. I kept it. Someone killed her."

"Didn't it strike you as odd that she'd want to meet so late?"

Deanna eyed Jenner over the rim of her cup. "Angela was fond of making odd demands."

"And were you fond of going along with them?"

"No, I wasn't. I didn't want to meet her at all. It's no secret that we weren't on friendly terms, and I knew we'd quarrel. The fact that we would made me nervous." Deanna set down her cup, curled up her legs. "I don't like confrontations, Lieutenant, but I don't run away from them, as a rule. Angela and I had a history that I'm sure you're aware of."

"You were competitors." Jenner inclined his head a fraction. "You didn't like each other."

"No, we didn't like each other, and it was very personal on both sides. I was ready to have it out with her, and a part of me hoped that we could settle things amicably. Another part was looking forward to yanking out a few handfuls of her hair. I won't deny I wanted her out of my way, but I didn't want her dead." She looked back at Jenner, calmer now, steadier. "Is that why you're here? Am I a suspect?"

Jenner rubbed a hand over his chin. "The victim's husband, Dan Gardner, seems to think you hated her enough to kill her. Or have her killed."

"Have her killed?" Deanna blinked at that and nearly laughed. "So now I hired a convenient hit man, paid him to murder Angela, knock me unconscious and roll tape. Very inventive of me." She sprang up, color washing back into her cheeks. "I don't even know Dan Gardner. It's flattering that he should consider me so clever. And what was my motive? Ratings points? It seems to me I should have arranged it so that I didn't miss the November sweeps."

The bruised, helpless look was gone, Jenner noted. She was fired up, burning on indignation and disgust. "Miss Reynolds, I didn't say we agreed with Mr. Gardner."

She stared for a moment, eyes kindling. "Just wanted a reaction? I hope I satisfied you."

Jenner cocked a brow. "Miss Reynolds, did you visit Miss Perkins at her hotel on the night she was murdered?"

"No." Frustrated, Deanna raked a hand through her hair. "Why should I have? We were meeting at the studio."

"You might have gotten impatient." Jenner knew he was reaching. Deanna's fingerprints hadn't been found in the suite, certainly they weren't on the extra champagne flute.

"Even if I had, Angela told me that she'd be busy until midnight. She had meetings."

"Did she mention with whom?"

"We weren't chatting, Detective, and I had no interest in her personal or her business plans."

"You knew she had enemies?"

"I knew she wasn't particularly well liked. Part of that might have been her personality, and part of it was because she was a woman with a great deal of power. She could be hard and vindictive. She could also be charming and generous."

"I don't imagine you found it charming when she arranged for you to walk in on her and Dr. Pike, in compromising circumstances."

"That's old news."

"But you were in love with him?"

"I was almost in love with him," Deanna corrected. "A very large difference." Oh, what was the point of all this? she wondered, and rubbed at the headache brewing dead center of her forehead. "I won't deny it hurt me, and it infuriated me, and it changed my feelings about both of them irrevocably."

"Dr. Pike tried to continue your relationship."

"He didn't look on the incident in the same way I did. I wasn't interested in continuing anything with him, and I made that clear."

"But he did persist for quite a while."

"Yes."

Jenner recognized the emotion behind the clipped response. "And the notes, the ones you've been receiving with some regularity for several years. Did you ever consider that he was sending them?"

"Marshall?" She shook her head. "No. They're not his style."

"What is?"

Deanna's eyes shut. She remembered the photographs, the detective's report. "Perhaps you should ask him."

"We will. Have you been involved with anyone other than Dr. Pike? Anyone who might have been so disturbed by the announcement of your engagement to Mr. Riley that they would break into your office, or Mr. Riley's home?"

"No, there's been—what do you mean, break in?" She gripped the wing of the chair she stood beside.

"It seems logical that whoever sent the notes is also responsible for the destruction of your office and the house you share with Mr. Riley," Jenner began. And, he believed, for Angela's murder.

"When?" Deanna could barely whisper the word. "When did this happen?"

Intrigued, Jenner stopped tapping his pencil on his pad. The rosy glow anger had brought to Deanna's cheeks had drained, leaving her face white as bone. Riley hadn't told her yet, he realized. And the man wasn't going to be pleased to have been scooped. "The night Angela Perkins was shot, Finn Riley's house was broken into."

"No." Still gripping the chair, she shifted, lowered herself before her legs buckled. "Finn didn't—no one told me." She squeezed her eyes shut, fighting the kick of nerves in her stomach. When she opened them again, they were dark as pitch and burning dry. "But you will. I want to know what happened. Exactly what happened."

There was going to be more than a little tiff when Finn Riley returned, Jenner decided. As he related the facts, he watched her take them in. She winced once, as though the words were darts, then went very still. Her eyes remained level, and curiously blank until he had finished.

She said nothing for a moment, leaning forward to pour more tea. Her hand was steady. Jenner admired her poise and control, particularly since he'd seen the ripple of horror cross her face.

"You think that whoever's been sending the notes, whoever broke into my office and my home, killed Angela."

It was a reporter's voice, Jenner noted. Cool and calm and without inflection. But her eyes weren't blank any longer. They were terrified. For some reason he remembered a report she'd done years before, a woman in the suburbs who'd been shot to death by her husband. Her eyes hadn't been blank then, either.

"It's a theory," he said at length. "It makes more sense for only one person to be involved."

"Then why not me?" Her voice broke, and she shook her head impatiently. "Why Angela and not me? If he was so angry, so violently angry with me, why did he kill her and leave me alive?"

"She was in your way," Jenner said briskly, and watched as the full impact struck Deanna like a blow.

"He killed her for me? Oh Jesus, he did it for me."

"We can't be sure of that." Jenner began, but Deanna was already shoving out of her chair.

"Finn. Good God, he could come after Finn. He broke into the house. If Finn had been there, he would have . . ." She pressed a hand to her stomach. "You have to do something."

"Miss Reynolds—"

But she heard the sound of tires on gravel. She whirled, racing the dog to the door, shouting for him.

Finn was already cursing the other car in the drive when he heard her call his name. His annoyance at the intrusion faded as he saw her sprint out of the house. She leaped trembling into his arms, choking back sobs.

Finn gathered her close, his eyes hot and lethal as they skimmed over her shoulder to where Jenner stood on the porch. "What the hell have you done?"

"I'M SORRY." IT WAS THE BEST Finn could think of to say as he faced Deanna across the living room. Jenner had left them alone. After, Finn thought bitterly, he'd dropped his bomb.

"What for? Because I found out from Jenner? Or because you didn't trust me enough to tell me in the first place?"

"That it happened at all," he said carefully. "And it wasn't a matter of trust, Deanna. You're barely out of the hospital."

"And you didn't want to upset my delicate mental balance. That's why the television is conveniently on the blink. That's why you wanted to go to the store alone, and didn't bring back the paper. We wouldn't want poor little Deanna to hear any news that might upset her."

"Close enough." He plunged his hands into his pockets. "I thought you needed some time."

397

"You thought. Well, you thought wrong." She spun around, headed for the stairs. "You had no right to keep this from me."

"I did keep it from you. Damn it, if we're going to fight, at least do it face to face." He stopped her on the landing, grabbing her arm, turning her around.

"I can fight when I'm packing." She shook him off and stalked into the bedroom.

"You want to go back, fine. We'll go back after we've settled this."

She dragged an overnight case out of the closet. "*We* don't have to go anywhere. I'm going." She tossed the case onto the bed, threw open the lid. "Alone." In quick, jerky moves, she plucked bottles and jars from the dresser. "I'm going back to my apartment. I can get whatever I've left at your house later."

"No," he said, very calmly, "you're not."

She heaved a perfume bottle toward the open case. It bounced merrily on the bed.

"That's exactly what I'm doing." With her eyes on his, she pried his fingers loose. "You lied to me, Finn. If Jenner hadn't come out here for some follow-up questions, I wouldn't have known about the break-in, or that you'd interviewed Dan Gardner and that hotel maid. I wouldn't have known anything."

"No, and you might have gotten a few nights' sleep."

"You lied," she repeated, refusing to see past that. "And don't tell me keeping the truth from me is different than lying. It's the same. I won't continue in a relationship that isn't honest."

"You want honest. That's fine." He turned, shut the door with a quiet click. A final click. "I'll do anything and everything in my power to protect you. That's a fact." Eyes steady, he walked back to her. "You're not walking out on me, Deanna. That's a fact. And you're not using some bullshit about rights and trust as your escape hatch. If you want out, then at least be honest."

"All right." She shifted so that he couldn't see the way her hands shook as she packed. "I made a mistake when I agreed to marry you, and I've had time to think it through. I need to concentrate on my career, on my own life. I can't do that if I'm trying to make a marriage work, if I'm starting a family. I talked myself into thinking I could do it all, but I was wrong." The diamonds on her finger winked mockingly at her. She couldn't quite bring herself to take the ring off. Not yet. "I don't want to marry you, Finn, and it's not fair to either of us to continue this way. My priority right now is my work, and getting it back on track."

"Look at me, Deanna. I said look at me." With his hands firm on her shoulders, he turned her to face him. The sensation of panic faded into steely confidence. "You're lying."

"I know you don't want to believe—"

"Jesus Christ, Deanna, don't you know that I can see it in your face. You could never lie worth a damn. Why are you doing this?"

"I don't want to hurt you any more than necessary, Finn." She held herself rigid in his arms, stared over his shoulder. "Let me go."

"Not a chance in hell."

"I don't want you." Her voice cracked. "I don't want this. Is that clear enough?"

"No." He jerked her forward, covered her mouth with his. She trembled immediately, her body shuddering against his, her lips heating. "But that is."

"It's not the answer." But her body yearned for his, for the warmth, the strength.

"You want me to apologize again?" Gently now, he stroked a hand over her hair. "Fine. I'm sorry, and I'd do exactly the same thing. If you want to call it lying to you, then I'd lie. I'd do whatever I had to do to keep you safe."

"I don't want to be protected." She broke away, curled her hands into impotent fists. "I don't need to be protected. Can't you see? Don't you understand? He used *me* to kill her. He used *me*. He isn't going to hurt *me; I* don't need to be protected. But God knows who else he might hurt because of me."

"Me," he said quietly, furiously. "That's what this is all about. You think he might try for me. The best way to prevent that is to dump me, right? To make sure everyone knows you've broken it off."

Her lips trembled before she pressed them together. "I'm not going to argue with you, Finn."

"You're absolutely right about that." He picked up her case and upended the contents. "Don't ever try that with me again. Don't ever use my feelings on me like that again."

"He'll try to kill you," she said dully. "I know he will."

"So you lied, to try to protect me." When she opened her mouth, shut it again, he smiled. "Quid pro quo, Deanna. We'll call it even. So you don't want to be protected—neither do I. What do you want?"

She lifted her fisted hands to her cheeks, then let them fall. "I want you to stop watching me as though I were going to fall apart."

"Done. What else?"

"I want you to swear you won't keep anything from me, no matter how much you think it'll upset me."

"Deal, and same goes."

She nodded slowly, watching him. "You're still angry."

"Yeah, I'm still angry. It's a residual effect when the woman I love cuts me in half."

"You still want me."

"God, yes, I still want you."

"You haven't made love with me since this happened. Whenever I'd turn to you, you'd soothe and you'd cuddle, but you haven't touched me."

"No, I haven't." He felt the blood begin to swim in his veins. "I wanted to give you time."

"I don't want time!" she shouted at him, felt the first sweet snap of release. "I'm not fragile or weak or delicate. I want you to stop looking at me as though I were, as though I'd crumble. I'm alive. I want to feel alive. Make me feel alive."

He reached out, brushed his knuckle down her cheek. "You should have asked for something more difficult."

He kissed her. She could feel the sparks of fury he was struggling to bank, taste the hot frustration, the searing need.

"Don't," she murmured. "Don't be gentle. Not now."

He wanted to be. But she was pulling him down on the bed, her hands already frantic as they tugged at his clothes. He couldn't be gentle, couldn't tap the well of tenderness when her mouth was driving him beyond caution into madness.

Her body vibrated against his as she arched and strained and writhed. More was all she could think. More of him. More of that simmering violence she had watched him fight to chain for days. She wanted him to release it now, inside her.

She could hear her own heart drum heavily in her ears, feel each separate pulse throb. Her muffled cry was one of triumph as he ripped her shirt aside, seeking flesh.

The wind kicked against the windows, rattling glass. It hooted down the chimney, struggling to puff smoke into the room. But the fire blazed in the hearth and burned brighter with the threat of the storm.

On the bed they rolled like thunder.

His mouth was on her, ravenous, teeth scraping skin already damp with passion. His breath was hot and quick, his hands bruising in their hurry to possess. She reared up to meet him, her head falling back, her moan long and feral.

Faster. Faster. The desperation peaked as he yanked at her jeans, his hungry mouth racing down her shuddering torso toward the violent heat. Her hands dived into his hair, pressed him closer, closer. Her nails scraped unfelt down his back as the first orgasm pummeled her.

"Now." She nearly wept it, dragging him up, frantic for him to fill her. Her hands clutched at his hips, her legs wrapped around his waist. "Now," she said again, then cried out when he drove himself into her.

"More." He yanked her body up, plunged deeper, thrusting hard, still harder while the ferocity of pleasure racked through him.

His body felt like an engine, tireless, primed to run. He mated it with hers, steel cased in velvet, pumping faster each time he felt her muscles contract like a moist fist around him.

When she arched, straining, he pulled her to him until they were torso to torso. Her teeth sank into his shoulder even as her body moved like wet silk against his. Again she went rigid, her body stiffening, then breaking into shudders. Her eyes sprang open, staring glazed into his while she went limp.

"I can't."

He shoved her back, grasping her hands and dragging them over her head. "I can."

He devoured her, letting the animal take over, ripping each new response from her with impatient teeth, enticing new fires with tongue and lips.

His breath was burning in his throat, his blood pounding in his head, in his loins. The final wave of sensation swamped him, flooded through his system like light—white and blinding. He thought she cried out again, just his name, as he emptied himself into her.

Chapter Twenty-four

Marshall Pike's office looked like an elegant living room. But no one lived there. It reminded Finn of an ambitious model home, decorated for prospective buyers who would never slouch on the brocade sofa or wrestle on the Aubusson rug. There would certainly never be a careless ring left by a careless glass set on the Chippendale coffee table. No child would ever play hide-and-seek behind the formal silk draperies or cuddle up to read in one of the deep-cushioned chairs.

Even Marshall's desk seemed more of a prop than a usable fixture. The oak was highly polished, the brass fittings gleamed. The desk set of burgundy leather fit seamlessly into the color scheme of wines and ferns. The ficus tree by the window wasn't plastic, but it was so perfect, its leaves so radically dust-free, it might as well have been.

Finn had lived with easy wealth all of his life, and the material trappings it could buy, but he found Marshall Pike's pristine office, with its low hum of an air filter discreetly sucking impurities, soulless.

"I would, naturally, be happy to cooperate with the police."

Piously, Marshall tugged the sleeves of his jacket over the monogrammed cuffs of his crisp white shirt. "As I explained to you, they haven't found it necessary to question me. Why would they? I have nothing to say to the press."

"As I explained to you, I'm not here as a member of the press. You're not obligated to talk to me, Pike, but if you don't . . ." Finn spread his hands. Jenner was going to be pissed, he thought, that he hadn't cleared this interview with the police. But this particular contact was personal. "Some of my associates might appreciate having their memory jogged about a certain incident between you and Angela. One that slipped through the cracks a couple of years ago?"

"I can't imagine that something so trivial would be of interest to anyone."

"It's amazing, isn't it, what grabs the viewer's attention? And what, if presented with a certain angle, will intrigue the police."

The man was reaching, of course, Marshall assured himself. There was nothing, absolutely nothing to connect him with Angela but a momentary lapse of judgment. And yet . . . a word to the wrong person could result in publicity his practice couldn't afford.

A few questions, he decided, a few answers wouldn't matter. He was, after all, an expert at communication. If he couldn't handle an overexposed reporter, he didn't deserve the degrees hanging prominently on the wall behind him.

More, he would enjoy outwitting the man Deanna had chosen over him.

"My last appointment for the day canceled." He shook his head as if in pity for the unhappy couple who wouldn't benefit from his skills. "I don't have another engagement until seven. I can spare you a few moments."

"That's all I'll need. When did you hear about Angela's death?"

"On the news, the morning after the murder. I was shocked. I understand that Deanna was with her in the studio. As you know, Deanna and I had a relationship. Naturally, I'm concerned about her."

"I'm sure that will help her sleep easy at night."

"I have tried to contact her, to offer my support."

"She doesn't need it."

"Territorial, Mr. Riley?" Marshall asked with a curve of the lips.

"Absolutely, Dr. Pike," Finn answered.

"In my profession, it's essential to be fair-minded." He continued to smile. "Deanna meant a great deal to me at one time."

With some interviews you prodded, with others you planted. In Marshall's case, Finn noted that the shorter the question, the more expansive the answer.

"Did she?"

"A great deal of time has passed. And Deanna is engaged to you. Regardless, I would still offer whatever support or help I could to someone I was fond of, particularly under such shocking circumstances."

"And Angela Perkins?" Finn leaned back in his chair. However relaxed his pose, he was alert, watching every flick of Marshall's eye. "Were you fond of her?"

"No," he said shortly. "I was not."

"Yet it was your affair with Miss Perkins which ended your relationship with Deanna."

"There was no affair." Marshall linked his hands on the desktop. "There was a momentary lapse of control and common sense. I came to understand rather quickly that Angela had orchestrated the entire incident for her own reasons."

"Which were?"

"In my opinion? To manipulate Deanna and to cause her distress. She was successful." His smile was thin and humorless. "Although Deanna did not accept the position Angela had offered her in New York, she did sever ties with me."

"You resent that?"

"I resent, Mr. Riley, that Deanna refused to see the incident for what it was. Less than nothing. A mere physical reaction to deliberate stimuli. There was no emotion involved, none at all."

"Some people are more emotional about sex than others." Finn smiled wider, deliberately baiting him. "Deanna's very emotional."

"Indeed," he said, and left it at that. When Finn remained silent, annoyance pushed him on. "I don't understand how my unfortunate misstep could be related to the investigation."

"I didn't say it was," Finn said pleasantly. "But, just to clear up that matter, why don't you tell me where you were on the night of the murder? Between the hours of eleven and two?"

"I was home."

"Alone?"

"Yes, alone." Confident now, Marshall relaxed. His eyes were mild. "I'm sure you'd agree, if I'd been planning on murder I would have had the simple intelligence to provide myself with an alibi. However, I had dinner, alone, spent a few hours working on case studies, then went to bed."

"Did you speak with anyone? Receive any phone calls?"

"I let the service take my calls. I don't like to be interrupted when I'm working—barring emergencies." He smiled cockily. "Do you advise me to contact my lawyer, Mr. Riley?"

"If you think you need one." If he was lying, Finn mused, he was cool about it. "When was the last time you saw Angela?"

For the first time in the interview there was a flash of genuine pleasure in Marshall's eyes. "I haven't seen Angela since she made the move to New York. That would be over two years ago."

"Have you had any contact with her since that time?" "Why would I? We did not have a love affair, as I explained."

"You didn't have one with Deanna, either," Finn commented, and had the satisfaction of wiping the smile from Marshall's face. "But you've continued to contact her."

"Not for nearly a year. She is not forgiving."

"But you have sent notes. Made calls."

"No, I haven't. Not until I heard about this. She hasn't returned my calls, so I must assume she neither wants nor needs my help." Assured he'd been more than reasonable, he tapped his cuff again, rose. "As I said, I do have an appointment at seven, and I need to go home and change for the evening. I must say, this was an interesting interlude. Be sure to give Deanna my best."

"I don't think so." Finn rose as well, but made no move to leave. "I've got another question. You can call this one from reporter to psychologist."

Marshall's lips jerked into a sneer. "How could I refuse?"

"It's about obsession." Finn let the word hang a moment, watching for any sign: an avoidance of eye contact, a tic, a change in tone. "If a man, or a woman, was fixed on someone, long-term, say, two or three years, and he had fantasies but he couldn't bring himself to approach this person, face to face, and in these fantasies he felt he'd been betrayed, what would he be feeling? Love? Or hate?"

"A difficult question, Mr. Riley, with such little information. I can say that love and hate are as intricately entwined as the poets claim. Either one can take control, and either one, depending on circumstances, can be dangerous. Obsessions are rarely constructive, for either party. Tell me, are you planning a show on the topic?"

"Could be." Finn reached for his coat. "As a layman, I wonder if someone who was dealing with that kind of obsession might be able to hide it. Go through the day-to-day motions without letting the mask slip." He studied Marshall's face now. "The old John Smith who mows down half a dozen people in a K Mart. The neighbors say what a nice, quiet guy he was."

"It happens, doesn't it? Most people are very clever at allowing others to see only what they wish to be seen. And most people only see what they choose in any case. If the human race were simpler, both of us would be looking for other means of employment."

"You have a point. Thanks for your time."

As Finn walked out of the office, through the reception area and to the bank of elevators, he wondered if Marshall Pike was the type who could calmly blow a woman's face off and walk away. There was cold blood there. That much he was sure of.

Smarm under the polish, Finn mused. It could have been pure animal reaction, he supposed, a territorial instinct. No, Finn concluded, that unease came from the reporter in him. The man was hiding something, and it was up to him to ferret it out.

It wouldn't hurt to take a run by the hotel and see if anyone had spotted Marshall in the area on the night of Angela's death.

IN HIS OFFICE, MARSHALL sat behind his desk. He waited, and waited, until he heard the faint rumble of the elevator. And he waited again until he heard nothing at all. Snatching up the phone, he punched in numbers, wiped his damp palm over his face.

He heard Finn's voice relay the information he already knew: Deanna wasn't there. Marshall slammed down the phone and buried his head in his hands.

Goddamn Finn Riley. Goddamn Angela. And goddamn Deanna. He had to see her. And he had to see her now.

"YOU SHOULDN'T HAVE COME back yet." Jeff stood in Deanna's office, his pleasant, homely face set in stubborn lines of worry. The smell of paint was still fresh.

They both knew why the walls had been painted, the rug replaced. There were long, jagged scratch marks marring the surface of Deanna's desk. The police had unsealed the room only forty-eight hours before and there hadn't been time to repair or replace everything.

"I was hoping you'd be glad to see me."

"I am glad to see you, but not here." Since it was just past eight in the morning, they were alone. Jeff felt obligated to convince her to give herself more time. When the rest of the staff arrived, he had no doubt they would add their weight. But now it was up to him to watch out for her. "You've been through a nightmare, Dee, and it hasn't even been a week."

Yes it had, she thought. One week tonight. But she didn't correct him. "Jeff, I've already been through this with Finn—"

"He shouldn't have let you come in."

Her hackles rose, but she bit back the first furious retort. Perhaps her nerves were still raw, she decided, if she was ready to snarl at poor Jeff. "Finn doesn't *let* me anything. If it makes you feel better, he agrees with you completely about my taking more time. I don't." She eased a hip down on the wide sill of the plate-glass window. Behind her, wet snow fell in thick, listless sheets. "I need to work, Jeff. Angela's death was horrible, but hiding my head under the covers isn't going to make it, or my part in it, go away. And I need my pals." She held out a hand. "I really do."

She heard him sigh, but he crossed to her and took her hand. "We wanted to be there for you, Dee. All of us."

"I know you did." She squeezed his hand, urging him down on the sill with her. "I guess this hasn't been easy on anyone. Did you have to talk to the police?"

"Yeah." He grimaced, shoving at his glasses. "That Detective Jenner. 'Where were you on the night in question?'" Jeff demanded in such a perfect mimic of Jenner that Deanna laughed. "We all got the treatment. Simon was sweating bullets. You know how he is under pressure. Wringing his hands, gulping audibly. He got so worked up that Fran made him lie down, then tore into the cop for harassment."

"Sorry I missed it." She leaned her head against Jeff's shoulder, content to be back with friends. "What else did I miss?" She could feel his body tense and she squeezed his hand in reassurance. "I'd feel better if I knew, Jeff. I've only gotten some sketchy details about how the office was torn up. I miss our Christmas tree." Her smile was brief and sad. "Silly, isn't it? When you think of everything that was destroyed in here, I miss that stupid tree."

"I'll get you another one. Just as ugly."

"Impossible." But she let it go. "Tell me."

He hesitated a moment. "The office was pretty messed up, Dee. But it was mostly cosmetic damage. Once the cops let us in, Loren had it cleaned out, repainted, recarpeted. He was royally pissed. Not at you," he said quickly. "It was the whole deal, you know. The fact that somebody got in and ... did what they did."

"I'll call him."

"Deanna ... I'm sorry. I don't know what else to say. I'm so damn sorry you had to go through all that. I wish I could say I'm sorry about Angela, but I'm not."

"Jeff—"

"I'm not," he repeated, and tightened his grip on her hand. "She wanted to hurt you. She did everything she could to ruin your career. Using Lew, making up lies, dragging that whole business with that creep football player into the public. I can't be sorry she won't be around to try something else." He let out a long breath. "I guess that makes me pretty cold."

"No, it doesn't. Angela didn't inspire great love and devotion."

"You do."

She lifted her head and turned to smile at him, when a sound in the doorway made them both jump.

"Oh, God." Cassie stood, a paperweight in one hand, a brass sculpture in the other. "I thought someone had broken in again." She pressed the hefty glass paperweight to her heart.

On watery legs, Deanna managed the two steps to a chair. "I came in early," she said, trying desperately to sound calm and in control. "I thought I might start catching up."

"I guess that makes three of us." With her eyes on Deanna, Cassie set the sculpture and paperweight aside. "Are you sure you're okay?"

"No." Deanna closed her eyes for a moment. "But I need to be here."

PERHAPS HER NERVES WERE raw and her temper short, but by midmorning Deanna found some comfort in the basic office routine. Bookings had to be rearranged and rescheduled, others fell through completely due to the time lapse. New story ideas were devised and discussed. Once word spread that Deanna was back in harness, the phones began to shrill. People from the newsroom popped upstairs, out of both genuine concern and pure curiosity.

"Benny's hoping you'll do an interview," Roger told her. "An exclusive for old times' sake."

Deanna passed him half the sandwich she was nibbling at her now overburdened desk. "Benny thinks a lot of old times' sake."

"It's news, Dee. And pretty hot when you consider it happened right here at CBC and involved two major stars."

A major star, she thought. What was the difference between a major star and a minor one? She knew what Loren would have said: A minor star sought airtime. A major star sold it.

"Give me some time, will you?" She rubbed at the tension in the back of her neck. "Tell him I'm thinking about it."

"Sure." His gaze wandered from hers to his own hands. "I'd appreciate it, if you decide to do it, if you let me do the interview." His eyes cut back to her, then away again. "I could use the boost. There are rumors of cutbacks in the newsroom again."

"There are always rumors of cutbacks in the newsroom." She resented the favor he was asking, and wished she didn't. "All right, Roger, for old times' sake. Just give me a couple of days."

"You're a peach, Dee." And he felt like sludge. "I'd better get down. I've got some bumpers to tape." He rose, leaving the sandwich untouched. "It's good to have you back. You know if you need a friendly ear, I've got two."

"Off the record?"

He had the grace to flush. "Sure. Off the record."

She held up both hands as if to gesture the words back. "Sorry. I'm touchy, I guess. I'll have Cassie set up an interview in a day or two, all right?"

"Whenever you're ready." He walked to the door. "This really sucks," he murmured as he shut the door behind him.

"You bet." Deanna leaned back in her chair, closing her eyes, letting herself hear only the impersonal murmur of the television across the room. Angela was dead, she thought, and that made her a hotter news item than she had ever been when she was alive.

The really horrid bottom line, Deanna knew, was that she was now hot news as well. And hot news made for hot ratings. Since the murder, *Deanna's Hour*—reruns of *Deanna's Hour*, she corrected—had spurted up in points, pummeling the competition. No game show or daytime drama could hope to withstand the mighty weight of murder and scandal.

Angela had given her greatest rival the success she'd hoped to take away. She'd only had to die to do it.

"Deanna?"

Her heart flew to her throat, her eyes sprang open. On the other side of her desk, Simon jumped as violently as she. "Sorry," he said quickly. "I guess you didn't hear me knock."

"That's okay." Disgusted with her reaction, she chuckled weakly. "My nerves don't seem to be as strong as I thought. You look exhausted."

He tried to smile, but couldn't bring it off. "Having trouble sleeping." He fumbled out a cigarette.

"I thought you'd quit."

"Me too." Embarrassed, he moved his shoulders. "I know you said you wanted to start taping on Monday."

"That's right. Is there a problem?"

"It's just that . . ." He trailed off, puffing hard on the cigarette. "I thought, under the circumstances—but maybe it doesn't matter to you. It just seemed to me . . ."

Deanna wondered if she grabbed onto his tongue and pulled, if the words would spill out. "What?"

"The set," he blurted out, and passed a nervous hand over his thinning hair. "I thought you might want to change the set. The chairs . . . you know."

"Oh God." She pressed a fist to her mouth as the vision of Angela, sitting cozily, sitting dead in the spacious white chair, flashed into her mind. "Oh God, I haven't thought."

"I'm sorry, Deanna." For lack of something better he patted her shoulder. "I shouldn't have said anything. I'm an idiot."

"No. No. Thank God you did. I don't think I could have handled . . ." She imagined herself striding out on the set, then freezing in shock and horror. Would she have run screaming, as she had done before? "Oh, Simon. Oh, sweet Jesus."

"Dee." Helplessly he patted her shoulder again. "I didn't mean to upset you."

"I think you just saved my sanity. Put the set decorator on it, Simon, please? Have him change everything. The color scheme, the chairs, tables, the plants. Everything. Tell him—"

Simon had already taken out a notebook to scribble down her instructions. The simple, habitual gesture somehow cheered Deanna.

"Thanks, Simon."

"I'm the detail man, remember?" He tapped out the half-smoked cigarette. "Don't worry about it. We'll have a whole new look."

"But keep it comfortable. And why don't you knock off early? Go get yourself a massage."

"I'd rather work."

"I know what you mean."

"I didn't know it would affect me like this." He tucked the pad away. "I worked with her for years. I can't say I liked her much, but I knew her. I stood right here, in this spot, when she was sitting there." He glanced up again, meeting Deanna's eyes. "Now, she's dead. I can't stop thinking about it."

"Neither can I."

"Whoever did it was in here, too." Warily, he scanned the room, as if he expected someone to lunge out of a corner wielding a gun. "Jesus, I'm sorry. All I'm doing is scaring the shit out of both of us. I guess it's eating on me because her memorial service is tonight."

"Tonight? In New York?"

"No, here. I guess she wanted to be buried in Chicago, where she got her big break. There's not going to be a viewing or anything, because . . ." He remembered why and swallowed hard. "Well, there's just going to be a service at the funeral parlor. I think I should go."

"Give the details to Cassie, will you? I think I should go, too."

"THIS ISN'T JUST STUPID," Finn said with barely controlled fury. "It's insane."

Deanna watched the windshield wipers sweep at the ugly, icy sleet. The snow that had fallen throughout the day had turned to oily gray slop against the curbs. The sleet that replaced it battered down, cold and mean.

It was a good night for a funeral.

Her chin came up and her jaw tightened. "I told you that you didn't have to come with me."

"Yeah, right." He spotted the crowd of reporters huddled outside the funeral parlor and drove straight down the block. "Goddamn press."

She nearly smiled at that, felt a giddy urge to laugh out loud. But she was afraid it would sound hysterical. "I won't mention anything about pots and kettles."

"I'm going to park down the block," he said between his teeth. "We'll see if we can find a side or a back entrance."

"I'm sorry," she repeated when he'd parked. "Sorry to have dragged you out to this tonight." She had a headache she didn't dare mention. And a raw sick feeling in her stomach that promised to worsen.

"I don't recall being dragged."

"I knew you wouldn't let me come alone. So it amounts to the same thing. I can't even explain to myself why I feel I have to do this. But I have to do it."

Suddenly, she twisted toward him, gripping his hand hard. "Whoever killed her could be in there. I keep wondering if I'll know him. If I look him in the face, if I'll know. I'm terrified I will."

"But you still want to go inside."

414

"I have to."

The sleet helped, she thought. Not only was it cold, but it demanded the use of long, disguising coats and shielding umbrellas. They walked in silence, against the wind. She caught sight of the CBC van before Finn ducked around the side of the building. He hustled her inside, drenching them both as he snapped the umbrella closed.

"I hate goddamned funerals."

Surprised, she studied his face as she tugged off her gloves, shed her coat. She could see it now. More than annoyance with her for insisting on attending, more than concern or even fear, there was dread in his eyes. "I'm sorry. I didn't realize."

"I haven't been to one since ... in years. What's the point? Dead's dead. Flowers and organ music don't change it."

"It's supposed to comfort the living."

"Not so I've noticed."

"We won't stay long." She took his hand, surprised that it would be he rather than she who needed comfort.

He seemed to shudder, once. "Let's get it over with."

They walked out of the alcove. They could already hear the murmur of voices, the muted notes of a dirge. Not organ music, he realized, horribly relieved, but piano and cello in somber duet. The air smelled of lemon oil, perfume, flowers. He would have sworn he smelled whiskey as well, sharp as a blade cutting through the overly sweetened air.

The thick carpet was a riot of deep red roses and muffled their footsteps as they walked down a wide hall. On both sides heavy oak doors were discreetly shut. At the end they were flung open. Cigarette smoke added to the miasma of scent.

When he felt her tremble, Finn tucked his arm more firmly around her waist. "We can turn around and leave, Deanna. There's no shame in it."

She only shook her head. Then she saw the first video camera. The press, it seemed, wasn't merely huddled outside. Several had been allowed in, complete with camera crews, microphones and lights. Cables were strewn over the garden of carpet in the main viewing room.

In silence, they slipped inside.

The cathedral ceiling with its painted mural of cherubim and seraphim tossed the murmuring voices and chinking glasses everywhere.

The room was crowded with people. As Deanna looked from face to face, she wondered if she would see grief or fear or simply resignation. Would Angela feel she was being mourned properly? And would her killer be here, to observe?

No one wept, Finn noted. He did see shock and sober eyes. Voices were muted respectfully. And the cameras recorded it all. Would they, he wondered, inadvertently record one face, one that couldn't quite hide the knowledge, and the triumph? He kept Deanna close to his side, knowing that the murderer could be in the room, watching.

There was a photograph of Angela in a gold frame. The flattering publicity shot sat atop a gleaming mahogany coffin.

It reminded Finn, much too vividly, of what lay inside the discreetly closed lid. Feeling Deanna shudder beside him, he instinctively drew her closer.

"Let's get the hell out of here."

"No."

"Kansas—" But when he looked at her he saw more than the shock and fear. He saw what was missing on so many of the other faces that crowded the room: grief.

"Whatever her motives," Deanna said quietly, "she helped me once. And whoever did this to her used me." Her voice broke. "I can't forget that."

Neither could he. That was what terrified him. "It would be better if Dan Gardner doesn't spot either one of us."

Deanna nodded, spotting him at the front of the room, accepting condolences. "He's using her too, even though she's dead. It's horrible."

"He'll ride her press for a while. She'd have understood that."

"I suppose."

"An interesting scene, isn't it?" Loren commented when he joined them. He gave Deanna a hard, searching look, then nodded. "You're looking well."

"No I'm not." Grateful for the lie, she kissed his cheek. "I didn't think you'd come."

"I could say the same." He warmed her chilled hands between his. "It seemed necessary somehow, but I'm already regretting it." His expression changed to one of disgust as he looked over his shoulder at Dan Gardner. "Rumor is he plans to air clips from this viewing along with the special Angela taped for next May. And he's demanding another five thousand a minute from sponsors. The son of a bitch will get it, too."

"Bad taste often costs more than good," Deanna murmured. "There must be five hundred people in here."

"Easily. A handful are even sorry she's dead."

"Oh, Loren." Deanna's stomach clenched like a fist.

"I hate to admit I'm one of them." Then he sighed and shrugged off the mood. "She'd have gotten an ego boost out of that piece of news." To clear the emotion from his voice, Loren coughed gently into his hand. "You know, I can't decide if Angela deserved Dan Gardner or not. It's a tough call."

"I'm sure she didn't deserve you." The tears burning in her eyes made Deanna feel like a hypocrite since they weren't for Angela. "We're not staying, Loren. Why don't you come with us?"

"No, I'm going to see this through. But I think you should avoid any publicity here tonight. Slip out quietly."

When they were back in the alcove, Deanna turned into Finn's arms. "I had no idea he still loved her."

"I don't think he did, either." He tipped her face up until their eyes were level. "Are you all right?"

"Actually, I'm better." She turned her head until her cheek rested on his shoulder. Most of the fear had ebbed, she realized. That jittering panic she'd nearly grown accustomed to feeling in her stomach had quieted. "I'm glad we came."

"Excuse me." Kate Lowell's sultry voice had Deanna turning her head. She stood in the doorway, sleek and somber in black silk, her hair waves of flame over her shoulders. "I'm sorry to interrupt."

"You haven't," Deanna responded. "We were just leaving."

"So am I." She glanced over her shoulder toward the sounds of voices and music. "It's not my kind of party." She smiled slightly. "She was a bitch," Kate said. "And I hated her guts. But I'm not sure even Angela deserved to be used quite so blatantly." She sighed once, moving her shoulders as if to shrug it all away. "I'd like a drink. And I need to talk to you." She looked at Finn and frowned. "I suppose it'll have to be both of you, and it hardly matters at this point." She watched Finn's brow rise, and smiled again, with more feeling. "Really gracious, aren't I? Listen, why don't you find us a bar? I'll buy us all a drink and tell you a little story you might find interesting."

Chapter Twenty-five

"To Hollywood," Kate said as she raised her glass of scotch. "Land of illusions."

Puzzled, Deanna nursed her wine while Finn stuck with coffee.

It wasn't the sort of bar where one would expect to find one of Hollywood's major stars. The piano player was glumly noodling out the blues so that the notes rose sluggishly on air thick with smoke. Their corner was dim, as Kate had requested. On the table scarred with nicks their drinks rested near a chipped amber glass ashtray.

"You came a long way for the funeral of someone you didn't like." Deanna watched Kate's elegant nails tap the table in time with the piano.

"I was in town. But if I hadn't been, I'd have made the trip. For the pleasure of making sure she was dead." Kate sipped her scotch again, then set the glass aside. "I don't imagine you cared for her any more than I did, but this might be rougher on you, since you found her." Kate's eyes softened as she stared into Deanna's. "As the story goes, it wasn't a pretty sight."

"No, it wasn't."

"I wish it had been me," Kate said under her breath. "You're a softer touch, always were. Even after everything she did, and tried to do, to you. I know a lot more about that than you might imagine," she added when Deanna studied her. "Things that didn't make it into the press. Angela liked to brag. She hated you." She inclined the glass toward Finn. "Because you didn't come to heel when she snapped her fingers. And she wanted you for exactly the same reason. She figured Deanna was in her way, from all manner of angles. She'd have done anything to remove you."

"This isn't news." Noting that Kate's glass was dry, Finn signaled for another. The lady, he concluded, was stalling.

"No, it's just my little prelude." She stretched back, but the sinuous gesture was all nerves. "I don't suppose you'd be surprised to know that Angela went to some trouble and expense to dig up that business from your past, Deanna. The date rape. It backfired, of course." Her lips curved into a lovely smile. "Some of her projects did. That's what she called them. Not blackmail." She sulked a moment, fingers tapping, tapping, tapping. "Rob Winters was one of her projects. So was Marshall Pike." She didn't glance at the waitress, but nudged the glass aside even as it was set in front of her. "There are plenty more. Names that would astonish you. She used a P.I. named Beeker. He's in Chicago. Angela kept him very busy documenting data for her projects. It cost me five thousand dollars to shoehorn his name out of Angela's secretary. But then, everybody has a price. I had mine," she added quietly.

"You're saying Angela blackmailed people?" Deanna leaned forward. "She traded secrets for money?"

"Occasionally. She preferred trading secrets for favors. Her terms again." Absently, she reached into the plastic bowl of mixed nuts. "'Do me a little favor, darling, and I'll keep this tidbit of information all to myself.' 'Your wife has a drug problem, Senator. Don't worry, I won't breathe a word if you just do me a favor.' What multi-Grammy winner was a victim of incest? What popular television star has ties to the KKK? Ask Angela. She made it her business to know what skeleton was in what closet. And if she was confident she had her hooks in you deeply enough, she might tell you what closet. It was a way of flexing her power. She was confident she had her hooks in me."

"And now she's dead."

Kate acknowledged Finn's comment with a nod. "Funny, now that she's no longer a threat to me, I feel compelled to do what she always threatened to do. I'm going public. Actually, I'd decided to do so on the very night she was murdered. The police might find that convenient, don't you think? Like a bad script. I saw her that night." She read the horror in Deanna's eyes. "Not at the studio. At her hotel. We argued. Since there was a maid in the next room, I imagine the police already know about it."

She lifted a brow at Finn. "Yes, I can see at least you knew about it. Well then. I'm going to go in and make a statement before they come to me. I believe I even threatened to kill her." Kate closed her eyes. "There's that bad script again. I didn't kill her, but you'll have to decide whether to believe me when I'm finished."

"Why are you telling us?" Deanna demanded. "Why don't you go directly to the police?"

"I'm an actress. I like the chance to choose my audience. You were always a good one, Dee." She reached out then in a quick, fleeting gesture of friendship. "And, in any case, I think you're entitled to know the whole story. Didn't you ever wonder why I backed out of coming on your show? Why I've never been available to appear on it?"

"Yes. But I think you've answered that. Angela was blackmailing you. And the favor was for you to boycott my program."

"That was one of them. I was in a precarious and fascinating position a couple of years ago, when you approached me. I had two whopping box-office successes. And the critics loved me. The wholesomely sexy girl-next-door. Don't believe that hype about stars not reading their reviews. I pored over mine. Every word," she said with a long, dreamy smile. "I could probably still quote a few

421

of the best ones. All I ever wanted was to be an actor. A star," she corrected with an easy shrug. "And that's what they called me. The first movie star of the new generation. A throwback to Bacall and Bergman and Davis. And it didn't take me years. One supporting role in a film that took off like a rocket, and an Academy nomination. Then I costarred with Rob and we burned up the screen, we broke hearts. The next movie, my name was over the title. My image was locked in. A woman who charms with a smile." She laughed at that, drank again. "The good girl, the heroine, the woman you'd like your son to bring home for dinner. That's the image. That's what Hollywood wants from me, that's what the public expects. And that's what I've delivered. They've given me plenty of credit for talent, but the image is every bit as important."

Her eyes slitted. "Do you think the top producers and directors, the players, the men who decide what project flies and what project gets buried would flood my agent with offers if they knew their perfect heroine, the woman who won an Oscar for playing the desperately devoted mother, had gotten pregnant at seventeen, and had given up the child without a second thought?"

She laughed when Deanna's mouth opened. But it wasn't a merry sound. "Doesn't fit, does it? Even in these enlightened times, how many of those ticket buyers would shell out seven bucks to watch me play the long-suffering or feisty heroine?"

"I don't . . ." Deanna stopped, waiting for her thoughts to settle. "I don't see why it should matter. You made a choice, one I'm sure was anything but easy for you. And you were a child yourself."

Amused, Kate glanced at Finn. "Is she really that naive?"

"About some things." He was, despite his pride in being a sharp judge of character, doing some rapid mental shuffling. "I can see why an announcement like that would have shaken things up. You'd have taken some knocks in the press. But you'd have pulled out of it."

"Maybe. I was afraid. Angela knew that. And I was ashamed. She knew that, too. She was very sympathetic at first. 'How hard it must have been on you, dear. A young girl, with her whole life in flux because of one tiny mistake. How difficult it must have been for you to do what you thought was best for the child.'"

Annoyed with herself, Kate flicked a tear away. "And you see, since it had been difficult, even horrible, and because she was sympathetic, I broke down. Then she had me. She reminded me that it wouldn't do for certain Hollywood brass to discover that I'd made this tiny mistake. Oh, she understood, she sympathized completely. But would they? Would the ticket-buying public who'd crowned me their valiant princess understand?"

"Kate, you were seventeen."

Very slowly, Kate lifted her gaze to Deanna's. "I was old enough to make a child, old enough to give her away. Old enough to pay for it. I hope I'm strong enough now to face the consequences." She frowned at her glass. If she didn't survive, if she crashed and burned, it would kill her. Angela had known that. "A few years ago, I wasn't. It's as simple as that. I don't think I could have survived the hate mail then, or the tabloids, or the bad jokes." She smiled again, but Deanna saw her pain. "I can't say I'm looking forward to it now. But the simple fact is, the cops are bound to track me down. Sooner or later they'll dig up Beeker and all of Angela's nasty files. I'm going to choose my own time and place for my public announcement. I'd like to do it on your show."

Deanna blinked. "Excuse me?"

"I said I'd like to do it on your show."

"Why?"

"Two reasons. First, for me it would be the ultimate payback to Angela. You don't like that one," she murmured, seeing the disapproval in Deanna's eyes. "You'll like this better. I trust you. You've got class, and compassion. This isn't going to be easy for me, and I'm going to need both. I'm scared." She set her drink down. "I hate that reason, but I might as well admit it. I lost the child through my ambition," she said quietly. "That's gone," she said fiercely. "I don't want to lose what I've got, Deanna. What I've worked for. Angela's just as dangerous to me dead as she was alive. At least I can pick my time and place this way. I've got a lot of respect for you. I always have. I'm going to have to talk about my private life, my personal griefs. I'd like to start off talking with someone I respect."

"We'll juggle the schedule," Deanna said simply. "And do it Monday morning."

Kate closed her eyes a moment, gathered what resources she had left. "Thanks."

THE SLEET HAD STOPPED BY the time they arrived home, leaving the air chill and damp and gloomy. Clouds hovered, thick and black. There was a light on in one of the front windows, streaming gold through the glass in cozy welcome. The dog began to bark the moment Finn slipped the key into the lock.

It should have been a homecoming. But there was the ever-present smell of paint reminding them their home had been violated. Drop cloths were spread in the hallway, and the dog's barking echoed emptily. So many of the rooms had been cleared out of broken crockery, damaged furniture. It was like being greeted by a mortally ill friend.

"We can still go to a hotel."

Deanna shook her head. "No, that's only another way of hiding. I can't help feeling responsible for this."

"Then work on it."

She recognized the impatience in his voice. She stooped to pet the dog as Finn peeled off his coat. "They were your things, Finn."

"Things." He shoved his coat on the hall rack. In the mirrored surface he saw her head bent over the dog's. "Just things, Deanna. Insured, replaceable."

She stayed where she was but lifted her head. Her eyes were wide and weary. "I love you so much. I hate knowing he was here, that he touched anything that was yours."

He crouched beside her, causing the dog to roll belly up in anticipation. But Finn took Deanna by the shoulders, his eyes suddenly fierce. "You are the only thing I have that's irreplaceable. The first time I met you, the first time, I knew that nothing that had happened to me before, or that would happen after, would mean as much. Can you understand that?" His hand moved roughly into her hair. "It's overwhelming what I feel for you. It's terrifying. And it's everything."

"Yes." She brought her hands to his face, guided his mouth to hers. "I can understand that." Emotions welled up, pouring into the kiss so that her lips were urgent and edgy. Even as Finn tugged at her coat, the dog wriggled between them, whining.

"We're embarrassing Cronkite," he murmured, drawing Deanna to her feet.

"We should find him a wife."

"You just want to go to the pound again and liberate another mutt."

"Now that you mention it . . ." But her smile faded quickly. "Finn, I have to talk to you about something."

"Sounds serious."

"Can we go upstairs?"

She wanted the bedroom, since it was almost fully restored. He'd seen that the work there had been completed first. The things that hadn't been destroyed had been placed there. Above the bed, where she knew a desperate message had been scrawled, the paint was fresh and clean. He'd hung the painting there—the one he had bought out from under her in the gallery so long ago.

Awakenings. All those vivid splashes of color. That energy and verve. He'd known she'd needed it there, a reminder of life. And so the room had become a haven.

"Are you upset about Kate?"

"Yes." She kept her hand in his as they climbed the stairs. "But this is about something else." She walked into the bedroom, moved to the fireplace, the window, then back. "I love you, Finn."

The tone put him on guard. "We've established that."

"Loving you doesn't mean I have the right to intrude in every area of your life."

Curious, he tilted his head. He could read her like a book. She was worried. "Which areas do you consider off limits?"

"You're annoyed." Baffled, she tossed up her hands. "I can never quite understand how easily I can set you off, especially when I'm trying to be reasonable."

"I hate it when you think you're being reasonable. Just spill it, Deanna."

"Fine. What did Angela have on you?"

His expression altered subtly, from impatience to utter confusion. "Huh?"

"Don't do that." She ripped off her coat and tossed it aside. In her tasteful black suit and damp shoes, she paced the room. "If you don't want to tell me, just say so. I'll agree that anything you've done in the past isn't necessarily connected to our relationship."

"Slow down, and stop stalking around the room. What do you think I've done?"

"I don't know." Her voice sounded shrill to herself. "I don't know," she said more calmly. "And if you think I don't need to know, I'll try to accept it. But once the police question this Beeker character, your secret is bound to come out anyway."

"Hold on." He held up both hands as she unbuttoned her suit jacket. "If I'm reading this correctly—and stop me anytime if I veer off—you think that Angela was blackmailing me. Have I got that part?"

Marching to the closet, she yanked out a padded hanger. "I said I wouldn't intrude if you didn't want me to. I was being reasonable."

"You certainly were." He came over, clamped his hands on her shoulders and steered her rigid body to a chair. "Now sit down. And tell me why you think I was being blackmailed."

"I went to meet Angela that night because she said she knew something about you. Something that could hurt you."

He sat himself then, on the edge of the bed, as a new kind of fury ate at him. "She lured you to the studio by threatening me?"

"Not directly. Not exactly." She dragged a hand through her hair. "There was nothing she could tell me that would change my feelings for you. I wanted to make sure she understood that. That she left us both alone."

"Deanna, why didn't you come to me?"

She winced from the simple, rational question. "Because I wanted to handle her myself," she shot back. "Because I don't need you or anyone running interference for me."

"Isn't that precisely what you misguidedly tried to do for me?"

That shut her up, but again, only for a moment. It was, she knew, master interviewer against master interviewer. And it was a competition she didn't mean to lose. "You're evading the issue. What would she have told me, Finn?"

"I don't have a clue. I'm not gay; I don't use drugs; I've never stolen anything. Except a couple of comic books when I was twelve—and nobody could prove it."

"I don't think this is funny."

"She wasn't blackmailing me, Deanna. I had an affair with her, but that was no secret. She wasn't the first woman I'd been involved with, but there haven't been any deviant sexual encounters I'd want to hide. I don't have any ties to organized crime, never embezzled. I'm not hiding any illegitimate children. I never killed anyone."

He broke off abruptly, and the impatient amusement drained out of his face. "Oh Jesus." He brought both hands to his face, pressing the heels to his eyes. "Jesus Christ."

"I'm sorry." Competition forgotten, she sprang up to go to him. "Finn, I'm sorry, I should never have brought it up."

"Could she have done that?" he said to himself. "Could even she have done that? And for what?" He let his hands drop, and his eyes were haunted. "For what?"

"Done what?" Deanna asked quietly, her arms still around him.

Finn drew back, just a little, as if what was working inside him might damage her. "My best friend in college. Pete Whitney. We got hooked on the same girl. We got drunk one night, really plowed, and tried to beat the crap out of each other. Did a pretty good job. Made sure it was off campus. Then we decided, hell, she wasn't worth it, and we drank some more."

His voice was cool, detached. His newscaster's voice. "That's the last time I've been drunk. Pete used to joke that it was the Irish in me. That I could drink or fight or talk my way out of anything." He remembered the way he'd been then—angry, rebellious, belligerent. Determined to be absolutely nothing like his chilly and civilized parents. "I'm not much of a drinker anymore, and I've figured out that words are generally a better weapon than fists. He gave me this." Finn tugged the Celtic cross out from under his shirt, closed his hand around it. "He was my closest friend, the closest thing to family I ever had."

Was, Deanna thought, and ached for him.

"We forgot about the girl. She wasn't as important to either of us as we were to each other. We killed off another bottle. My eye was swollen up like a rotten tomato, so I tossed him the keys, climbed into the passenger seat, passed out. We were twenty, and we were stupid. The idea of getting into a car filthy drunk didn't mean anything to us. When you're twenty, you're going to live forever. But Pete didn't.

"I woke up when I heard him scream. That's it. I heard him scream and the next thing I remember is waking up with all these lights and all these people and feeling as if I'd been run over by a truck. He'd taken a turn too fast, hit a utility pole. We'd both been thrown from the car. I had a concussion, a broken collarbone, broken arm, lots of cuts and bruises. Pete was dead."

"Oh, Finn." She wrapped her arms around him again, held on.

"It was my car, so they figured I'd been driving. They were going to charge me with vehicular manslaughter. My father came down, but by the time he got there they'd already found several witnesses who had seen Pete take the wheel. He wasn't any more or any less dead, of course. It didn't change that, or the fact that I'd been drunk and stupid, criminally careless."

He tightened his fingers around the silver cross. "I wasn't hiding it, Deanna. It's just not something I like to remember. Funny, I thought about Pete tonight, when we walked into Angela's funeral. I haven't been to one since Pete's. His mother always blamed me. I could see her point."

"You weren't driving, Finn."

"Does it really matter?" He looked at her then, though he already knew the answer. "I could have been. My father gave the Whitneys a settlement, and that was pretty much the end of it. I wasn't charged with anything. I wasn't held responsible."

He turned his face into Deanna's hair. "But I was. I was just as responsible as Pete. The only difference is I'm alive and he's not."

"The difference is, you were given a second chance and he wasn't." She closed her hand over his, so that they both held the cross. "I'm so sorry, Finn."

So was he. He'd spent his adult life making himself into the man he was, as much for Pete as for himself. He wore the cross every day as a talisman, yes, and as a reminder.

"Angela could have dug up the facts easily enough," Finn said. "She could even have made it appear that the Riley money and power influenced the outcome. But she would have blackmailed you, not me. She'd have known if she'd come to me, I'd have told her to take out an ad."

"I want to tell the police."

He eased her back on the bed so that they were curled together, wrapped close. "We'll tell them a lot of things. Tomorrow." Gently, he tipped her face toward his. "Would you have protected me, Deanna?"

She started to deny it, but caught the gleam in his eye. She knew he'd recognize a lie. "Yes. So?"

"So, thanks."

She smiled as she lifted her mouth toward his.

NOT SO FAR AWAY SOMEONE was weeping. The tears were hot and bitter, scalding the throat, the eyes, the skin. Photographs of Deanna looked on, smiling benignly at the sobbing form. Three candles tossed the only light, their flames, straight and true, high-lighting the pictures, the single earring, the lock of hair bound in gold thread. All of the treasures on the altar of frustrated desire.

There were stacks of videotapes, but the television screen was silent and dark tonight.

Angela was dead, but still that wasn't enough. Love, deep, dark and demented, had triggered the gun, but it wasn't enough. There had to be more.

The candleglow shot the shadow of a form hunched into a ball, racked with despair. Deanna would see, had to see that she was loved, cherished, adored.

There was a way to prove it.

FINN WOULD HAVE PREFERRED to handle the interview alone. Jenner would have preferred to do the same. Since neither of them could manage to shake the other loose, they drove to Beeker's office together.

"Might as well make the best of it," Jenner said. "I'm doing you a favor, Mr. Riley, letting you tag along."

That statement earned Jenner a frigid stare. "I don't tag along, Lieutenant. And let me remind you that you wouldn't know about Kate Lowell or Beeker if we hadn't come to you with the infor-mation."

Jenner grinned and rubbed his chin, which he'd nicked shaving. "And I get the feeling you wouldn't have come to me if Miss Reynolds hadn't insisted."

"She feels easier knowing the police are on top of things."

"And how does she feel about your being involved in the investigation?" Silence. "Doesn't know," Jenner concluded. "As a man married thirty-two years last July, let me mention that you're skating on thin ice."

"She's terrified. And she's going to continue to be terrified until you have Angela's killer under wraps."

"Can't argue with that. Now, this Kate Lowell business. Being a reporter, you might not agree, but I think she's entitled to her privacy."

"It's tough to argue for privacy when you make your living in the public eye. I believe in the right to know, Lieutenant. But I don't believe in blackmail, or in poking telescopic lenses into someone's bedroom window."

"Got your dander up." Pleased, Jenner scooted through a yellow light. "Me, I feel sorry for her. She was a kid, probably scared."

"You're a soft touch, Lieutenant."

"Like hell. You can't be a cop and be a soft touch." But he was, damn it. And since it embarrassed the hell out of him, he took the aggressive route. "She still could've killed Angela Perkins."

Finn waited as Jenner doubled-parked, then flipped the officer-on-duty sign over on the dash. "Entertain me."

"She argues with Angela at the hotel. She's fed up with Angela, enraged at being made to suffer for something that happened when she was still wet behind the ears."

"There's that soft touch again. Keep going," Finn prompted as he climbed out of the car.

"She's tired of Angela holding it over her head and threatens her. She hears the maid in the bedroom so she leaves. But she follows Angela to CBC, confronts her in the studio, murders her. Then Deanna comes in, and she gets creative. She's been in films for years. She knows how to set up a camera."

"Yes." There was a quick, nippy breeze that smelled of the lake. Finn drew it in, the easy freshness of it as they crossed the street.

"Then she decides to disguise her motive by going public with exactly what she killed Angela over. Better the world knows she's an unwed mother than a murderer."

"It doesn't play," Jenner concluded.

"Not for me. If Beeker has half the dirt Kate thinks, we'll have a dozen more scenarios by dinnertime." They walked into the office building, Jenner flashing his badge at the security guard in the lobby.

Upstairs, Jenner scanned the wide corridor. The oil paintings were originals and very good. The carpet was thick. Tall, leafy plants were tucked into niches every few feet.

The doors of Beeker Investigations were glass and whispered open into an airy reception area complete with a tidy miniature spruce for the holiday season.

A trim, thirtyish brunette piloted a circular reception desk fashioned from glass blocks. "May I help you?"

"Beeker." Jenner offered the receptionist his ID for inspection.

"Mr. Beeker is in conference, Lieutenant. Will one of his associates be able to help you?"

"Beeker," he said again. "We'll wait, but I'd buzz him if I were you."

"Very well." Her friendly smile chilled a few degrees. "May I ask what this is in reference to?"

"Murder."

"Nice touch," Finn murmured when they wandered over to the deep-cushioned chairs in the waiting area. "Real Joe Friday stuff." He took another look around. "Very elegant surroundings, for a P.I."

"A couple of clients like Angela Perkins means this guy nets in a month what I do in a year."

"Lieutenant Jenner?" The receptionist, obviously miffed, stood in the center of the room. "Mr. Beeker will see you now." She guided them through another set of glass doors, past several offices. She knocked lightly on the door at the end of the hall, and opened it.

Clarence Beeker was like his office, trim, subtly elegant and serviceable. He stood, a man of average height and slim build, behind his Belker desk. The hand he extended was fine-boned.

His hair was graying dashingly at the temples, and he had a finely drawn face that was more handsome with the lines and crevices etched by time. His body was obviously trim beneath his Savile Row suit.

"Might I see some identification?" His voice was smooth, like cool cream over rich coffee.

Jenner was disappointed. He'd expected Beeker to be sleazy.

He examined the shield after slipping on silver-framed reading glasses. "I recognize you, Mr. Riley. I often watch your show on Tuesday nights. Since you've brought a reporter along, Detective Jenner, I assume this is an unofficial visit."

"It's official enough," Jenner corrected. "Mr. Riley's here as a special liaison of the mayor's." Not by a flicker did Jenner or Finn react to the glib lie.

"I'm honored. Please sit. Tell me what I can do for you."

"I'm investigating Angela Perkins's murder," Jenner began. "She was a client of yours."

"She was." Beeker settled behind his desk. "I was shocked and distressed to read about her death."

"We have information leading us to believe that the deceased was blackmailing a number of people."

"Blackmail." Beeker's graying brows rose. "It seems a very unattractive term to be connected to a very attractive woman."

"It's also an attractive motive for murder," Finn put in. "You investigated people for Miss Perkins."

"I handled a number of cases for Miss Perkins over our ten-year association. Given the nature of her profession, it was advantageous for her to be privy to details, backgrounds, the personal habits of those she would interview."

"Her interest, and her use of those personal habits, might have led to her death."

"Mr. Riley, I investigated and reported for Miss Perkins. I'm sure you understand both those functions. I had no more control over her use of the information I provided than you do over the public's use of the information you provide to them."

"And no responsibility."

"None," Beeker agreed pleasantly. "We provide a service. Beeker Investigations has an excellent reputation because we are skilled, discreet and dependable. We abide by the law, Detective, and a code of ethics. Whether or not our clients do so is their business, not ours."

"One of your clients got her face shot off," Jenner said shortly. "We'd like to see copies of the reports you wrote for Miss Perkins."

"I'm afraid, as much as I prefer to cooperate with the police, that would be impossible. Unless you have a warrant," he said pleasantly.

"You don't have a client to protect, Mr. Beeker." Jenner leaned forward. "What's left of her is in a coffin."

"I'm aware of that. However, I do have a client. Mr. Gardner has this company under retainer. As the deceased's husband and beneficiary, I am morally bound to accede to his wishes."

"Which are?"

"To investigate his wife's murder. To be frank, gentlemen, he's dissatisfied with the police investigation to date. And as he was my client during his wife's life, and continues to be after her death, I can't ethically turn over my files without the proper warrant. I'm sure you understand my position."

"And you'll understand mine," Finn said pleasantly. "Liaison or not, I am a reporter. As such, I have an obligation to inform the public. It would be interesting to inform the public of the kind of work you did for Angela. I wonder how many of your other clients would appreciate that connection."

Beeker had stiffened. "Threats, Mr. Riley, aren't appreciated."

"I'm sure they're not. But that doesn't make them any less viable." Finn glanced at his watch. "I think I have enough time to squeeze in a quick feature on the evening news. We'd be able to do an in-depth version tomorrow."

Jaw clenched, Beeker lifted his phone, buzzed his secretary. "I'll need copies of Angela Perkins's files. All of them." He cradled the phone again, linked his fingers. "It will take a little time."

"We've got plenty," Jenner assured him. "While we're waiting, why don't you tell us where you were on the night Angela Perkins was shot?"

"I'd be happy to. I was at home, with my wife and my mother. As I recall, we played three-handed bridge until about midnight."

"Then you won't object to us questioning your wife and your mother?"

"Of course not." Though he wasn't pleased at being out-maneuvered, Beeker was a practical man. "Perhaps I can offer you gentlemen coffee while we wait for the files?"

Chapter Twenty-six

MARSHALL PIKE HAD BEEN WAITING IN HIS CAR IN THE CBC parking lot for more than an hour when Deanna finally walked out. He felt the quick, unbidden tightening of his muscles in response at the sight of her: part anger, part lust. For the past two years, he had been forced to content himself with images of her on the TV screen. Seeing her now in the gloom of dusk, short-skirted, her legs flashing as she hurried toward a dark sedan, exceeded his memories.

"Deanna," he called to her, climbing quickly out of his own car.

She stopped, glanced toward him, peering through the rapidly deepening night. The quick, friendly smile of greeting faded. "Marshall, what do you want?"

"You never returned any of my calls." He cursed himself for sounding petulant. He wanted to appear strong, dynamic.

"I wasn't interested in speaking with you."

"You're going to speak with me." He clamped his hand over her arm. His gesture made Deanna's driver spring out of the car.

"Call off your dog, Deanna. Surely you can spare five minutes?"

"It's all right, Tim." But she removed Marshall's hand before turning to her driver. "I won't keep you waiting long."

"No problem, Miss Reynolds." He gave Marshall a measured look, then tipped his cap. "No problem at all."

"If we could be private." Marshall gestured across the lot. "Your guard will be able to see you, Deanna. I'm sure he'll leap to your rescue should I try to manhandle you."

"I think I can handle you alone." She crossed the lot with him, hoping the meeting would be brief. The wind was bitterly cold and she didn't relish speaking with him. "Since I can't think of anything we'd have to discuss on a personal level, I assume you wanted to talk to me about Angela."

"It would have been difficult for you. Finding her."

"Yes, it was."

"I could help you." He put his hand on her arm again.

"Professionally?" Her brow quirked. The wind, and anger, brought color to her cheeks, a snap to her eyes. "No thanks. Tell me what you want."

For the moment, he stared at her. She was still perfect. Fresh, seductive. All luminous eyes and moist lips. "Have dinner with me," he said at last. "The French place you always liked so much."

"Marshall, please." There was no anger in her voice, only pity. It scraped like rusty blades over his ego.

"Oh yes, I seem to have forgotten to congratulate you on your engagement to our dashing correspondent."

"Thank you. Is that all?"

"I want the file." At her blank look he tightened his grip. "Don't pretend you don't understand. I know Angela gave you a copy of her investigator's report on me. She told me. She gloated over it. I didn't ask for it before because I'd hoped that you'd come to realize what I could offer you. Now, under the circumstances, I need it."

"I don't have it."

Rage darkened his face. "You're lying. She gave it to you."

"Yes, she did." Her arm was throbbing now, but she refused to struggle. "Do you really think I would have kept it all this time? I destroyed it ages ago."

He gripped both her arms now, nearly lifting her off her feet. "I don't believe you."

"I don't give a damn what you believe. I don't have it." More furious than frightened, she struggled against him. "Can't you understand I didn't care enough to keep it? You weren't important enough."

"Bitch." Too incensed to think clearly, he dragged her toward his car. "You won't hold that file over my head." He grunted, his wing tips skittering on the pavement as he was yanked from behind. He went down painfully, bruising his hip and his dignity.

"No, Tim, don't." Though she was shaking, Deanna grabbed her driver's arm before he could haul Marshall to his feet and knock him down all over again.

Tim adjusted his bulky coat, seeing Marshall was quelled. "You okay, Miss Reynolds?"

"Yes, I'm fine."

"Hey!" A baseball cap shielding his eyes, a camera on his shoulder, Joe raced across the lot. "Dee? You okay?"

"Yes." She pressed a hand to her temple as Marshall got to his feet. Perfect, she thought. Pictures at ten. "Yes, I'm okay."

"I was just pulling into the lot when I saw this guy hassling you." Joe's eyes narrowed. "The shrink, right?" He slapped a hand on Marshall's chest before Marshall could step toward his car. "Hold on, pal. Dee, you want me to call the cops, or should Tim and I just show this creep what happens to men who push women around?"

"Just let him go."

"Sure?"

She looked into Marshall's eyes. There was something dead in them now, but she couldn't find any pity. "Yes. Let him go."

"The lady's giving you a break," Joe muttered. "If I catch you bothering her again, I won't be so nice."

Silently, Marshall got into his car. He locked the doors, fastened his seat belt, before driving out of the lot.

"Are you sure he didn't hurt you, Miss Reynolds?"

"No, he didn't. Thank you, Tim."

"No problem." Tim sauntered proudly back to the car.

"I wish you'd let me punch him." Joe gave a regretful sigh before looking back at Deanna. "Spooked you, huh?" He glanced at the camera on his shoulder, grimaced. "I got so pissed I didn't get any tape of it."

That, at least, was something. "I guess there's no point in my asking you not to mention this in the newsroom."

He grinned as he walked her to her car. "No point at all. News is news."

SHE DIDN'T WANT TO TELL Finn, but they'd made a deal. No holding back. She'd hoped Finn would have to work late, but as luck would have it, he opened the door and greeted her with a long, sloppy kiss.

"Hiya."

"Hi yourself." She rocked back on her heels and gave Cronkite the caress he was whining for.

"We had a change in schedule, so I got home a little early." The change in schedule had been canceling all of his appointments and spending his afternoon with Jenner reading through Beeker's files. "Made dinner."

Cooperating, Deanna sniffed the air. "Smells great."

"New recipe." With one brow cocked, he tipped a finger under her chin. "What?"

"What, what?"

"You're upset."

She scowled and pushed his hand away. "Damn it, Finn, that's irritating. Don't you know a woman likes to think she has some mystery?" Still hoping to stall, she peeled out of her coat and hung it on the hall rack.

"What happened, Kansas?"

"We'll talk about it later. I'm starving."

He merely shifted and blocked her path. "Spill it."

She could argue, but since an argument was precisely what she was hoping to avoid, what was the point?

"Will you promise to hear me out and not overreact?"

"Sure." He smiled at her as he swung an arm around her shoulders and led her to the steps. They sat together near the bottom landing, with the dog happily at their feet. "Is it about Angela?"

"Not directly." She blew out a long breath. "It was Marshall. He sort of ambushed me in the parking lot."

"Ambushed?"

His icy tone alerted her. But when she looked up at Finn, his eyes seemed calm enough. Curious, a little annoyed, but calm. "Just a figure of speech. He was upset. You know I haven't returned his calls." When Finn said nothing, she let the rest tumble out. "He was just angry and upset, that's all. About that. And about the files Angela had sent to me. I told you about them. Marshall has it in his head that I kept them. Of course, with the investigation going on he's worried. Naturally."

"Naturally," Finn said pleasantly.

He'd hear about the rest anyway, Deanna reminded herself. From Joe, or someone else in the newsroom. That would be worse. "We had a little scuffle."

There was a dangerous light in Finn's eyes. "Did he put his hands on you?"

Deanna shrugged, hoping to lighten the mood. "In a manner of speaking. It was really just one of those push-shove sort of things. But Tim was there," she added quickly. "And Joe. So it was nothing. It was really nothing."

"He put his hands on you," Finn repeated. "And he threatened you?"

"I don't know that I'd call it a threat. It was just—Finn!" He was already up, removing his coat from the rack. "Finn, damn it, you said you'd be reasonable."

He shot her one look, one stunningly frigid look that had her heart stopping. "I lied."

Her knees were knocking together, but she was on his heels as he strode out of the house. The cold and the look in Finn's eye had her teeth chattering as she struggled into her coat. "Stop this now. Right now! What are you going to do?"

"I'm going to go explain to Pike why he should keep his hands off my woman."

"Your woman?" That tore it. She bounded ahead of him, slapping both hands onto his chest. "Don't you pull that macho bullshit on me, Finn Riley. I'm not going to . . ."

Her voice slid back down her throat when he propped his hands under her elbows and lifted her off the ground. His eyes were blazing.

"You are my woman, Deanna. That's not an insult, that's a fact. Anybody who manhandles you, anybody who threatens you has to deal with me. That's another fact. Got a problem with it?"

"No. Yes." Her feet hit the ground with a thump and she ground her teeth. "I don't know." How was she supposed to think when all she could see were those furious, deadly eyes boring into her. "Let's go back inside and talk this through reasonably."

"We'll talk when I get back."

She raced to the car after him. "I'm going with you." There was still a chance, a slim one, that she could talk him down.

"Go inside, Deanna."

"I'm going with you." She opened the door, climbed in and slammed it shut. He wasn't the only one who could slice flesh with a look. "If *my man's* going to go make a fool of himself, I'm going to be there. Got a problem with that?"

Finn slammed the door and turned the key. "Hell no."

THE BEST DEANNA COULD hope for now was that Marshall wouldn't be home.

The wind had picked up and held a fresh threat of snow. It raced

441

through Finn's hair, sent it flying around his face as he stalked up to Marshall's door. He had only one thing on his mind and, like a skilled reporter, easily blocked out all distractions: Deanna's mumbled curses, the occasional swish of tires on the street, the numbing chill in the air.

"He's not worth it," Deanna said for the hundredth time. "He's just not worth your making a scene."

"I have no intention of making a scene. I'm going to talk to him, and he's going to listen. And then, unless I'm very much mistaken, you'll never see or hear from him again."

He had been wanting a confrontation since the day Deanna had rushed out of the CBC Building in tears, and into his arms. Finn could already feel the grim satisfaction of pleasure postponed.

Deanna saw his eyes slit like a predator's as the door opened. Her stomach clenched and she had one wild thought: to jump between them.

But Finn didn't lunge, as she'd been half terrified he would. He simply strolled across the threshold and into the foyer.

"I don't believe I invited you in." Marshall ran a finger over the black tie of his tuxedo. "And I'm afraid I'm on my way out."

"We'll make this as quick as possible, since I don't believe Deanna's comfortable being here."

"Deanna's always welcome in my home," Marshall said stiffly. "You are not."

"What you don't seem to understand is that we're a team. When you threaten her, you threaten me. I don't react well to threats, Dr. Pike."

"My conversation with Deanna was personal."

"Wrong again." Finn stepped closer. The feral gleam in his eyes had Marshall stepping back. "If you come near her again, if you ever put your hands on her again, I'll bury you, in every way you can imagine."

"There are laws to protect a man against a physical attack in his own home."

"I have better ways of dealing with you. Angela's file on you made very interesting reading, Pike."

Marshall's eyes slid to Deanna. "She doesn't have the file. She destroyed it."

"No, Deanna doesn't have it. But you don't know what I have, do you?"

Marshall's attention snapped back to Finn. "You have no right—"

"I've got the First Amendment. Steer clear, Pike, way clear. Or I'll break you in half with it."

"You bastard." Fear of exposure propelled Marshall forward. He swung out, more in panic than design. Finn easily avoided the blow and followed it by one punishing fist to the midsection.

It was over in seconds. Deanna had done no more than squeak in response. Marshall had done no more than moan. And Finn, she realized as she gaped, had made no sound at all.

Then he crouched down, impossibly graceful and smooth. "Listen carefully. Don't ever come near Deanna again. Don't call, don't write, don't send a telegram. Are you getting this?" He was satisfied when Marshall blinked. "That should conclude our little interview." He stepped back to where Deanna still stood, openmouthed, on the stoop. Quietly, he shut the door. "Let's go."

Her legs were jelly. She had to lock her knees to keep from swaying. "Good God, Finn. Good God."

"We're going to have to reheat dinner," he said as he guided her to the car.

"You just—I mean you—" She didn't know what she meant. "We can't just leave him there."

"Of course we can. He doesn't need paramedics, Deanna. I only wrinkled his tux and bruised his ego."

"You hit him." Once she was seated, strapped in, she pressed both hands to her mouth.

His black mood had passed. He felt almost sunny as he drove

fast through the windswept night. "Not exactly my style, but since he swung first, it worked for me."

She turned her head away. She couldn't explain, couldn't *believe* what she was feeling. The way he'd sliced Marshall with words. Sharp and cold as a sword. Then he'd shifted his body aside, graceful as a dancer. She hadn't seen the blow coming any more than Marshall had. He'd moved so fast, so stunningly. She pressed a hand to her stomach and bit back a little moan.

"Pull over," she said in a muffled voice. "Right now."

He did, terrified she was about to be sick, disgusted because he hadn't reined in his temper long enough to make her stay home. "Take it easy, Deanna. I'm sorry you had to see that, but—"

Whatever else he'd intended to say was lost as she lunged at him. In one fluid move, she tore off her seat belt and whipped toward him. Her mouth was hot and wet and hungry. Through his shock, and instant arousal, he felt the violent thud of her heart.

And her hands. Jesus. Her hands.

Cars sped by them. He could only groan as she dived deeper into his mouth, her tongue greedy, her teeth vicious.

Both of them were panting for air when she leaned back.

"Well," he managed, but his mind was wiped as clean as glass. "Well."

"I'm not proud of it." She flopped back in her seat, face flushed, eyes bright. "I don't approve of intimidation or fighting. I absolutely don't. Oh God." With a half laugh, she squeezed her eyes shut. Her body was vibrating like an overheated engine. Intellect, she discovered, could be completely overpowered by glands. "I'm going to explode. Drive fast, will you?"

"Yeah." His aching hand trembled a bit as he turned the key again. Then, as he punched the accelerator, he started to grin. The grin became a hard, deep-throated laugh. "Deanna, I'm crazy about you."

She had to curl her fingers into fists to keep herself from tearing at his clothes. "We're both crazy," she decided. "Drive faster."

MARSHALL COMFORTED HIMSELF as best he could, pampering his bruised stomach muscles, taking a painkiller. Shame and fury had driven him out of the house. He opted for a drink first, then two, before keeping his date at the opera.

He hadn't thought he'd enjoy the music, or the company. But both had soothed him. He was a civilized man, he reminded himself. A respected man. He would not be intimidated by some grandstanding reporter like Finn Riley. He would simply bide his time, calmly.

Enchanted by the diva's final aria, he still felt peaceful when he pulled in to his driveway, even though his stomach ached dully. Another dose of painkiller would take the edge off, he knew. Fury and frustration had been eased by Mozart's music. Humming lightly, Marshall set the security on his car. If Deanna had the file, and he could no longer be sure, he would convince her to return it to him. But he'd wait until Riley was away on assignment.

They would talk, he promised himself, and finally set the past behind them. As Angela was behind them.

His eyes gleamed as he reached for his keys. He thought he sensed a movement to his left. He had time to turn, time to understand. He didn't have time to scream.

FINN WAS WATCHING DEANNA sleep when the phone rang. They'd started on each other in the foyer, worked their way up the steps. Halfway up they'd decided, tactically, that they'd made it far enough.

It made him grin to remember how she'd torn at his clothes. Attacked him, he thought smugly. Of course, he'd been a willing victim, but she'd shown surprising energy, and amazing resilience.

He almost thought it a shame he hadn't dealt so satisfactorily with Pike before.

He dismissed all thoughts of Pike as he settled back, pleasantly aroused when Deanna curled her body against his.

He wouldn't wake her, though it was very tempting to do so. He was too relieved that she no longer tossed and turned or awakened quaking as she had for several nights after Angela's murder. Instead, he simply enjoyed the way her body fit to his.

He swore when the phone rang and she woke.

"Take it easy." Like Deanna, he expected to hear nothing but breathing when he lifted the receiver.

"Finn? It's Joe."

"Joe." He saw the tension dissolve from Deanna's shoulders. "I guess it would be pointless to mention it's after one A.M."

"Got a tip for you, pal. I was whiling away some time with Leno and monitoring my police scanner. We had us a murder over at Lincoln Park."

"I'm not on the crime beat."

"I checked it out, Finn. Figured you'd want to know right away, instead of catching it on the early news. It was Pike. You know, the shrink who hassled Dee today. Somebody did him."

Finn's gaze cut to Deanna's. "How?"

"The same way as Angela. In the face. My police connection wouldn't give me much. But he bought it right on his own doorstep. A neighbor reported hearing gunshots around midnight. A black-and-white checked it out and found him. I'm calling from the cop shop. We've got a unit on it. Story'll break top of the hour on *Sunrise*."

"Thanks."

"I figured Dee would take it better from you."

"Yeah. Keep me posted?"

"You bet."

He hung up, dispirited.

"Something's wrong." She could see it in his face, in the way the air had seemed to thicken around him. "Just tell me straight out, Finn."

"Okay." He covered her hands with his. "Marshall Pike's been murdered."

Her hands jerked once, then went still. "How?"

"He was shot."

She already knew, but had to ask. "The same as Angela? It was the same as Angela, wasn't it?"

"It looks that way."

She made a strangled sound in her throat, but eased back when he reached for her. "I'm all right. We need to tell the police about what happened after work today. It has to be connected."

"It's possible."

"Don't circle around it," she snapped out, and pushed off the bed. "Marshall harassed me today, and we went over there. Hours later, he's shot. We can't pretend that one had nothing to do with the other."

"And if it is connected, what can you do?"

"Whatever I can." She dragged a sweater over her head, snatched trousers from the closet. "Even though I didn't pull the trigger, I am the cause, and there has to be something I can do."

She didn't resist when he put his arms around her, but clung to him, pressing her face to his shoulder.

"I have to do something, Finn. I can't bear it otherwise."

"We'll go see Jenner." He cupped her face in his hands, kissed her. "We'll figure something out."

"Okay." She finished dressing in silence. She was sure he wouldn't feel guilty about facing down Marshall only hours before, because he would see what he had done as pure and simple justice. And perhaps he was right.

Is that what whoever had leveled a gun at Marshall's face had thought as well?

The idea sickened her. "I'll wait downstairs," she said as he pulled out his boots.

She saw the envelope before she reached the bottom landing. It lay crisp and white against the glossy floor of the foyer, inches inside the door. There was a quick pain, a twist in the gut like a fist punching muscle. Then she went numb, crossing the polished wood, bending down.

She opened the envelope as Finn came down behind her.

"Goddamn it." He took it from her limp fingers, and read.

He'll never hurt you again.

When they left the house, someone was watching, a heart bursting with love and need and terrible grief. Killing for her had been nothing. It had been done before, and needed to be done again.

Perhaps she would see, at last.

Chapter Twenty-seven

JEFF STOOD IN THE CONTROL BOOTH OVERLOOKING THE studio, biting his lip in agitation. Deanna was about to film her first show since Angela's death.

"Camera Three, on Dee." He barked out orders. "Take Two, zoom out. Wider on One, pan. Give me Dee tight, Three, music in. Great, great applause. Start the playback tape."

He applauded himself, as did the others in the booth. From their perch overlooking the stage they could see the audience surge to its feet and cheer.

"Ride it," Jeff ordered. Oh yeah, he thought, sharing the triumph. She's back. "Ride the applause."

Down below Deanna stood on the new set with its jewel tones and banks of cheery holly bushes and let the waves of applause wash over her. It was, she knew, a show of support, a welcoming home. When her eyes filled she didn't bother to blink back the tears. She didn't think about it.

"Thanks." She let out a long, unsteady breath. "It's really good to be back. I . . ." She trailed off while she scanned the crowd. There were familiar faces dotted among the strangers. Faces from the newsroom, from production. Pleasure glowed on her face. "It's really good to see you. Before we get rolling, I'd like to thank you all for your letters and phone calls over the past week. Your support has helped me, and everyone involved with the show, through a difficult time."

And that, she thought, was all the space she could give, would give, to the past.

"Now I'd like to bring out a woman who's given us all so many hours of entertainment. She's incandescent. Luminous. With a talent as golden as her eyes. According to *Newsweek*, Kate Lowell can 'ignite the screen with a sweep of the eyelash, by the flash of her signature smile.' She's proven both her popular and her critical appeal by holding the number-one box-office position for two straight years, and by winning an Oscar for her portrayal of the heroic, unforgettable Tess in *Deception*. Ladies and gentlemen, Kate Lowell."

Again, the applause erupted. Kate swept into it, looking confident and fresh and every bit the star. But when Deanna took her hand, she found it cold and trembling. Deliberately Deanna wrapped her in an embrace.

"Don't do anything you're not ready to do," she murmured in Kate's ear. "I'm not going to push you into any revelations."

Kate hesitated a moment. "Oh God, I'm glad you're here, Dee. Let's sit down, okay? My knees are shaking."

It wasn't an easy show, from any angle. Deanna was able to guide the first ten minutes through juicy Hollywood chitchat, keeping the audience amused to the point where she assumed Kate had changed her mind about the announcement.

"I like playing women of strength, and character." In a fluid movement that rustled silk, Kate crossed her long, million-dollar legs. "And there do seem to be more scripts being written for strong women, women who are not just bystanders but who have beliefs and standards they're willing to fight for. I'm grateful for the chance to play those women, because I didn't always fight for what I wanted."

"So you feel as though you're able to do that now, through your work?"

"I relate to many of the characters I've played. Tess in particular. Because she was a woman who sacrificed everything, risked everything for the sake of her child. In an odd sort of way, I mirrored Tess. Mirror images are opposites. And I sacrificed my child, my chance with my child, when I gave it up for adoption ten years ago."

"Damn." In the control booth, Jeff's eyes popped wide. The audience had dropped into stunned silence. "Damn," he said again. "Camera Two, tight on Kate. Man, oh man."

But even as he worriedly bit his lip again, he focused on Deanna's face. She'd known, he realized, and let out a long, calming breath. She'd known . . .

"An unplanned pregnancy at any time, under any circumstances, is frightening." Deanna wanted her audience to remember that. "How old were you?"

"I was seventeen. I had, as you know, Dee, a supportive family, a good home. I'd just begun my modeling career, and I thought the world was at my feet. Then I discovered I was pregnant."

"The father? Do you want to talk about him?"

"Was a nice, sweet boy who was every bit as terrified as I. He was my first." She smiled a little now, remembering him. "I was his. We were dazzled by each other, by what we felt for each other. When I told him, we just sat there, numb. We were in LA, and we'd gone to the beach. We sat there and watched the surf. He offered to marry me."

"Some people might feel that would have been the answer. You didn't?"

"Not for me, or the boy, or the child." Kate continued, using all of her skill to keep her voice level. "Do you remember the way we used to talk about what we wanted to do when we grew up?"

"Yes. I do." Deanna linked her fingers with Kate's. "You never had any doubts."

"I'd always wanted to be an actress. I'd made some progress modeling, and I was going to conquer Hollywood come hell or high water. Then I was pregnant."

"Did you consider abortion? Discuss the option with the father, with your family?"

"Yes, I did. As difficult as it was, Dee, I remember how supportive my parents were. I'd hurt them, disappointed them. I didn't realize how much until I was older and had some perspective. But they never wavered. I can't explain to you why I decided the way I did. It was a purely emotional decision, but I think my parents' unflagging support helped me make it. I decided to have the baby and give it away. And I didn't know, not until it came time to do just that, how hard it would be."

"Do you know who adopted the baby?"

"No." Kate dashed a tear away. "No, I didn't want to know. I'd made a deal. I had chosen to give the child to people who would love and care for it. And it wasn't my baby any longer, but theirs. She would be ten years old now, nearly eleven." Eyes swimming, she looked toward the camera. "I hope she's happy. I hope she doesn't hate me."

"Thousands of women face what you faced. Each choice they make is theirs to make, however difficult it is. I think one of the reasons you play admirable, accessible women so well is that you've been through the hardest test a woman can face."

"When I played Tess, I wondered how everything would have worked out if I'd chosen differently. I'll never know."

"Do you regret your choice?"

"A part of me always will regret I couldn't be a mother to that child. But I think I've finally realized, after all these years, that it really was the right one. For everybody."

"We'll be back in a moment," Deanna said to the camera, then turned to Kate. "Are you all right?"

"Barely. I didn't think it would be so hard." She took two deep breaths, but kept her eyes on Deanna rather than look out at the

452

audience. "The questions are going to come fast and furious. And God, the press tomorrow."

"You'll get through it."

"Yes, I will. Dee." She leaned forward and gripped Deanna's hand. "It meant a lot to me, to be able to do this here, with you. It seemed, for a minute or two, as if I were just talking to you. The way we used to."

"Then maybe this time you'll keep in touch."

"Yeah, I will. You know, I realized while I was talking why I hated Angela so much. I thought it was because she was using me. But it was because she was using my baby. It helps knowing that."

"HELL OF A SHOW." FRAN fisted her hands on her hips as Deanna walked into the dressing room. "You knew. I could tell you knew. Why the hell didn't you tell me? Me, your producer and your best friend."

"Because I wasn't sure she'd go through with it." The strain of the past hour had Deanna's shoulders aching. Rolling them in slow circles, she went directly to the lighted mirror to change makeup. Fran was miffed. She understood that, expected it. Just as she understood and expected it would wear off quickly. "And I didn't feel it was right to talk about it until she did. Give me a gauge on audience reaction, Fran."

"After the shock waves died off? I'd say about sixty-five percent were in her corner, maybe ten percent never got past the stunned stage, and the remaining twenty-five were ticked off that their princess stumbled."

"That's about how I figured it. Not bad." Deanna slathered her face with moisturizer. "She'll be all right." She lifted a brow at Fran's reflection. "Where do you stand?"

After a moment of stilted silence, Fran exhaled hard, fluttering her choppy bangs. "In her corner, one hundred percent. It must have been hell for her, poor kid. God, Dee, what made her decide to go public that way?"

"It all has to do with Angela," Deanna began, and told her.

"Blackmail." Too intrigued now for even mild annoyance, Fran let out a low whistle. "I knew she was a bitch, but I never thought she'd sunk that low. I guess the list of suspects just expanded by several dozen." Her eyes widened. "You don't think Kate—"

"No, I don't." Not that she hadn't considered it, thoroughly, Deanna thought, logically, and she hoped objectively. "Even if I thought she killed Angela, which I don't, she doesn't have any reason to have killed Marshall. She didn't even know him."

"I guess not. I wish the cops would figure it out and lock this lunatic up. It worries me sick that you're still getting those notes." Now that all was forgiven, she moved over, automatically massaging Deanna's stiff shoulders. "At least I can rest easier knowing Finn won't be going out of town until this is over."

"How do you know that?"

"Because—" Fran caught herself, looked quickly at her watch. "Gosh, what am I doing sitting around here talking? I've got a hundred things—"

"Fran." Deanna stood and stepped in front of her. "How do you know that Finn's not going out of town until this is over? The last I heard he was scheduled to go to Rome right after Christmas."

"I, ah, I must have gotten mixed up."

"Like hell."

"Damn it, Dee, don't get that warrior look on your face."

"How do you know?"

"Because he told me, okay?" She tossed up her hands in disgust. "And I was supposed to keep my big mouth shut about the fact that he's canceled the Rome shoot and anything else that takes him out of Chicago."

"I see." Deanna lowered her eyes, brushed a speck of lint from her teal silk skirt.

"No, you don't see because you've got your blinders on. Do you really expect the man to fly gleefully across the Atlantic while this is going on? For Christ's sake, he loves you."

"I'm aware of that." But her spine was rigid. "I have things to do myself," she said, and stormed out.

"Good going, Myers." Muttering oaths, Fran snatched up the dressing room phone and called up to Finn's office. If she'd inadvertently started a war, the least she could do was tell him to be fully armed.

IN HIS OFFICE ABOVE THE newsroom, Finn replaced the receiver and sent a scowl at Barlow James. "You're about to get some reinforcements. Deanna's on her way up."

"Fine." Pleased, Barlow settled back in his chair, stretched his burly arms. "We'll get all this settled once and for all."

"It is settled, Barlow. I'm not traveling more than an hour away from home until the police make an arrest."

"Finn, I understand your concerns for Deanna. I have them, as well. But you're short-sheeting the show. You're overreacting."

"Really?" Finn's voice was cool, deceptively so. "And I thought I was taking two murders and the harassment of the woman I love so well."

Sarcasm didn't deflate Barlow. "My point is that she can obtain round-the-clock protection. Professionals. God knows a woman in her financial position can afford the very best. Not to slight your manhood, Finn, but you're a reporter, not a bodyguard. And," he continued before Finn could respond, "as skilled a reporter as you are, you are not a detective. Let the police do their job and you do yours. You have a responsibility to the show, to the people who work with you. To the network, to the sponsors. You have a contract, Finn. You're legally bound to travel whenever and wherever news is breaking. You agreed to those terms. Hell, you demanded them."

"Sue me," Finn invited, eyes gleaming in anticipation of a bout. He glanced up as the door slammed open.

She stood there in her snazzy silk suit, eyes flashing, chin angled.

455

Each stride a challenge, she marched to his desk, slapped her palms on the surface.

"I won't have it."

He didn't bother to pretend he didn't understand. "You don't have any say in this, Deanna. It's my choice."

"You weren't even going to tell me. You were just going to make some lame excuse about why the trip was canceled. You'd have lied to me."

He'd have killed for her, he thought, and shrugged. "Now that's not necessary." He leaned back in the chair, steepled his fingers. Though he was wearing a sweater and jeans, he looked every inch the star. "How did the show go this morning?"

"Stop it. Just stop it." She whirled, jabbing a finger at Barlow. "You can order him to go, can't you?"

"I thought I could." He lifted his hands, let them fall. "I came from New York hoping to make him see reason. I should have known better." With a sigh, he rose. "I'll be in the newsroom for the next hour or so. If you fare any better than I did, let me know."

Finn waited until the door clicked shut. The sound was as definitive as that of the bell in a boxing ring. "You won't, Deanna, so you might as well accept it."

"I want you to go," she said, spacing each word carefully. "I don't want our lives to be interfered with. It's important to me."

"You're important to me."

"Then do this for me."

He picked up a pencil, ran it through his fingers once, twice, then snapped it neatly in two. "No."

"Your career could be on the line."

He tilted his head as if considering it. And damn him, his dimples winked at her. "I don't think so."

He was, she thought, as sturdy, as unshakable and as unmovable as granite. "They could cancel your show."

"Throw out the baby with the bathwater?" Though he wasn't feeling particularly calm, he levered back, propped his feet on the

456

desk. "I've known network execs to do dumber things, so let's say they decide to cancel a highly rated, profitable and award-winning show because I'm not going on the road for a while." He stared up at her, his eyes darkly amused. "I guess you'd have to support me while I'm unemployed. I might get to like it and retire completely. Take up gardening or golf. No, I know. I'll be your business manager. You'd be the star—you know, like a country-western singer."

"This isn't a joke, Finn."

"It isn't a tragedy, either." His phone rang. Finn picked up the receiver, said, "Later," and hung up again. "I'm sticking, Deanna. I can't keep up with the investigation if I'm off in Europe."

"Why do you need to keep up with it?" Her eyes narrowed. "Is that what you've been doing? Why there was a rerun last Tuesday night? All those calls from Jenner. You're not working on *In Depth*, you're working with him."

"He doesn't have a problem with it. Why should you?"

She spun away. "I hate this. I hate that our private and professional lives are becoming mixed and unbalanced. I hate being scared this way. Jumping every time there's a noise in the hall, or bracing whenever the elevator door opens."

"That's my point. That's exactly how I feel. Come here." He held out a hand, gripping hers when she walked around the desk. With his eyes on hers, he drew her into his lap. "I'm scared, Deanna, right down to the bone."

Her lips parted in surprise. "You never said so."

"Maybe I should have. Male pride's a twitchy business. The fact is, I need to be here, I need to be involved, to know what's happening. It's the only way I've got to fight back the fear."

"Just promise me you won't take any chances, any risks."

"He's not going after me, Deanna."

"I want to be sure of that." She closed her eyes. But she wasn't sure.

*

AFTER DEANNA LEFT, Finn went down to the video vault. An idea had been niggling at him since Marshall's murder, the notion that he'd forgotten something. Or overlooked it.

All Barlow's talk about responsibilities, loyalties, had triggered a memory. Finn skimmed through the black forest of video cases until he found February 1992.

He slipped the cassette into the machine, fast-forwarding through news reports, local, world, weather, sports. He wasn't sure of the precise date, or how much coverage there had been. But he was certain Lew McNeil's previous Chicago connection would have warranted at least one full report on his murder.

He got more than he'd hoped for.

Finn slowed the tape to normal, eyes narrowing as he focused in on the CBC reporter standing on the snowy sidewalk.

"Violence struck in the early morning hours in this affluent New York neighborhood. Lewis McNeil, senior producer of the popular talk show *Angela's*, was gunned down outside his home in Brooklyn Heights this morning. According to a police source, McNeil, a Chicago native, was apparently leaving for work when he was shot at close range. McNeil's wife was in the house . . ." The camera did its slow pan. "She was awakened shortly after seven A.M. by the sound of a gunshot."

Finn listened to the rest of the report, eyes fixed. Grimly, he zipped through another week of news, gathering snippets on the McNeil murder investigation.

He tucked his notes away and headed into the newsroom. He found Joe as the cameraman was heading out on assignment.

"Question."

"Make it a quick one. I'm on the clock."

"February ninety-two. Lew McNeil's murder. That was your camerawork on the New York stand-up, wasn't it?"

"What can I say?" Joe polished his nails on his sweatshirt. "My art is distinctive."

"Right. Where was he shot?"

"As I recall, right outside his house." As he thought back, Joe reached into his hip pocket for a Baby Ruth. "Yeah, they said it looked like he was cleaning off his car."

"No, I mean anatomically. Chest, gut, head? None of the reports I reviewed said."

"Oh." Joe frowned, shutting his eyes as if to bring the scene back to mind. "They'd cleaned up pretty good by the time we got there. Never saw the stiff." He opened his eyes. "Did you know Lew?"

"Some."

"Yeah, me too. Tough." He bit off a hefty section of chocolate. "Why the interest?"

"Something I'm working on. Didn't your reporter ask the cops for details?"

"Who was that—Clemente, right? Didn't last around here very long. Sloppy, you know? I can't say if he did or not. Look, I've got to split." He headed for the stairs, then rapped his knuckles on the side of his head. "Yeah, yeah." He headed up the steps backward, watching Finn. "Seems to me I heard one of the other reporters talking. He said Lew caught the bullet in the face. Nasty, huh?"

"Yeah." A grim satisfaction swam through Finn's blood. "Very nasty."

JENNER MUNCHED A MIDMORNING danish, washing down the cherry filling with sweetened coffee. As he ate and sipped, he studied the grisly photos tacked to the corkboard. The conference room was quiet now, but he'd left the blinds open on the glass door that separated it from the bull pen of the precinct.

Angela Perkins. Marshall Pike. He stared at what had been done to them. If he stared long enough, he knew he could go into a kind of trance—a state of mind that left the brain clear for ideas, for possibilities.

He was just annoyed enough at Finn for emotion to interfere with intellect. The man should have told him the details of his

459

conversation with Pike. However slight it had been, it had been police business. The idea of Finn interviewing Pike alone burned Jenner more bitterly than the station house coffee.

He remembered their last meeting, in the early hours of the morning that Pike had been murdered.

"WE'RE CLEAR THAT THE shooter knows Miss Reynolds." Jenner ticked the fact off on a finger. "Was aware of her relationship, or at least her argument, with Pike." He held up a second finger. "He or she knows Deanna's address, knew Pike's and had enough knowledge of the studio to set up the camera after killing Angela Perkins."

"Agreed."

"The notes have shown up under Deanna's door, on her desk, in her car, in the apartment she still keeps in Old Town." Jenner had lifted a brow, hoping that Finn would offer some explanation for that interesting fact. But he hadn't. Finn knew how to keep information to himself. It was one of the things Jenner admired about him. "It has to be someone who works at CBC," Jenner concluded.

"Agreed. In theory." Finn smiled when Jenner let out a huff of breath. "It could be someone who *worked* there. It's possible it's a fan of Deanna's who's been in the studio. A regular audience member. Lots of people have enough rudimentary knowledge of television to work a camera for a still shot."

"I think that's stretching it."

"So let's stretch it. He sees her every day on TV."

"Could be a woman."

Finn let that cook a moment, then shook his head. "A remote possibility. Let's shuffle that aside for a minute and try out this theory: It's a man, a lonely, frustrated man. He lives alone, but every day Deanna slips through the television screen right into his living room. She's sitting right there with him, talking to him, smiling at him. He's not lonely when she's there. And he wants her there all the time. He doesn't do well with women. He's a little afraid of them.

He's a good planner, probably holds down a decent job, a responsible one, because he knows how to think things through. He's thorough, meticulous."

Impressed, Jenner pursed his lips. "Sounds like you've done your homework."

"I have. Because I'm in love with Deanna I think I understand him. Thing is, he's got this temper, this rage. He didn't kill in a rage. I think he did that coolly." And that was what chilled Finn's blood. "But he trashes my house, Deanna's office. He writes his feelings of betrayal on the wall. All but splatters them there. How did she betray him? What changed from the time she got the first note to Angela's murder?"

"She hooked up with you?"

"She'd been involved with me for two years." Finn leaned forward. "We got engaged, Jenner. The official announcement had barely hit the streets when we had Angela's murder and the break-ins."

"So he killed Angela because he was ticked at Deanna Reynolds?"

"He killed Angela, and Pike, because he loves Deanna Reynolds. What better way to show his devotion than to remove people who upset or annoy her? He trashed her things, taking special care with the wedding-gown sketches, the newspaper reports of the engagement, photographs of Deanna and me. He was enraged because she'd announced, publicly, that she preferred another man to him. That she was willing to take vows to prove it."

Nodding slowly, Jenner doodled on a sheet of paper. "Maybe you didn't get your psychiatrist's degree at Sears. Why hasn't he gone after you?"

Instinctively, Finn reached up to run his fingers over his sleeve. Beneath it was a scar from a bullet. A bullet that hadn't come from the sniper or the SWAT team. But he couldn't be sure. "Because I haven't done anything to *hurt* Deanna. Marshall did, on the day he was killed, and a couple of years ago, when he fell into Angela's trap."

"I should have talked to him." Jenner tapped a fist lightly on his files. "He could have known something, seen something. It's possible he'd received threats."

"I doubt that. He was the type who'd have come running to the cops. Or he would have told me when I talked with him."

"You were too busy beating him up."

"I didn't beat him up." Finn folded his arms across his chest. "He swung, I swung. Once. In any case, I meant he would have told me when I talked to him at his office a few days ago."

Jenner stopped doodling. "You went to see him about Angela Perkins's murder?"

"It was a theory."

"One you didn't feel necessary to share?"

"It was personal."

"Nothing's personal on this, nothing." Jenner edged forward, eyes narrowed. "I've let you in on this investigation because I think you're a smart man, and I sympathize with your position. But you cross me and you're out."

"I'll do what I have to do, Lieutenant, with or without you."

"Reporters aren't the only ones who can harass. Keep that in mind." Jenner closed his file, rose. "Now I have work to do."

NO, JENNER THOUGHT NOW, sympathy and admiration aside, he wasn't about to let Finn go off on his own. He might be wearing blinders to the fact that his life was in danger, but Jenner knew better.

He rose to refill his coffee cup, and glanced through the glass door. "Speak of the devil," he murmured. Jenner pulled open the door. "Looking for me?" he asked Finn, and waved away the uniform who was blocking Finn's path. "It's all right, officer. I'll see Mr. Riley." He nodded briefly at Finn. "You've got five minutes."

"It's going to take a little longer." Finn studied the police photos on the board dispassionately. There were snapshots of both victims taken prior to and after death. Side by side, they were like before-and-after shots gone desperately wrong. "You're going to need to put one more set up there."

TWENTY MINUTES LATER, Jenner completed his conversation with the detective in Brooklyn Heights. "They're faxing us the file," he told Finn. "Okay, Mr. Riley, who knew that McNeil was passing information on to Angela?"

"Deanna's staff. I'd be certain of that. I'd also give odds that it would have leaked downstairs." There was an excitement brewing in him now. The kind he recognized as energy from a puzzle nearly solved. "There's always been a lot of interaction between Deanna's people and the newsroom. Are we on the same wavelength here? Three people are dead because they threatened Deanna in some way."

"I can't comment about that, Mr. Riley."

Finn shoved back from the table. "Damn it, I'm not here as a reporter. I'm not looking for a scoop, the latest tidbit from an unnamed police source. You want to frisk me for a mike?"

"I don't think you're after a story, Mr. Riley," Jenner said calmly. "If I'd ever thought that, you never would have gotten your foot in the door. But maybe I think you're too used to doing things your own way, to running your own show, to handle the delicate matter of cooperation."

Finn slammed his hands down on the table. "If you think you're going to brush me off, you're wrong. You're right about the harassment, Lieutenant. One phone call and I can have a dozen cameras dogging your every move. I can put so much pressure on you that you won't be able to sneeze without someone sticking a mike up your nose. Before you catch your next breath Chicago will be buzzing about a serial killer. The commissioner and the mayor will love that, won't they?" He waited half a beat. "You use me, or I'll use you. It's your choice."

Jenner folded his arms on the table, leaned forward against them. "I don't like threats."

"Neither do I. But I'll do a lot more than threaten if you try to block me out now." He looked at the victims on the board. "He could lose it." He spoke quietly now, carefully. "He could lose it anytime and try to put her up there. You're pissed because I did some tracking on my own, fine. Be pissed. But use me. Or by God I'll use you."

Objectively, Jenner buried his irritation, calculating how much damage would be done by a media war. Too much, he mused. It was always too much.

"Let's do this, Mr. Riley. Let's say we theorize that McNeil was the first victim of three—and we'll want to keep that under our hat."

"I told you I'm not interested in a story."

"Just laying down the ground rules. We'll theorize that, and that only a limited number of people had the knowledge that would lead to motive for his murder." He gestured to a chair, waiting for Finn to sit again. "Tell me about those people. Start with Loren Bach." In the spirit of compromise, Jenner opened the file on Loren that Angela had commissioned from Beeker.

CASSIE WALKED INTO DEANNA'S office, then let out a long, long sigh. Deanna stood on a stool in the center of the room, the seamstress at her feet. Yards of shimmering white silk billowed.

"It's gorgeous."

"It's barely started." But Deanna was almost sighing herself as she brushed a hand over the sweeping skirt neatly pinned to the lacy bodice. Irish lace, she mused. For Finn. "But you're right."

"I've got to get my camera." Inspired, Cassie bolted for the door. "Don't move."

"I'm not going anywhere."

"You must be still," the seamstress complained over a mouthful of pins. Her voice was raspy, as if she'd already swallowed more than her share.

Deanna used all her willpower not to shift from foot to foot. "I am being still."

"You're vibrating like a spring."

"Sorry." Deanna took a long, steadying breath. "I guess I'm nervous."

"The bride-to-be," Cassie recited as she walked back in with a Palmcorder blocking her face. "Deanna Reynolds, the reigning queen of daytime TV, has chosen an elegant gown of . . ."

"Italian silk," the seamstress prompted. "With touches of Irish lace and a sea of freshwater pearls."

"Exquisite," Cassie said soberly. "And tell us, Miss Reynolds—" with an expert's touch, she zoomed in on Deanna's face—" how do you feel on this exciting occasion?"

"Terrified." She crossed her eyes. If the fitting took five minutes over the allotted hour, she'd be making up time all week. "And partially insane. Other than that I'm enjoying every minute of it."

"If you'll just stand perfectly still, I'll do a little circle around so that our viewers can get the full effect." Cassie sidestepped, panned back. "This'll go in my growing library of life behind *Deanna's Hour.*"

Deanna felt her smile stiffen. "Do you have a lot of tape?"

"Oh, a little of this, a little of that. Simon pulling what's left of his hair out. Margaret tossing spitballs. You racing for the elevator."

Beneath the sparkling bodice, Deanna's heart thudded thickly. "I guess I've never paid much attention. So many cameras around. You always keep that at hand, don't you?"

"You never know what historical, or humiliating, moment you might capture."

Someone had captured her, Deanna remembered, while she'd slept at her desk. Coming to work, going from, shopping, playing with Fran's baby in the park.

They'd captured her unconscious in the studio beside Angela's body.

Cassie, who was in and out of the office dozens of times a day. Cassie, who knew every detail of Deanna's schedule. Cassie, who had dated one of the studio camera operators.

"Turn it off, Cassie."

"One more second."

"Turn it off." Her voice sharpened, and Deanna set her teeth to steady it.

"Sorry." Obviously baffled, Cassie lowered the camera. "I guess I got carried away."

"It's all right. I'm just edgy." Deanna managed to smile again. It was ridiculous, she told herself. It was insane even to speculate that Cassie would be capable of murder.

"It's your first day back." Cassie touched her hand and Deanna had to force herself not to jerk away. "God knows it was a madhouse around here after the show with all those calls coming in about Kate Lowell. Why don't you give yourself a break after you've finished the fitting, and go home? I can reschedule the rest of the afternoon's business."

"I think that's a good idea." She spoke slowly over the erratic thud of her heart. "I've got a lot of things to deal with at home."

Cassie's mouth thinned. "I didn't mean you should jump out of one madhouse into another. You're not going to get any work done there, with all those painters and carpenters slogging away. I think—" She saw that Deanna's eyes had focused behind her and turned. "Jeff." Her mouth softened at the admiration on his face. "She looks fabulous, doesn't she?"

"Yeah. Really." He glanced at the camera Cassie held. "You got pictures?"

"Sure. Capture the moment. Listen, unless it's a crisis, hold it off, will you? This is a momentous occasion. Dee's going home early."

"Oh, good idea. Finn called, Deanna. He said to tell you he had a meeting and he'd see you at home. He thought he might get there by four."

"Well, that's lucky. Maybe I'll beat him there."

"Not if you don't hold still," the seamstress muttered.

*

BUT IT WAS BARELY THREE-THIRTY when Deanna slipped into her shoes and grabbed her briefcase. "Cassie, can you call Tim?"

"Already done. He should be waiting downstairs."

"Thanks." She stopped by the desk, feeling ashamed and foolish about her earlier thoughts. "I'm sorry about before, Cassie. The camera business."

"Don't worry about it." Cassie zipped open one of the daily letters that heaped on her desk. "I know I'm a nuisance." She chuckled. "I like being a nuisance with it. See you tomorrow."

"Okay. Don't stay late."

More at ease, Deanna walked to the elevator, checking her watch as she punched the Down button. With any luck, she could surprise Finn by arriving first. It wouldn't take much effort, she knew, to persuade him to fix some blackened chicken and pasta. She was in the mood for something spicy to cap off her first day back in harness.

She could deal with a mountain of paperwork and phone calls there. Then, if she scheduled a break, she could slink into something designed to drive Finn crazy.

They'd have dinner late. Very late, she decided, and swung out of the elevator.

Maybe she'd wrap a few last-minute Christmas gifts, or talk Finn into baking some cookies. She could run a couple of the new segment ideas by him.

The flash of sunlight had her reaching automatically for her tinted glasses. Slipping them on, she climbed into the back of the waiting limo.

"Hi, Tim." She closed her eyes and stretched. The limo was beautifully warm.

"Hi, Miss Reynolds."

"Turned out to be a beautiful day." Out of habit, she reached for the bottle of chilled juice that was always stocked for her. She looked up idly at the back of her driver. Despite the car's warmth, he was huddled inside his coat, his cap tipped low.

467

"Sure did."

Sipping the juice, she flipped open her briefcase. She set the file neatly labeled "Wedding Plans" aside and reached for the daily correspondence Cassie had culled for her to read. She'd always considered the drive to and from the office part of the workday. In this case, she had to make up the time she'd taken with the fitting, and for knocking off early.

But by the third letter, the words were blurring. There was no excuse for being so tired so early in the day. Annoyed, she slid her fingers under her glasses to rub her eyes clear. But they blurred all the more, as if she'd swabbed them with oil. Her head spun once, sickly, and her arm fell heavily to the seat beside her.

So tired, she thought. So hot. As if in slow motion, she tried to shrug out of her coat. The papers fluttered to the floor, and the effort of reaching for them only increased the dizziness.

"Tim." She leaned forward, pressed a hand against the back of the front seat. He didn't answer, but the word had sounded dim and far away to her own ears. As she struggled to focus on him the half-empty bottle of juice slipped from her numbed fingers.

"Something's wrong," she tried to tell him as she slid bonelessly to the plushly carpeted floor of the car. "Something's very wrong."

But he didn't answer. She imagined herself falling through the floor of the limo and into a dark, bottomless pit.

Chapter Twenty-eight

DEANNA DREAMED SHE WAS SWIMMING UP THROUGH red-tinted clouds, slowly, sluggishly pulling herself toward the surface, where a faint, white light glowed through the misty layers. She moaned as she struggled. Not from pain but nausea that rolled up, burning in her throat.

In defense, she kept her eyes closed, taking long, deep breaths and willing the sickness back. Drops of clammy sweat pearled on her skin so that her thin silk blouse clung nastily to her arms and back.

When the worst had passed, she opened her eyes cautiously.

She had been in the car, she remembered. Tim had been driving her home and she'd become ill. But she wasn't home now. Hospital? she wondered dully when she let her eyes carefully open. The room was softly lit with delicate violets trailing up the wallpaper. A white ceiling fan gently stirred the air with a whispering sound of blades. A glossy mahogany bureau held a collection of pretty, colored bottles and pots. A magnificent poinsettia and a miniature blue spruce decorated with silver bells added seasonal flair.

Hospital? she thought again. Groggily, she tried to sit up. Her head spun again, hideously, shooting that fist of nausea back into her stomach. Her vision doubled. When she tried to bring her hand to her face, it felt weighted down. For a moment she could only lie still, fighting back the sickness. She saw that the room was a box, a closed, windowless box. Like a coffin.

A spear of panic sliced through the shock. She reared up, shouting, stumbling drunkenly from the bed. Staggering to a wall, she ran her fingers over the delicate floral wallpaper in a dizzy search for an opening. Trapped. She wheeled around, eyes wide. Trapped.

She saw then what was on the wall over the bed. It was enough to crush the bubbling hysteria. A huge photograph smiled sassily down at her. For several stunned moments Deanna stared at Deanna. Slowly, with the sound of her own heartbeat thudding in her ears, she scanned the rest of the room.

No, there were no doors, no windows, just flowers, bowers of them, wall to wall. But there were other photographs. Dozens of pictures of her were lined on the side walls. Candid shots, magazine covers, press photos stood cheek by jowl against the dainty wallpaper.

"Oh God. Oh God." She heard the whimpering panic in her own voice and bit down fiercely on her lip.

Looking away from her own images, her eyes glassy with shock, she stared at the refectory table, its snowy white runner stiff with starch as a backdrop for silver candle holders, glossy white tapers. Dozens of little treasures had been arranged there: an earring she'd lost months before, a tube of lipstick, a silk scarf Simon had given her one Christmas, a glove of supple red leather—one of a pair that had disappeared the winter before.

There was more. She eased closer, straining against the tidal wave of fear as she studied the collection. A memo she'd handwritten to Jeff, a lock of ebony hair wrapped in gold cord, other photographs of her, always of her, in elegant and ornate frames. The shoes she'd been wearing in the limo were there as well, along with her jacket, neatly folded.

The place was like a shrine, she realized with a shudder. The sound in her throat was feral and frightened. There was a television in the corner, a shelf of leather-bound albums. And most terrifying, cameras bracketed the upper corners of the room. The pinpoints of their red lights beamed like tiny eyes.

She stumbled back, fear soaring like a slickly coated bird. Her gaze sliced from one camera to the other.

"You're watching me." She fought back the terror in her voice. "I know you are. You can't keep me here. They'll look. You know they'll find me. They're probably looking already."

She looked down at her wrist to check the time, but saw that her watch was gone. How long? she wondered frantically. It might have been minutes, or days, since she'd passed out in the car.

The car. Her breath began to hitch. "Tim." She pressed her lips together until the ache snapped through the need to weep. "Tim, you have to let me go. I'll try to help you. I promise that. I'll do whatever I can. Please, come in here, talk to me."

As though only her invitation had been required, a section of the wall slid open. In reflex, Deanna surged forward, only to bite back a moan of despair as her head spun in sickening circles from the drug. Still, she straightened her shoulders and hoped that she hid the worst of her fear.

"Tim," she began, then only stared in confusion.

"Welcome home, Deanna."

His face flushed with shy pleasure, Jeff stepped into the room. He carried a silver tray on which rode a wineglass, a china plate of herbed pasta and a single red rosebud.

"I hope you like the room." In his unhurried and efficient way, he set the tray on the bureau. "It took a long time for me to get it just right. I didn't want you to be just comfortable. I wanted you to be happy. I know there's no view." He turned toward her, eyes too bright, though apology quavered in his voice. "But it's safer this way. No one will bother us when we're in here."

"Jeff." Calm, she ordered herself. She had to stay calm. "You can't keep me here."

471

"Yes I can. I've planned it all carefully. I've had years to work it out. Why don't you sit down, Dee? You're probably feeling a little groggy, and I want you to be comfortable while you eat."

He stepped forward, and though she braced, he didn't touch her.

"Later," he continued, "after you understand everything, you'll feel a lot better. You just need time." He lifted a hand as if to touch her cheek, but drew it away again as if he didn't want to frighten her.

"Please try to relax. You never let yourself relax. I know you might be a little afraid right now, but it's going to be all right. If you fight me, I'll have to . . ." Because he couldn't bear to say the words, he slipped a hypo out of his pocket. "I don't want to." Her instant recoil had him pushing the needle out of sight again. "Really, I don't. And you wouldn't be able to get away."

Smiling again, he moved a table and chair closer to the bed. "You need to eat," he said pleasantly. "You always worried me when it came to taking care of yourself. All those hurried or skipped meals. But I'll take good care of you. Sit down, Deanna."

She could refuse, she thought. She could scream and rant and threaten. And for what? She'd known Jeff, or thought she'd known him, for years. He could be stubborn, she reminded herself. But she'd always been able to reason with him.

"I am hungry," she told him, and hoped her stomach wouldn't rebel. "You'll talk to me while I eat? Explain things to me?" She gave him her best interviewer's smile.

"Yes." The smile burned across his face like a fever. "I thought you might be angry at first."

"I'm not angry. I'm afraid."

"I'd never hurt you." He took one of her limp hands in his and squeezed lightly. "I won't let anyone hurt you. I know you might be thinking about getting past me, Deanna. Getting through the panel. But you can't. I'm really very strong, and you're still weak from the drug. No matter what you do, you'll still be locked in. Sit down."

As if in a dream, she did as he told her. She wanted to run, but even as the thought communicated from brain to body, her legs folded. How could she run when she could barely stand? The drug was still in charge of her system. It was precisely the kind of detail he would have thought of. Precisely the kind of detail that had made him such an invaluable part of her team.

"It's wrong to keep me here, Jeff."

"No, it's not." He set the tray on the table in front of her. "I've thought about it for a long, long time. And this is for the best. For you. I'm always thinking of you. Later on, we can travel together. I've been looking into villas in the south of France. I think you'd like it there." He touched her then, just a brushing caress on her shoulder. Beneath her blouse her skin crawled. "I love you so much."

"Why didn't you ever tell me? You could have talked to me about the way you felt."

"I couldn't. At first I thought it was just because I was shy, but then I realized that it was all like a plan. A life plan. Yours and mine."

Anxious to explain, he pulled up another chair. As he leaned forward, his glasses slid down his nose. While her vision blurred, then cleared, she watched him shove them up again—an old habit, once an endearing one, that now chilled her blood.

"There were things you needed to do, experiences—and men— you had to get out of your system before we could be together. I understood that, Dee. I never blamed you for Finn. It hurt me." Resting his hands on his knees, he let out a sigh. "But I didn't blame you. And I couldn't blame him." His face brightened again. "How could I when I knew how perfect you were? The first time I saw you on TV, I couldn't get my breath. It scared me a little. You were looking right at me, into me. I'll never forget it. You see, I was so lonely before. An only child. I grew up in this house. You're not eating, Deanna. I wish you would."

Obediently, she picked up her fork. He wanted to talk. Seemed eager to. The best way to escape, she calculated, was to understand. "You told me you grew up in Iowa."

"That's where my mother took me later. My mother was wild." The apology crept back into his voice. "She would never listen to anyone, never obey the rules. So naturally, Uncle Matthew had to punish her. He was older, you see. He was head of the family. He'd keep her in this room, trying to make her see that there were proper ways to do things, and improper ways." His face changed as he spoke, tightening around the mouth and eyes, growing somehow older, sterner. "But my mother never learned, no matter how hard my uncle tried to teach her. She ran away and got pregnant. When I was six, they took her away. She had a breakdown, and I came to live with Uncle Matthew. There was no one else to take me in, you see. And it was his family duty."

Deanna choked down a bite of pasta. It stuck like paste in her throat, but she was afraid to try the wine. He could have drugged it, she thought, like the bottle of juice. "I'm sorry, Jeff, about your mother."

"It's okay." He shrugged it off like a snake shedding skin. His face smoothed out again like a sheet stroked with careful hands. "She didn't love me. No one's ever loved me but Uncle Matthew. And you. It's just wine, Dee. Your favorite kind." Grinning at the joke, he picked up the glass and sipped to show her. "I didn't put anything in it. I didn't have to, because you're here now. With me."

Drugged or not, she avoided the wine, unsure how it would mix with the drugs in her system. "What happened to your mother?"

"She had dementia. She died. Is your dinner all right? I know pasta's your favorite."

"It's fine." Deanna slipped another bite through her stiff lips. "How old were you when she died?"

"I don't know. Doesn't matter, I was happy here, with my uncle." It made him nervous to talk about his mother, so he didn't. "He was a great man. Strong and good. He hardly ever had to punish me, because I was good, too. I wasn't a trial to him, like my mother was. We took care of each other." He spoke quickly now, fresh excitement blooming. "He was proud of me. I studied hard and I didn't hang out with other kids. I didn't need them. I mean, all they wanted to do was ride in fast cars and listen to loud music and fight with their parents. I had respect. And I never forgot things like cleaning my room or brushing my teeth. Uncle Matthew always told me I didn't need anybody but family. And he was the only family I had. Then, when he died, there was you. So I knew it was right."

"Jeff." Deanna used all her skills to keep the conversation flowing, to steer it in the direction she wanted. "Do you think your uncle would approve of what you're doing now?"

"Oh, absolutely." He beamed, his face sunny and innocent and terrifying. "He talks to me all the time, up here." He tapped his head, winked. "He told me to be patient, to wait until the time was right. You know when I first started sending you letters?"

"Yes, I remember."

"I dreamed about Uncle Matthew for the first time then. Only it wasn't like a dream. It was so real. He told me I had to court you, the way a gentleman would. That I had to be patient. He always said that good things take time. He told me that I would have to wait, and that I had to look out for you. Men are supposed to cherish their women, to protect them. People have forgotten that. No one seems to cherish anyone anymore."

"Is that why you killed Angela, Jeff? To protect me?"

"I planned that for months." He leaned back again, rested one bent leg across his knee. Conversations with Deanna had always been a high point of his life. And this, he thought, was the very best. "You didn't know that I let her think I was taking Lew's place."

"Lew's? Lew McNeil's?"

"After I killed him—"

"Lew." Her fork rattled against the china when it slipped through her fingers. "You killed Lew."

"He betrayed you. I had to punish him. And he used Simon. Until I started to work with you, I never really had friends. Simon's my friend. I was going to kill him, too, but I realized he'd been used. It wasn't really his fault, was it?"

"No." She said it quickly, punctuating the word by laying her hand over Jeff's. "No, Jeff, it wasn't Simon's fault. I care very much about Simon. I wouldn't want you to hurt him."

"That's what I thought." He grinned, a child praised by an indulgent adult. "You see, I know you so well, Deanna. I know everything about you. Your family, your friends. Your favorite foods and colors. Where you like to shop. I know everything you're thinking. It's as though I were right inside your head. Or you're inside mine," he added slowly. "Sometimes I'd think you were inside mine. I knew you wanted Angela to go away. And I knew you'd never hurt her yourself. You're too gentle, too kind." He turned his hand over to squeeze hers. "So I did it for you. I arranged to meet her in the parking lot at CBC. She sent her driver away, just like I'd told her to. I let her in, took her down to the studio. I'd told her that I had copied papers from the office. Story ideas, guests, plans for remotes. She was going to buy them from me. Only she didn't tell me you were coming." Incredibly, his bottom lip poked out in a pout. "She lied to me about that."

"You killed her. And you turned the cameras on."

"I was angry with you." His mouth quivered, his eyes lowered. Deanna gripped her fork again with some idea of using it as a weapon. The effects of the drug were wearing off, and she felt stronger. She thought she could thank fear for that. But his eyes lifted to hers and the searing light in them had her fingers going numb.

"I knew it was wrong, but I wanted to hurt you. I nearly wanted to kill you. You were going to marry him, Dee. I could understand your sleeping with him. Weak flesh. Uncle Matthew explained all about how sex can pervert, and how weak people can be. Even

476

you." The hand that covered hers tightened, tightened, until bone rubbed bone. "So I understood, and I was patient, because I always knew you'd come to me. But you couldn't marry him, you couldn't take vows. I knew it was you when you opened the door. I always know when it's you. I hit you. I wanted to hit you again, but I couldn't. So I carried you to the chair, and I put Angela in the other one and turned on the camera. I wanted you to see what I'd done for you. I'd already been upstairs, in your office." He compressed his lips, sighed and gently released her throbbing hand. "It was wrong of me to wreck your office. I shouldn't have gone to Finn's house, either. I'm sorry."

He said it as though he'd neglected to keep a luncheon appointment.

"Jeff, have you ever told anyone about your feelings?"

"Just my uncle, when we talk in my head. He was sure you'd understand soon, and come home with me. And after I heard what that creep did to you in the parking lot, I knew it was nearly time."

"Marshall?"

"He tried to hurt you. Joe told me how he'd acted, so I waited for him. I killed him the same way I'd killed the others. It was symbolic, Deanna. My vision destroyed their vision. It's almost holy, don't you think?"

"It's not holy to kill, Jeff."

"You're too forgiving." His eyes scanned her face, adoringly. "If you forgive people who've hurt you, they'll only hurt you again. You have to protect what's yours."

He remembered the dog that had come into their yard time after time, digging up Uncle Matthew's flowers, spoiling the grass. He'd cried when his uncle had poisoned the dog. Cried until Uncle Matthew had explained to him why it was right and honorable to defend your own against any intruder. With that in mind, he got up and went to the bureau. He opened the top drawer and took out a list.

"I've planned it," he told her. "You and I always make lists and plan things out. We're not the type who run off without thinking, are we?" Beaming again, he offered the list to her.

LEW MCNEIL
ANGELA PERKINS
MARSHALL PIKE
DAN GARDNER
JAMIE THOMAS
FINN RILEY?

"Finn," was all she could say.

"He's not for sure. I put him down in case he hurt you. I nearly did it once before. Nearly. But at the last minute I realized I was only going to kill him because I was jealous. It was like Uncle Matthew was there, and he jerked the rifle at the last minute. I was really glad I didn't kill him when I saw how upset you were that he'd been shot."

"In Greektown," Deanna said through trembling lips. "That day in Greektown. You shot him?"

"It was a mistake. I'm really sorry."

"Oh God." Horrified, she cringed back. "Oh my God."

"It was a mistake." His voice was sulky, dangerously so. Jeff looked away from her. "I said I was sorry. I won't do anything to him unless he hurts you."

"He hasn't. He won't."

"Then I won't have to do anything about him."

Her palm dampened against the paper, and her heart began to beat heavily in her throat. "Promise me you won't, Jeff. It's important to me that Finn's safe. He's been very good to me."

"I'm better for you."

There was a child's petulance on his face now. Deanna exploited the moment. "Promise me, Jeff, or I'll be very unhappy. You don't want that, do you?"

"No." He struggled between her needs and his own. "I guess it doesn't matter now. Not now that you're here."

"You have to promise." She clamped her teeth together to keep the desperation from her voice. Reason, she told herself. Calm reason. "I know you wouldn't break your word to me."

"All right. If it makes you happy." To show his sincerity, he took out a pen and scratched Finn's name off the list. "See?"

"Thank you. And Dan Gardner—"

"No." His voice sharp, he folded the page. "He's already hurt you, Dee. He's said terrible things about you; he helped Angela try to ruin you. He has to be punished."

"But he doesn't matter, Jeff. He's nothing." Calm, she reminded herself. Calm but firm. Adult to child. "And Jamie Thomas, that was years and years ago. I don't care about them."

"I do. I care. I'd have killed him first, right away, but he was in Europe. Hiding out," he said scornfully. "It's not easy to get a weapon through customs, so I was patient." Now he beamed. "He's back now, you know. He's in New Hampshire. I'll be going there soon."

The drug was no longer making her ill, but the nausea rolled greasily in her stomach. "I don't care about him. About any of them, Jeff. I don't want you to hurt them for me."

He turned his face away, sulking. "I don't want to talk about this anymore."

"I want—"

"You have to think about what I want, too." He shoved the list back in the drawer, slammed it hard enough to rattle bottles. "I'm only thinking of you."

"Yes, I know. I know you are. But if you go to New York to kill Gardner, or New Hampshire for Jamie, I'll be all alone here. I don't want to be locked up alone, Jeff."

"Don't worry." His tone gentled. "I've got plenty of time, and I'll be very careful. I'm so glad you're here."

"Would you let me go outside please? I need some air."

"I can't. Not yet. It isn't part of the plan." He sat again, leaning forward. "You need three months."

Horror drained her blood. "You can't keep me locked up like this for three months."

"It's all right. You'll have everything you need. Books, TV, company. I'll rent movies for you, cook your meals. I've bought clothes for you." He sprang up to slide open another panel. "See? I spent weeks choosing just the right things." He gestured inside to the closet full of slacks and dresses and jackets. "And there's shirts and sweaters, nightclothes and underthings in the bureau. Over here . . ." He pushed open another hidden door. "The bathroom."

He flushed, stared at his shoes. "There aren't any cameras in there. I swear. I wouldn't spy on you in the bathroom. I stocked your favorite bath oils and soaps, your cosmetics. You'll have everything you need."

Everything you need. Everything you need. The words spun around and around in her head. She couldn't keep the hitch out of her voice. "I don't want to be locked up."

"I'm sorry. That's the only thing I can't give you right now. Soon, when you've really come to understand, it'll be different. But anything else you want, I'll get for you. Whenever I have to leave, you'll be all right here. The room's secure, soundproofed. Even if someone came into the house, they wouldn't find you. Outside the door is a bookcase. It's really cool. I designed it myself. No one would ever guess there was a room in here, so you'll be safe and sound whenever I'm gone. And when I'm busy around the house, I can watch you." He pointed toward the cameras. "So if you need me, I'll know."

"They'll come and find me, Jeff. Sooner or later. They won't understand. You have to let me go."

"No, I have to keep you. Do you want to watch TV?" He crossed over, picked up the remote from the nightstand. "We have full cable."

Fighting back a hysterical laugh, she pressed her fingers to her eyes. "No, no, not now."

"You can watch whenever you want. And the shelf is full of

480

videos. Movies, and tapes I've taken of you. And the scrapbooks."
He bustled around the room, an energetic host anxious to entertain. "I've kept them for you. Everything that's ever been written
up on you is in here. Or there's the stereo. I have all your favorite
music. There's a little refrigerator in the bathroom that I stocked
with drinks and snacks."

"Jeff." She could feel that bubble of panic swelling. Her hands
shook as she stood. "You've gone to a lot of trouble. I understand
that. And I understand that you've done what you thought you had
to do. But this is wrong. You're keeping me prisoner."

"No, no, no." He came to her quickly, grabbing her hands when
she jerked back. "You're like the princess in the fairy tale, and I'm
protecting you. I'm cherishing you. It's like you're under a spell,
Dee. One day you'll wake up and I'll be here. And we'll be happy."

"I'm not under a spell." She yanked away, fury simmering under
fear like an exotic stew. "And I'm not a goddamn princess. I'm a
human being, with the right to make my own choices. You can't
lock me up and expect me to be grateful because I've got bathroom
privileges."

"I knew you'd be angry at first." Disappointment sighed
through his voice as he reached down for her dinner dishes. "But
you'll calm down."

"The hell I will." She leaped at him, striking out with her free
hand. The first blow glanced off his cheekbone. China shattered on
the floor and flew like bullets. Snarling, she scrambled after a shard.

She screamed, fighting like a madwoman as he wrestled her to
the floor. He was strong, so much stronger than he looked with
those long, gangly arms. He made no sound, no sound at all,
simply clamped a hand painfully on her wrist until her fingers
opened to release the makeshift weapon.

He dragged her to the bed, stoically suffering her flailing feet
and fists. When she was pressed under him, his erection hard
against her thigh, her terror doubled.

There were worse things than being locked in. "No!" She tried to buck him off, her fingers fisting and unfisting while he clamped her hands over her head.

"I want you, Deanna. God, I want you." His fumbling kiss dampened her jaw. The sensation of her body writhing beneath his had a red haze of need cloaking his vision. Her heart was chugging like a piston against his, and her skin was soft as water, hot as fire. "Please, please." He was almost weeping as his mouth covered hers. "Just let me touch you."

"No." Sickened, she turned her head. Control. She grasped onto her only hope. "You'd be no better than Jamie. You're hurting me, Jeff. You have to stop hurting me."

Tears tracked down his cheeks when he lifted his head. "I'm sorry. Deanna, I'm so sorry. It's just that I've waited so long. We won't make love until you're ready. I swear it. Don't be afraid of me."

"I am afraid." He wouldn't rape her, she realized, and was almost ashamed that she was willing to settle for that. "You have me locked up. You've told me no one can find me. What if something happened to you? I could die here."

"Nothing's going to happen. I've planned everything, every detail. I love you, Deanna, and I know under it all, you love me too. You've shown me in hundreds of ways. The way you smile at me. The way you touch me, or laugh. The way you'll catch my eye across the room. You made me your director. I can't begin to explain what that meant to me. You trusted me to guide you. You believed in me. In us."

"It's not love. I don't love you."

"You're just not ready yet. Now you need to rest." He braceleted her wrists in one hand, fought the hypo free with the other.

"No. Don't." She twisted, wrenched, begged. "Please don't. I can't go anywhere. You've said I can't get away."

"You need to rest," he said quietly, and slid the needle under her skin. "I'll watch out for you, Deanna."

Her head lolled back, and his tears fell to mix with hers. He waited, miserably, until her struggles to fight off the drug ceased. When her body went limp, he clamped down on the urge to stroke his hands over it.

Not until she's ready, he reminded himself, content to brush the dampness from her cheeks. Gently, he shifted her onto the pillows and placed a chaste kiss on her brow.

His princess, he thought, studying her as she slept. He'd built her an ivory tower. They'd live there together. Forever.

"Isn't she perfect, Uncle Matthew? Isn't she beautiful? You'd have loved her too. You'd have known she was the one, the only one."

He sighed. Uncle Matthew wasn't speaking to him. He'd been wrong to allow sex to twist his plans. He'd have to be punished. Bread and water only for two days. That's what his uncle would have done. Meekly he crouched down to clean up the broken dishes. He tidied the room, turned the lights down. With one last, longing glance at Deanna, he slipped out of the room, shutting the panel silently.

"I THINK IT WOULD BE BEST if you'd take Miss Reynolds home." Jenner rode up in the elevator with Finn. He still resented Finn's earlier pressuring but he covered it with quiet dignity. "I'd prefer that she was out of the office when we re-interrogate her staff."

"The minute she finds out that's what you intend to do, she won't budge." Pleased that matters seemed to be moving forward, Finn leaned against the wall. "I'll do what I can to convince her to stay out of the way, but that's the best I can offer. Deanna's fiercely loyal. She won't want to accept that one of her own people is involved."

"She may have to." Jenner headed out of the car the moment the doors opened. "If she kicks up too much of a fuss, we can take her people in to the station. She'll like that less."

"You can try. You don't know her the way I do, Lieutenant. Cassie," he said as he walked into the reception area. "She in?"

"No." Baffled, she stopped gathering the stacks of mail she'd intended to post on the way home. "What are you doing here?"

"Cassie Drew?" Jenner inclined his head. "We'd like to ask you some more questions. I wonder if you could get the rest of Miss Reynolds's staff together?"

"I—I don't know who's still in the building. Finn?"

"Why don't you buzz everyone," he suggested. "And find Deanna for me, will you?" He wanted to get her out, and quickly. Some instinct told him to hurry. He intended to heed it. "Tell her I'm in the mood to cook."

"She's gone home. She left right after you called."

"I called?" He felt uneasy. "Did Deanna tell you I called?"

"No, you left a message about a meeting, and getting home early. It came in during her fitting, and she left as soon as she was done."

Finn shoved open the door to Deanna's office, took one quick scan. "Did you take the message?"

"No, I was in with her when it came in. Jeff took it."

His eyes were like blue ice when he turned back. "Did he say he spoke to me?"

"Yes—I guess. Is something wrong?" Fear began to gnaw through confusion. Cassie's gaze darted from Jenner to Finn and back again. "Is something wrong with Deanna?"

Rather than answer, Finn grabbed the phone and punched in his home number. Two rings later, he heard the answering machine click on. With his teeth set, he waited through the message. "Deanna? Pick up if you're there. Pick up the phone, damn it."

"She'd have to be home by now. She left more than an hour ago. Finn, what's going on?"

"What did Jeff tell her?"

"That you'd called, just as I said."

"Why didn't you answer the phone?"

"I—" Frightened, and not knowing why, she put a hand on the desk to keep her balance. "I didn't hear the phone. I didn't hear it."

"Where's Jeff?"

"I don't know. He—"

But Finn was already racing down the hall. He burst into one room, found Simon in consultation with Margaret. "Hey, Finn. Don't bother to knock."

"Where's Jeff?"

"He wasn't feeling well. He went home." Simon was rising from the desk as he spoke. "What's the problem?"

"Finn." Though her hands were stiff with cold, Cassie tugged on Finn's sleeve. "I called for Tim myself. I talked to him. He met her downstairs."

"Get him on the line. Now."

"Mr. Riley." Jenner spoke calmly as Cassie rushed off to obey. "I've got a black-and-white on its way to your house right now. Odds are Miss Reynolds wasn't answering the phone. That's all."

"What the hell's going on?" Simon demanded. "What's happened now?"

"Tim doesn't answer his page." Cassie stood in the hallway, a hand at her throat. "I got his machine on his home phone."

"Give me the address," Jenner said briskly.

Chapter Twenty-nine

"Mr. Riley, I know you're upset, but you're going to have to let me handle this."

Jenner stood on the sidewalk in front of Jeff's suburban home, aware he was only temporarily blocking Finn from storming the door.

"She's in there. I know it."

"Not to belittle your instincts, but we can't know that. We only know that Jeff Hyatt delivered a message. We're going to check everything out," Jenner reminded him. "The same way we checked out the driver, Tim O'Malley."

"Who wasn't home," Finn ground out, staring at the windows behind Jenner. "And the company car wasn't in the lot. And no one's seen O'Malley since sometime in the afternoon." His gaze, icy still, cut like a blade back to Jenner. "So where the hell is he? Where the hell is Deanna?"

"That's what we're going to try to find out. I'm not going to waste my time telling you to get back in your car and go home, but I am telling you to let me handle this with Hyatt."

"So handle it."

His voice might have been cold, his eyes frosty, but Jenner recognized a powder keg ready to explode. The melodious sound of church bells rang out when Jenner pressed the doorbell. Beneath his feet was a mat with the word WELCOME woven in black. In the center of the door was a glossy Christmas wreath topped by a bright red bow. Colored lights had been neatly strung around the frame. Jeff Hyatt appeared ready for the holidays.

He'd known they would come, and he was ready. Clad comfortably in a tattered sweater and baggy sweats, Jeff descended the stairs. He'd watched them arrive from his bedroom window. He smiled to himself as he paused before the door. This, he knew, was the next step toward freeing Deanna. Toward binding her.

He pulled open the door. "Hey, Finn." Confusion clouded his eyes as he looked at his visitors. "What's up?"

"Where is she?" Finn spaced each word precisely. Yes, there was a powder keg inside him, and only the knowledge that it could explode over Deanna kept it tapped. "I want to know where she is."

"Hey." His grin tilted into confusion. Jeff stared blankly at Finn, then at Jenner. "What's going on? Is something wrong?"

"Mr. Hyatt." Jenner stepped neatly between the two men. "I need to ask you some questions."

"Okay." Jeff rubbed his fingertips against his temple. "No problem. Do you want to come in?"

"Thank you. Mr. Hyatt," Jenner began, "did you relay a message to Miss Reynolds at approximately three o'clock this afternoon?"

"Yeah. Why?" Wincing, Jeff continued to massage his temple. "Jesus. Can we sit down? I've got this monster headache." He turned into the living area. The furnishings were straight out of a catalogue. Matching tables, matching chairs, twin lamps, a soulless, practical suite favored by uninspired bachelors or newlyweds on a strict budget. Only Jeff sat.

"You told her I called?"

"Sure I did." Jeff's smile was cautious. His eyes were wary. "Your assistant said to tell Dee you had this meeting and were planning on getting home early."

"You didn't talk to Mr. Riley?" Jenner demanded.

"No. I thought it was kind of weird that the call came through my office, but when I went to tell Dee, I saw that she and Cassie were all involved. Dee was getting her wedding dress fitted. She looked incredible."

"Why did you leave the office early?"

"This headache. I haven't been able to ditch it all day. It makes it hard to concentrate. Listen." He stood again, obviously impatient and bewildered. "What's this all about? Is it some kind of crime to deliver a phone message?"

"What time did you leave the office?"

"Right after I talked to Dee. I came home—well, I went to the store first, picked up some more heavy-duty aspirin. I thought if I laid down awhile . . ." His voice trailed off. "Something's happened to Dee." As if his legs wouldn't support him, he lowered slowly to the couch again. "Oh my God. Is she hurt?"

"She hasn't been seen since she left the office," Jenner told him.

"Oh God. Jesus. Have you talked to Tim? Didn't he drive her home?"

"We're unable to locate Mr. O'Malley."

On a shaking breath, Jeff rubbed his hands over his face. "It wasn't a message from your assistant, was it, Finn? I didn't ask any questions. I wasn't paying attention." His jaw quivered when he dropped his hands again. His eyes were dark with an emotion disguising itself as fear. "All I could think about was getting home and going to bed. I just said, sure, I'll tell her. And I did."

"I don't believe you." Finn didn't move a muscle, but the words cracked toward Jeff like a slap. "You're a meticulous man, Jeff. That's how Deanna describes you." And the minutes were ticking away. "Why would you, with everything that's been going on, pass along a half-baked message like that?"

"It was supposed to be from you," Jeff shot back. The way Finn studied him, as if he could see all the secrets swimming in his brain, put Jeff on edge. "Why wouldn't I pass it along?"

"Then you won't mind if we go through the house." Finn turned to Jenner. "Through every inch of it."

"You think I—" Jeff snapped his mouth shut, pushed himself from the couch. "Go ahead," he said to both men. "Search it. Go through every room. I want you to."

"We appreciate your cooperation, Mr. Hyatt. It would be best if you came with us while we do."

"Fine." Jeff stood for a moment, staring at Finn. "I know how you feel about her, and I guess I can't really blame you for this."

They went through every room, searching through closets, cupboards, through the garage, where Jeff's undistinguished sedan was parked. It took less than twenty minutes.

Finn noted the tidy, practical furnishings, the well-pressed, practical clothes. As a director for a number-one show, he'd be well compensated financially. And Finn could see that he sure as hell wasn't spending any money on himself.

Just what, he wondered, was Jeff Hyatt saving his pennies for?

"I wish she was here." Jeff felt a quick, gleeful surge as they walked past the bookcase. "At least she'd be safe. I want to help. I want to do something. We can start with the press. We can get national coverage. By morning we'll have everyone in the country looking for her. Everybody knows her face." He looked beseechingly at Finn. "Someone will see her. He can't keep her locked in a tower somewhere."

"Wherever he has her"—Finn never took his eyes off Jeff's—"I'll find her."

Without a backward glance, Finn strode out of the house. Seconds later, the sound of his engine roared.

"I can't blame him," Jeff muttered. He looked toward Jenner. "No one could."

He locked up carefully behind the policeman. His smile grew wider, wider, wider as he climbed the stairs. They might come back. A small, grinning part of him hoped they would. Because he would lead them right through the house, right by the hidden room where his princess slept.

They would never find her. And eventually they would go away. He and Deanna would be alone. Always.

He turned on the television in his room. The evening news didn't interest him. He flipped a switch on the splitter behind the set and settled down to watch Deanna.

She slept on, still as a doll behind the glass of the screen. The tears he wept now were of simple joy.

Jenner caught up with Finn at home. He made no mention of the speed limits Finn had ignored. "We'll be checking out Hyatt and O'Malley thoroughly. Why don't you be a reporter and get the story on the air?"

"It'll be on the air." Standing in the chill December wind, Finn struggled to stave off panic. "Hyatt looked as innocent as a newborn lamb, didn't he?"

"Yes, he did." Jenner blew out a smoky breath. Three days until Christmas, he thought. He would do everything in his power to be certain it was a day of celebration.

"I had some trouble with that house," Finn said after a moment.

"What kind?"

"Nothing out of place. Not a crooked picture, not a dustball. Books and magazines lined up like soldiers, furniture all but geometrically arranged. Everything centered, squared and bandbox clean."

"I noticed. Obsessive."

"That's how it strikes me. He fits the pattern."

Jenner acknowledged that with a slight nod. "A man can be obsessively neat without being obsessively homicidal."

"Where was the Christmas tree?" Finn muttered.

"The Christmas tree?"

"He's got the wreath, he's got the lights. But no tree. You'd think he'd have a tree somewhere."

"Maybe he's one of those traditionalists who don't put it up until Christmas Eve." But the omission was interesting.

"One more thing, Lieutenant. He claims he came home early to lie down. The bed in his room was the only thing mussed up. Pillow scrunched a bit, bedspread wrinkled. We got him up from his nap."

"So he says."

"Why did he have his shoes on?" Finn's eyes gleamed in the lowering light. "The laces were tied in double knots. Someone that neat doesn't lie down on his bed with his shoes on."

He'd missed that clue, damn it, Jenner thought. "I believe I mentioned this before, Mr. Riley, you have a good eye."

HE COULDN'T STAY AT HOME. Not without her. Finn did the only thing that seemed possible. He went back to the station, avoiding the newsroom. He couldn't bear to answer questions, to be asked questions. He went to his office, brewed a pot of strong coffee. He added a healthy dose of whiskey to the first cup.

He booted up his computer.

"Finn." Fran stood in the doorway, her face splotchy, her eyes swollen and red. Before he'd risen completely, she took a stumbling step forward. "Oh God, Finn."

He stroked her shaking shoulders, though he felt no well of comfort that he could offer. It was just the routine, the show of comfort that meant nothing to anyone.

"I had to take Kelsey to the pediatrician for her checkup. I wasn't here. I wasn't even here."

"You couldn't have changed anything."

"I might have." She shoved away, eyes fierce now. "How did he get to her? I've heard a dozen different stories."

"This is the place for them. Truth or accuracy, which do you want?"

"Both."

"One's not the same as the other, Fran. You've been in the game long enough. Accurately, we don't know. She left early, went out to the lot where her car and driver were supposed to be waiting. Now she's gone. Her driver seems to have vanished into thin air."

She didn't like the cool control of his voice or the workaday hum of his computer. "Then what's the truth, Finn? Why don't you tell me what the truth is?"

"The truth is that whoever has been sending her those notes, whoever killed Lew McNeil, Angela and Pike, has Deanna. They've got an APB out on her, and one on O'Malley and the car."

"Tim wouldn't. He couldn't."

"Why?" The single word was like a bullet. "Because you know him? Because he's part of Deanna's extended family? Fuck that. He could have." Finn sat down, drained half his coffee. The shock of caffeine and whiskey spread through him like velvet lightning. "But I don't think he did. I can't be sure until he turns up. If he turns up."

"Why wouldn't he?" Fran demanded. "He's worked for Dee for two years. He's never missed a single day."

"He's never been dead before, has he?" He swore at her, at himself when her color faded to paste. Rising, he poured her whiskey, straight. "I'm sorry, Fran. I'm half out of my mind."

"How can you sit in here and say things like that? How can you work, think about work, when Dee's out there somewhere? This isn't some international disaster you're covering, goddamn it, where you're the steady, unflappable journalist. This is Dee."

He jammed useless hands in his pockets. "When something's important, vital, when the answer means everything, you sit, you work, you think it through, you take all the facts and create a scenario that plays. Something that's accurate. I think Jeff's got her."

"Jeff." Fran choked on whiskey. "You're crazy. Jeff's devoted to Dee, and he's harmless as a baby. He'd never hurt her."

"I'm counting on that," he said dully. "I'm betting my life on it.

I need everything you've got on him, Fran. Personnel records, memos, files. I need your impressions, your observations. I need you to help me."

She said nothing, only studied his face. No, his eyes weren't cold, she realized. They were burning up. And there was terror behind them. "Give me ten minutes," she said, and left him alone.

She came back in less than her allotted time with a stack of files and a box of computer disks. "His employment record, résumé, application for employment. Tax info." Fran smiled weakly. "I lifted his desk calendars. He keeps them from year to year. They were all filed."

Meticulous. Obsessive. Though his blood iced, Finn accessed the first disk.

"That's his personnel file from CBC. I hope you don't mind breaking the law."

"Not a bit. This application is from April eighty-nine. When did Dee go on air at CBC?"

"About a month before that." Fran reached for the whiskey to unclog her throat. "It doesn't prove anything."

"No, but it's a fact." The first he could build on. "Same address he's got now. How'd he afford a house like that when he'd been working as a radio gofer?"

"He inherited it. His uncle left it to him. Finn, I had to call Dee's family." She pressed a hand to her mouth. "They're getting the first flight out in the morning."

"I'm sorry." He stared hard at the screen. Families. He'd never had one to worry about before. "I should have done it."

"No, I didn't mean that. I just—I don't know what to say to them."

"Tell them we're going to get her back. That's the truth. Fran, see if you can find the date in his calendar when Lew McNeil was killed. It was February ninety-two."

"Yeah, I remember." She opened the book, flipped through the pages, skimming Jeff's neat, precise notations. "We had a show that day. Jeff was directing. I remember because we had snow and every-body was worried that the audience would be thin."

"Do you remember if he came in?"

"Sure, he was here. He never missed. Looks like he had a ten o'clock meeting with Simon."

"He'd have had time," Finn murmured.

"Christ Almighty, do you really think he could have gone to New York, shot Lew, come back and waltzed into the studio to direct a show, all before lunch?"

Yes, Finn thought coldly. Oh yes, he did. "Fact: Lew was killed about seven—that's Central time. There's an hour's time difference between Chicago and New York. Speculation: He flies in and out, maybe he charters a plane. I need his receipts."

"He doesn't keep his personal stuff here."

"Then I'll have to get back in his house. You make sure he comes in tomorrow morning. And you make sure he stays."

She got up, poured coffee into her whiskey. "All right. What else?"

"Let's see what else we can find."

SHE'D LOST TRACK OF TIME. Day or night, there was no differ-ence in the claustrophobic world Jeff had created for her. Her head was cotton from the drug, her stomach raw, but she ate the break-fast he'd left for her. She didn't open the plain white envelope he'd left on her tray.

For a timeless, sweaty interlude, she tried to find an opening in the wall, had pried and poked with a spoon until her fingers had cramped uselessly. All she'd accomplished was to mar the pristine wallpaper.

She couldn't be sure if he was gone, or how long she'd been alone. Then she remembered the television and jumped like a cat on the remote.

Still morning, she thought, her eyes filming with tears as she scanned the channels. How easy it was to time your life around the familiar schedule of daytime TV. The bright laughter of a familiar game show was both mocking and soothing.

She'd slept through her own show, she realized, and choked back a bitter laugh.

Where was Finn? What was he doing? Where was he looking for her?

She rose mechanically, walked into the bathroom. Though she'd already checked once, she repeated the routine of standing on the lip of the tub, climbing onto the lid of the toilet and searching for hidden cameras.

She had no choice but to trust Jeff that he wouldn't pry in this room. She slid the door closed, tried not to think about the lack of a lock. And she stripped.

She had to bite back the fear that he would come in when she was most vulnerable. She needed the cold, bracing spray to help clear her mind. She scrubbed hard, letting her thoughts focus as she soaped and rinsed, soaped and rinsed.

He hadn't missed a detail, she thought. Her brand of shampoo, of powder, creams. She used them all, finding some comfort in the daily routine. Wrapped in a bath sheet, she walked back into the bedroom to go through the drawers.

She chose a sweater, trousers. Just the sort of outfit she would pick for a day of relaxing at home. Ignoring the fresh shudder, she carried the outfit, and the lacy underwear he'd provided, into the bathroom.

Dressed, she began to pace. Pacing, she began to plan.

FINN PARKED HIS CAR HALF a block down, then backtracked on foot. He walked straight to Jeff Hyatt's front door. He didn't bother to knock. Since he'd just hung up his car phone with Fran, he knew Jeff was in the office.

Finn had the extra set of keys Fran had taken from Jeff's

bottom desk drawer. There were three locks. A lot of security, he mused, for a quiet neighborhood. He unbolted all three and, once inside, took the precaution of locking up again.

He started upstairs first, clamping down on the urge to dive wildly into desk and files. Instead he searched meticulously, going through each drawer, each paper with his reporter's eye keen for any tiny detail. He wanted a receipt, some proof that Jeff had traveled to New York and back on the day of Lew's murder.

The police might overlook his reporter's instinct, but they wouldn't overlook facts. Once they had Jeff in custody, they would sweat out of him Deanna's whereabouts. He kept his eyes open, too, for some proof that Jeff had another house, a room, an apartment. He might be holding her there.

He wouldn't believe she was dead.

The pattern so far was to kill people in public places.

He shut the last drawer of the desk and moved to the files.

By the time he'd finished, his palms were damp. Biting back the taste of despair, he strode from the office into Jeff's bedroom. He'd found nothing, absolutely nothing except proof that Jeff Hyatt was an organized, dedicated employee who lived quietly and well, almost too well, within his means.

WHILE FINN SEARCHED THE bedroom, Deanna paced the floor beneath him. She knew she would have only one chance, and that failure would be more than risky. It might be fatal.

IN THE ROOM ABOVE, FINN scanned row after row of videotapes. The man was beyond a buff, Finn mused. He was fanatical. The neat labels indicated television series, movies, news events. Over a hundred black cases lined the wall beside the television. Finn juggled the remote in his hand, deciding if he had time after searching the house, he'd screen a few to see if there was anything more personal on tape.

He set the remote down, only a push of a button away from bringing Deanna to life on screen. He turned to the closet.

The scent of mothballs, an old woman's odor, tickled his nostrils. Slacks hung straight and true, jackets graced padded hangers. The shoes were stretched on trees. The photo album he found on the shelf revealed nothing but snapshots of an elderly man, sometimes alone, sometimes with Jeff beside him. His jaw seemed permanently clenched, his lips withered to a scowl. Beneath each shot was a careful notation.

Uncle Matthew on 75th birthday. June 1983. Uncle Matthew and Jeff, Easter 1977. Uncle Matthew, November 1988.

There was no one else in the book. Just a man, young, a little thin, and his hard-faced uncle. Never a young girl or a laughing child, a romping pet.

The book felt unhealthy, diseased, in his hand. Finn slid it back on the shelf, careful to align the edges.

Details, he thought grimly. Two could play.

Underwear was tucked into the top dresser drawer. All snowy white boxers, pressed and folded. There was nothing beneath them but plain white paper, lightly scented with lilac.

It was almost worse than the mothballs, Finn thought, and moved down to the next drawer.

None of the usual hiding places was utilized. He found no papers, no packets taped to the undersides or backs of drawers, no valuables tucked into the toes of shoes. The nightstand drawer held a current *TV Guide* with selected programs highlighted in yellow. A pad and a sharpened pencil and an extra handkerchief joined it.

He'd been in the house for nearly an hour when he hit pay dirt. The diary was under the pillow. It was leather-bound, glossy and locked. Finn was reaching in his pocket for his penknife when he heard the rattle of a key in the lock.

"Goddamn it, Fran." He glanced back at the closet, rejecting it instantly not only as a cliché, but also as a humiliating one. He'd rather face a foe than hide from one. He stepped forward toward the bedroom door just as Jeff walked down the hallway, whistling on his way to the kitchen.

"Don't seem too devastated, do you? You son of a bitch." Muttering under his breath, Finn slipped toward the stairs.

HE COULDN'T WAIT TO SEE HER. Jeff knew he was taking a chance leaving the office when Fran was so insistent that he stay. But he'd slipped out, antsy to get home. To get to Deanna. The office was in an uproar, he thought. No one could work, and he could always claim to have needed to be alone. Nobody would blame him.

He poured a glass of milk, arranged fancy tea cookies on a china plate and put them all on a tray with another single rose.

She'd be rested now, he was certain. She'd be feeling better, more at home. And soon, very soon, she would see how well he could care for her.

Finn waited at the top of the stairs. He heard Jeff whistling and the sound of dishes ringing together. He heard the footsteps, a quiet click, followed moments later by another.

Then he heard nothing at all.

Where did the bastard go? he wondered. Moving quietly, he descended the stairs. He slipped like a shadow from room to room. By the time he reached the kitchen, he was baffled. He saw the bakery box of cookies, caught the candy scent of icing. But the man had vanished like smoke.

"YOU LOOK WONDERFUL." Secure in the soundproofed room, Jeff smiled shyly at Deanna. "Do you like the clothes?"

"They're very nice." She willed herself to smile back. "I took a shower. I can't believe you went to all the trouble to pick out all my favorite brands."

"You saw the towels? I had them monogrammed with your initials."

498

"I know." Her stomach rolled. "It was very sweet of you, Jeff. Cookies?"

"They're the ones you like best."

"Yes, they are." Watching him, she walked over, fighting not to grit her teeth. She kept her eyes on his as she chose a cookie, bit in delicately. "Wonderful." She saw his gaze lower to her mouth as she licked at a crumb. "You were gone a long time."

"I came back as soon as I could. I'm going to turn in my resignation next week. I have plenty of money put away, and my uncle invested. I won't have to leave you again."

"It's lonely here. By myself." She sat on the edge of the bed. "You'll stay with me now, won't you?"

"As long as you want."

"Sit with me." In a subtle invitation, she touched the bed beside her. "I think if you explain things to me now, I'd be ready to understand."

His hands trembled as he set the tray down. "You're not angry?"

"No. I'm still a little scared. It frightens me to be locked in here."

"I'm sorry." He eased down beside her, careful to keep an inch of space between them. "One day it'll be different."

"Jeff." She made contact by laying her hand over his. "Why did you decide to do this? How did you know this was the time?"

"I knew it had to be soon, before the wedding. When I came in yesterday and saw you in your wedding dress—I couldn't wait any longer. It was like a sign. You were so beautiful, Dee."

"But it was a terrible risk. Tim was downstairs waiting."

"It was me. I was waiting. I used his hat and his coat, the sunglasses. I had to get Tim out of the way."

"How?" When he looked down, staring at their joined hands, her heart dropped. "Jeff. Is Tim dead?"

"I didn't do it the way I did the others." Eager, anxious, he looked back at her, his eyes as hopeful as a child's. "I wouldn't have done that. Tim didn't hurt you. But I had to get him out of the way, and fast. I liked him, too, really. So I was real quick. He didn't

499

suffer. I put him in the trunk of the car after—and then when I'd brought you here, I drove the car to a parking lot downtown. I left it there and I came home. To be with you." His face crumbled when she turned hers away. "You've got to understand, Deanna."

"I'm trying to." *Oh, God. Tim.* "You haven't hurt Finn?"

"I promised I wouldn't. He's had you all this time, and I've been waiting."

"I know. I know." Instinctively she soothed. "They're looking for me, aren't they?"

"They won't find you."

"But they're looking."

"Yes!" His voice rose as he pushed off the bed. Everything had gone perfectly up till now, he reminded himself. Perfectly. But he felt as though he were standing on the edge of a cliff, and couldn't see the bottom. "And they'll look and look. And then they'll stop. And nobody will bother us. Nobody."

"It's all right." She rose, too, though her legs trembled. "You know how curious I am about everything. Always asking questions."

"You won't miss being on television, Dee." He used his sleeve to wipe a tear away. "I'm your best audience. I could listen to you for hours and hours. I do. But now I won't have to watch a tape. Now it can be real."

"You want it to be real, don't you?"

"More than anything."

Her heart slammed against her ribs as she reached out to stroke his cheek. "And you want me."

"You're all I've ever wanted." His face twitched under her palm. "All these years, you're all I've wanted. I've never been with another woman. Not like Pike. Not like Riley. I was waiting for you."

She wished she could harden her heart, but part of her wept for him. "You want to touch me." She steeled herself and lifted his hand, placed it on her breast. "Like this."

"You're soft. So soft." There was something pathetic and

terrifying about the way his hand shook against her, even as his fingers moved to caress.

"If I let you touch me, the way you want, will you let me go outside?"

He jerked back as though she'd burned him. Bitter betrayal welled in his throat. "You're trying to trick me."

"No, Jeff." It was all right for her desperation to show, she told herself. Let him see her weakness. "I don't like being closed in. It frightens me. I only want to go outside for a few minutes, get some air. You want me to be happy, don't you?"

"It's going to take time." His mouth set in a stubborn line. "You're not ready."

"You know how I have to keep busy, Jeff." She stepped toward him, careful to keep her eyes fixed on his. When she slid her arms up his chest, his eyes clouded, darkened. "Sitting here like this, hour after hour, is upsetting me. I know how much you've done for me." And she felt the outline of the syringe in his pocket. "I know you want us to be together."

"We are together." He brought his unsteady hand back to her breast. When she didn't flinch, he smiled. "We'll always be together."

He lowered his head to kiss her. She slipped the needle from his pocket.

"Deanna," he murmured.

Her sharp indrawn breath betrayed her. She twisted, fighting to plunge the needle into him as they grappled to the floor.

Searching for Jeff finally brought Finn back to the bookcase. He had seen what he and Jenner had missed on their first search. The dimensions, he thought, as the spit in his mouth dried to dust. The dimensions were wrong. The bookcase couldn't be an end wall. Couldn't be.

She was in there, he realized. Deanna was in there. And she wasn't alone. He had one panicked notion of hurling himself bodily against the shelves. His body quivered with the effort of

501

holding back. It wasn't the way. God knew what Jeff would do to her in the time it took him to break through.

Struggling for calm, he began to search methodically for a mechanism.

SHE WAS LOSING. THE HYPO squirted out of her fingers when he rolled over her. She screamed as her head rapped hard against the floor. Though her vision blurred, she could see him above her, his face distorted, his tears running. And she knew he could kill. Not only others, but her.

"You lied," he cried out in an agony of despair. "You lied. I have to punish you. I have to." And sobbing, he closed his hands around her throat.

She used her nails to rake his face. The blood surged to the surface and ran like his tears. When he howled in pain, she squirmed free. Her fingers brushed over the syringe as he snagged her ankle.

"I loved you. I loved you. Now I have to hurt you. It's the only way you'll understand. It's for your own good. That's what Uncle Matthew says. It's for your own good. You'll have to stay in here. You'll have to stay and have bread and water until you're ready to behave." He chanted the words as he dragged her back toward the bed. "I'm doing my best for you, aren't I? I gave you a roof over your head. I put clothes on your back. And this is the way you thank me? You'll just have to learn. I know best."

He snagged her hand, yanked up her arm.

She plunged the needle into him.

FINN HEARD THE SOUND OF sirens in the distance, but they meant nothing. Every ounce of concentration was focused on the puzzle at hand. There was a way in. There was always a way. And he would find it.

"It's here," he murmured to himself. "Right here. The son of a bitch didn't walk through the wall." His finger hit a nub. He twisted. The panel opened in well-oiled silence.

Deanna stood beside the bed, the syringe gripped in one hand. Eyes glazed, murmuring her name, Jeff crawled across the mattress toward her.

"I love you, Deanna." His hand brushed hers before he went limp.

"Oh, Jesus. Deanna." In one leap, Finn had her in his arms.

She swayed, the needle dropping from her loose fingers. "Finn." His name burned her bruised throat and felt like heaven. From what seemed like a long, long distance, she heard him swear when her body jerked with a shudder.

"Did he hurt you? Tell me if you're hurt."

"No. No, he wanted to take care of me." She buried her face in Finn's shoulder. "He only wanted to take care of me."

"Let's get out of here." He carried her through the opening, down the hall, where he dragged at the locks.

"I kept asking him to let me go outside." She breathed in the raw air like wine. "He shot you, Finn. He was the one who shot you. And he killed Tim."

She jolted at the sound of screeching brakes.

"Well." Jenner climbed out of his car, moments ahead of two black-and-whites. The picture of Finn carrying Deanna down the front steps wasn't what he'd expected to see after he'd gotten the frantic call from Fran Myers. But it was an image that satisfied. "Went off on your own again, Mr. Riley."

"You can't trust a reporter, Lieutenant."

"Guess not. Good to see you, Miss Reynolds. Merry Christmas."

DEANNA STUDIED HER REFLECTION in the dressing room mirror. The bruises had faded from her throat, and the haunted look had ebbed from her eyes.

But her heart was still sore.

As Joe had often told her during her reporting days, she had one that bled too easily.

She couldn't afford for it to bleed now. She had a show to do in thirty minutes.

"Hey."

She glanced over, saw Finn. Smiled. "Hey back."

"Can you spare a minute?"

"I've got several for you." She swiveled in her chair, held out her hands. "Don't you have a plane to catch?"

"I called the airport. My flight is delayed two hours. I've got time on my hands."

Suspicion gleamed in her eyes. "You're not going to miss that plane."

"I know, I know. You've already laid down the law. I've got a job to do, and you're not going to support me if I screw it up. I'm going to Rome. Only a week off schedule." He bent down, kissed her. "I figured I had time to give one more shot at talking you into coming with me."

"I've got a job to do, too."

"The press is going to be all over you."

She arched her brows. "Promises, promises." She stepped off the chair, turned a circle. "How do I look?"

"Like something I don't want to be several thousand miles away from." He tipped up her chin, looked deep into her eyes. "You're hurting."

"I'm better. Finn, we've been through this." She saw his face change, harden. "Don't."

"I don't know how long it's going to take before I close my eyes and stop seeing you in that room. Knowing you were there all those hours, and I'd walked right by you." He pulled her roughly against him. "I still want to kill him."

"He's sick, Finn. All those years of emotional abuse. He needed to escape, and he used television. And one day, the day he found his uncle dead, I walked out of the screen and into his life."

"I don't give a damn how sick he is, how warped or how pathetic." He drew her back. "I can't, Deanna. I don't have it in me to care. And I can't stand hearing you blame yourself."

"I'm not. Really, I'm not. I know it wasn't my fault. Nothing he did was my fault." Still, she thought of Tim, whose body had been found in the trunk of her company car in a downtown parking lot. "I was never real to him, Finn. Even all the time we worked together, I was never anything but an image, a vision. Everything he did he did because he'd twisted that image. I can't blame myself for that. But I can still be sorry."

"Dee." Fran stepped into the doorway, winked at Finn. "We need the star in five."

"The star's ready."

"I can postpone the flight, stick around for the press conference after the show."

"I can handle reporters." She kissed Finn firmly, on the mouth. "I've had plenty of experience."

"Want to get married, Kansas?" With his arm around her, he walked her into the corridor, down toward the set.

"You bet I do. April third. Be there."

"I never miss a deadline." He turned her around to face him. "I'm crazy about you." And winced. "Bad choice of words."

She wasn't surprised that she could laugh. Nothing surprised her now. "Call me from Rome." Marcie leaped forward to repair Deanna's lipstick. "And don't forget, you have to handle the flowers for the church and reception. You have the list I made you?"

Behind her back, he rolled his eyes. "Which one?"

"All of them."

"No you don't." Marcie threw up a hand before Deanna could lean into another kiss. "You've got thirty seconds, and I don't want my work smeared."

"Stay tuned, Kansas. I'll be back."

Deanna took another step toward stage. "The hell with it." She whirled around, flew into Finn's arms. Over Marcie's groan, she clamped her lips to his. "Hurry back," she told him, and rushed toward the stage, nailing her cue.

The floor director stabbed a finger toward her. Over the sound of applause, she smiled into the camera's glass eye and slipped seamlessly into millions of lives.

"Good morning. It's good to be home."